Praise for the
Novels of Faith Hunter

Raven Cursed

"Faith Hunter has outdone herself in *Raven Cursed*. . . . A master of plotting, Hunter hooks the reader from the first line, weaving in enough complex layers to keep the reader guessing and turning pages. My one caution is to start this book early unless you don't mind staying up all night . . . rife with snarky dialogue, vivid descriptions, and enough hairpin turns to keep a fantastic driver busy."   —SF Site

"Faith Hunter is on my list of the top ten urban fantasy writers today. . . . *Raven Cursed* was amazing and I can give it nothing less than five stars!"   —Night Owl Reviews

Mercy Blade

"Fans of Faith Hunter's Jane Yellowrock novels will gobble down *Mercy Blade*, the third installment in this series, which has all the complexity, twists, and surprises readers have come to expect . . . a thrill ride from start to finish . . . Hunter has an amazing talent for capturing mood."   —SF Site

"There was something about the Jane Yellowrock series that drew me in from the very beginning. That hunch was solidified with each book I read into a feeling of utter confidence in the author. . . . *Mercy Blade* is top-notch, a five-star book!"
                    —Night Owl Reviews

"I was delighted to have the opportunity to read another Jane Yellowrock adventure. I was not disappointed, but was somewhat overwhelmed by the obvious growth in Faith Hunter's writing skill."   —*San Francisco Book Review*

"A thrilling novel. . . . Fans of suspenseful tales filled with vampires, weres, and more will enjoy this book. Jane is a strong hero   f a situation and kick
butt   ance Reviews Today

"Fai   rite characters, ever.
Jane   . . . As with the other
bool   from clear-cut, with
sym   haracters with shades
of gray. Highly recommended."   —Fresh Fiction

continued . . .

Blood Cross

"Mystery and action are at the forefront here, but the romance from the first book continues to build slowly. Readers eager for the next book in Patricia Briggs's Mercy Thompson series may want to give Faith Hunter a try." — *Library Journal*

"In a genre flooded with strong, sexy females, Jane Yellowrock is unique.... Her bold first-person narrative shows that she's one tough cookie, but with a likeable vulnerability ... a pulse-pounding, page-turning adventure." — *Romantic Times*

Skinwalker

"Seriously. Best urban fantasy I've read in years, possibly ever." — C. E. Murphy, author of *Walking Dead*

"A fantastic start to the Jane Yellowrock series. Mixing fantasy with a strong mystery story line and a touch of romance, it ticks all the right urban fantasy boxes." — *LoveVampires*

"Stunning ... plot and descriptions so vivid, they might as well be pictures or videos. Hunter captures the reader's attention from the first page and doesn't let go." — *SF Site*

"A fabulous tale with a heroine who clearly has the strength to stand on her own ... a wonderfully detailed and fast-moving adventure that fills the pages with murder, mystery, and fascinating characters." — *Darque Reviews*

"A promising new series with a strong heroine.... Jane is smart, quick, witty, and I look forward to reading more about her as she discovers more about herself." — *Fresh Fiction*

Host

"Hunter's world continues to expand in this highly original fantasy with lively characters where nothing can ever be taken for granted." — *Publishers Weekly*

"Hunter has created a remarkable interpretation of the aftermath of Armageddon in which angels and devils once again walk the earth and humans struggle to find a place. Stylish storytelling and gripping drama make this a good addition to most fantasy collections." — *Library Journal*

"Readers will admire [Thorn's] sacrifice [in] placing others before herself.... Fans will enjoy reading about the continuing end of days." — *Midwest Book Review*

"With fast-paced action and the possibility of more romance, this is an enjoyable read with an alluring magical touch."

—Darque Reviews

Seraphs

"The world [Hunter] has created is unique and bleak ... [an] exciting science fiction thriller." —*Midwest Book Review*

"Continuing the story begun in *Bloodring*, Hunter expands on her darkly alluring vision of a future in which the armies of good and evil wage their eternal struggle in the world of flesh and blood. Strong characters and a compelling story."

—*Library Journal*

"This thrilling dark fantasy has elements of danger, adventure, and religious fanaticism, plus sexual overtones. Hunter's impressive narrative skills vividly describe a changed world, and she artfully weaves in social commentary ... a well-written, exciting novel." —*Romantic Times*

Bloodring

"A bold interpretation of the what-might-be.... With a delicate weaving of magic and Scripture, Faith Hunter left me wondering: What's a woman to do when she falls in love with a seraph's child?" —Kim Harrison

"Entertaining ... outstanding supporting characters.... The strong cliff-hanger of an ending bodes well for future adventures." —*Publishers Weekly*

"Hunter's distinctive future vision offers a fresh though dark glimpse into a newly made postapocalyptic world. Bold and imaginative in approach, with appealing characters and a suspense-filled story, this belongs in most fantasy collections."

—*Library Journal*

"It's a pleasure to read this engaging tale about characters connected by strong bonds of friendship and family. Mixes romance, high fantasy, apocalyptic, and postapocalyptic adventure to good effect." —*Kirkus Reviews*

"Hunter's very professionally executed, tasty blend of dark fantasy, mystery, and romance should please fans of all three genres." —*Booklist*

"Enjoyable ... a tale of magic and secrets in a world gone mad." —*Romantic Times*

DEATH'S RIVAL

A Jane Yellowrock Novel

WITHDRAWN

Faith Hunter

A ROC BOOK

ROC
Published by New American Library, a division of
Penguin Group (USA) Inc., 375 Hudson Street,
New York, New York 10014, USA
Penguin Group (Canada), 90 Eglinton Avenue East, Suite 700, Toronto,
Ontario M4P 2Y3, Canada (a division of Pearson Penguin Canada Inc.)
Penguin Books Ltd., 80 Strand, London WC2R 0RL, England
Penguin Ireland, 25 St. Stephen's Green, Dublin 2,
Ireland (a division of Penguin Books Ltd.)
Penguin Group (Australia), 250 Camberwell Road, Camberwell, Victoria 3124,
Australia (a division of Pearson Australia Group Pty. Ltd.)
Penguin Books India Pvt. Ltd., 11 Community Centre, Panchsheel Park,
New Delhi - 110 017, India
Penguin Group (NZ), 67 Apollo Drive, Rosedale, Auckland 0632,
New Zealand (a division of Pearson New Zealand Ltd.)
Penguin Books (South Africa) (Pty.) Ltd., 24 Sturdee Avenue,
Rosebank, Johannesburg 2196, South Africa

Penguin Books Ltd., Registered Offices:
80 Strand, London WC2R 0RL, England

First published by Roc, an imprint of New American Library,
a division of Penguin Group (USA) Inc.

First Printing, October 2012
10 9 8 7 6 5 4 3 2 1

ALWAYS LEARNING   PEARSON

To my own Renaissance Man,
who takes me Class III kayaking, Zip-lining through
mountain trees, who writes the songs, and rubs my feet.

ACKNOWLEDGMENTS

A book is not a solo endeavor; it takes a village. In addition to all the usual suspects, I am giving a huge "thank-you" to my editor at Roc Books, Jessica Wade. This book was so complicated in terms of the progression of the clues, that it needed a lot of work and effort from outside sources (read: fresh, well-trained, professional eyes). You are the BEST! I also must thank the wonderful copy editor, Dan Larsen, who caught dozens of errors. Jesse Feldman was a huge help, and ferried requests to all the right people. To Rosanne Romanello—thank you for letting me use your name and some personal details for the vamp MOC character in Sedona. You were great. As always, my agent, Lucienne Diver of the Knight Agency, was invaluable. I literally (koff-koff) could not have written *Death's Rival* without all of you. My humble thanks.

And I wish a huge thank-you to my fans. You made Jane Yellowrock a bestseller. You told your friends, you shared your excitement for her and for Beast and Leo and Bruiser and Rick and Molly and Angelina and . . . all the others. You took Jane to the stars, and I know how much I owe you, each and every one. So to honor that trust, I promise to write the very best book I can, every single time. No cutting corners. No silliness. No stupidity. My word of honor.

CHAPTER ONE

I'm Gonna Need Some Stitches

"Vamps don't get sick," I said. "They may go nuts at the least provocation, but they don't get sick." Air currents buffeted the small jet; I held on to the phone and the seat arm with white-knuckled grips. Inside me, Beast was purring, enjoying the ride entirely too much for a creature who used to be afraid of flying.

Static fuzzed the connection, but I made out the words "—two of these did. And maybe the third one, don't know." If Reach didn't know something, it was better hidden than the identity of Kennedy's killer—assuming that there really *was* a coven of blood-witches on the grassy knoll. Conspiracy theorists have a consensus on that, but there never was any evidence to back it up. "I'm still searching," Reach said, "but it looks like the masters of the city of Sedona and Seattle are still showing signs of malaise. Boston's MOC has vanished, and rumor has it the suckhead's dead."

Malaise, I thought, unamused, reading the description of their symptoms. It was a heck of a lot more than malaise. In spite of what I'd said, the vampires *were* sick—maybe dying. "Give me details."

"According to my latest timeline, this vamp came out of nowhere two months ago and vamps started getting sick, which should be impossible, I know," he agreed. "Once they were sick, they each got an ultimatum from an unknown vampire to swear him loyalty in a blood-ceremony, or face that master in a Blood Challenge, not something they could survive while sick. As soon as they swore allegiance to the new guy, the vamps got somewhat better. He didn't kill them once he deposed them, but left them to run the cities as his loyal deputies. Each went from masters of independent strongholds to completely loyal subjects overnight. He's successfully created a new power base and no one knows how he did it or who he is. Yet."

"No vamp is *loyal*," I said. "They're all egocentric blood-sucking fiends."

"True. But *rich* egocentric blood-sucking fiends, which is why we work for them."

I grunted. I hated to think of myself that way, but he had a point. I'm Jane Yellowrock, and I used to kill vamps for a living. Until I started working for them. It wasn't easy money, and I'd dumped the contract with Leo Pellissier, the chief fanghead of the Southeastern U.S., when the retainer ran out. But when Leo had requested my help yesterday, I'd re-upped to resolve this problem, because it was the right thing to do. Leo and his people had been attacked under my watch. Humans had been injured. Blood-servants had died. I'd killed some of them. No one knew who this new enemy was, and now vamps were sick, maybe dying, and a new, powerful vamp had entered the vampire political scene.

Which was why I was in a Learjet flying at way-too-dang-high. I didn't like flying. Well, I didn't like flying in planes. Wings are different.

Reach continued to update me on two months of data and to answer a lot of questions. I'd need it. We'd touch down in Sedona in minutes, and assuming I got out alive, I'd be off to Seattle almost immediately. Listening to Reach's matter-of-fact tone helped to keep my mind occupied and my heart out of my throat. Sorta.

"Okay," I said. "And you're—" Leo's Learjet dropped several feet before leveling out. My mind went blank and I swallowed my dinner—again. "And you're *sure* the attack on Leo in Asheville was this same guy who took over Sedona, and Seattle?"

My question wasn't argumentative. The attack on Leo had happened before any of the others, and had been purely weapon-based, a frontal attack, no disease, no ultimatum, no nothing. I didn't know what to make of the discrepancy. "If it's the same vamp," I said, "his attack on Leo falls completely outside his subsequent M.O. Of course, he did try to kick sand in Leo's face, and Leo's people busted his chops. Maybe when that happened he tried this new tack." I hated guesswork.

The sound of leather squeaking reminded me to relax my grip on the seat arm. I took a breath, blew it out, and drank half a bottle of water to settle my stomach. Computer keys clacked in the cell's background, sounding like a quartet of castanets as Reach—the best research and intel guy in the business—worked.

"I stopped believing in coincidence," he said, "about ten seconds before I stopped believing in Santa Claus. It's like this. Leo visits Asheville, is attacked in a hotel, and wins a gun battle. Within weeks of the attack on Pellissier, Lincoln Shaddock and three of his vamps in Asheville become ill with a brand-new vamp disease. Then Sedona gets sick, then Seattle, and now Boston. They got challenged, swore loyalty, and got better. Leo's Asheville vamps are still sick, unlike in cities where the MOCs got sick, challenged and defeated, and then received treatment. Shaddock's peeps are dying— as if it's a punishment rather than a takeover tool."

Which thought made me sit up in my chair. Vamps were big on sneak attacks and vengeance. This scenario made all kinds of sense. Shaddock was bound to Leo and an attack on Shaddock was, by extension, an attack on Leo.

Reach went on, "Yeah, it's outside the attacking vamp's modus operandi, but the symptoms of Lincoln's peeps are exactly the same as those of the other masters of the city who fell through the looking glass."

"Peeps," I muttered. I knew those vamps. Among the sick ones was Dacy Mooney, Lincoln's heir. The two were vicious killing machines. The fact that I sorta liked them may have said something not quite sane about me. "We only *think* the other vamps were treated. We don't have empirical evidence," I said.

"Yeah, yeah, yeah. But the disease is circumstantial evidence I'm willing to bet on. I think our BBV"—*Big Bad Vamp,* I thought with a smile—"started in Asheville with a frontal attack, and had to abandon his plans there when Leo's people kicked his butt, and he left the disease as a punishment, a calling card, a warning, and a threat. The evidence you obtain in Sedona and Seattle will either confirm or deny that theory."

"Ahhh," I said. "That makes sense, which is why I pay you the big bucks." The jet bumped up as if slapped high by a giant hand; then the bottom fell out. The small craft dropped what had to be a thousand feet before catching itself. On air. "*Crap*," I whispered.

My things in an overhead compartment thumped around as gravity was again defeated. I wrenched my seat belt so tight it nearly cut me in two.

Inside me, my Beast huffed with amusement.

Beast is the soul of a mountain lion that I absorbed when I was a child and fighting for my life. It had been accidental, as much as black magic can ever be an accident. When I shifted, Beast's was the form I most often took, and her thoughts and opinions counted nearly as much as my own. *Fun,* she thought. *Like chasing rabbits in hills.*

I slapped my brain back on, swallowed my dinner yet again, and focused. "Agreed," I said, wishing I'd turned down this job. "But that theory still leaves questions. Why did the attacking master choose vamp strongholds so far apart on the map? Running three cities at a distance has to be a pain. Why not announce to the world who he is and what he's doing? Every vamp I know is a megalomaniac and would publicize his conquest. This guy hasn't." And the newly subdued master vamps weren't talking about what had happened on their turf or who their new master was— at all—which was another reason for this flight.

"The attacker is cheating, not challenging, according to the Vampira Carta," Reach said.

I grunted again. The Vampira Carta and its codicils were the rule of law for the vamps—or Mithrans, as they liked to be called—and it contained laws and rules for proper behavior between vampires, their scions, blood-servants, blood-slaves, and cattle—meaning the humans they hunted. It provided proper protocols for everything, including challenging and killing each other in a duel called the Blood Challenge. The new vamp had challenged his conquests, but there had been no fights. None at all. And Boston, attacked a week ago, had gone off the grid. There had been no communication from that MOC in days. He was presumed to be true-dead.

Reach said, "If an unknown vamp is making a major power play, one that involves vamps getting sick, and Leonard Pellissier, Master of the City of New Orleans, is attacked, and then Leo's scions get sick, it's the same dude."

"That isn't quite ipso facto. It's still more than half speculation."

"Ipso facto? Janie knows her Latin. I'm sending you a folder on the vamp you're visiting—the ex-master of Sedona. It's put together from the files you loaned me to collate and organize."

Back when I had a working relationship with the head of NOPD's *weird cases* (not that the New Orleans Police Department used those words to describe the official department. Local cops called it lots of things, none of them very flattering), I'd had access to NOPD's supernatural crime's hard-copy files. It was kept in the woo-woo room, and I copied copious amounts of info directly into my own electronic files. I was paying Reach an arm and a leg to organize the info.

Reach said, "The ex-MOC's name is Rosanne Romanello. Check your e-mail."

Peeling my fingers off the armrest again, I pulled the Lear's laptop across the table to me and logged on, checking e-mail. The Lear had all the office and party bells and whistles and its electronic gear was easier to use at jet speeds than my own. "Yeah. Got it. Thanks."

"Your business is my pleasure and profit."

"You oughta get that trademarked." I hung up the jet's phone and sat back with the laptop, reading the collated records—which was way easier than finding and reading scraps in individual files. Not that I'd tell Reach that. No way. He'd find a way to make a bigger profit off my now effortless search.

Rosanne Romanello had an exceptionally well-documented history. She had been born in 1787 in a small town in Calabria, the eldest child of grape and olive growers and olive oil exporters. A beautiful woman, she had been turned in a violent confrontation with a young rogue. Rescued by her fiancé, Luca, she appeared to die and was placed in the church for the death watch, which ended when she rose on the third night, killed the acolyte who had fallen asleep in the nave, and vanished into the hills. She survived there for four years, a rogue in hiding, until Leo Pellissier, traveling through the countryside one night, saw and chained her so she could grow out of the posttransformation insanity vamps called the devoveo. He had taken her west with him when he returned to the United States, and set her free seven years later, sane and strong.

According to Reach's notations, there were indications that the relationship between Rosanne and Leo had been more than just passing friendly. Well, duh. Leo believed in something he called the Dark Right, an authority that gave him the right to rule, and that permitted him to sleep with and drink from anyone under his power or his scions' power. Leo was charming and charismatic, but he was an old-time sleazeball too. I had a lot of sleazeballs in my life right now, and some important people who were seemingly out of my life for good. Old grief welled up in me, but I shoved it back down, hard. There was nothing I could do about the past. Not a thing. And I could grieve the lost relationship with Rick LaFleur later. Much later. I went back to the dossier.

Rosanne had emancipated herself from Leo and risen slowly in the ranks of the U.S. vamps, moving west until she claimed and settled in Sedona. She had been the blood-master of that city for nearly two hundred years, comfortable in her stronghold—literally. Romanello had started an olive oil business much like her family's, and built an Italian-style fortress-home where she still lived. Over the centuries, she had made friends with several blood-covens of witches and, with their power base, had protected her land and her scions. Until now.

Now things had changed. She had lost in direct Blood Challenge to an unknown master—and she was sick. The digital photos accompanying the file were hard to look at. In one, taken only last month at the full moon ceremonies with her witch allies, she had been stunning, pale-skinned, dark-eyed, almost ethereal in her delicate beauty. The poor-quality photo that arrived in Leo's headquarters e-mail yesterday showed a very different woman. Wasted, wan, with dark circles under her eyes and a dark crust at her nostrils that was presumed to be blood, she looked like death warmed over. Or worse—death still chilled. On the back of her hand was a lump, which looked like a pustule. I didn't know who had sent the file photo, as it came through a circuitous route and an e-mail account that went nowhere, but it was clearly a cry for help. I was betting on the MOC herself sending it to her former lover and friend, and Reach agreed it was likely.

Leo wanted her healed and restored, his Asheville scions healed and restored, the new master vamp identified so he could kill the bastard, and the vamp disease wiped off the face of the earth. To achieve that end, Derek Lee, my second-in-command, was going to Asheville to get blood samples from Shaddock, and I was supposed to obtain a few vials of Rosanne's blood. Just walk in and say, "Hey, Ro. Feel like making a donation?" Right. Like that was gonna happen.

Even less likely was my obtaining blood and a cogent report from the vamp-stronghold in Seattle, another conquered master of the city who was reputed to be sick. The should-be-impossible vamp-disease seemed like it was everywhere.

The door to the cockpit opened and the first mate, Tory, stuck his head out. "We're approaching Sedona's Mountaintop Airport and will be landing in fifteen minutes. Can I get you anything before we land?"

I thought about my stomach and shook my head. The smoked salmon he'd served, cold, with toast points, a salad, and a light beer, just after takeoff in New Orleans, was still sitting uneasily in my stomach. "No offense, but I'll just be happy to get my feet on the ground. Locked in this tin can with the *mild turbulence* you talked about back in New Orleans has not been fun."

He grinned. "This tin can is a Bombardier Learjet 85, valued at over fifteen million dollars."

I gulped and tried not to let my shock show. By the way Tory laughed, I knew I hadn't been successful. Tory was mid-thirties, not bad looking, standing about five-ten, with a lithe and wiry build, big thighs, like a cyclist, and it was clear that he found me amusing. It had to be the flight nerves.

"If you need anything just press your call button." He disappeared behind the closed door and I looked around. I was pretty sure most Learjets were not laid out like this one. The cabin was decorated in muted shades of white and taupe. It held four, fully adjustable, heated leather seats, with a galley and full bath between the seating area and the casket in back. Well, not really a casket, and I had been careful not to call it that out loud; vamps didn't care much for the fictional assumptions that they sleep in caskets filled with dirt from their homeland burial grounds. But the back portion of the cabin was a cramped bedroom with no windows and stacked bunks. It slept four—six in a pinch—strapped in to the single bunks, in perfect security, allowing vamps to fly by daylight, safe from sunlight, the doors and hatches sealed on the inside. But still. Fifteen million dollars. "Crap," I whispered.

I went back to my reading, trying to ignore the bumpy ride. Fifteen minutes later, at Tory's polite request, which I interpreted as orders, I yanked the seat belt again, cutting off the circulation in my legs, and grabbed the armrests as tightly as I could. The small jet dropped—this time on purpose, as the pilot descended for the landing at the private airport outside Sedona.

As a skinwalker—a supernatural being who can change into animal shapes, provided I have enough genetic material to work with—I've actually flown, and I far prefer wings and feathers to engines and metal. I knew what it felt like and what it took to land, in terms of wing feathering and variation, flight-feather positional changes, reaching out with front clawed feet, back-winging, tail feathers dropping, and I was relatively certain that the tin can—no matter if it was worth a rather large fortune—did not have the ability to do any of that. Or if it did, a human—a being never designed to fly—was in charge, which was doubly frightening. I'd rather be feathered and in charge.

Deep in the darks of my mind, Beast huffed. Beast didn't like it when I took the form of an animal other than hers—the *Puma concolor*—the mountain lion. She especially didn't like it when I changed mass into something smaller, because she didn't get to hang around for the ride, though I was pretty sure she had made strides in that regard. After a century and a half—give or take—Beast was evolving, something that might have been helped along by access to an angel named Hayyel not long ago. Long story.

Moments later we touched down. Hard. My teeth clacked together. Relief washed over me like a wave. I took a deep breath, released the armrests, and pushed at the leather upholstery that was now twisted and dimpled by my fingers. They didn't move back into proper position. *Permanent damage to Leo's toy. Crap.*

As we taxied to wherever the Learjet was going to hang out while I did Leo's bidding, I pulled the laptop to me again and sent Reach a text. "Still waiting on Seattle financial info." It was a nudge that he didn't need, but needling Reach to speedier work wasn't something I got to do often, and was not about to pass up now.

Reach sent back a series of dollar signs by way of an answer. "$$$$$$."

"Funny guy," I muttered. "Charge Leo all you want."

I texted back "What about the CS canisters?" The CS canisters were a potential new weapon in the war on rogue-vamps, pressurized colloidal silver water. Vamps didn't breathe often, but in combat they did sometimes take a breath. If the air had a mist of colloidal silver vapor, the vamps would inhale the poison. It wouldn't kill them, but it would slow them down. Maybe. And the poison might kill them later. It would certainly hurt them, even maybe burn their skin. I could hope.

Reach immediately sent back "Done. Untested. Delivered to your place soonest."

An e-mail beeped into my in-box, and I frowned, suddenly feeling helpless and useless. It was from Adelaide, the blood-servant daughter of Dacy Mooney. I opened it and read the short message. It was the same as the last three I'd gotten from her. "Any word? Any cure?" I typed back "Not yet. Will know more by morning." Of course, her mother and the other vamps in Asheville could die anytime, bleeding out from the new vamp disease. Just another reminder that time was of the essence.

I remembered to unplug my cell from the jet's battery

chargers. That reactivated the cell's GPS tracking device and gave Leo the ability to track me, my calls, my e-mails, and texts all in real time. For all I knew, it gave him the power to listen in on non-phone-call conversations. But the guy was paying me *very* well, so I wasn't complaining. Much. And I had two throwaway cells in my luggage for my private calls.

I tossed my go-bag on the seat as the small jet taxied and slowed. I wasn't going to be in Sedona long enough to get to shift, which ticked Beast off. She knew most everything I did and that meant she knew that mountain lions had been sighted near here. Two large males, probably litter mates, as they had learned the unlikely ability of pack hunting. Instead of going solitary, they were taking down prey together. Like African lions.

Good hunters. Need strong mate, she sulked. Which she had been doing a lot lately.

They're too dangerous. They're being hunted. They'll be dead soon, I thought at her.

Beast growled in anger, but there wasn't anything I could do about two wild big-cats who had learned a new trick. Not a dang thing. Snarling, she retreated into the depths of my mind, silent, distant, as she had been for weeks, since that accidental run-in with the angel Hayyel.

When the plane finally stopped and the engine whine decreased, Tory appeared in the cabin and opened the door to the outside. The smells of the world blew in on a hot gust. I stopped. Lips parting, eyes closing. On top of everything was the reek of petroleum products, heated plastic and metal, rubber, exhaust, and asphalt, but underneath that was a blend of subtle scents all fused together, unknown trees, flowers, hot sand, minerals I didn't recognize, herbs still carrying the heat of the day.

Beast rose fast and took over, holding me down, her claws in my mind, painful. I held on to the seat arms again, breathing in through mouth and nose, smelling, tasting, parsing the scents. It was . . . amazing was too trite a word. Too overused. I had no word for the aromatic mixture. It was yellow like sunlight, and red like iron-rich earth. It sang of scarlet and sun and iron, with rare blues and greens, and the land stretched out farfarfar. Magic tingled on the air, the magic of the earth itself, still alive here in this place. Beast wanted to *Hunt! Now!*

With a hard shove, I pushed Beast back down and unbuckled the belt. Stood. Pulled on my boots—Lucchese western dress boots, dark green snakeskin with a four-inch toe and a three-inch heel—seriously cool boots, the color matching the green vest I wore over the black silk button-front shirt that was unbuttoned to show off a bit of chest.

I unlocked the weapons cabinet where my weapons—both edged and handguns—had been secured for the trip and did a quick but careful check of each. They had thumped around a bit in flight, but nothing had been damaged. I strapped on the shoulder harness for the Heckler & Koch nine-mil under my left arm, checked the .32 six-shooter in one boot holster, and slid a two-shot derringer under my braids. All the guns were loaded for vamp, with silver—which worked well on blood-servants too. I'd checked the weapons exhaustively in New Orleans, and I'd check them again in the car. It wasn't obsessive-compulsive disorder. Really. It was survival instinct, honed over the years.

I adjusted a new vamp-killer in the sheath of my other boot, carefully and deliberately not recalling the way I lost the old one. That was one of the memories I tried not to think about. The blade was half knife, half small sword, with a deep blood groove along its eighteen-inch length and heavy silver plating except for the sharp, steel cutting edge. Strapped to my waist, under the vest, went two more silvered blades and three backup silver stakes in sheaths and loops. I was going armed to the teeth, into the clan home of a vamp who had once been loyal to Leo and now was under the control of another. A sick vamp. Vampires were unpredictable at best. As Leo's self-proclaimed *Enforcer*—which was going to cause me trouble, I just knew it—I was expected to be armed. Everywhere, everywhen.

Normally, half a dozen silver crosses were around my neck, my waist, and tucked into my clothes, but at the moment, there was no reason to cause pain to my hostess on my unexpected and unannounced visit. I carried only one, sterling, in a lead-foil-lined vest pocket. I twisted my tightly braided black hair into a fighting queue around the derrin-

ger, and slid four silver-tipped, ash-wood stakes into the
bun as hair sticks. I hooked the silver-over-titanium collar
around my neck. Protection against vamp-fangs, vamp-
hunger, and vamp-anger. Into a pants pocket I tucked a
mountain lion fang. I had begun to carry the fetish I used
for emergency shifting more often, as my job working for
vamps, rather than just staking them, seemed to result in
more life-threatening violence, not less.

Lastly, I pulled on my summer-weight wool jacket and
clumsily adjusted the fit. It was a gesture I'd been taught to
do by the woman who had designed the clothing. It felt silly,
but the small tug made my weapons hang right. Though it
was November, it was too warm for my silver-studded, armored leather, and I felt naked without it; nothing protected against vamp claws and fangs like silver and leather.
But, despite the weapons, this visit was not a challenge, a
hunt, or an act of war; it was a fact-finding mission to discover who the enemy was. With the letter of introduction in
my pocket, I was supposed to be safe even without the armor. Not that "supposed to be" ever meant anything in my
line of work.

And while working for vamps is never smart, Leo's money
was too much of a lure to do anything else just now. I did the
little jacket tug again and felt everything fall into place,
which was what should happen when a jacket cost nearly five
hundred bucks. Way too much for a jacket, but it wasn't my
money, it was Leo's. I was expected to look good. It was part
of my job description. I smeared on bright red lipstick and
dropped it into the same pocket as the official cell phone.

Satisfied, I looked up and met Tory's gaze. He was staring at me, a singularly acute and piercing look. Warmth rose
up my neck. I had, effectively, just gotten dressed in front of
him. How stupid was that? "Your car is out front of the
airport," he said. "The driver will have a sign in the window
that says 'JY.'"

First a Learjet, now a chauffeur. This felt downright
weird. My life was not . . . normal. Not anymore. "I'll be
back before dawn," I said, and was surprised when my voice
sounded professionally polite and not schoolgirl-silly.

I slung the tote with the blood-collection vials over a
shoulder and passed Tory on the way out, looking down on

his scalp and curly, deep-chestnut-colored hair. He was average height, but in the boots, I stood six-three, bringing my boobs about even with his face. *Right.* Smothering a sigh, I took in the small airport, or what I could make out from the top of the ramp. The sun had been setting when we took off from New Orleans, and it was only a bit later now than then, with the time changes.

I clattered down the steel steps and into the dusk. My boots made so much noise I missed the sound of cloth moving on cloth, but the scent caught me as I stepped onto the tarmac.

Blood-human-vampire, Beast thought. *Guns. Upwind.*

To my left.

I drew on Beast-speed and pulled the vamp-killer. Stepped right. Caught a glimpse of a shadow in my path. I smelled the gun oil and the fear-stink. I cut out right, hard. Impact jarred up my arm. A grunt. Reversed the knife and moved fastfastfast forward. Whirled. Into the light. Blinding my attackers. Two. Only two. Blood smell meant I'd hurt the one I'd cut at. On his blood I smelled vamp and something chemical. But there was no time to examine the scent. They came at me together. Moving faster than human. Nearly vamp fast. *Crap.*

I hit out, feinting, and leaped up, torquing my hips, rotating my body in midair, midkick, at the uninjured one. My heel flew around, speeding up on the pivot point. Time slowed into the consistency of cold maple syrup, each moment containing a snapshot clarity. The bright light and black shadows danced beside and below me. My target moved in the split second before the kick landed. My boot hit his shoulder. *Crap.* I'd been aiming at his chin.

I landed on my other foot, whirled, ducked, and struck out behind me with the knife. My blade hit metal, the sound the dull clang of a gun, followed by an "*oof*" of pain. Both attackers were injured now. This one cursed. I managed to drop the stupid blood-collection bag and pummeled the closest guy with a series of left-handed punches and right-handed cuts. Blocked his strikes. Hit him again, this time knocking the gun away. It spun in the air. Into the dark. I bounced back, fighting for balance on the three-inch heels. I came away with his blood on my fist. A shot exploded in front of my face, the muzzle flash blinding me. The ricochet echoed in the concussion.

I blinked hard, trying to restore vision. The first guy I had cut came at me out of the retinal glare. Blinking, I dodged, cut, bent, and whirled away, biding my time until my vision came back, moving fast to make a harder target of myself.

Heart thudding, I heard clattering. Tory. Joining the fight. *Idiot man.*

One man turned toward him. Pulled another gun. I opened my mouth to shout a warning, but Tory kicked, straight from the hip, his entire body in the move. A practiced, fluid motion that bent his body into a tight V and then snapped it open. I wondered what he studied.

The gun went flying. A shot rang out behind me, sounding dull beneath the concussive damage to my ears. Somebody had an extra gun. It sucks when the bad guys start thinking like me. Tory kicked again, but I smelled his blood. He'd been hit. *Enough.* I pulled a throwing knife and let it fly, the motion all one thing—pull blade, elbow back, wrist back, shoulder back, set up, throw, wrist snap, release. It took the shooter midchest, just left of his sternum. A lucky hit, between two ribs. The knife hilt thudded into his chest. Blood fountained out.

I whirled to the other guy. He was aiming at Tory, his extra gun in both hands in a Chapman stance. I dove forward. Grabbed his head. Our bodies impacted. I rode him down. Slammed his head into the tarmac.

He went limp. I didn't. Not even for a split second of victory. I'd been taught better. I banged his head again. Hard. And rolled, kipping to my feet. Tory was dropping back onto the metal steps, his movement so slow it looked arthritic. The fight was over. I remembered to take a breath. My heart thudded into my chest like a jackhammer. Time snapped back to normal speed. I huffed for breath as I checked the two bad guys. One no longer breathing, one down and out.

"How bad?" I asked Tory.

"I'm gonna need some stitches." He leaned left, hit the railing with his shoulder, and slid down. His blood flowed out, venous, not the fierce, arterial pumping of the man I'd just killed. But still, not good. Not good at all.

CHAPTER TWO

Oh, Goody. I Wasn't Gonna Get Sucked to Death

The pilot stuck his head out of the door above me, back inside, and then raced down the stairs. "I've called airport security and 911. They're sending an ambulance and the cops," he said.

I said something that would have gotten my mouth washed out by the house mother at the Christian children's home where I was raised. "Medical kit!" I demanded. But the pilot was ahead of me and knelt beside Tory, opening the small kit. With actions that were medic-fast, he ripped open boxes and plastic packages and applied a thick layer of gauze over Tory's wound. Over that he folded a blanket from the jet. The entry wound was low in the upper left quadrant, above his waist, below his ribs. I tried to remember what organs were there and came up with upper colon and maybe spleen. The exit wound was directly behind it and way bigger. The pilot adjusted Tory's limp body, stuffed another blanket over that one, and wrapped them in place with gauze and a sticky-wrap bandage. He leaned in, applying pressure, his knees on the tarmac. "Come on, boy. Don't die on me," he muttered. "Don't die. Fight. You can fight this."

I lifted Tory's feet and propped them on the steel step, got more blankets from inside, all treatment for shock. I'd taken an emergency medicine course between life in the children's home and life as an adult as the junior member of a security firm. I'd taken a lot of classes in a lot of things. Some of what I'd learned was even useful occasionally.

Needing to be doing something for the man who had thought I needed help, and knowing there was nothing I could do, I secured the unconscious attacker, hands and feet, with double zip strips, cleaned out his pockets, and made a fast reconnoiter of the area while I called Leo's to report in. Bruiser answered. "We've landed. Two blood-slaves—" I stopped. *Yeah. Multiple vamps had fed off them. Blood-slaves, not blood-servants. Expendable weapons.* "—attacked me as I got off the plane. I took them down, but the first mate, Tory somebody"—I slid a hand over my face. I didn't even know his last name—"jumped in to help. He's injured. The pilot called 911."

Bruiser swore. Vamps took care of their own, avoiding all human agencies when possible, but this time it was too late. "Dan's a part-timer. Leo's regular pilot is sick today," Bruiser said. The phone fell silent as he thought, probably going over the vamp-political implications of Leo's self-proclaimed and uninvited Enforcer killing someone in the city of another master. Unlike me, Bruiser had a political mind and an elegant surface in addition to his ruthless side, which was the reason he was Leo's *real* Enforcer. That and the fact that he had the blood-bond with Leo that I had refused. "Okay," he said. "I'll get someone there to handle things. You get to the Romanello Clan Home."

Which was what I'd known he would say, but the words were still cold and heartless. Something twisted deep inside me. As if he knew what I was feeling, Bruiser added, "Or you can stay and spend the next two days answering the questions of local law enforcement."

He was right. I knew it. Still . . . "Okay. But someone knew we were coming. That list is limited to the pilot and first mate, the pilot who called in sick, any of the vamps y'all told on your end, and Derek Lee and his guys on my end." Derek's old team all went by monikers based on vodka drinks: V. Martini, V. Lime Rickey, V. Chi-Chi, V. Hi-Fi, V. Sunrise, V. Angel Tit. Derek had been called V. Lee's Surrender—a joke with historic connotations. I trusted these guys.

"Derek has new men," he said.

I thought about that. In some way I had never questioned or understood, Derek was Leo's before he was my guy. And Derek was merging ten new men into his team, shooters fresh out of combat, honorably discharged, all with nicknames based on tequila drinks, like T. Sunrise, T. Cheek Sneak, T. Grenada, T. Blue Voodoo, T. El Diablo, and T. Firecracker. They were a mixed crew, not all from the same unit, as Derek's Vodka Boys were, but picked from several different units, or whatever the marines called them. I hadn't gotten to know them well enough yet to say what I thought of them, except they probably weren't part of our current stool pigeon problem. "Derek's new guys were in service overseas when we first got our leak back during the Asheville parley. No. It's not someone new, unless our bad guy covered his bases and used some big bad mojo to recruit *two* former military guys—which would be nigh unto impossible. So, I'm telling you, *again*, you got a leak in vamp security. You had one in Asheville, and you got one now."

"Noted. You have a mission. Get on it. And see if you can make the security footage of the fight disappear."

Post-9/11 means there are digital cameras at every mom-and-pop airport in the nation. I disconnected. Checked Tory. He was still breathing. I should have left, but I pulled my phone and called Reach.

"Evening again, Paycheck," he said.

"I need to make all the outdoor security footage from Sedona Mountaintop Airport disappear. Review it first and see if you can ID the blood-slaves who just attacked me."

He cursed, and there was a long silence on the other end. Then keys started clacking. "This is going to cost you, Little Janie."

"Yeah, yeah. Bill it to Leo. Can you do it?"

"Yes." The connection ended, but I had no doubt that Reach was ticked off. And maybe worried. If he got caught, it had to be a federal crime.

Security raced in on an electric golf cart, a red light on the top. I started laughing, and the sound had an edge, sharp and caustic. I cut off the laughter. Somehow, Tory was still alive ten minutes later, when the paramedics got there. I slid into the shadows as the real cops showed up, and made my way through the terminal, head down, away from cameras to the ladies' room, where I pulled off the jacket and washed my clothes, drying them under the hand dryer. It didn't take long. I had remarkably little blood on me, but I'd still smell like dinner to any vamp who got a whiff. And here I was, going into the clan home of one. My life was totally out of control. I dropped my weight onto the counter, the edge cutting into my palms. I stared at myself. I was shaking.

I'd just killed a man.

And my lipstick was still in place, vibrant against my coppery Cherokee skin. As if it never happened.

Nausea rose in my throat, but no tears started. My eyes didn't fill. They were glowing Beast-gold. I'd left the pilot and Tory to the cops. The blood-slave I'd tied up and the blood-slave I'd killed. I was a traitor and a coward. I closed my lids and breathed, finding a small calm place inside myself. Though he had attacked me, I offered up a prayer for the spirit of my enemy, Cherokee-style, to the Christian God I had worshipped for all the life I remembered. Wondering if there would come a time when God no longer heard me, or worse, when I no longer prayed. That happened sometimes when one wandered into unfamiliar spiritual areas.

When I opened my eyes again, they were my ordinary amber. I finished cleaning up. Jacket back over my weapons, I smoothed the wisps of black hair that had come free, up into the braid and fighting queue. Straightened the hair sticks. Tugged the jacket. I looked long and lean and fashionably unremarkable. No one noticed me as I exited the terminal, careful to avoid the metal detectors.

The car with my initials in the windshield, written in marker on a piece of white cardboard, was waiting out front, and I slid into the backseat. The driver pulled away but wanted to talk about the appearance of the cops. I looked behind us, as if just noticing them, and said, "Really? Huh." He took that as me not knowing anything, shrugged, and drove into the night.

The driver, gathering that I wasn't the chatty type, concentrated on the road, for which I was grateful. It took us over forty minutes to reach the Romanello Clan Home on the outskirts of Sedona, a long, silent drive. I opened the e-file of the Romanello family dossier and tried to read, but the dark pulled at me. As the city fell away, the sky was so black it looked like being in space, and I had never seen so many stars, not ever, anywhere, not even in the Appalachian Mountains a century ago, before electricity lit up the nights.

There wasn't enough light to sightsee, but I cracked a window and the smells kept my nose busy. The car's headlights lit red stone bluffs, spiky foliage, low trees, scrub. I was quickly able to pin certain smells on specific plants. A coyote trotted across the road, stopped, and looked at the slowing car before trotting on. I smelled rodents and maybe some kind of squirrel. Baked earth. Smelled an animal with a musky, odd underscent—armadillo roadkill— half roasted from the late autumn sun.

The clan home of the former blood-master of the city was in a canyon, about halfway up, on a ledge. It was in a position that would have been easily defended in the eighteen and nineteen hundreds. The only way to attack it today, barring helicopter, parasailing, ultralight plane, or parachute, was the road. Or a really horrible hike, a mountain climb, and rappel down from the cliff behind the manor hall.

A mile out, a wrought-iron gate blocked the road. We slowed and stopped at a dynamic camera, one that could be operated via joystick from a security console elsewhere. It was a top-of-the-line model with every bell and whistle on the market: motion-sensor, heat-detector, low-light capability, a PIR sensor—passive infrared—and traditional optical. The screws holding it in place were fresh and shiny. The system was new. The fence that trailed out from the road had motion sensors on it and a current running through its wires.

I rolled my window down and heard a mechanical voice say, "State your business."

I repeated the words Leo had told me to say. "I am Jane Yellowrock, seeking shelter and hospitality, here under parley rules, sent by Leonard Eugène Zacharie Pellissier, Blood Master of the Southeastern United States. I am armed, an Enforcer, but offer my word and guarantee that none shall be harmed by my hand except in defense."

"Wait."

Well, that was sweet. The camera swiveled to center on my face. I let them stare while I drew on Beast's night vision and studied the house in the distance. Constructed of brick and the red stone of the land, it was large, with a wrap-around porch, huge arched openings on the outside of the porch that protected matching arched windows on the house wall. The windows were uncovered, revealing the inside. Rugs and wood and plaster interior walls met my enhanced gaze, and though I couldn't see them, I knew there would likely be automatic steel shutters on the inside to protect against sunlight and attack—vamp security.

A red clay roof had a solar array on its south side and three windmills. Two were modern, tall pipes, white against the black sky, with whirling, spinning tops that looked like serrated blades encased in steel. The third one looked more like a traditional windmill, and on the night breeze I could smell water. Only a little water, maybe pumped into an underground cistern, but a sharp contrast to the arid land.

It was a place of wealth and power, two stories tall, nearly impregnable. I'd seen specs of the clan home, such as existed, drawings made by visitors, but I knew how poorly most people remembered exact dimensions. And no one had mentioned a lair, neither for the vamps nor for their chained-scions, young vamps still in the devoveo of madness after being turned. So there was a lot I didn't know about the house. I would be flying by the seat of my pants, which I was good at, but it was never safe, and eventually I'd pay the price for my lack of knowledge. I always did.

"Go ahead," the mechanical voice said. The gate opened with a soft whir and Driver Dude pulled forward, up the hill toward the house. As we moved, low lights along the sides of the drive came on, brightening our way, and screwing with my night vision. Deliberate, I was sure. I closed one eye, peering at the world through the lashes of the other eye.

At the top of the rise, in the shadows of the house, I spotted five men. Each carried guns I could make out in the low light. I couldn't tell what kind, but I could guess they were modified fully automatic and fully illegal weapons. *Ducky. Just freaking ducky.* My heart rate sped, and a slow trickle started down my spine. I took a deep breath and blew it out, forcing away the nerves. Fear—and anything close to fear—is not wise when one is in the presence of vamps. They can smell it, and they sometimes like to play with their dinner before sucking it dry.

A dark shadow stood out against a broken-rock wall just ahead, a black triangular shape with coppery glints where the stars picked out brass rounds. Even in the dark, I thought I recognized a belt-fed machine gun, maybe an HK 21 .308 Shorty, one with the standard nine-inch barrel. My breath caught, and, oddly, my fear subsided. If I was right, it was a rare gun and I wished I could just walk over and take a peek. But since it was pointed at me and the guy manning it was wearing nighttime camo and expected to be unseen, I figured that might get me shot. I grinned, showing teeth, feeling better for some reason I couldn't name.

The driver pulled to a stop in front of the house. Calmer, I studied the house's perimeter, taking in the rest of the security measures. Three men and a woman exited the front door and stood, widely spaced, in a semicircle around the car. If I planned to jump out shooting, I'd never get them all before I was brought down. Each of the welcoming committee was standing out of the way of direct line of fire of the gunmen. Excellent positioning.

Driver Dude turned off the car and tossed the keys over the back of the seat, which I caught. "I'll be hiking back to the road for my ride. You leave the car back at the airport. We'll pick it up."

My brows rose, though there was no way he could have seen my reaction in the dark. I hadn't been paying attention to actual turns on the ride, just the scents. Stupid move. I wondered how I was getting back to the airport. "This thing got GPS?"

"GPS-linked, voice-activated HDD navigation system. Just push this button and you're on." He opened his door and got out.

Ooookaaaay. I got out too and looked over the car. Lexus sedan, new, a fancy car. I'd have noted all this right away if it had been a motorcycle, and maybe oohed and aahed a bit. Cars were just transportation for me. I pocketed the keys. He waved to the welcoming committee and started jogging back the way we had come. In the distance, I saw headlights moving along the road. His ride, presumably.

I turned to the blood-servants and the vamp awaiting me and repeated the little speech Leo had made me memorize. When I was done, I shut my mouth and waited. No one said anything. The silence stretched. By pulling on Beast's hearing, I could make out night breezes soughing over rock, tough-leaved plants clacking together with a dry, slithering sound, and the click of insects, hard carapaces and chitinous legs noisy as they ran. I could count the breath of the humans and pinpoint the one, still vamp.

They let the silence build, and it felt dangerous on the night, but Beast was a hunter. Patient. Unmoved by ploys. And so I stood, appearing relaxed, waiting. Once upon a time, and not so very far in my past, this little game would have left me with my knees knocking. I was getting better at vampire games and didn't know if that was a good thing or not.

Finally the vamp said, "You stink of danger. Of the scent of predator, but not one I know."

"Fancy that," I said, my voice carrying no trace of emotion. The first time I met Leo and Katie, his heir, they had both hated my scent, but when Leo accepted me, all his vamps had done so too, without a word being spoken. Interesting tidbit to be dissected later. If I lived.

"And you stink of blood. A fresh kill, for Pellissier's Enforcer?"

The vamp's tone was harsh and pitiless and demanding. Pretty good for so few words. I said, "I was attacked at the airport. I was forced to kill a blood-slave." Before he could draw a breath to reply, I added, "Not one of yours, I'm sure." And I was sure, because I didn't taste the -slave's scent on the wind and hadn't detected any scent I smelled here on either attacker. But I wasn't gonna add that. Let my comment be considered a polite disclaimer with a hint of uncertainty in it.

"We were not expecting visitors."

I didn't reply to that, letting the silence work for me now.

"My mistress will not accept you in her sanctuary for long. You have a letter of passage?" the vamp asked. I detected a hint of accent in his tone, maybe Russian or one of the formerly Russian countries.

"I do. I carry a letter of concern for your mistress."

"Our mistress is unwell."

"So I hear. Leo sends his regards and his well-wishes to his longtime friend."

The night fell silent again for a whole minute, which is a

long time in the dark with guns pointed at me, before the vamp spoke again. "Come this way." The light fell on him when he turned, and I recognized Nicolas Nivikov, a former vamp stray, from his photo; the Russian was Rosanne Romanello's heir. Ro took in all sorts of strays—vamps with no master and no hunting ground. This one had been a rival until they fell in love, and now he was her protector and her heir.

The blood-servants fell in behind me as I followed Nicolas up the low steps into the house. I didn't like that, but there was no way to refuse. The door opened, held by a blood-servant, ugly muscle who looked me over, taking in the weapons. He didn't like me carrying and wanted me to know it. I nodded once at him, a single downward thrust of chin. *Duly noted.*

The interior shutters I'd expected to see were in place, stacked back against the sides of the windows. The décor was done in Italian antiques juxtaposed against modern, southwestern art, with contemporary updates like comfy but traditional Italian leather furniture and soft Hopi-patterned rugs over Italian marble floors. Not that I knew much about Italian stuff, but the dossier on Sedona's master of the city had been detailed. Very detailed. The place smelled of leather and sage and blood and something vaguely sickly sweet I couldn't identify.

I was shown into the library, where the smell of leather was strong, mixed with the scent of old paper, ancient ink, and the mold that likes books. There, I waited for over half an hour as various blood-servants and house-vamps came and went, introducing themselves, offering coffee, tea, wine, a snack, a full-course dinner, and an opportunity to freshen my toilette, which I interpreted as a chance to use the little girls' room. I turned them all down. No way was I accepting anything to eat or drink in this place or back into a closed space with my britches down. I thought it was odd that Ro's Enforcer didn't show up and scope me out, but maybe he was watching on the well-hidden security cameras in the corners of the room. I thought about making faces at them, but controlled myself. I understood why the vamps and servants kept me constant company. The vamps wanted to sniff me, and the servants wanted to get a good look in case they had to kill me tonight.

At the thought, Beast rolled over deep in my mind, pulling her paws close under. It was a good position if she needed to launch her body—a strike posture, which meant she was paying close attention to everything, in spite of her silence. My growing sense of unease dissipated slightly knowing that she was awake and aware.

I was perusing the library's titles when Nikki-Babe appeared in the doorway. "This way, if you please," he said. I followed him through a receiving parlor into a small office, where a vamp sat in the shadows. The photo I'd seen of her had obviously been taken in this room, but Rosanne's illness had progressed since. Now she had pustules up her neck and across one cheek. Another was on her lip, as if the disease liked mucous membranous tissue.

She clutched a handkerchief, and blood dotted it. Her nose was bleeding. I had never seen a vamp bleed except from a wound. Had never seen one sick. Freedom from bodily complaints, illness, or needs—with the exception of blood and sex—was supposed to be a benefit of being a vamp. But no more, it seemed. The sickly sweet smell was Ro—the scent of disease and decaying blood.

The room was filled with an odd tension, electric and gluey, as if it stuck to me when it brushed past. I had paused too long, let the silence grow too deep. I didn't want to approach, but I had been schooled by Bruiser in Mithran visitation etiquette. I had to present my letters of introduction. I stepped to the table and laid the envelopes before her. The official one, Ro handed to Nik. She opened the privately addressed one, the one written in Leo's own hand with lots of old-fashioned flourishes, the words *Ro, mi amore* on the envelope. They both read, and when Rosanne was done, she folded her letter and placed it in her desk drawer, which she locked with a small key hanging on a chain around her neck.

"Nikki tells me you were attacked." Her voice sounded weak and whispery. "They were not mine."

"I know," I said gently.

"He also prepared me for your scent, but I find it not entirely unpleasant. You smell of predator and aggression, but also of contact with my Leonardo. He is well? I had heard . . ." She stopped to breathe, little desperate gasps, which nearly made my eyes bug out. Master vamps did *not* need to breathe except to talk and to fight, and this one had to stop and re-oxygenate. Not good. "I had heard he had not recovered from the death of his son. I liked Immanuel immensely."

"He recovered," I said shortly. Leo's state of mind and the death of his supposed son wasn't a subject I wanted to talk about, since I had killed the creature masquerading as Immanuel. "He's now concerned about *you*."

Rosanne made a very Italian gesture, a slow throwing of her fingers, as if the subject was unimportant. "I was offered a Blood Challenge. I did not contest it. I have a master now." She shook her head, and with the movements, her sick scent floated into the room. "It has been long since I was . . . mastered. It was difficult at first. But he has left me in control of my own hunting grounds. He has made me his heir of this land."

This part was the tricky part. To mention her diseased state might be considered insulting. I'd been warned that if I was attacked after entering and being welcomed, it would be when I brought up the obvious. But she had mentioned Leo's illness, so maybe I had some leeway there too. "Leo is concerned that his old friend is not recovering as quickly as she should."

The tendrils of tension wrapped around me like the prickly webs of a spider, close and sticking. "I have been sent a treatment by my new master. However, there is only one, and I may not drink as often as I need."

I thought about that for a moment until I found the trans-lation. The new master had sent her blood-servant or -slave who had the "treatment" in his blood, but if she drank too much he'd die. She had a human drug, a human antibiotic factory to feed on. She was getting enough to keep her alive, but not enough to heal totally. Talk about a way to control your subordinates. Her new master had probably been the one to make her sick and now only he had the power to heal, or at least to keep her alive. No way was she going to thwart him. "And his name?" I asked. When Rosanne didn't re-spond, I clarified, "The name of your new master?"

"I may not answer."

Without turning my head, I glanced at Nikki. His face was closed, as unyielding as a marble statue. No answer there either. *Well, crap.* "May I ask another question about your master, without giving offense?" *What I'd like to do is beat it out of you, but I have my orders.*

Ro chuckled, almost as if she had heard my thoughts. Vamps are as adept as any predator at reading body language and interpreting vocal tones as cues, so maybe in a way she had. "Do you know how you were infected?" I asked. "Is the disease associated with your new boss?"

Ro said nothing, but Nikki laughed, and the tone was not happy. "This illness is a scourge upon all of us."

Which I took as a yes, but that didn't really help me much. From my memory, I pulled up the formal words for my next request—which was the primary reason for my visit, and the biggest reason I might not walk out of here under my own power. "The Master of the City of New Orleans," which was Leo's less formal title, "has dependable and confidential physicians in his employ who might assist with finding a cure. He requests . . ." I took a steadying breath. This was the most dangerous part. ". . . that you allow me to draw a sample of your blood for testing."

Nikki stepped toward me, vamp fast. I stepped back, toward the door. *Beast does not run from predators.* The voice in my head reminded me that running from vamps activated the chase instinct. Not that it mattered. The opening was suddenly filled with a blood-servant—the big, bad, ugly guy who had held the door, all brawn and speed and no brains. The tension in the room shot up like a wildfire hitting a stand of dry pine.

On reflex, I ducked right, backed into the corner of the room, pulled the nine-mil and a vamp-killer, the one I'd killed the blood-slave with. I knew the vamps would smell the fresh blood, even after the thorough cleaning I'd given the blade in the ladies' room.

Nikki-Babe followed so fast I didn't see him move. He was so close I could smell who he'd had for dinner. I heard the distinctive click of fangs snicking down on the little hinged mechanism in the roof of his mouth. In a single heartbeat, his eyes vamped out. "Pellissier must still be caught in the *dolore* of grief to ask such a thing," he said, black pupils the size of quarters spreading into bloodred sclera. "He is insane still, from the loss of his son." No trace of white or iris remained in Nikki's eyes, and no trace of humanity. This was going to hell in a handbasket fast.

I shoved the gun up under Nikki's chin. "Silver shot," I warned, on a whisper. He stilled, his eyes twisting back to Rosanne. "Look, lady," I said to her, "I don't want trouble. Leo just wants to help. Girrard DiMercy is back with him, and Leo is sane again."

Ro lifted a hand. The pressure in the room died. "Girrard has returned to him?"

"Yes, and Leo thinks his private lab can find a cure to the sickness."

She thought about that for a moment. "You know how to do this taking of blood?" I nodded. "You may." Nikki-Babe started in with a barrage of oddly accented Italian, clearly disagreeing with her decision, but I ignored him. According to the Vampira Carta, she was in charge. I slid away from Nik, keeping him in my side vision, and stepped to the desk. Ro rolled up her sleeve. Oh, goody. I wasn't gonna get sucked to death.

I holstered the weapons and opened the small tote, taking out the blood drawing kit. I wasn't skilled at taking blood, but I knew how to do it. I pulled on gloves and tied the tourniquet around Rosanne's arm. The pustules were here as well, and the smell of the sickness was gag-inducingly strong this close to her. There was a vein right in the middle of her arm, slightly plumped by the tourniquet. I cleaned the bottles and tubes, each with different-colored tops and containing different anticoagulants, with alcohol, and then the sticking site with foamy brown soap and Betadine. I pulled the cap from the needle and stuck the sharp needle under her skin. She didn't flinch, though I wasn't experienced with the procedure. If it had been a stake, maybe then . . .

I stifled the thought and pushed the first bottle on, then the next, then four more tubes in succession. When I was done, I popped the tourniquet. Put a square of gauze above the insertion site and removed the needle. Flipped the safety cap closed.

I met Ro's calm eyes, and she smiled slowly, tilting her head the barest fraction. The expression on her face suggested that she had accomplished a goal, and I was reminded of the photo that arrived at Leo's from an anonymous

source. Yeah. Ro had sent the photo and had known that
Leo would send help. She might have preferred an armed
rescue, but she trusted Leo or she wouldn't have allowed me
to draw the blood. Vamps were sneaky. I liked that about
them. I nodded back slightly to show I understood.

I held the site while I dropped the torn packages, the
bottles, and tubes into a zip-lock baggie and sealed it up. I
was supposed to label the tubes with name, date, and time,
but that could wait. I was ready to get out of here and so
was Beast. I could feel her unease padding through my
mind like a lion in a cage, back and forth, back and forth.

Chilled moisture soaked my thumb and I glanced at the
puncture site to see blood oozing up from beneath my grip.
I grabbed more gauze, applied it, and held harder, but the
blood welled faster. Vamps don't bleed. Not like this. "Crap,"
I whispered.

Nik pushed me aside and took Rosanne's arm. And he
did something I'd never seen a vamp do before. Instead of
licking it clean, he wiped the puncture site, tossing the
bloody gauze into the garbage. A vamp ignored blood.
Didn't lick it. And then he spat onto the wound. I almost
said *eeeewwww* but caught myself in time. I realized he was
worried she was contagious.

Vampire saliva closes wounds, causing the veins and skin
to contract and constrict. It's usually applied with a tongue
laving. This was weird. Okay. This gig was making me re-
think everything I thought I knew about vamps, and I had
been on a steep learning curve ever since I hit New Orleans.

The tiny wound stopped bleeding. Nikki-Babe looked at
me and I nodded my thanks. "I'll be going now," I said.

"I don't think so," a voice said behind me. I turned and
saw a man, human—or as human as the fangheads' dinners
ever are. I knew this guy wasn't one of Ro's usual blood-
servants; even if I hadn't been able to smell the new master
on him, he wasn't in the dossier. He was maybe seventy
years old, looked twenty-five, and was powerful—meaning
that he had fed on the blood of a master for a very long
time. Bald, six feet and a smidge, blue eyes, reddish beard
needing a trim, casual clothes, shirt half-tucked, as if he'd
dressed and gotten here in a hurry. He was a righty.

And he had a gun pointed at my chest.

CHAPTER THREE

I Started to Squeeze the Trigger

Holding his eyes, I slid the tote strap around my shoulders, shoved it back out of the way, and walked straight toward him. Keeping loose. Letting Beast bleed into my bloodstream and into my eyes. My heart rate sped as her adrenaline pumped into my body. His blue eyes widened. Beast-fast, I swerved right, forcing him to move cross-hand. And back left, into his personal space. I body-slammed him. Hard. Hooked his ankle as he shifted and shoved.

The gun went off. Wild shot. Toward the ceiling. I caught his gun hand, flipped him, and landed one knee in the middle of his spine with all my weight. Took his gun away while he tried to remember how to breathe. Banged his head on the floor so hard he had to see stars.

Fun, Beast thought. *More!*

The shadow over me shifted. I lifted my eyes. Nikki-Babe was standing over me, still vamped out, blocking the light. Fangs latched down, claws out, waiting. If I really tried to hurt the stranger, he'd kill me, and I didn't know why. Ignoring the looming shadow, I leaned in and sniffed. Blue Eyes smelled of witchy-power, not his own, but something he had obtained from a powerful witch or coven—probably an amulet of some sort. The witchy stench nearly overrode the blood-signature scent of his master, but not quite. It was a vamp-scent I recognized. The undertang made me hesitate, but only for a moment. For now the amulet was more important. Whatever spell he had was underneath him, inactivated, and I had better keep it that way. I pulled his arms back and secured them with a zip strip. Then added three more strips. He was a blood-servant to someone very powerful, with a witchy charm on his person. I wasn't taking chances.

I flipped him over, slamming his head against the marble floor. He grunted.

"Have a care with our *guest*," Nikki said, his mouth near my ear. The last word was nearly spitting, as if he would have used another, less kind and less hospitable term. *Curiouser and curiouser.*

"I'm taking care," I said, my voice flat. I fished in Blue Eyes' pocket and pulled out a pocket watch. It was neither old nor new, cheap nor expensive. It was something no one would ever notice twice, but it was charmed. I sniffed the amulet, and the magics smelled like blood. Like meat. Weird. I tucked it into my lead-lined pocket with the silver cross while Blue Eyes was still disoriented, and patted him down. I searched for wallet, ID, or a cell, but he was clean. *Figures.*

I leaned in again. Now he smelled only of his master. A close perusal of the blood-signature proved that the master wasn't someone I knew, not someone I had ever met, but I had killed a blood-servant belonging to the vamp recently. In Asheville, when I'd been attacked in my hotel room. Once again, everything went back to Asheville and I didn't know why. Beast didn't have the olfactory memory of a bloodhound, but she was no slouch either. She remembered this scent, though it was much stronger than the last time she had scented it. It was peaty and spicy and, oddly, a little beery. The servant also had a funky chemical top-note, acrid and clear as a desert sky, in Beast's synesthesia. A nonguest in the house of a deposed master . . .

I put it all together and looked over at Rosanne. She was leaning her weight on her elbows on her desk, as if it took all her strength to hold herself upright. "This is your treatment, isn't it? You suck on him and his blood fights the disease in you. Kill him and you die." When no one disputed my claim, I looked up. "Back off, Nikki-Babe. I'm not gonna kill your mistress' antibiotic."

Nik took a single step back but didn't let his eyes bleed back to human. I grabbed Blue Eyes' head and banged it against the floor again. Leaped to my feet before Nik could react. Shrugged. "Didn't say I wasn't gonna hurt him a little. I want him out until I'm ready to go. Is he the only one for Ro to feed on?"

"Yes," she whispered. "And he is not enough."

"And he's to call his master at prearranged times," I said, "to let his boss know everything is okay here, right?" When she nodded again, moving as if her neck and head hurt, I asked, "Are you going to be able to handle this—my being here and knocking your new boy around—or do you need backup?"

"We will be fine," she whispered. She sounded certain, unwavering, and maybe it was just her trying to get rid of me, but I nodded.

"Okay. I'm gone. If you change your mind and need help—"

"We need nothing from you," Nik said through his fangs.

I looked him over, thinking, *You let your mistress get defeated in a Blood Challenge. And now someone else has to fix your screwup. Seems to me you needed* something, *Nikki-Babe.* But I didn't say it. If I had given in to temptation, I'd have had another fight on my hands and I'd done enough for one night.

I walked between the score of blood-servants and clan-vamps and out the front door. The night smelled wonderful here. Huge and free and heated. Beast wanted to hunt, but even she wanted to get down off this cliff first. I got in the car and fished out the key, drove down the drive and out through the soundless gate. Following the GPS directions, I made it back to Sedona proper without incident and pulled in next to a FedEx drop box. I labeled the blood tubes and bottles, wrapped them in bubble wrap, taped them up, boxed them, added more tape, and affixed Leo's mailing label to the front. There were laws about putting biohazard-ous materials through the mail, and I was breaking all of them, which is why I used Leo's address as both return and sender. If my plane crashed, at least the blood wouldn't go down with me. I dropped the blood into the drop box and heard it hit other packages with a soft, slithering thump.

I texted my ETA to the pilot, with the question "Can we use current plane?" at the bottom. With the police involved, Leo's personal jet might be grounded. Unless Leo pulled strings, I might be getting on a charter. Satisfied, I whirled the steering wheel and pulled back onto the road. Following the directions of the GPS voice, I headed back to the airport. The pilot texted back a succinct "Yes," which I read before tossing the phone into the passenger seat.

My primary mission was accomplished, which meant a nice fee would be electronically deposited into my account as soon as Leo got the package. Mentally, I calculated my payment for the travel part of this gig. I was getting a base fee for each visit, travel pay, hazard pay, and I was getting a bonus for each sick vamp who let me bleed him or her. A *very* nice bonus, because vamps didn't give up their blood to anyone who wasn't family, scion, servant, master, or slave. Never. Now if it was just as easy to get a sample from the Seattle MOC, I'd be set.

Behind me down the road, headlights pulled onto my street. I took note of their shape and the outline of the car they were attached to. GMC sedan. Another car moved parallel to mine one street over, which could be a standard tailing procedure, but when I turned right at the next intersection, the cars didn't follow. They pulled on past and disappeared. I didn't know Sedona at all, but maybe they were just leaving a club. Or getting off work somewhere on the night shift.

It was long after midnight when I dialed Leo's number, but it's never too late to call a vamp. Bruiser answered, his voice like a long, low caress. "Jane."

I couldn't help my smile. Or Beast's inner purr. Beast likes Bruiser—George Dumas—and though my cat had been oddly quiescent, she always paid attention to Bruiser. He was Leo Pellissier's right-hand blood-meal, and arguably the most powerful nonvamp in New Orleans. He probably had more political clout than the governor and he definitely had better looks and charisma than any purely human politician.

I opened my mouth to say, "I have a report." What came out was "Hi." And a soft, sexy-sounding "Hi," at that. I clamped my mouth shut. Bruiser chuckled at my tone, that secure, masculine laugh men get when they know a woman is interested. Which ticked me off.

Two months ago, I had lost my first boyfriend since my early twenties and I was *not* in the market for another. Especially one who was bound to a vamp for his very existence. Blood-servants like Bruiser must have drops and sips of vamp blood on a regular basis to keep their vamp-blood-induced extended-youth thing going. I was not taking second place behind Leo. So even though Bruiser was sex on a stick, he was not going to be mine.

Mine, Beast murmured.

I firmed my tone and said, "I have a report."

I could hear the smile in his voice when he said, "Go ahead."

I talked for twenty minutes as I drove out of the city, toward the stark country of red hills, cliffs, bluffs, and buttes, detailing everything that had happened. The sky was black overhead as I drove, too big, too dark, with too many stars. Beast liked it. Sedona was a pale glow, like a halo on the horizon. I finished with "Ro wouldn't name her new master. She looks and smells sick. She's covered in pustules. She's bleeding from her nose, and when I took her blood—"

"You obtained her blood?"

"I got it. It's in the FedEx box. But when I stuck her she didn't stop bleeding on her own. Nik had to spit on her arm to stop it. Which, by the way, was gross."

"Spit? Not lick?"

A familiar pair of headlights pulled behind my car. GMC sedan. Behind it was another car, about a quarter mile back; it had the same configuration as the car riding parallel to me earlier. *Beast is not prey,* she whispered into my mind. "Right," I said to them both. "I'm being followed. If I'm not back at the airport in an hour, tell the pilot to—" I stopped. The substitute pilot who had been one of the few people who knew exactly where I was going and when I'd get there. Before I could say all that to Bruiser, the sedan launched at me. I tossed the cell. Took the wheel in two hands. And floored the car.

I wasn't fast enough. The sedan roared up. I gripped the wheel hard enough to make the leather groan. The car rammed me. My spine whiplashed. The seat belt cut into my chest and abdomen before slamming me back into the seat.

"Jane?" Bruiser's voice, tinny. Far away. From the floor.

The sedan raced closer. Rammed me again. The tail of my car spun into the oncoming lane. I hit the brakes. The antilock braking system kicked in. The car danced across the road. *That shouldn't have happened,* was my last thought as my car hit something slick on the road and its slight spin turned into a twisting spiral. Off the road and down.

The car bucked over the rough terrain. Up into the air, the headlights illuminating the red stone of a low cliff wall and the night sky, and down, into a ditch. The car's frame shrieked, contorting as its own momentum forced it at an angle up the other side. My window flexed and shattered, raining me with rounded nodules of safety glass. Down the car went again, at a sharp angle, a long, fast slide. A bouncing, jouncing ride that ended suddenly. Too hard. Whiplash took me again, from my toes to the top of my head. The air bags released with explosions of sound. Socked me in the face. I saw stars and then nothing.

I roused to the sound of an engine hissing. My headlights picked out a spiny cactuslike plant through the bashed windshield. Bruiser's voice called me from somewhere, insistent. Frantic. My ears were ringing and I couldn't focus to locate the cell. But my brain was starting to work again.

Footsteps were approaching the car. One pair, booted. Skidding downhill over the rock and dirt. In the far distance, maybe near the road, I heard a voice talking, the words lost in the buzzing aftermath of being hit in the face. The breeze shifted, blowing into the car. I smelled gun oil and cheap aftershave. Over it all, I smelled the scent of a blood-servant. But not Rosanne's. Another vamp. Not quite a stranger, yet not entirely familiar. But exactly like the blue-eyed man I had left bound on Rosanne's floor.

I fumbled with the seat belt, but the car was at an angle and I was bound by the flex and gravity, leaning into the car's console. I pushed against it, and when I took a breath, something stabbed me in the chest; I was pretty sure I'd busted a rib. I tasted blood, salty. I'd bitten through my tongue.

Beast flooded my system with strength, claws sinking into my mind, more *here* than she had been in weeks. The pain in my side faded beneath her claws. My night vision sharpened into silvery blues and crisp greens, the night a thousand shades of black. My heart, beating erratically, smoothed out, fast and strong. I fumbled under my jacket and managed to pull my nine-mil. Focused on the night sky through the broken window. Stars. Millions and billions of them.

The footsteps stopped. To see inside the car, my attacker would have to lean over and in. I steadied my aim at the window opening.

Shuffling of booted feet. He leaned in. I started to squeeze the trigger. He slipped and nearly fell. I didn't fire, didn't move. He reappeared in the corner of the open space. Anglo. Light-colored hair. Big-assed gun. Though humans don't have good night vision, he seemed to see me and adjusted his aim at the same time I fired. Three shots.

He ducked and fired twice, our reports overlaying one another. The muzzle flash blinded me, but I fired again, through the door. He rose into my window, moving freaky fast, and fired two more shots. A punching pain hit me, like a hard strike delivered by a black belt with something to prove. Burning and icy. Chest shot. He'd hit me.

I fired back, emptying my gun before I harnessed my fear. *Stupid. Crap! Dumb, dumb, dumb.* But I smelled blood, his as well as mine. Blinded by the flashes, deaf from the concussive explosions, I felt along my boot for my backup. My chest stabbed with pain and I couldn't reach the holster.

Frantic, I pulled a throwing knife. But he didn't reappear to shoot me again. Long moments later, I saw headlights start to move, bouncing off the red-rock walls as two cars drove away. I dropped my head back. Pain flooded through me, a tsunami of agony. I was tired. So tired. But I had to stay awake. Had to get out of here. I pushed at the seat belt, trying to remember how they worked.

Something wet and warm pooled in my palm holding the hilt of the knife. *Blood.* I was bleeding out. I needed to shift. Fast. I struggled to get the mountain lion tooth out of my pocket, but my fingers didn't seem to work. I tried to drop into a meditative trance, but the earth spun when I closed my eyes, a sickening lurch. My gorge rose, tasting of blood, and I gagged. The night sky twirled and tightened down, becoming a pinpoint of velvet black sprinkled with white light. I could hear my heartbeat. Thump-thump, thump-thump, fastfastfast. Too fast. I tried again to find the calm in the center of myself, but there was nothing there, no center, no peace. Just the sound of my speeding heart and wet, raspy breath. I was worse off than I thought. Maybe a lot worse.

I didn't have the time to shift into my beast to save my life. *Beast?* I called in my mind. She didn't answer. No snarky comment. No insult. Nothing. *Beast?*

Feet padded in the dark, barely heard. Coming closer. I laughed, the sound little more than a wet, raspy moan. I closed my eyes. Beast pressed her claws into my mind again, the pain sharp and demanding. Forcing me down. I dropped. Deeper. Into the darkness inside my own past, where ancient, tenuous memories swirled in a world of shadow-gray and uncertainty. I heard a distant drum, smelled herbed wood smoke. The night wind coming through the broken window chilled my skin, smelling foreign and hot and dry. Beast forced me deeper, memories firmed, memories that, at all other times, were forgotten, both mine and Beast's.

In the memories, I saw a deer with fawn and knew I would not hunt her just now, but only after the fawn was grown. I saw an old woman bending over a fire, her silver hair in braids, her wrinkled face catching light and shadow like the cliffs and valleys of a river gorge. Her eyes were yellow like mine. I saw a kit straying toward the cliff edge and padded over, taking it in my mouth, his entire head in my killing teeth, held gently. I tasted/smelled/felt the kit struggling, heard his mewling cries. Breathed in his scent. *Mine.*

My heart rate began to slow. To stutter. The blood pooling in my hand felt chilled. I had held cold blood before. Had placed my hands in it, in the cavity of my father's chest. And then wiped my fingers across my face in a promise of vengeance. A vengeance I had never taken. The old promise, never fulfilled, scourged me, hatred unfulfilled. *A wrong never avenged, never forgiven,* I thought. But the concepts of vengeance and forgiveness melted away.

As I had been taught so long ago, I took up the snake that rests in the depths of all beasts. Beast. Beast's snake, remembered, even without actually touching the fetish tooth in my pocket. Beast's snake was a part of me. I fell within. Like water trickling down a cliff face. Like fog slowly obscuring the world. Grayness enveloped me, sparkling and cold. The world fell away. I was in the gray place of the change.

My breathing stopped. My heart faltered. My bones ... slid. Skin rippled. Fur, tawny and gray, brown and tipped with black, sprouted. Pain, like a knife, slid between muscle and bone.

She fell away. My nostrils widened, drawing deep. The scent of blood. Jane's and the predator who had stalked her. Night came alive—wonderful, new scents, heavy on dry, hot air, thick and dancing. Blood. Salt. Humans. Sweat. Strange car. *Blood.* Faint trace of vampire. I panted. Listened for sounds. In the floor of car, Bruiser's voice still called, full of fear. But there were no cars, no music, no voices talking over one another. I pushed away the seat belt and pawed from the boots and clothes. Gathered limbs beneath and pushed, balancing on plastic between seats and placing front paws on door/window/opening. Ugly man-made light was far away. Nothing here was thief-of-vision. The world was clear, sharp. *She* never saw like this. Scented like this. Attackers were gone. I yawned and stretched front legs and chest, pulling against legs, spine, belly.

Gathered Jane's clothes and dropped them over the car door onto the dirt. Boots. The gun she had killed, emptying its noisy heart out. Dropped everything and turned back for cell phone. Bruiser was shouting for Jane on cell. Sounded angry-afraid. I looked at it on the floor. Sniffed at it, pulling in air over tongue and roof of mouth with soft *scree* of sound. Cell phone carried Jane-scent, and Bruiser could track her with cell phone. Could track Jane-scent on cell from far away. I did not understand how he did this, but Bruiser was good tracker of Jane.

I thought. *Bruiser could find Beast!* I stared at cell. Did

not know what to do. I looked inside, to Jane, asleep in corner of mind-den. I swatted her, without claws. But she did
not move. I looked back outside mind-den, at cell. I bent
into floor of car and picked up cell phone in killing teeth.
Foot slipped off plastic. Teeth bit down. Cell phone shattered into many parts, broken. Bruiser's voice went silent. I
pawed cell and sniffed. Jane had told me about machines,
like guns and Bitsa and cars, that were alive but not alive
and that did not bleed blood. I did not understand stupid
human things. Cell phone had no blood, yet it was dead. I
killed it, like foolish yearling puma with first litter, killing
kit with teeth. *Stupid Beast.* I batted bloodless cell parts into
backseat. Did not know what to do. Did not know if Bruiser
could track Jane now, but did not think that Jane wanted
Bruiser to find Jane-clothes and Jane gone.

Looked out at night, sniffing strange new air. New scents
made Bruiser-worry go away. Cell was dead. I could not
make it alive again. I chuffed. Growled. Scented. Listening
to world. I was safe here until Bruiser sent help. Then big-
cat would be prey to white man's guns. Again. Bruiser did
not know Beast. Would kill Beast. This hunt was not a good
hunt. Beast needed Jane, but Jane still slept. I thought,
Could hide Jane!

I took boots into killing teeth and leaped up, over, and
down, *lithe* and *lissome*—her words for me. Liked those
words. Landed on dirt. Hunger tore into belly. Shifting used
much food, gave much hunger. But there was no meat here
without hunting, and no hunting until Jane was safe

I carried Jane's boots across the ditch and into the dark.
Went back to car, to Jane's bag and top-half clothes. Went
back again for her bottom-half clothes. Snuffled her pants.
They were full of Jane's blood, and spattered with her attacker's blood. Jane had shot him. Jane is good hunter, even
without claws and killing teeth. Found hunter's blood on
ground and bent over it, opened mouth, pulled back lips,
sucking in air over tongue and scent sacks in roof of mouth.
Tasting and smelling with *scree* of sound. Learning. Scent
was human and vampire and something hard and metallic
and ugly. Did not know this smell.

I bumped Jane's pants with nose. Smelled tooth of puma
concolor in small trap called pocket inside of pants. Smelled

cross and smelled magics of amulet. Jane thought amulet was important. It was safe in pocket-trap of Jane-clothes. Beast wore one suit of skin and fur. Humans wore skin and clothes—many clothes instead of fur. Would have been smarter to grow fur, but humans were never smart. Walking backward, dragged Jane's pants along Beast's paw-print trail. Hid paw trail. Hid her clothes. Jane was safe now from predator who might hunt her.

Hopped on top of boulder. Studied world. Smelled for mountain lions. Jane said mountain lions had been seen here. Two males, smart males who hunted as a pair. But I smelled no big-cat. Only goat smell. Not far away. Wanted to eat goat. Listened for Jane in mind. Jane still slept. I chuffed and snarled, claiming goats. And padded into night.

I ate. Long canines tore into throat of goat. Large goat still kicked, still dying. But I was hungry. I bit into meat. Drank down pumping blood. Ripped into goat and filled stomach. Hot blood. Good hunt. Over fences. Scared away large dog, as big as Beast. Took stringy old male, not baby goat, so that Jane would not be angry. Carried old goat back over fence into night. Ate. Afterward, licked blood from whiskers and face. Rolled over, belly to sky, paws in air. Happy. *Beast is good hunter.*

Overhead, a loud bird flapped wings in night, shining lights onto earth. Not an owl. Owls are good hunters. This bird was stupid hunter, noisy, frightening prey. But big. Beast liked big. Bird ducked and rose and circled, its heart an engine like Jane's bike, Bitsa. Alive but not alive. I remembered helicopter Jane had ridden in. Did not like helicopter, riding in belly of loud helobird. Liked Learjet, smelling of leather and vampire.

Beast, sleepy and full of old goat, lay on back and watched helobird. Helobird was like angel Hayyel, and not like. Hayyel was bright and fast and flew like helobird, but without humans in his belly. Hayyel had offered Beast freedom. Had offered Beast new life. Beast had refused. Did not want to leave Jane. Overhead, big helobird flew away.

Drew in night air. Cool. Clean. Delicate nostril membranes fluttered. Many new smells, some with value, some without. Unimportant: smell of flowers, spiky plants, hot earth, small creatures cowering in rocks, small snakes and big snakes. *Rattlers*. Dangerous hunters, stupid hunters. Would strike even at Beast, who was too big for them to eat.

Foul smells were distant: gasoline, rubber, hot road, oil on road. Men were not many here. Ridge of land, not far away, looked out over empty-of-man world. On ridge, Beast could see/smell/hear farfarfar. Beast would walk to ridge, take in new world. Maybe look for brothers who hunt together. Beast needed new mate. Strong mate would be good. Strong, smart mate would be better. Even better still, to have two of them.

CHAPTER FOUR

The Man Who Killed Me

I woke with my head on my boots, my body veiled by my hair. A spider perched only inches away, a big black hairy thing thrown into monster-sized silhouette by a dark gray dawn. It skittered way, shrinking to palm sized, as I pushed to my hands and knees and then to my feet. I threw back my hair and studied the situation. The car I'd been driving when forced off the road, then crashed, then been shot in, was canted at an angle, the engine silent. I could smell the road nearby, an overlay of exhaust placing it to my right.

Overhead, a hawk flew, black against the dark sky. It called, greeting the day with a piercing cry. I was muzzy-headed. And shivering. And hungry. Confused. Yeah. Confused. But I knew that it was too early for most species of hawk to hunt. Something had disturbed it.

My clothes were in a pile at my feet, which was weird, because I'd been in the car, and no way had I made it here before shifting into big-cat. I'd been too close to death. Beast had forced a shift when I couldn't, but I didn't remember anything after that, which wasn't normal. Even in the worst of shifts, when I was on the brink of death and only a shift into another form brought healing, I always, eventually, found myself inside Beast's body, along for the ride, just as Beast was along for the ride when I was in human shape.

I always remembered at least something of my time in fur. I didn't remember anything this time. Yet I was alive. I bent and found my panties and bra and pulled them on, making a face at the dried blood. I pulled on the ruined pants and stuck my fingers through the hole in the shirt. Two fingers. One hole. Yeah. It had been a big-assed gun. I found the new scar under my left arm and between my ribs, which corresponded to the hole in the shirt, and tried to figure what had been hit to make me bleed out so fast. And then I found the other scar on the right side, a little lower. The bullet had blown straight through me at an angle, probably taking out a kidney, maybe the bottom tip of my lung, and the top of my liver on the right. Bowel for sure. But kidney and liver were the likely kill spots; both organs had juicy blood supplies. I had an indentation on the right side big enough to put two knuckles in, so a big chunk of tissue had been taken out. I'd have to shift several times to smooth that out, and like the other, older kill shot on my upper chest, it might never go away completely. The old scar seemed to be permanent, I figured, because I had only shifted the one time, before I wandered out of the woods to be found by humans, and I had stayed in human form for years. These days, I shift often enough that most of the lethal wounds disappear. Most. Eventually. Even the scars on my neck from several near beheadings. Vamp hunting is dangerous business. My stomach cramped with hunger. I needed to eat. Soon.

Headlights lit up the road in the distance and I hurriedly finished dressing, shoving the empty gun into my waistband, holstering the others, and pulling the boots on over my bare feet. My socks were nowhere to be found. My black jacket hid some of the dried blood, clothing damage, and weapons, but not enough to allow me to safely hitch a ride once the sun was high. No one would stop for a bloody, armed, Amazon-sized woman on the side of the road, so I had to get moving before the sun rose.

I checked the ground as I made my way back to the car. No boot prints led away. No blood splatters marked the ground. No indication I had come this way. Just the rare sliding mark.

I stopped and bent, studying the ground up close as the

sun peeked over a butte. Red light spread out over the earth, a rosy crystal clarity of illumination that revealed a paw print to the side of the slide mark. I blinked. Beast had come this way, and something had then covered her tracks. I looked back at the rock I had waked up near, and back to the car. And down at my filthy pants, long streaks of dust marking them. "Son of a gun," I murmured. "Smart girl." It almost seemed like she was getting smarter, more intelligent, more able to cope with the human world, though she would have hated that thought. Beast didn't answer.

I moved on to the car and gathered up my weapons and gear, trying to see what had happened. I'd wounded the man who killed me. His blood trail was easy to follow. I bent and sniffed, smelling the vamp who had fed the blood-servant, and something metallic underneath the vamp-scent. Odd. They had followed me, shot me, one had been shot, and they left. The blood trail got heavier the closer to the road it got. I wondered if the man had made it to a hospital or died on the way. It was getting time to ditch the nine-mil. There were too many shootings tied to it, and if a surgeon or a coroner found a silver bullet, one of the rare, expensive hand-loaded rounds made especially for killing vamps, it would come back to haunt me. I opened the tote and pulled the top off a blood collection tube. Scooped up some dirt and dried blood. Resealed the tube. I didn't know if anyone could test a dirt/blood mixture, but if they could, it would be nice to know whatever the lab tests could tell me.

I slung the tote over my shoulder and trudged to the road, thinking about the phone in the Lear. I really shoulda brought a second cell.

At the airport, I stepped off the running board of the big-wheeled truck and handed the cell phone back to the old man who had given me a ride. I'd given him a fifty and fed him breakfast, watching him laugh as I ate enough food to feed a platoon of soldiers. Men seemed to like to watch me eat, which was weird, but if it kept them happy and out of my business I was content. It took a lot of calories to shift, and four fast-food paper bags and more than a dozen wrappers littered the floor of the truck cab. He waved and gunned the cranky motor even before the door closed. He was color-blind and hadn't noticed the blood; I'd been lucky. Not so much with the pilot—the pilot I was halfway convinced had told someone where I'd be today.

Dan—which I hadn't remembered from his name tag—studied me as he walked over, not missing the dirt, dried blood, or my general state of mess. "You're late."

I lifted a shoulder as if to say, *Sue me,* but I said nothing.

"This way," he said. "Stay close so no one sees the blood." Personable, talkative fellow. He should be on radio. I buttoned my jacket and held the tote over my bloody shirt. The flyboy avoided the metal detectors, leading me through the back of the terminal where only VIPs and flight personnel go, to the Learjet. I stopped at the base of the stairs as the pilot climbed up.

The blood had been washed off the pavement. There was no crime scene tape. No indication that I had fought for my life and Tory had been injured. "Is Tory okay?" I asked.

"He'll live." Flyboy didn't turn around.

"Chatty, aren't you?"

He didn't reply. "See you in Seattle, then," I told him. I climbed the stairs, grabbed my luggage, and went straight to the shower, where I took a long hot one before we taxied out. And then I pulled on sweats, hid my bloody clothes, stuffed the vial of dirt and blood and the blue-eyed blood-servant's pocket watch into my duffel. I stuffed the duffel under a bunk and studied the door. I wasn't happy about sleeping in a small confined space with a possible enemy only feet away, and I figured that if vamps slept here by day, they would have a mechanism to lock the door. They did. I slammed home two steel braces that were built into the door, arranged so they would lock into the steel frame of the jamb. Nice. Secure, I strapped myself into a bed in the sleeping cabin, fumbled for the Lear phone, and called Bruiser.

He answered with "Details." He didn't sound happy. I had called him on the old geezer's cell and reported that I was alive, but that the fancy cell Leo had provided was dead. Bruiser had been gratifyingly relieved to hear my voice, and irritated when I wouldn't use up Geezer's minutes on a full report. I had taken his time by sharing my concerns about the pilot instead. Bruiser was a step ahead of me and had already launched a full-scale, deep background investigation into Flyboy Dan, his finances, lifestyle, and love life. Because he was a part-time contract guy, the original background search hadn't been as intense as the one for the regular pilot had been. Now his life was getting the fine-tooth-comb deal.

Safe in the Lear, I gave the demanded detailed report, leaving out any mention of Beast, of course, filling in the time between the crash and the call on Geezer's phone with being knocked unconscious. Though I'm sure they had their suspicions, Leo and his people didn't really know what I was. Bruiser had tried to find me, but the GPS on the phone and the GPS on the car both went out with the accident. Though there had been flyovers by helicopters in the general vicinity, which was news to me; no one had spotted the wreck. Bruiser had called every hospital and law enforcement agency in a hundred miles of Sedona and discovered that one man had come in with "self-inflicted, accidental" GSW—gunshot wound. *Yeah. Right.* The man had gone into surgery and then disappeared from the recovery room. Like, literally disappeared. He didn't even show up on security cameras. He just vanished. Poof. But at least there wouldn't be any pesky cop questions.

"Get some sleep," Bruiser said when I was done. He clicked off. If I had been hoping for some sweet chat or pillow talk, I was disappointed. I rolled over, tucked the phone in its little nook, and closed my eyes. I was aware when we landed, the rising roar of the engines and the bump of touchdown, but I didn't wake. I slept until just before four p.m.

And woke to the smell/sizzle of steak wafting under the door. I got up, dressed in clean clothes, black jeans this time with a black velvet jacket, black silk shirt, braided hair, and holstered guns. I'm not girlie, so dressing didn't take long. The weapons, however, did.

I wasn't satisfied with the weapons I'd carried last night. I wanted more than just a nine-millimeter loaded with silver shot. I hadn't had enough firepower to stop the bad guys at the crash site—who had been human, not vamp. I wanted everything I had and I wanted every possible bad guy to know I carried it. Walk softly and carry a big stick. Or stomp loudly and carry enough firepower to start a small war. Whatever worked.

The weapons harnesses were problematic, having to be strapped on separately, yet align themselves to give me freedom of movement. I wore two matching, scarlet-gripped Walther PK380s; the one under my arm was loaded with nonstandard, hollow-point ammo; the one at the small of my back was the Walther's twin, loaded with silver for vamp and were-animal—just in case. The semiautomatic handguns were lightweight, ambidextrous, with bloodred polymer grips, and reengineered so the safety block wouldn't break off. I had practiced with them enough that I knew how they fired, how likely they were to jam in rapid-fire situations, and how they reacted to various kinds of ammo. I'm not a shooter, not a sniper, not into techno-porn. But I liked guns, and if I'd had all mine on me last night, I'd have finished the goon without effort. Or at least without dying. Into my boot holster went a six-round Kahr P380, a small semiautomatic with a matte black finish. It was loaded with standard ammo. Under my right arm, low on my chest, I wore my H&K nine-millimeter, loaded with nonsilver hollow-point rounds that would explode on impact. If I missed a center-mass kill shot, I'd maim an attacker, even a vamp. I inspected the weapon. I hadn't cleaned it, which was stupid, but I'd only emptied one clip, so the guilt wasn't particularly intense. Extra clips went onto my belt, under the velvet jacket.

My shotgun, a Benelli M4 Super 90, was slung over my back, belted on top of my jacket, the grip within easy reach over my shoulder. It was loaded for vamp with hand-packed silver-fléchette rounds that would work on human antagonists too. I carried one silver cross in my belt, hidden under my jacket, and stakes, secured in loops at my jeans-clad thighs. My braided hair was twisted around my head in a crown that would be hard to grab. Hip-length hair was a handle in a fight, and I had been advised to cut it long ago. It was the only suggestion by all of my senseis that I had ever ignored. I shoved silver stakes into the crown and stepped from the sleeping quarters just as a stranger placed a two-pound steak on the small table.

He froze when he saw me. He was wearing the white

shirt and black pants of the company Leo used for his part-timers, the patches on his shirt naming him Chris, the new first mate. Lovely. Now I had a flyboy pilot who might be an enemy and a first mate who might be his partner. I didn't think Leo was trying to kill me anymore, but one never knew. He swallowed before he asked, "M-M-Miss Yellow-rock?"

I slid in front of the steak and dropped the napkin across my lap, picked up the knife and fork, and closed my eyes. The prayer lasted half a heartbeat. I wasn't leaving my eyes closed for any reason. I cut into the steak and chewed, and then broke my own rule with a groan and a gourmand's closed eyes. Holy crap, it was good. Three bites later I looked up and remembered the first mate had spoken. Around a mouthful of steak I said, "Hi, Chris. I'm Jane. Good steak. I may have to marry you."

He swallowed and turned back to the kitchen, but I heard him murmur, "It'd be like sleeping with a scorpion." Which I thought was very funny, and almost told him so, but he was bringing me tea, and the steak was so good that I wanted to be nice. I ate the whole thing, plus the sautéed mushrooms and grilled zucchini he set on the side. Delicious. Ten minutes after I finished the meal, I was on my way, without ever seeing Flyboy Dan.

It was still an hour before sunset when I got to the clan home of the Master of the City of Seattle. The house—okay, it was a mansion, but my standards had changed the longer I worked in close proximity to vamps—now I called it a house and didn't feel like an impostor when the driver pulled up out front. The clan home was a hundred years old, three stories, brick, stucco, and wood on an acre of land, lakefront. It had heavily landscaped grounds and a circular drive off Lake Washington Boulevard, and all the houses near it were mansions too. I had no idea about property values, but I was guessing two mil easy. I gathered my things and stopped, dragging my eyes back to the Seattle Clan Home. Something wasn't— The lack jumped out at me. No security, no armed blood-servants patrolling. Not even a gardener on the grounds. The place looked deserted. My shoulders tightened as I got out, slung the blood-collecting bag over one shoulder, and closed the door. "You're waiting, right?" I said to the taxi driver.

"You're not a hit man, right?"

"Right. Just a bodyguard, applying for a job." *Liar, liar, pants on fire.*

"I'll wait unless I hear gunfire. Then I'm outta here."

"Fair enough. Thanks for the phone," I said, tucking it in my pocket. He had brought me a new one—no bells or whistles, but at least in one piece and functioning—on the orders of Leo. Having learned my lesson, I had another in my back pocket.

I spun on a heel and walked to the front door. It was a double door, wavery panes of leaded glass in the doors and side lights. One door hung open.

A Walther was in my hand in an instant, the Benelli sliding from the back sheath. From inside, I smelled a familiar sickly-sweet scent, heard raspy breathing and an irregular moaning. Using a toe, I pushed open the door.

The foyer looked immaculate, twelve-foot-tall ceilings, walls a pale cream, wainscoting a muted beige, and the millwork at ceiling and floor in a yellow the color of twenty-four-karat gold in candlelight. I slid inside and to my left into the formal room. Hardwood floors, Oriental rugs, marble fireplace surrounded by massive millwork. Cloth upholstery on couches and chairs, which was weird. Vamps liked leather; the feel of skin against theirs appealed to their predatory instincts. But I saw no leather anywhere. And even more odd, the shutters were open. Sunlight poured into the front room.

I moved on to the left, into the music room/library. A baby grand piano stood in the middle of the room, and couches and bookshelves lined the walls. The lower floor of the house was set up in a circular pattern for formal entertaining. I kept on circling to my left, into the breakfast room that looked out over the water and toward the Seattle cityscape, through the kitchen—lots of copper and brass, even on the walls and ceiling—and into the dining room, which had a table that would seat twelve. I hadn't seen anyone. No security cameras. Nothing. The sickly smells were all coming from upstairs.

I took the stairs to the second floor cautiously, the M4 pointed up, the handgun covering my backside. There were four bedrooms and ten sick blood-servants. Crap. There was no info anywhere on blood-servants getting sick. This was new, and not in a good way. The humans were sick like I had never seen anyone sick before, covered in pustules, many of them ruptured and seeping onto the bedding. The closest thing I could have guessed was smallpox. They were the source of the raspy breathing and moans.

I climbed the stairs to the third floor, which was empty, and then into the finished attic. The smell of rot about blew me away, and with Beast's experience, I can take a lot of decomposition. The upper floor was an apartment, and on the floor lay a woman. She had died by multiple gunshots. She had been beheaded, the way one would kill a vamp or were, to make certain of death. I kept the Benelli on the doorway to the stairs and slid the handgun into its holster. Avoiding the body fluids, I dropped to one knee at her side and reached into her mouth, feeling for fangs. Nothing. Human teeth. So why the beheading?

In the corner, something moved in the air currents. A bright blue feather, downy, fluffy. I swiveled on my knee and studied the rest of the floor. There were a lot of blue feathers, everywhere. But no bird or boa to explain why.

I drew a steel blade and pulled on Beast's vision to look at the woman. She still looked human. With the blade, I sliced down. Fast. Hard. And for an instant, I saw, not a woman, but a huge blue- and rosy-hued bird. "Crap," I whispered. The woman was an Anzu—a Mercy Blade. The supernatural species lived under a blanket of glamours that could be disrupted momentarily by the proper application of a steel blade. They were fierce fighters. If she was dead, then the clan home had been physically attacked as well as the vamps made sick. There was no sign of them here; they were likely hiding in their lairs.

I went back to the second floor and asked permission of the sick humans who were conscious, and took their blood, promising to call for ambulances. Oddly, they weren't panicked or worried, and even insisted that they were getting better, which sounded just plain weird, unless the disease affected their brains, like meningitis. The one I stuck last seemed the most lucid, and I asked, "What happened here? I thought your MOC had accepted a new master."

"Our Mercy Blade said we must fight, not accept the fist at our throats. She said we would win with her fighting at our sides. It was a mistake." Tears leaked from her eyes. "They killed her. They killed Mithrans, and then they ... spent some time with us."

I had a feeling that "spent some time with us" had been really, really bad. "Did any of your vamps survive the attack? Are they in their lairs?"

"Some died true-dead. Some didn't," she whispered. "We killed four of theirs, though they were old and powerful. But when we were overwhelmed, I told my masters to run. I haven't seen them since then."

After I obtained her blood, I washed my hands thoroughly in the hall bath. Even with gloves, I wasn't taking chances. Like Ro, the humans had kept bleeding and I had to apply pressure bandages at the puncture sites.

Back downstairs, I found an Apple laptop and shoved it into my tote with the blood, grabbed up several cell phones, and added them in too. Maybe the call histories would tell us something. I also found a business card tacked to a corkboard near a rack of cell chargers. It was black, white, and red, with a stylized drawing of a neck with holes in it, bleeding fresh blood, like a blood-whore's calling card. The name on the card was Blood-Call, the number and address local. It was the only thing on the board, which was odd, so I pocketed the card. On a desk, I found several other business cards, most of them of local businessmen: lawyers, accountants, a PR firm, people who might conceivably want a vamp's business and money. I found another Blood-Call card, this one creased and folded as if it had been carried around for a while. I took all the cards.

Standing just inside the front door, breathing fresh air through the open crack, I dialed Leo's number and told his *secundo* to wake Bruiser. He did it without demur and when Bruiser came on, he sounded chipper and alert, even though it was his sleep schedule. I told him what I'd seen and done, everything but the part about Mercy Blade being Anzu. I wasn't sure that the vamps knew that part. "I have blood samples from four human individuals, and had a devil of a time getting them to stop bleeding.

"You have any idea why these guys are still sick when their master gave in to the vamp we're chasing?"

"Someone rebelled after the fact, and the new master is teaching them a lesson." Which was totally something a vamp would do. Bruiser went on. "I'll find Gee DiMercy and tell him about the Mercy Blade. You get out of there and back here. I'll handle calling ambulances and alerting the authorities about the pla—the disease."

I hung up and stepped outside, still thinking about the word he had almost used for a disease that had attacked vamps *and* humans. *Plague.*

The stench clung to me, so bad even the patient driver's nose curled, so I tipped him two twenties when he dropped me off at the small, private airport in the boonies outside Seattle. The terminal was a single-story building with all the charm of a saltbox, but it lit up the early night like a beacon. This afternoon, I had passed through with a minimum of effort, even carrying the weapons, guessing that Leo's money had greased enough palms to make that happen. But there had been three people in the terminal. Now, as I stepped inside, there was no one.

My hackles rose. The car that brought me, and was the fastest way outta here, drove off, tires abrading on cement. I stepped to the right of the windowed door, wall at my back. I pulled the M4 and the Walther that was loaded with silver. It didn't have the stopping power of the H&K, but it was the weapon of choice when there was a likelihood of collateral damage—innocent humans who might get killed. The Benelli would take care of any vamps.

I felt the door close beside me with a little puff of air. Standing just inside, I slid to my right, along the wall. If I'd had a pelt, it would have bristled. Something was very wrong here.

The terminal was silent except for the hum of electronics and the whir of an overhead fan. The air was permeated with an acrid sting of overheated electronics and dissipated gun smoke. I breathed in, scenting for traces of blood, urine, feces—the body fluids that escape when humans die. The terminal didn't seem to contain any dead humans; nor did it smell like it had when I left. Beneath the reek of smoke, it stank of fear and blood-servant and the now-familiar vamp. And the burned powder of fired weapons.

A soft scrape like skin on something smooth sounded from the office door. I moved silently around the room, my back to the walls where possible, knowing that I was a sitting duck to anyone outside, hidden by the darkness. My reflection moved with a catlike effortlessness, and seeing myself in the windows gave me a weird feeling of déjà vu I couldn't specify but that felt like being tracked by another predator. My weapons swept the room. I used the windows to check behind the counter. Nothing. No one. But that soft scrape sounded again.

I ducked my head into the office and back out. Letting the image of the room resolve itself in my mind. Cheap metal folding table. Chairs. Papers scattered on the floor. Barrage of busted electronics still leaking smoke. Bullet holes in the equipment, walls, computers.

A bundle of body on the floor. Human. Tied up. Lying on his belly, hands secured behind his back, feet tied together, and then the ties laced through the binding on his hands and tightened, pulling him into an uncomfortable squashed C shape. Hog-tied.

There was a ball of something in his mouth. I edged into the doorway, forced to turn my back to the windows, which I hated. The man on the floor was wide-eyed, bobbing his head emphatically. His hands were dark purple, and I guessed that he had been tied up for at least twenty minutes. I moved in fast, looked behind the door, stepped to the side, and opened the closet, securing the room. It was clear.

I knelt beside the man and set the handgun on the floor, so I could work the wad out of his mouth. It was wet and gooey with blood and saliva and was wedged in tightly. Nothing is ever as easy in real life as it is on TV. As I worked, I whispered to him, "When this comes free, talk softly. Tell me three things. How many? Were you alone? And where are the people who did this? If you shout or talk too loudly, I'll stuff it back in. Understand?"

He grunted what might have been an affirmative. When the mushy cloth plopped out he said, "Three. One a fang-head. I was alone, but Beatrice will be back any minute with supper. They went back to the aircraft. I heard screaming. A lot of screaming. Then they drove off without walking back through here. Which is crazy because the fencing is twelve feet high with razor wire at the top and they didn't have time to cut—"

"Shut up," I said. He did, gasping for breath. "You're bound with plastic and it'll take time to free you. I don't have that time. I'll be back." I stood and breathed in and out, hard, pulling on Beast-speed. She wasn't talking to me much, but I could still access her traits. I raced out of the room and through the back terminal doors. Outside. Slammed my back against the wall. Took a quick look around as I ran into the shadows that would make me a less-easy target. Beast-vision made everything green and silvery and bright. No one was here.

Up the stairs of the Learjet. The smell of blood hit me hard. Fresh blood is not a smell humans can detect. But I can. Wet, sweet, and a lot of it. Blood in massive quantities aerated by arterial spraying.

I stopped just inside the hatch.

I share my soul with a predator, a big-cat who doesn't mind if her prey is still struggling when she starts to feed, who likes to play blood-games with her food. I'm used to death. But this blood-game had been played with a human. And it was bad.

CHAPTER FIVE

Deer Antlers Piercing Through His Shoulders

The carpet was soaked scarlet. The walls had been spray painted crimson. The leather chairs had been painted. The rounded roof ran with red rivulets. A naked body had been tacked beside the entrance of the sleeping quarters. The body was bluish white skin everywhere except for the raw, gaping wounds, still leaking. His limbs spread in a grotesque X. Nails, huge six-inch-long nails, held him in place on the bulkhead wall. Steel nails though his wrists and above his ankles. *Crucified*.

It was the part-timer, Flyboy Dan.

My scalp tingled. My vision telescoped down to the bloody man hanging on the wall. The vision of the nailed man triggered something deep inside, in some dark and shadowy place in my soul, some memory of fear and pain. It was like a tight, scarlet bud, the flower of some unseen, un-remembered horror still concealed in bloody, deadly petals.

Crucified. But not like the Christ. Like something else.

I smelled blood and the stink of bowels released in death. Heard the soft, wet sound of a drop of blood falling to the saturated carpet. I took a slow, deep breath and the darkness receded, the flower of old pain softened and blurred, losing its power over my mind.

But in some tiny, logical place of my brain that was still

functioning, I thought, *It isn't like the suckheads to let blood go to waste.*

Stupid thought. Stupid, stupid, stupid thought. I forced myself to breathe, breathe, slowly, deeply. Underneath the blood-death-stink I smelled vamp. Now-familiar vamp. The vamp I was chasing. I drew my weapons back into firing readiness. I'd let them drop at the sight of the man. Stupid rookie mistake. Stupid thoughts. I blinked away tears I didn't know I'd cried and scanned the small jet, looking for anything alive or undead.

There was no way to avoid stepping in blood, but I did my best as I peeked into the cockpit and then circled around to the galley. Both were empty. I flipped the light switch in the sleeping quarters. There was no blood here. No. The vamp had left me a different kind of message. The new part-time first mate was naked, positioned on the bed where I had slept. Dead, with two holes in his neck, still trickling blood. A smile on his face. An envelope lying on his fish white belly.

It had my name on it.

I toed off my bloody boots, walked barefoot to the bed, and took the envelope. Tucked it into the blood-bottle tote. Grabbed my belongings and slid back into my boots. Not sure where the calm actions were coming from. Training or instinct. Maybe a bit of both, taking over when my mind went on hiatus and my soul was aching. I paused at the hatch and looked back at the crucified man.

The ancient, blooming horror opened before me, in fast forward.

I had a momentary vision of another man, white, bearded, bloodied, hanging over hot coals, deer antlers piercing through his shoulders, ropes leading up from the antlers into the dark of night. The sound of drums. The smell of herbed smoke and blood. A phantom memory, new, yet oldoldold. And then it was gone, as if it had never been real. As if the memory was a dream, half lost upon waking.

I went down the steps, leaving bloody footprints, and washed my boots at a low faucet on the terminal building wall. Entered the terminal. I was sawing at the bindings on the hog-tied air traffic controller when the tears that were gathered in my eyes started to fall. This was crazy. People were being drained, were being crucified. People were dying of *plague*. I was on a mission of peaceful parley that should have been known only to a few specific people, but it felt as if my every move had been telegraphed to Leo's enemies and I didn't know how, or who was giving away inside information. More people were dead by violent means and I didn't know why. I didn't know a lot of stuff, and it had come back to haunt me.

I blinked and saw the man stuck to the Learjet wall like a bug on felt. I took a steadying breath. I could mourn later. I bore down on the bindings holding the air traffic controller. Dulling my blade. Because his hands had swollen around the plastic strips, it took all my strength and concentration to saw through the strips on his wrists and not cut him badly. One of the zip strips parted. I bent into the struggle with the plastic. It took a whole minute and several cuts to his hands and wrists, even with my highest-quality steel edges, to free him. Whoever had trussed up the air traffic controller had known what he was doing. When the last binding on his hands broke through, the man collapsed on the floor, pulling his hands up to shoulder height. They looked awful, but I thought they would be okay. Tying up someone's hands that tight can result in permanent damage from something called compartment syndrome. I'd seen it before and it wasn't pretty. "See a doctor," I said shortly, not letting my relief sound in my voice.

I cleaned his blood from the blade by wiping it on his pants and put it away in a sheath not easy to hand. I didn't want to draw it again until it had some attention. I should question him again. Hard and thoroughly. Just because he had been trussed up at a crime scene like a young calf didn't mean he hadn't been culpable on some level. Maybe he let the bad guys in. Maybe he did something else. But I wouldn't interrogate him. I would take the coward's way out and vanish. I stood and said, "Is there video surveillance of the attackers?"

Using one purpled palm, he pushed up and rolled over, looking at the destroyed computer and electronic equipment. He laughed, a pained chuffing sound. "I doubt it. Looks like they shot up the whole works."

"I need transportation."

"I have a Yamaha Super Ténéré bike beside the building out front. Can you ride?"

"I'm a Harley girl. Yeah."

"Keys in my pocket." He tried to move his fingers and hissed through his teeth at the pain.

"Give me ten minutes before you call the cops," I said. "Mr. Pellissier will make it worth your time." I fished for the keys and left through the front door. The bike was in the shadows at the side of the building, hidden from the parking lot, helmet on the back. It was a sleek, sporty street bike, all black, built for speed and comfort. I stored my weapons and clothes in the aluminum side cases and strapped the Benelli to the bike along my knee. The weight and balance were different from Bitsa, and it used a key start, which I had always thought was a wussy way to start a bike, but I wasn't complaining. I keyed it on and it had the nice steady purr of a well-kept engine. The last thing I did before leaving the airport was to throw the new cell phone as far as I could and let my braids down from the crown to put on the helmet. It smelled of the air traffic controller but wasn't too horrible. I'd been around worse smells today. I tucked the braids into my collar and was on the road in seconds, heading toward the city lights.

Popular wisdom says it's supposed to rain all the time in Seattle, but it was dry and balmy for November, in the high seventies, even this late. Scudding clouds were advancing across the sky, and the night was black with buffeting winds and unfamiliar scents, mostly fecund earth and dense greenery, exposed rock, still warm from the sun. I shifted gears and climbed a hill, gaining speed. Putting the past behind me. Right now no one knew where I was. No one could contact me. If I wanted, I could take off and just disappear. Start over.

Beast does not run away, she growled softly.

But I could. If I wanted. A large part of me did want to head for the hills. Every time I blinked I saw the man I had left in the Learjet. *Black road. Blink. Bloody body hanging on the jet's bulkhead wall. Open eyes.* The man I had left alone, unprotected, to be tortured by vamps. *Black road. Blink. Bloody body. Open eyes. Black road.* The hanging, bloody man had been familiar, part of an old memory, a memory from my Cherokee past. Familiar, but fading. Already the vision of the man in the past had merged with the dead man of tonight. The familiar, hanging pose. The distant memory tumbling into the present, yet not quite sliding into place. I had seen such a thing when I was a young child. I was nearly certain. Nearly.

For months, little bits and pieces of my current life had fallen away or were ripped from me, much like the man's flesh had been flayed off. But my grief had all been internal—not overt—and therefore easily pushed away, shunted aside in favor of more immediately important matters. Ignored. But at the sight of the tortured flyboy, and the half-recalled memory, the enormity of my life changes had socked me in the face like some dark demon risen from hell.

Black road. Blink. Bloody body. Open eyes. Black road. Grip bike. Apply more speed. Bend into the turn. Wind beating at me. My breath was hot under the faceplate, almost panting. Almost a sob.

I'd lost my best friend, Molly, when I killed her sister. I could still feel the eighteen inches of vamp-killer-blade sliding into Evangelina. Her demon-heated blood, pumping across my hand.

I'd lost my boyfriend Rick LaFleur when he was attacked by werewolves and were-cats, and I had been unsuccessful in helping him with his shift-to-furry problem. I had been forced to say good-bye to him while he went to a special training camp outside Quantico for agents of Big Brother—PsyLED—the Psychometry Law Enforcement Division of Homeland Security.

I was, for the first time in my adult life, essentially homeless, friendless, empty, and alone. Just as I had been at age twelve when I wandered out of the forest after being stuck in Beast form for decades. But this time, I remembered some of my past, and the memories left me flayed just as the pilot had been. Just as the man had been in the old memory. Had he? I remembered blood. I think. But the distant past was shifting and changing and drifting away. *Black road. Blink. Bloody body. Open eyes. Black road.* My own bleeding was all internal.

I was stupid and pathetic and spineless. Everything I'd done, every decision I'd made, had taken me to a place I had never intended to go—working long-term for the vamps instead of just beheading the crazy ones. Learning that some of them were thinking, feeling creatures. Not human—but not worthy of death just because of their vamp-nature. *Black road. Blink. Bloody body. Open eyes. Black road.*

Tears started to fall behind the face-shield, caught by the air currents sweeping up underneath like mini tornadoes, cool and damp across my face and into my hair. I deserved losing my best friend because I'd killed her sister. I had blood on my hands and on my soul and I'd added to the toll tonight—it was my fault that the men in the jet were dead, because I hadn't considered that someone would come after me, because I hadn't taken precautions. I didn't recognize myself anymore in the killing machine I was becoming.

Jane is killer. Only killer, Beast murmured.

"Go away," I shouted into the teeth of the wind. She growled and went silent. I gave the engine gas, speeding into the dark, passing headlights that left smears on my retinas. Bent low over the bike, leaning into the turns, taking chances that would have been deadly to anyone with human reflexes. *Black road. Blink. Bloody pilot. Bloody bearded man. Nails. Antlers. Open eyes. Black road.* The bloody body was a nightmare memory brought forward in time. Was the man from my past someone I had cared for? A white man? How would that be possible? And I'd never know, not for sure.

Lost. They were all lost. Everyone I knew from my first life. *Etsi*, my mother, *Edoda*, my father, *Elisi*, my grandmother. All gone. All dead. Decades and decades ago. And now everyone I truly loved and truly trusted from my current life, Molly and Rick, were gone. I screamed out my grief, in long, hoarse sobs as the miles and black pavement raced beneath me, and wind buffeted the misery that dogged me. I screamed until there was only the wind against my clothes and the road beneath my tires. *Black road. Blink. Bloody pilot. Open eyes. Black road.*

When the tears finally stopped, my voice was hoarse and my throat was raw. I was empty and purposeless and useless. *Jane is killer only,* Beast thought at me.

"Shut up," I whispered. "I didn't kill the man with the antlers through his body."

Jane is killer only.

In a small town outside Seattle, I passed a bank with a well-lit ATM and pulled over. If I had to go to ground, I needed money. I inserted my card and punched in the special PIN that allowed me a onetime withdrawal of an unlimited amount of cash. I removed five thousand dollars and added it to the wad of money Bruiser had given me for this gig. I wasn't sure why I might need to go into hiding, but the imperative was there. Take money. Stock up. Be prepared. Now I had to get back to New Orleans, which meant flying commercial, so I had to get rid of my weapons.

Two blocks over, in a brand-new strip mall, I found a one-stop shopping spot, most stores still open. In a high-end luggage store I paid cash for two hard-bodied cases used for shipping electronic musical equipment. Outside, I took my weapons apart so they couldn't fire, packaging the pieces in separate shipping containers, so that if someone stole one case, there weren't enough parts to make a whole weapon. It isn't easy to ship firearms and I didn't want any problems. In a UPS franchise store that was trying to close, I purchased a third container and shipping materials for the bladed weapons. The fifty I tipped the manager ensured that he stopped making noises about needing to close the store and got helpful, handing me padding and foam and layers of cardboard to keep the knives from shifting in transit. I kept only two weapons—two wooden stakes that I could use as hair sticks. If I got stopped by airport security, I wouldn't mind tossing them, and I'd feel safer if I had something on hand to defend myself.

I paid for insurance and overnight shipping to New Orleans and though it was an exorbitant price, I didn't blink at the cost. Another way the vamps had ruined me. Money meant a lot less now, was a lot less dear. *Blink. Bloody body. Open eyes.* I put the latest blood vials into a bubble-wrap envelope without telling the helpful clerk about the blood, and then secured them into the shipping container so they wouldn't roll around and burst.

I saw my reflection in the windows against the night outside. I looked like I'd been crying, my face strained and flushed. I took my receipts and left.

Inside the little town I also found a pay phone. I hadn't

seen one of those in forever. I went back to the UPS store and held a twenty up to the locked door, mouthing, "Change? Please?" Maybe it was the tear streaks on my face, but something worked because he cleared all the change out of his cash register for me. I tipped him another five. He was a happy camper. But he'd surely remember me.

Standing in the dark, I inserted coins and called Bruiser on the pay phone. He answered with a simple hello. He sounded very British in that moment, though he hadn't been British since the early nineteen hundreds. He also sounded distant and unapproachable. If Leo told him to kill me, would he do it? I honestly didn't know, and it was dangerous to be attracted to a man whose loyalties lay elsewhere. "Hello?" he repeated. *Blink. Bloody body. Open eyes.*

"Your pilot is dead," I said. "Stuck to the bulkhead wall by nails just like a bug on display. His blood was sprayed all over the Lear." My voice sounded hollow, empty, and rough as broken stone. "Your new first mate was drained and left on the bunk I slept on. The air traffic controller was injured. It was done by two blood-servants, one vamp. They knew where I'd be." I placed a hand over the envelope in my pocket, the one I had taken from the drained body of the new first mate. It bent under the pressure but didn't crinkle, a heavy cotton fiber paper. Bruiser started to reply but I interrupted with "You have a serious leak. I'll get home on my own. We'll talk then." I hung up, walked back to the bike, and lifted the helmet. The phone rang. Dang caller ID. I walked over and picked up. "What?"

"You, little girl, are not human. And I have the security tape."

I chuckled. "Reach. I *know* that was not a threat. Your clients would be horrified if they ever learned you could be enticed to blackmail."

"Not blackmail. Self-protection. I don't know what you are, but if I feel threatened, this will go viral so fast that cheap, pixeled-out video of you carrying a dead cop out of a cave will look like child's play."

My past was always coming back to haunt me, ghosts of the dead. I had nearly died killing off a whacked-out family of vamps in a closed gem mine in the Appalachian Mountains. I had survived but hadn't been able to save the cop. Another failure I carried on my shoulders. A camper had caught the video on his camera as Molly and I exited the cave, the dead cop over my shoulder. "I'm not your enemy, Reach. But Leo would be, should I tell him you're monitoring his incoming and outgoing calls. For now, let's just call it even. I'll keep your secrets. You keep mine." I hung up again and got on the bike. The phone rang again as I rode away. I didn't look back.

I rode back to Seattle, taking in the sights as the clouds grew more ominous overhead and rain started to spit down in hard, widely spaced drops. The buildings were a charming mixture of new and old, towering and modest-height, nestled into the terrain as if they'd been tossed and landed where happenstance chose. The pace of life here, this late at night, was leisurely, with only moderate traffic and no sense of urgency.

The Space Needle was amazing, and Beast peeked out to get a good look, snarling, *Too tall to use for watching prey. Stupid human buildings.* After that, she disappeared from the forefront of my brain again. In spite of her disdain, part of me thought I'd like living here.

Underneath the usual white-man smells of modern life, Seattle smelled of fish, stone, raw wood, and green earth. It smelled of rain—lots of rain—tropical-forest quantities of rain—and freshwater lakes and the Pacific Ocean and a sense of freedom I hadn't expected. Though part of that might be from getting out from under Leo's and Bruiser's and even Reach's thumbs. Unless I gave them opportunity, like with the pay phone call, they couldn't find me tonight without a lot of work and a lot of luck. I stopped for gas and washed more blood, now dry, off my boots. It ran in thin trails across the pavement.

Near the Fisherman's Terminal, at the wharf, I found a coffee shop still open and wheeled the bike in. I got an extra-large chai latte and a big blueberry scone and pulled out the laptop I'd stolen from the vamp house. I went online and did some research into flights out of the city. There were plenty of commercial red-eyes leaving, heading east, but nothing direct to New Orleans until morning. I'd be getting in near ten. I needed to be there a lot sooner, but I had no choice. I booked a direct flight with one stop, but no flight change, which cost me over five hundred dollars, but I didn't quibble, and—not able to use cash for a flight since 9/11—I used the one credit card I was pretty sure no one knew about. I borrowed the coffee shop's phone and left a message at the shot-up airport where the borrowed bike would be, then rode the bike to Sea-Tac, Seattle Tacoma International Airport, and left it in short-term parking with a hundred-dollar bill in the saddlebag.

With two hours left until my six a.m. flight to New Orleans, I cleaned up in the ladies' room and ate in a terminal restaurant that served overpriced, overcooked, undertasty food. I settled in for a long night. Having brooded myself into a total funk, I pulled out the fancy, heavy cotton envelope and turned it over. My name was on the front in a flowery, curlicue, old-fashioned script that looked like calligraphy. Old vamps had the best penmanship. They'd had centuries to perfect it. Whoever had written the two words had managed to imbue my name with elegance and menace, or maybe that was just me projecting. Or maybe it was the spot of bloodred wax sealed with the imprint of a bird with a human head, maybe an Anzu.

Sniffing the envelope, I detected a faint blood-scent: peaty, spicy, and a little beery—the now-familiar blood-scent of the vamp who drained the first mate. It was an odd scent for a vamp. Even without being in Beast form, I knew it was the same vamp who had sent my attacker in Asheville, and all the ones since.

Deflecting a spurt of apprehension, I slit open the envelope and pulled out the single sheet, unfolded and scrutinized it. The words were oddly capitalized, like the way old English words were capitalized in documents to indicate their importance. Again, it was written in the calligraphy of someone who had written in script back when that was a prized skill.

You killed my Enforcer, Ramondo Pitri.
You will Die with your Master,
in a massacre such as you have never seen.
This, at a time of my choosing.

Ramondo Pitri was the name of the blood-servant I'd killed in Asheville. He had come into my hotel room, carrying a gun with a silencer, and smelling of unknown vamp. I had shot him, killed him, before I ever knew that he was a made man out of New York, not the usual vamp fodder. He hadn't smelled like any vamp I knew, or been formally attached to any of Leo's clans. All that had caused us to assume he was a hired killer. But as an Enforcer, Ramondo should have been known to the general vamp population and should not have entered any other master's territory without proper papers or an invitation. And he should have stunk of his master's blood and been deeply under the blood-bond, rather than smelling of a distant and irregular feeding. Of course, I was an Enforcer—sort of—and I had no blood-bond at all.

I turned the paper over as if looking for clues that simply were not there. I had killed another master's Enforcer and now I had to die? And Leo had to die? And the blood-slave at the Sedona Airport had to die? And the pilot stuck to the wall of a jet had to die, as did the drained corpse of the first mate? All because I . . . what? Shot first and asked questions later?

The grief I had given into on the harrowing bike ride receded a pace, leaving a small blank slate of uncertainty on my soul. Grief, like guilt, may not always be warranted.

I folded the letter back into the envelope. I needed a cup of strong tea, but there was nothing in the airport except teabags, so I walked to a bar and ordered a pint of Guinness Draught, not because I could get a rush out of the alcohol— skinwalker metabolism is too fast for that—but because I wanted something in my hands to help me think. Holding the big glass, I sipped.

The taste brought Beast to the forefront of my mind again. *Smells like vampire,* she thought, and she was right, which might, subconsciously, account for me ordering the beer in the first place. Peaty and beery. Yeah. Like the vamp. I drank long, killing half the beer, feeling tension begin to drain away. I was tired and sleepy, but I pulled the letter from my pocket again and studied it. Midnight had come and gone. This read like some kind of vamp-challenge, the fanged Hatfields meet the vamped-out McCoys. If a challenge had been issued to Leo, I hadn't been notified. I looked at a clock and discovered it was now after five a.m., Pacific time. Maybe the letter meant midnight tomorrow. Or next week. The new moon was days away.

Smells like vampire, Beast thought again. *Is important.*

It was the first time she had taken such an interest in my life in weeks, and I couldn't help my internal smile. *Okay,* I thought back at her. *But why?* She didn't answer. *Big help you are.*

I debated calling Bruiser and asking, and I decided it could wait. This vamp threat would be contained in the Vampira Carta or its codicils, which I had on file on my own laptop back in New Orleans and could access soon enough.

Old vampires are patient hunters, Beast thought. *Like snakes, lying on rocks all day in the sun. Not moving until a rabbit—or a puma—comes by. Then striking, fastfastfast with killing teeth. Even if snake is too small to eat its prey.*

Sooo. The vamp attacks me, I thought back, *in the cities he's conquered. Like a snake. Sneaky. That's part of his war on Leo?*

Again, Beast didn't answer. *Dang cat.* I didn't want to use Reach for this. Maybe it was nothing, but he'd known about each of my stops on this little excursion. Maybe my best research help was also my new worst enemy.

I pulled out a throwaway cell and considered calling Derek Lee. I thought about how he had been Leo's ally first, then mine through a process I wasn't sure I understood, except for the money. I had made sure he was paid for his kills of rogue-crazy-nutso-vamps, and he had backed me up on several gigs. Money created either honorable bedfellows or cheating partners, one or the other. And then there were his new guys—who might be safer and more trustworthy than his older, dependable guys. Or not. There were too many new faces to keep track of.

"Derek Lee," he answered, succinct.

I smiled into my beer. Took a long slurp, so he could hear it, and said, "I need some intel."

"Legs," he said, using the nickname he and his men had given me. "And I should help you, why?"

"Because I keep life interesting," I said. He snorted. "And because I have money and something else you want, although you haven't figured out what, yet. No questions asked." Derek Lee went quiet at that. I had just offered a future favor, whatever he needed, whenever he needed it. "I need intel on Ramondo Pitri, a made man, of Corsican descent, if I remember right, out of New York."

"That's the guy you shot in your hotel room," he said, his interest sharpening.

"Yeah. Turns out he was the Enforcer of an unknown vamp, who intends to challenge Leo soon. He thinks I need to die along with Leo."

"Damn suckheads. Uh. Sorry."

The men knew I didn't curse and that often made them uncomfortable, as if they had mistakenly said a bad word in front of their grandma, in church. I laughed, the sound curt and bitter. "My sentiments exactly. One of your guys, Angel Tit, if I remember right, is from New York. Maybe he has contacts there he can use to dig up some history that isn't on record." Angel Tit was the nickname of Derek's electronics guy, a hacker as good as Reach. Well, nearly as good as Reach.

"What? A black guy from New York should know the mob?"

"He can ask his buddies and they can ask around. That's all I'm asking."

I heard Derek talking in the background, the sound muffled. "He says okay, but his guys are scattered. He doesn't know what he can find out. It's gonna cost you, Legs. Money to grease the way."

"It always does, Derek. It always does. Before you hang up, I need some specialists. I want an intel guy and a security guy on retainer, to meet me at dusk, at my house. The security guy needs to be someone with Special Forces training, but doesn't have to be a marine or SEAL. Army's fine." He snorted his opinion of the army. "I'll give you a finder's fee, but they'll belong to *me*." I put delicate emphasis on the word. "Not you." A silence stretched out. I waited, knowing that I had insulted him by saying the men I wanted had to belong to me and not him, and knowing that most people would have said something—anything—to end the silence. I didn't.

"Money talks," he said at last, the words almost spitting. "I'll send you some guys. I can't vouch for them personally, but they have good records."

"That's all I can ask."

"Legs, you ask everything of a man."

The connection ended and I had no idea what he meant.

I arrived back at Louis Armstrong New Orleans International Airport at ten a.m., exhausted, sleepless, and shaky from lack of food. Peanuts don't go far when one is stuck on a plane for hours. I dragged into my freebie house and stared longingly at the stove. I wanted food, but I needed something else. I divested myself of anything that might be considered a weapon—including the two hair sticks and the magic amulet, the pocket watch I'd stolen off the blood-servant in Sedona. I tucked it into the Lucchese boot box I use for jewelry. The box wasn't pretty, but it did the trick.

After a quick shower, I pulled on clean jeans and a tee and checked my e-mail. I had a succinct one from Reach. It read "Subjects on video at airport are not identified. Not in any database."

"I can't get a break here," I muttered. Irritated, I took off on Bitsa. I had things I needed to know, things that might be stuck somewhere inside me, like grease and hair in a drain, or trees in a creek, backing things up. I was frustrated and tired and wanted to hit something. Not a good way to be when I needed to think clearly.

I made my way out of the city to Aggie One Feather's house. Aggie was a Cherokee elder, and I thought her mother might be a Cherokee shaman—sha-woman?—of sorts, not that I knew enough of my own heritage to say for sure if that was even possible. But Aggie had been working with me to find my past, the memories that were stuck so far deep inside me that they had become part of the framework of who I was, rather than separate moments that helped to shape me. And while I didn't like a lot of the things that had shaken loose inside me, I was learning stuff I needed, and, as she put it, freeing up my spirit to continue on its journey.

In the Lake Cataouatchie area—which is mostly mosquito-infested swamp—I pulled into the shell-asphalt street, smelling smoke, and onto Aggie's white crushed-shell drive-way. The house was small, a 1950s gray, asbestos-shingled house of maybe twelve hundred square feet, with a screened porch in back. The house was well kept, with charcoal trim and a garden that smelled of tomatoes and herbs in the morning warmth.

At the back of the property was a small building, a wood hut with a metal roof—a sweathouse—and smoke was leaking from it, smoke that carried the scents of my past, herbed smoke infused with distant memories, all clouded with fear and blood. Smoke that spoke of the power of The People. *Tsalagiyi*—Cherokee, to the white man.

I turned off the bike and set the kickstand. Propped the helmet on the seat and walked up the drive, shells crunching under my feet. Not much stone in the delta; they used what was handy, shells. I took the steps to the porch, and pushed the bell. It dinged inside. Almost instantly, a slender, black-haired woman in jeans and a silk tank opened the door. Her face was composed, her eyes were calm, but she didn't speak. She just looked at me. Waiting. *"Egini Agayvlge i,"* I said in the speech of The People. "Will you take me to sweat?"

For a long moment, she said nothing, studying my face, reading my body language, which always gave away too much to her. "I have taken one to sweat today already. I am tired. Come back tomorrow."

She started to close the door and I said, quickly, "Please."

Her eyes narrowed, but the door stopped closing. *"Dalonige i Digadoli,* Golden Eyes Golden Rock," she said with something like asperity, "you have hidden yourself away from the eyes of your own spirit, hidden yourself away from me, so that I cannot help you. What do you seek?"

"To know why nothing matters but finishing a job. To know why I'd compromise everything to see through to the end of a responsibility I accepted, even when it hurts me and the people I love. To see why I remember an image of a bearded man, tortured and hanging from antlers."

"You killed a man in your hotel room," she accused, her tone without heat. "You killed the sister of your friend. I saw it on TV."

I closed my eyes, weariness making me sway on my feet. "Yes."

"Go add wood to the coals. Make yourself ready. Clear your mind of useless thoughts and unnecessary pain. I will come." The door closed in my face. Rudeness from an elder of The People was almost unheard of, but I had a way of pushing people's buttons. Go, me.

In the back of the windowless hut, hidden from the street, I stripped and hung my clothes on a hook, ran cold water over me from the high spigot, dried off on a clean, coarsely woven length of cloth, and tied it around me. I ducked and entered the low sweathouse, stepping onto the clay floor.

I hadn't told Aggie what I was, but she knew bits and pieces of my story and probably guessed a lot more. I had originally come here, hoping she could help me find the child that I once had been so very long ago, before Beast, before I lost my memories, before the hunger times, which I remembered only vaguely, and before I was found wandering in the Appalachian Mountains, scared, scarred, naked, and with almost no memory of human language. I kept coming back because she was doing much more than I asked. She was showing me also who I was now.

Finding an elder here in New Orleans shouldn't have been a surprise — The People lived all over the States — but it still felt like a weird coincidence the universe tossed my way, like scraps to a dog. Like fate or kismet or whatever, though I didn't believe in any of that stuff.

I stirred the coals and added cedar kindling. Flames rushed up and lit the twigs, sending shadows dancing over the wood walls. Aggie had done some work (or hired it out, but I was betting on her doing it herself) in the sweathouse. She had added some more river rocks to the fire ring, and I pushed them closer to the flames. They were already warm to my hands, but not warm enough for what Aggie wanted. She had replaced the seating. A six-foot-long log had been cut in half lengthwise, sanded smooth on the flat sides, and lacquered until the benches shone. Then they had been placed on low cradle-shaped stands so people could sit on them instead of on the clay floor. These low benches were slightly higher than the old ones. I was guessing that old knees were more comfortable at that height. Maybe she was the president of the local elders, and they held elder meetings here. Assuming she wasn't the only elder round about. And assuming they held meetings. . . .

I was clouding my mind with inanities. I had a feeling

that Aggie would make me wait until she thought I had gotten past that part of the process to make an appearance. *"Make yourself ready. Clear your mind of useless thoughts and unnecessary pain."* Yeah. She'd make me wait. I sighed and added more wood. Time passed. The wood crackled and hissed. I moved from the log to the floor, sitting as modestly one could in a sweathouse, and I sweated.

When the coals had burned down and the rocks had taken their heat, I dipped water over them with the hand-carved wooden ladle, from the Cherokee stoneware pitcher that I coveted. Steam rose, and I sweated some more. When the coals were a red glow below a coating of ash, I reached into a woven basket and pulled out a tied bundle of dried herbs, like a very fat cigar: twigs of rosemary, sage, tobacco, which was a new one, a hint of camphor, other things I couldn't identify, lots of sweetgrass. I set it in the coals. The herbs smoked and the smell filled the sweathouse.

I closed my eyes and dropped into the dark of my own soul. Into the cavernlike place where memories of the *Tsalagiyi* resided. The firelit, smoky cave of my soul home. I had been here before, in this half-remembered cavern with its sloped ceilings and shifting midnight shadows, with the far-off plink of dripping water and the scent of burning herbs, of the steady beat of a tribal drum, hypnotic and slow.

I heard the door of the sweathouse open, a shaft of light across my lowered lids, quickly darkened as the door closed. Bare feet padded close. Aggie sat across from me in the cavern of my soul home. I couldn't smell her scent, only sweetgrass and smoke and a single breath of the cool, damp air of the cave of my soul.

Warm, wet heat and darkness surrounded us, steam rising from red coals and heated rocks piled in the center of my spirit place. She started music—drums, steady, resonant. I think I slept. And dreamed.

Long hours later, I heard a voice in my dreams, softer than the quiet drums. *"Aquetsi, ageyutsa."* Granddaughter . . . "Tell me what you did not finish."

My mouth refused to open, as if I was caught in a dream, trapped, trapped, *trapped*. I sucked in a breath so deep and hard it hurt my ribs. I forced open my lids and they parted sluggishly, revealing Aggie through my tangled eyelashes.

Aggie's eyes were black in the dark, calm and quiet, like deep pools of water in a slow mountain stream. She cocked her head, as if she were a robin staring at a juicy worm. We were no longer in the sweathouse, but in the cave where she took me sometimes, and I didn't know if this was vision or reality or some esoteric blending of the two.

The drum was deep, a reverberating beat, hollow against the cavern walls of my mind. A heartbeat of sound, steady and soothing. I couldn't get my mouth to work to ask my question. I didn't know what *to* ask.

Aggie smiled into the scented darkness. "You are stubborn. You are full of resentment. Only failure of the worst sort would cause you to resent failure. To fear it. To grow a tough hide that would make you never back down. Only failure." She reached into the basket and brought out another smudge stick, fat and aromatic even before she held it to the fire. Yellow flames licked out and up, and light caught her copper-colored cheeks and forehead, darkening the shadows at the sides of her mouth, making her look older than she really was. Drawing out her mouth into a muzzle. *Like a wolf.*

I tried to tense, but my muscles failed me. I tried to push upright, but the world whirled around me as if I were drunk or stoned. Aggie's mother was *ani waya*, Wolf Clan, Eastern Cherokee. Her father was Wild Potato Clan, *ani godigewi*, Western Cherokee. Aggie had magic I had only guessed at. Her snout stretched out. Her shadow on the cavern wall was all wolf. Teeth, wolf teeth, glinted in the firelight.

"My, what big teeth you have, Grandmother," I mumbled.

I knew I was trapped in a dream when the wolf laughed. She held the smoking smudge stick into the air and saluted the four directions, north, east, south, west, and north again. The trailing smoke made a pale, thinning square in the darkness. "What did you fail at, *Dalonige i Digadoli*?"

I recalled a vision of shadows on the wall. A man riding a woman. My mother. Remembered the stink of semen and death. The soft cries of fear and pain. The slick feel of cooling blood. "I didn't kill the killer of my father. I didn't kill the white men who raped my mother." I told the story of the fractured memories.

CHAPTER SIX

I Never Had a Chance to Say Good-bye

"You were a child of five. You were no match for the white man." Through my tangled lashes, I saw Aggie One Feather's wolf snout tilt, like a robin, the motion unsettling, part wolf, part bird, all dream.

"I swore an oath on my father's blood," I said. "I wiped it on my face, in promise."

"Are you certain you failed?" Her head tilted far to the side. "Who did you tell of this great crime? Who did you go to?"

Instantly, I remembered the sharp stick piercing my foot as I ran through the dark, my pale nightgown catching the moonlight through the stalks of corn. The corn towered over my head, the garden never seeming so large in the daylight. Down the hill to my grandmother's house, the longhouse where she lived with her daughters and their husbands. This was a new memory, and my breath caught before I said, unsteadily, "I went to *Uni Lisi*, grandmother of many children, *Elisi*, the mother of my father." I saw my hand banging on the door. Pounding on it. Saw the door open and the light/heat/brilliant colors blast out. Voices so loud they pulsed against my eardrums. My screaming. The women grabbing up weapons. A hoe. A long knife. My grandmother holding a shotgun. And the long horrible run back through the corn, racing ahead, *Elisi* letting me lead the way.

In the sweathouse, my heart raced with an uneven beat, like a broken drum, as my body reacted to the memory and its terror. I saw again my mother, in a heap on the ground, naked in the moonlight. The white men gone. The smell of horses. And man stuff. The sound of her crying. The warrior-woman, my grandmother, putting me on a horse, in front of her, and galloping into the night, her arm a band holding me close. The smell of her sweat and her anger. The smell of the pelt she carried. The feel of her beast roiling under her skin — *tlvdatsi* — mountain lion. Yet the pelt she carried over her shoulder was black.

A black panther, my white mind murmured. *Elisi was a skinwalker. Like me. A protector of the Cherokee, a warrior of the tribe.*

The door opened, the vision shattered. I sat up.

Aggie One Feather stood in the doorway, fully human, freshly dressed in the coarse woven robe she wore in a sweat ceremony. Just entering for the session. "I was delayed. My apologies."

"No need to be sorry," I said, sitting up, standing, my legs feeling wobbly. "But I think I'm done for the day. Can I come back? Soon?"

Aggie tilted her head, just like she had in my vision, but there the resemblance ended. "Certainly. If you're sure?"

"Very sure. Thank you."

Back home, I showered, dressed, and fell on my bed, face in the pillow. It smelled musty. I needed to change the sheets. Wash clothes. Maybe get a life. On that thought, I slept.

The sun was setting when I heard a ringing and forced myself awake.

I was in my house, or, rather, the house I was using as long as I worked for the blood-master of New Orleans. It was a nice house, two hundred years old, give or take, remodeled to give it all the modern amenities and still have all the old-world charm, at a nice address in the Quarter.

Yawning, I made my way to the kitchen to see a cell

phone lying on two notes, both signed by Troll, Katie's primo blood-servant and protector. The top note said "Frm: Derek Lee. Angel Tit had no luck with New York contacts." The second was an invitation to dinner from Katie and her girls. I had missed the girls who lived and worked at Katie's, and it would be the first relaxing moment in my life recently. I needed some relaxing. The cell started ringing again, so I answered. And heard gunfire. And Bruiser shouting.

"Jane! Are you in New Orleans? We're under attack!" The phone shifted and I heard him shouting to the side, muffled, "Get him out of here! Alejandro, Estavan, take four men and get our master to Katie's! Set up a perimeter. *Keep them safe!* Hildebert, Koun, take over on the battle-field. Lorraine, Bettina, go with Alejandro. Guard your master and his heir! I charge you with—"

"I am going nowhere. This is my home! I *stay!*" Leo shouted, his voice guttural and vamped out. Even over the phone I could feel the power he was drawing upon, the power of all his clan. "I will not run from my enemies!"

Beast flooded into my system. Phone to my ear, I raced to the side door. I had heard a knock while I slept and hoped it was a delivery. I nearly ripped the door off its hinges. It slammed back against the wall, and I spotted the shipping containers full of my weapons.

"You are of no use to us burned alive," Bruiser said, going all upper-class British. "Get to a place of safety until we can formulate a plan. Please, Master!"

Master? Things were *bad* if he was calling Leo *Master.* I lifted the heavy containers and carried them as fast as I could to my bed. Gunfire sounded so close I held the phone away from my ear. I heard sirens, fire and police, and Bruiser's voice, grunting. I knew that sound, that specific tone of pain. He was hit. Hit bad. The phone fell and clattered away.

I never had a chance to say good-bye to my father. I had no intention of letting that happen to me again. I tore off the top of the shipping boxes and started to reassemble my weapons.

I bent over Bitsa, the wind tangling my hair, which streamed out in the wind, chilling the necklace of interlocked links that protected my throat from vamp-fang—the new neck-

lace of silver-plated titanium. I took the old bridge over the
Mississippi, the pebbled roadway a patterned hum beneath
the tires, weaving between cars and trucks of evening traffic,
ignoring both speed and safety laws with abandon. I nearly
flew into the countryside on the far side of the river. I could
see the light on the horizon miles away. A fire. A big fire.

The smell of smoke was hot on the wind. Wood, plastic,
metal, brick, each has its own scent markers as it burns. So
does the smell of burning flesh. Human. Foul and horrible,
like spoiled pork. I shifted my weight forward and lowered
my head over Bitsa, the Harley moving at the peak of her
engineering specs, taking curves at top speed. Beast shared
her night sight, the shadows glowing green and silver and
blue. Her reflexes allowing me to handle the greater speed.
Mine, she whispered into my thoughts. *Mine.*

I slowed, turning into the long drive, zigzagging between
cars and fire trucks and emergency trucks, red, white, and
blue lights strobing the dark, the artificial lights lost beneath the red-orange blaze of the conflagration. Men and
women shouted. Water plumed up and over, aiming into
broken dormer windows on the roof of the old wooden clan
home. Smoke and fire billowed out from the windows of
every story; sparks and flames leaped high into the air. Fire
demons—tornadoes that sometimes formed above raging
fires, sucking the flames into the gyre—spun high above the
madness. The smell of magic tingled on the air, hot and
spicy as cactus spines. Gunshots sounded in the distance,
punctuated by muffled screams and shouted orders. Ahead,
near the flames, I smelled Bruiser on the air, Bruiser and his
blood, a lot of blood.

I dropped my Harley and helmet against a tree far from
the fire, where the shadows would hide the Benelli strapped
to the bike. I raced in, bypassing the cops who tried to stop
me. Choosing the ambulance surrounded by the most people, I pushed through the throng, tripped over a hose. Shook
off a hand that tried to pull me back. Rounded the ambulance, my boots grinding with my speed. Smelling the blood
even over the smoke. Bruiser's blood. Everything in my life
narrowed to that one scent. I dodged another man who
tried to stop me, shouting it was too dangerous for onlook-
ers. I jumped into the ambulance. Bent over Bruiser,

touched his shoulder, and leaned in to breathe in his scent, my unbound hair sliding forward.

His shirt had been half cut away, bloody rags still on one arm and half tucked into his trousers. Blood smeared his chest, as did brown Betadine and swathes of white bandages centered on his upper left shoulder and his right chest below his pec. Bags of clear fluid hung from IV stands; one was a plasma expander, the other normal saline. His eyes were closed and his skin was chilled where my hands brushed over his chest. But he was full of vamp blood. He would have some residual accelerated healing.

I tried to say something, anything, thinking, *Are you okay?* Or something like that. Something normal. Instead what growled out of my mouth was "If you bleed to death, I'll kill you and Leo both."

A faint smile touched his face, but before he could reply, the paramedic said, "Ma'am, unless you're next of kin, get out, you." Frenchy patois. Cajun background.

"She's next of kin," Bruiser said, without opening his eyes.

"Your wife, she is?" The paramedic sounded incredulous. I ignored him.

"Sure. She can make any medical decisions for me. My lawyer has the papers."

Which was news to me, if it was true. And *wife?* I shook that away, even as Beast purred a satisfied *Mine*. "What happened?" I asked, knowing it had something to do with my trips and the vamp who was attacking other MOCs. "This is my fault," I said.

He tried to laugh, but his breath caught with pain. I thought I heard something wet and gurgly in his chest, but the paramedic didn't seem concerned and the sound stopped.

When he could speak, he said, "You struck the match? Carried the gasoline? Tried to kill my friend and master?"

Inside, I flinched at the two terms used together for Leo, who was both vamp and monster, but I kept it there, in the dark inside me. I shook my head no.

"Just after moonrise, Leo was sitting down to breakfast," Bruiser said. "We heard gunfire. Vamps and blood-servants attacked, killed the gardeners and three security men in the first ten seconds. Inside of fifteen they had us pinned down inside. By thirty seconds, they had firebombed the house and were taking off on trail bikes that they must have pushed in. Then we heard the second wave, gunfire from the surrounding property. It was well coordinated. They were professionals, well trained, and they are still fighting out there." He lifted a finger and pointed off behind the house. "How can any of that be your fault?"

I had seen the property from an all-terrain vehicle during my review of Leo's security systems, and hadn't liked the easy access to the house. But making Leo move into town and give up his family home hadn't been an option. When I'd suggested the move, he had lifted a narrow black brow and uttered a laconic "No." I hadn't argued and I should have. Now that decision was back to bite Leo. Worse was the knowledge that I was even more involved in today's fiasco.

"It's my fault because the man I killed in my hotel room was the Enforcer of the master vamp who's challenging and taking other vamps' territory."

Faint humor touched his features, his closed eyes crinkling slightly. "Why do you think that?"

"Leo's enemy left me a letter on a dead man."

"A? Z? Q?" the paramedic asked, and laughed at his own joke.

Bruiser's brown eyes came open slowly, as if they had been glued together. There was pain in his gaze, but also intense concentration and focus. He lifted a finger and touched my hand. I almost jerked away from the contact, his flesh as cold as a vamp's, but his fingers closed over mine. "When you first saw him in your hotel room, was his gun drawn?"

The question surprised me nearly as much as the gesture. "I don't know." I stared into his eyes, unable to block out his study of me. Unable to not remember. It had been months, and what I recalled about the man had been the initial lack of scent on his person. Unscented deodorant, no cologne, only gun oil and lubricants to mark him as armed, and later, the very, *very* faint taint of his master—which I could now identify as beerlike, hops and fermentation and the sweet smell of blood. I had been naked, asleep, when he entered the hotel suite, my body hidden behind the mounded bed linens. I had risen, whirling, grabbed the statue beside the

bed, and thrown it as both a diversion and a weapon, diving
for my Walther 380. His arm had been coming up. "He was
turned to the side, right arm down and out of sight, looking
at my weapons, going through my blades and stakes with his
left hand, when I threw the statue at him. It's all in the police reports. I didn't lie about anything."

"You shot first?"

I hadn't actually seen the weapon until he fired. Spats of
sound from an illegal suppressor, like books dropping flat
from shoulder height. Then the sound of my weapons firing.
The recoil in wrist and shoulder. The stench of gunfire and
blood. "No. He shot first." Which meant that my attacker
had been already holding a drawn weapon. An odd tightness in my chest eased.

"Self-defense. Did he say anything?"

"No. He went unconscious fast, even though there wasn't
a lot of blood. I thought he was going to live until they told
me that he . . . died. Later."

"The letter the master Mithran left you. Where is it?"

I slipped my hand from his and pulled the envelope from
my pocket. He chuckled, the laughter holding more pain
than comedy. "Read it to me."

I unfolded it and read the letter aloud. When I was done,
he took the single page and stared at the words. I heard
something stutter-thump-give-way, something from *inside*
him. Bruiser's hand fell to his stomach, the letter fluttering
to the floor. The paramedic cursed and pushed me to the
side. Bruiser didn't take another breath, his chest sunken in
and still. I pulled the new cell and speed-dialed a landline
number I seldom called. I was shocked when Katie—who
hated phones—answered with my name, "Jane Yellowrock." There was rage in the words, but I didn't think it was
directed at me.

I said, "Leo's primo is bleeding out. I need someone
strong to feed him. Fast."

"We have our own wounded. Leo is not alone to suffer
assault tonight. We too are under attack," she said, uninten-
tionally repeating Bruiser's words, from what felt like days
ago, as he told vamp-warriors to get Leo to safety and to
protect Katie. "My Alejandro and Estavan were injured as
their carriage drove up. The little priestess is in a healing

trance with them. The elder priestess is *missing*," she spat. "The others are fighting and dying to ensure our safety. Who do you suggest I send to feed a *human*?"

Fury spurted through, me, hot and blazing at her callous disregard of any but another vamp, even a *valuable human*, like the primo. "I don't care who you send," I ground out, "but it better be fast, or so help me, by all I hold holy, I'll stake and behead you myself, and rip out your fangs and mount them on my necklace." My breath came hard and fast, as if I'd been running.

"Deo. You would too. And Leonardo would let you," she hissed. "I will recall someone from the battlefield. He will be there in moments." The cell connection ended and the ambulance started to move.

"Stop," I said. When the paramedic ignored me, I swiveled on my heel and slid against the driver, shoving him. One handed, I opened the door and continued my momentum, pushing him off his seat and out onto the drive, even as I slid into the driver's seat, hit the brakes, and threw the ambulance into park. I looked down, ascertained that I hadn't run over the driver, and said, "If you'd been wearing your seat belt, this wouldn't have happened." I looked to the paramedic in back and started to tell him something, but the words died in my throat. He was doing CPR on Bruiser.

Time slowed into something spiked and thorny, as if each second, each compression to Bruiser's chest, were a wound stabbed into my soul with a cold iron blade. Again and again. The medic was shouting. Something about getting to the hospital. The driver, also a paramedic, opened the back ambulance doors and jumped inside, black boots landing with twin thumps, two cops behind him. I turned off the ambulance. Opened the door. Threw the keys into the dark. Just before the paramedic body-slammed me.

The world tilted. Smoky air rushed at me as I fell from the ambulance, following the trajectory the driver had taken. The driveway hit my shoulder, hip, one booted foot. Men piled up on me. Pressing me down. Burying me. I couldn't breathe. Didn't really want to. I'd lost Rick. Now I was losing Bruiser.

My arms were yanked behind me. My face ground into the pavement. Cuffs ratcheted down on my wrists, cold and metallic. The weight began to shift off me, one body at a time. No one searched me. I was a girl, skinny and hysterical. Why would I have weapons? Or maybe they just didn't care. Or more likely, they knew I couldn't get to anything useful, even the gun in the spine holster. When the last man rolled to his knees, I got a breath, painful and short and heavy with smoke. I heard Koun speak. "Get out of my way or I will gut you where you stand. I am here to heal the human."

I started laughing, coughing, abrading my face on the rough pavement. "He'll do it too," I said from the ground. "The blue tattoos are Celtic. Koun's one of Leo Pellissier's warriors. He's about a thousand years old and he's been fighting since he was in diapers."

"My father placed my first knife on my belly the very hour I was born."

"I stand corrected. Or I lie corrected. Let him heal Bruiser. He can save him. It's why I stopped the ambulance."

"Bruiser is what she calls the primo. She is in love with him and human women like pet names."

"I'm not—" I stopped. *In love with him? Human? Crap.*

I heard Koun enter the ambulance and the doors shut. After that, my world was sounds and flashing lights and smoke and the distant pop of gunfire. There was a battle taking place in the distance. The rhythmic three-cracks of semiautomatic handguns, the overlapping *thuts* of machine-gun-style, fully automatic and illegal weapons, the boom of shotguns, the guttural shouts of orders and the screams of the wounded. Koun had come from the battle.

I realized that the humans around me didn't seem concerned about the gunfire I had heard when I arrived. They didn't even seem aware of the small war in the distance. It was vamp-magic, something new I hadn't seen before. I smelled vamps on the wind, multiclans of them, only half of them recognizable by scent as Leo's, the rest the beery scent of his enemy. I smelled vamp-blood and blood-servant blood, a *lot* of blood-servant blood.

The house, not far from where I lay, burned hot and fast, until the walls started to fall in, loud, roaring crashes, the screech of heated wood. The water from the trucks was now being turned primarily on the trees, the barn, and the outlying buildings to keep the flames from spreading. The house was a total loss, according to the firefighters around me, pulling hoses across me and stepping over me.

Sometime later, the paramedic I had left doing CPR on Bruiser squatted near me. "Sorry, ma'am. I thought you had lost it. Didn't know you had called a fanghead to help him. I'll see if I can get you released." I grunted. Even later, another man straddled me, one boot to either side of my hips, and removed the cuffs from my wrists. My arms slithered down to my sides, boneless and bloodless and tingly, as circulation was restored. He helped me to stand, patted my shoulder, and walked off before I could get a good look at him. But I got a good whiff. I'd know him again.

The paramedic came back, staring at me, studying my face, my body, and only now noticing the array of weapons. His gaze lingered on my ringless left hand. "Are you really his wife?"

"I don't wear rings when I fight. They can get hung up on things." Which was a lie of omission and misdirection, but I didn't care. My voice went breathless. "Is he going to live?"

"We don't know. He has a sinus rhythm sometimes. A normal heartbeat," he clarified. "Sometimes not. My partner is bagging him."

"Bagging him" meant Bruiser wasn't breathing on his own. I blinked tears away just as Koun stepped from the back of the ambulance, licking his own wrist. I had been healed by vamps a few times, but I didn't know what it took to be healed from . . . death. Apparently blood, and from Koun's pale skin, a lot of blood. He was half-naked, dressed in sweat-slick skin, blue and black tattoos and a loincloth, sword at his side. Koun was taller than I was with the shoulders of a Viking and eyes like the North Sea. He was blondish, forever young, and mercy had long burned out of him. He looked and saw me. "I left my master's fight to heal a human," he snarled. "You owe me a boon, woman." He pulled his sword.

I stepped back, going for my Walther. But he was on me in an instant, moving faster than I could see, with a little pop of displaced air. His long blade coming at my throat. Time slid into slow motion. His sword sliced at me, level and lethal, catching the red of embers, wavering in the heat of the burning clan home. Beast slammed power to me. The blade slicked into my throat as I jumped away, still fumbling for the gun even as my feet went out from under me and my muscles went into a shoulder-tucked roll. I landed hard. Heard officers shouting, "Put down the weapon!" And, "Police!" like a chorus of the tone-deaf. Gunshots sounded and Koun stumbled, coming back up upright, the wounds not even slowing him. He stood over me, one foot to either side, much as the cop had stood, his sword held in both hands, blade down, over me. "A boon!" he demanded.

I thought a boon was a favor, but with more connotations, and I wasn't going to agree to the unknown without a negotiation, even if I sucked at them and I had a sword at my throat. "What boon?"

"I am weakened, and the primo requires yet more blood. You will fight in my place." With one hand, he pointed to the trees, in the general direction of the gunshots, which were coming closer, more distinct.

"Done," I said. He stepped back and I rolled to my feet. "How many are there? Who are they?"

"Perhaps three score of the enemy were still alive when I left, unless our attackers have reinforcements. They did not announce themselves by name or clan. We have half that many, fighting against shadows and cowards." At Koun's words, the humans nearby should have commented or questioned or at least said, "Huh? What?" They didn't. More vamp mojo I didn't understand.

I thought a score meant twenty, so sixty opponents. Crap. It was a small war. I turned my back to him and trotted across the pasture, stopping at Bitsa to pull the M4 and slide into the harness.

Fun, Beast thought at me. *Hunt.* She poured excitement and power into my bloodstream.

My breath deepened; my heart thumped like a bass drum against my ribs. "Not fun, so much," I said aloud. No leather and armor, no silver studs, no magical shield to protect me from bullets.

Jane does not have a magical shield. Jane has Beast.

I laughed. "Yeah. I do." I trotted past the barn, where horses milled, restless and anxious with the smell of blood and smoke. The scent of their fear was like an aphrodisiac to Beast, but the added reek of big-cat sent the horses into full-blown panic. Hooves struck stall walls, screams of terror and challenge bugled on the night air. I sped up to take my scent away from them. Ahead, smoke and lights danced drunkenly in a field, illuminating surrounding pine trees and another horse barn, the central barn doors open to the dark and the stall doors like half-open eyes, staring out over the field. This barn was older, without the telltale scent of fresh manure. By the smell, it was full of hay and diesel-powered machines. The pasture around it had been planted in hay, thigh deep and brown, ready for the final harvest of the long growing year.

Stopping behind a large-bole pine, I studied the scene through all my senses, the night too black and the lights too bright to rely solely on sight. There were five or six vamps and as many human blood-servants in the barn, some bleeding, stinking of sweat and vomit. I caught the strong tang of a chemical that I now recognized, bitter and metallic and artificial. Beneath the metallic tang I smelled the beery scent that belonged to the vampire who had challenged and defeated three master vamps and left them sick. It belonged to the vamp who had sent blood-slaves after me, and who had killed and drained the men on the Learjet. And I realized, standing in the trees, the air saturated with the stink, that though the beery scent was native to the master vamp, the metallic, chemical smell was man-made, not natural in any way.

I looked out over the field of hay and the circle of trees, smelling and hearing others, injured or dead, lying in the tall grasses, some of them the enemy's vamps and humans, some of them Leo's.

I smelled Derek Lee, close, only a few paces over, his body strong with the bitter scent of battle. He was speaking into his com unit, and I could hear the new men, the Tequila Boys, his newest former marines, home from Iraq or Afghanistan, talking back into his earpiece, their voices muffled. In the dark, I saw a guy in camo bend over a vamp half-hidden in the grass, and offer his wrist to feed on. It was Tequila El Diablo and it was unexpected that he would be generous to a vampire in need. Not many humans, and even fewer marines, liked vamps enough to spit on them if they were on fire, but maybe they knew one another, or more likely, money talks. Vamps were known to offer most anything when they were wounded and needed blood to heal. El Diablo was unusual for one of Derek's men. I liked him for reasons I couldn't name, except maybe his ready smile and his laughing eyes. Marines with laughing eyes are a rarity.

Farther on, I saw another new guy, Tequila Cheek Sneak, as he clubbed a vamp to the ground. It wasn't one of ours, so I didn't react, but I made a note to keep an eye on him.

Farther yet, at the edge of the woods, I saw two other Tequila Boys pulling an injured soldier off the battlefield. A vamp followed them to help with the healing; I thought it was Leo's former daughter-in-law, Amitee Marchand, which was weird on all sorts of levels. Amitee hated Leo, but maybe a common enemy had healed some wounds.

Closer, I scented Innara and her anamchara, Jena, the mind-joined female vamp leaders of Clan Bouvier. One moved, the light of weapons-flash catching her face, and I stepped back into the shadows. Innara was no longer the thin, petite, elegant vamp of our few meetings, but a warrior, lips pulled back in a snarl to expose fangs glistening in the dark, a silver-plated short sword in one hand and a handgun in the other, her eyes vamped out, the blood red sclera like openings into Hades. Her muscles were sharply defined and blood smeared her mouth and chin.

The hairs on the back of my neck rose and bristled. Beast hissed deep inside. I had never seen a vampire at war, and her vision didn't blink away, but reappeared in negative image on the inside of my lids. She was wearing a headset, a modern accouterment to her primitive fury.

She was upwind of me and so didn't know I was there until I said, softly, "Innara, coleader of Clan Bouvier."

Her head jerked and focused on me in the dark. She growled.

"It's Jane," I said. "Koun sent me to fight in his place. Will you tell the others so I don't get shot?" After a moment her lips relaxed and she nodded, speaking softly into her mic. Derek turned to me and I lifted a hand, seeing the low-light-vision goggles on his face. "Where do you want me?" I asked just as softly, trusting her vamp hearing.

Innara moved with the air-popping speed of her kind and appeared next to me. I tried not to jerk, but didn't quite manage it, and Innara smiled up at me. Not a human smile of amusement, but the hunting smile of the predator who saw prey flinch. "Leo's Mercy Blade was to lead the assault on the barn, with Koun at his side. In light of his removal from the field of battle, we are reconsidering our options, and then the master's Enforcer appears, well weaponed. How fortuitous."

Great. Just freaking great. I had no doubt that Koun meant for me to take his place in the assault too. I looked back at the barn. "I'll take Koun's place. Fill me in."

Instead, Innara spoke into her mic and a moment later I saw a form that seemed to float through the trees like a dark mist, like an owl in flight, his feet never appearing to touch the ground. "The little goddess will fight with me?" Gee DiMercy asked, his teeth flashing in the night. "We fought well in the past. This battle will be a joy and a thing of beauty to behold."

I flipped the long blade I held, letting it settle firmly in my hand. *Goddess. Yeah, right.* "And the tactics?"

"Attack from two sides at once, create a diversion, and leave the way open for the Mithrans to eat the fallen. The human soldiers may clean up the leavings."

"Wrong. No one eats or drains the vamps or the humans," I said.

Innara growled and the hairs on my neck quivered in atavistic response. "No one tells me who I may not drain on the field of battle."

I carefully did not make eye contact, to avoid ratcheting up the tension. "The vamps are diseased. And maybe on some chemical. Drug. Something. Can't you smell it?"

Innara lifted her nose and sniffed, her head moving like a snake, in little jerking motions with each breath. "I smell nothing."

"Well, I do. It smells metallic."

"Like silver? Many of our old masters were poisoned when a blood-slave drank colloidal silver and brandy and allowed them to drain her."

I knew that story. I lifted my blade and sniffed it, smelling the iron in the steel and the silver in the plating. I frowned. "Not silver. Not iron. But something metallic. Maybe a drug. Just don't drink from them and don't get bit.

Okay?" Innara studied me. The disparity in our heights should have allowed me to feel superior, but I didn't, I wasn't. Not next to the fierce little vamp, her fangs picking up the moonlight.

"You think their bite is dangerous?" she asked. "You think the blood of their servants is poisoned?"

I shrugged. "I smell something that isn't right." And vamps were getting sick. I didn't have to add that part.

"My anamchara and I will herd them into a small group. And then we will cut off their heads."

I chuckled softly at the bloodthirsty comment. "It would be nice to have something left to question after. Also there are cops nearby. I'm surprised they haven't shown up here already."

"The police are human, and humans can be swayed to see what we wish them to."

Which sooo did not make me happy.

Derek walked up, nearly silent in the night, with his soldier's training, but Innara and Gee DiMercy turned, hearing him coming. "I won't be part of a slaughter," he said, "even if the fangheads are naturally armed and bat-shit crazy."

"You will do as you are told, human," Innara hissed.

"Enough," I said. "Derek, do you have flashbangs?" At his nod, I said to Innara, "No slaughter. You and your vamps make a diversionary feint directly at the front of the barn. Gee, you go left with half of Derek's men, aiming for the open, middle stall door. Derek, you and the rest of your men go in on the right"—I pointed—"to that door, but behind me. When we get to the barn, we throw in every stun grenade we have. It isn't a confined space, which will limit the noise and concussion factor, but I'll take what we can get with the light.

"After the blasts, we go in." I pointed to Gee and me. "We'll take care of any vamp old enough to still be standing after the candle flash. Derek and his men will round up anyone blinded and temporarily disabled." Flashbangs produced enough noise and light to incapacitate a human and to blind vamps. Maybe permanently. But old vamps had enough power to survive things the young ones did not, and I'd never tested them on a master. Without a pause, I went on.

"Innara, you and your fan—vamps come in behind us. No drinking, no killing. I want them alive."

Her eyes lit up, bleeding back to human, her pupils shrinking, sclera paling down from scarlet to merely blood-shot. "So that we can make them tell us everything they know. Yes! I like your plan."

It wasn't much of a plan, but I didn't argue. For some reason they were listening to me. Maybe that ill-fated Enforcer situation. Derek handed two flashbangs to me and one to Gee, demonstrated the use of the military-grade, M84 stun grenades, which I was pretty sure he should not have had in his possession. He said, "We need to pull and throw together, otherwise the suckheads will have time to react and look away, cover their eyes. It'll be on three." He tapped his mouthpiece three times to demonstrate.

The vamps moved into the night like snakes in the grass, their bodies weirdly not human, disjointed. I dropped into the hay, Derek behind me. It wasn't a long crawl, but it wasn't going to be easy as loaded down with blades as I was. And wearing the wrong boots. And the wrong clothes. Not that I would gripe about it. I didn't have time to gripe about anything.

We crawled through the hay, crushing the stiff stalks, disturbing insects, sending rodents scurrying and snakes slithering. From one whispered curse, I gathered that Derek was not fond of reptiles. We also set up a cloud of mosquitoes as we moved. With all the activity, the vamps had to see and hear us coming. Great plan. We'd have been better to just charge, except that one group had done that, and engaged someone at the front of the barn. Blades clashed and voices shouted.

I stood up at one corner of the barn, Gee across from me. We met eyes, and the smaller man nodded. Derek tapped his mic. On one, I pulled the pin. On two, I stepped to the door, Derek behind me, mirroring my actions. On three, I threw the grenade. Derek's lofted high and at a different angle from mine. I pulled the pin on the second flashbang and tossed it, eyes closed, and continued the arc of the throw, bringing up my hands to cover my eyes and ears. A flashbang explodes at 170 decibels and a pyrotechnic metal-oxidant mix of magnesium and ammonium, at over six million candela. The night went white in a series of blasts. Moments later, we rushed in.

I figured it was useless, but I shouted as I ran, "Surrender and you'll live. Put down your weapons." Surprisingly, a few listened and surrendered. The fight with the rest was short and brutal. Derek and his men herded half-blind vamps and injured humans out into the night and dropped them onto the ground. Three enemy vamps who could still see went after Derek and his men, leaping off huge farm equipment and out of the hayloft at the former marines. Innara and her vamps attacked before they landed. Sneak Cheek moved off the side at a dead run and clubbed two vamps to the ground. They stayed down. Tequila Sunrise staked them in the lower bellies to immobilize them. It was nice work.

Gee and I turned to the two vamps rushing us from the corner. I fired the M4 at one, emptying both barrels, two hand-packed, silver fléchette rounds into his abdomen, the recoil reverberating through me. The vamp went down but was still alive, struggling back to his feet, even without any flesh between ribs and hips, and only a damaged spine holding him together. He was gripping a sword and an old six-shooter pistol. I kicked the gun away and blocked his human-slow-because-he-no-longer-had-blood-inside strikes until he fell for good.

Shotguns loaded with silver made fighting vamps way too easy, especially the old ones. They didn't have the mindset to fear guns and so took few precautions against them. But there was no fair in war. I stood over the vamp. "Yield and you'll live," I said.

"No," he gasped, his face set in stubborn, frantic lines as he bled into the dirt.

I waited until he stopped gasping for breath, until his blood stopped flowing, giving him a chance to surrender. Then, when he looked dead, I took his head to keep him from rising as a revenant.

Gee was a two-blade fighter, moving like the love child of a flamenco dancer and a bird of prey, his swords like two wings, sweeping together and apart, cutting and slicing, his feet balletic, his body graceful. After making sure there were no more vamps in the barn, I holstered the M4 and leaned against a wall, watching him play with the vamp.

And it was play, because though the vampire had obviously been fencing for centuries, he looked like a first-year student against the Mercy Blade. I had never fought against Gee DiMercy, and it was a good thing, as he would have cut me to ribbons. Literally. Just as he was doing with a fighter who was way better at swordplay than I was.

When he took mercy on his opponent and called for him to surrender, the man charged him, and Gee took his head. It was just like in the old TV shows and movies about the Highlander, and the saying "There can be only one." Only without the lightning and wind when the head fell. I couldn't help it. I clapped.

And Girrard DiMercy whirled with a flourish and bowed, one sword behind him like a wing, the other across his body, pointed down to the floor. "Very pretty," I said.

He rose with another dramatic flourish and said, "I am, aren't I?"

I snorted and followed him out of the barn, to find Innara casually staking a vamp.

CHAPTER SEVEN

I Whirled and Caught the Naked Man

She was using a silver-tipped wood stake, which was much longer than one of mine, and she wasn't aiming at the heart. She was stabbing him in the right side of his chest. He was screaming and bleeding, his chest already punctured several times. I raced up and caught her wrist, ripping the stake out of her hand. Innara whirled on me, her short blond hair flying. Before I could react, her fangs were at my throat.

And then she was ten feet away, screaming in pain, dancing like a burned child. Her lips were blistering, swelling as I watched. I touched my silver mesh necklace. I'd never seen it work quite so well on a vamp. Usually they had to bite me, or attempt to, and their tongues might sting a bit before they jerked away. But this—

A blur I halfway saw and totally felt tackled me from the side; her anamchara. My spine formed a sharp C shape and slapped me against the earth with a whiplash speed. I might have cursed again had I any breath. Instinct made me grab her hands, forcing her back and off me. I caught a breath and it hurt when my ribs moved. *Another broken rib. Great.* I held Jena off; her lips were blistered too, and she hadn't touched my necklace. Anamchara are mind linked, meaning that they know the other's thoughts and feelings, and apparently, if they are linked closely enough, their bodies react to the other's pain. Now I had both of them ticked off. Then I caught a whiff of the blood. Leo's blood.

I whipped my head to the vamp Innara had been torturing, and threw Jena from me. She let me, landing on her feet and backing away, half stumbling, arms out to the side like a wounded bird.

Derek and El Diablo were holding the vamp up, Derek with the vamp's hair in his fist, supporting his head. Diablo was still smiling, and this time the smile was calculated and cold. I was still holding Innara's stake, and I twirled it like a marching band baton as I strode to the vamp. I didn't even look at Derek. I bent over the vamp and breathed in his scent over tongue and mouth with a soft *scree* of sound. He hissed at me through two-inch fangs. Which I ignored. I leaned so close I could feel the grave-cold of his chest on my face as I sniffed. Yes. Leo's blood mixed with the blood of this vamp. I moved close to his face and caught the odor of Leo's blood on his mouth. I placed the tip of the stake against his heart and looked at Derek. "Do we know where Leo is?"

Derek's dark eyes were full of disdain, the disdain of the human for the nonhuman. Me. I smiled at his expression, showing my teeth, letting him know I had seen the scorn. He cocked his head in a "We'll have to fight one day" expression. I chuckled. We understood each other. "No," he said. "Fanghead boss got to Katie's front door, but was intercepted in the street. Three of my boys are injured. Leo's missing."

Leo's missing. On my watch. I looked at the vamp and let my teeth show in what was not a smile. "You know, doncha, Corpse? You know where Leo is, right? And we're going to find out. Take him to Katie's. Him and any other vamp still alive. Make sure they talk. I want to know everything."

"Torture seldom provides accurate intel," Derek said.

"True. But if Corpse talks, I'll make sure he lives and is adopted into a clan where he has a chance of moving up in the hierarchy. If he doesn't, I'll give him to Innara and Jena for dessert."

The vamp spat at me. I moved fast enough that he missed. Derek didn't like the speed, but I was getting tired of hiding what I was, feeling ashamed of what I was. I wasn't fully human, never had been. Or maybe was both fully human and fully other. Whatever.

With a whoosh of air, the scene in front of me blurred in the moonlight. Corpse was gone, ripped out of Derek's grip. I blinked and tried to focus, seeing Grégoire and Corpse rolling on the ground, vamp-speed making it impossible to tell their limbs apart. Grégoire's blond head was my only clue who was who. He was latched on the stranger vamp's throat. I leaned in and grabbed a handful of Grégoire's blond hair and yanked, pulling him off Corpse and to his feet. Grégoire was maybe a hundred pounds and short, having been changed at age fifteen by a vamp with a predilection for young boys. Pretty, young boys, but he wasn't pretty now. Grégoire was blood-smeared and vicious, wounded and smelling of the dead. He growled at me and struck out with fangs and claws. Derek and one of his men grabbed Grégoire's arms. Four others subdued Corpse. I shook Grégoire. "He's for info on where Leo is. He's not for killing."

"He drank from my master. I smell Leo on his mouth."

"Yeah, I know. Which is why we want him alive until he tells us what he knows, and if he tells us, he gets to live."

"I will hound him until the day of his true-death. I will challenge him in a blood-duel and chase him—"

Rage roared up in me. "Later!" I screamed. The night fell silent. Fury, like steam, boiled in my blood. I was breathing heavily. So were the other humans. But the vamps had stopped speaking, stopped breathing, and if their hearts ever beat, they went silent too. Like marble statues, they stood or kneeled or sat in the field of hay, immobile as stone. "You can sort it all out later according to the Vampira Carta and Leo's wishes. For now, I want to know what he knows, and I'm not picky how that's done." If he'd been human, I'd have been way picky, a small quiet part of me whispered, which was a double standard I'd look at later. Someday. Maybe.

"If Leo has been kidnapped," Grégoire said, "he will not survive until the new moon. The swine who calls himself a master Mithran, yet violates the Vampira Carta, will kill him."

"Swine?" Corpse spat, again. It seemed to be a personal tic, an unhygienic version of a sneer. "Your master's Enforcer killed my master's Enforcer without any good reason." He was speaking in a strong country accent, which still sounded weird coming from a vamp's mouth. "The Carta and its protocols say she cain't do that."

"Ramondo Pitri?" Derek asked.

Corpse stared at me, ignoring Derek, his body posture doing the whole "I'll never talk, no matter what you do to me" thing, all without him saying a word.

"I'll take that as a yes," Derek said softly. "I have all the intel on ol' Ramondo's made-man past on the streets of New York. So gut this piece of crap. We don't need him." Which was just the opposite of what Derek had said earlier. I took that to mean that we were back to playing good cop, bad cop, but with versatile roles.

"No. We'll give him an opportunity to talk," I said. "Who knows? His boss might want him alive and come to save him, which would give us the chance to take him. We need a place to hold you, Corpse." I looked at Grégoire. "And we need him and any of the others who are still breathing— even it's only when they chat over dinner—alive. Or un-dead. Whatever." My voice wandered to a halt as the fury in my blood drained away. Exhaustion tugged at me, a heavy weight.

"I have silver cages," Grégoire said. "Two of them." He smiled, and it was an eerie expression on the boyish, beauti-ful face. Terrifying. It made me not want to know what had been done to him when he was newly sane after being turned.

"Bring everyone still alive and your cages to Katie's," I said softly. "We'll talk with them there." I knew what I was saying. What I was condoning. I shivered that I could con-sider the torture of anyone, even a vampire. I wasn't sure what I was becoming, but *was* sure I didn't like me much.

I entered Katie's Ladies, one of the oldest still-operating whorehouses in New Orleans, through the front door. I was one of the last to arrive from Leo's and was greeted by Troll, a tall, bald, burly blood-servant with a voice like a hill of gravel being massaged by a shovel. His real name was Tom, but I'd called him Troll the first time I met him and it had stuck. "Jane. You're late to the *party*." His eyes and tone said he didn't approve of the festivities, or maybe just the guests, but because he was a blood-servant, his opinion wouldn't have been sought.

"Yeah. I had to deal with cops and fire trucks before I could get away from Leo's."

He leaned to me and sniffed. Blood-servants' sense of smell was better than that of humans, and his crinkled his nose. "You stink. How's the clan home?"

I smiled at the insult, but it fell off my face fast. "Gone."

Troll grunted and there was remorse in the tone. "I liked that old house. What about people?"

"We lost two of Leo's vamps, both from Clan Bouvier, Louise D'Argent and Peter Schansky. I didn't know either one, but from their injuries, they were ambushed, immobilized, drained, and then cut to pieces." I looked away. It had been bad—a slaughter. Whoever had killed them had wanted to leave a message, and it had been up to me to take their heads so that they didn't rise as a revenant at sunset. That didn't happen often, but when it did, it was bad. "We also lost two humans—their blood-servants. I had to deal with informing their clan masters."

"Sorry, Jane." Troll patted my shoulder. It should have felt awkward, but it didn't.

"Any word on Leo's location?" I asked.

He shook his head. "They're in the parlor. It isn't pretty," he warned.

"Yeah. Big surprise." I squared my shoulders and went on through the house, Troll following me. A thick Oriental rug muffled our footsteps in the entry, and I automatically checked out the security upgrades I had recommended, the cameras, sensors, and monitors tied into Katie's security console hidden behind the doors of a seven-foot-tall, black-lacquered chest with gold-leaf dragons capering across its doors. I might be heartsick, but I still had a job to do.

The house was stylish and elegant and only slightly overdone, recently decorated in hundreds of shades of gold from palest yellow to darkest golden brown, with paintings and statues and objets d'art everywhere, each of them probably worth more than I make in a year. The Christian children's schoolgirl inside me was always torn between cringing and staring when I came inside. "Where are the girls?"

"Katie canceled the clients for the night," Troll said, "and sent the girls to a hotel on St. Charles Avenue."

I lifted a hand to indicate I heard and took the twisty hallways the back way to the parlor, the place where the girls met with the *customers* before taking them upstairs for kinky games, which might include the transfer of blood, depending on whether the john was human or vamp. I passed the open doorway of Katie's office and was struck silent and still by the contents of the small room. All the stuff that usually lay on the leather surface of the massive, dark wood desk had been shoved to the floor, and two people lay on the cleared top—Bruiser and a black-skinned woman. Both were mostly naked, but it wasn't sex, not in any way I could ever think about sex, even with the nudity. It was something else entirely.

Bruiser lay on his back, spread-eagle, his skin death-pale and marbled blue, the veins appearing like waterways on a map. He was wearing socks. That's all. Socks. He wasn't breathing. The black vamp half sitting, half-curled on top of his hips was wearing a wildly patterned, full-circle skirt in shades of indigo, with a matching turban-thingy on her head. No shirt. Perky boobs with dark aureoles brushed Bruiser's unmoving chest. Bethany Salazar y Medina, one of the vamp priestesses, had slit her wrists and they lay over his mouth, her blood dripping into him. Her fangs were buried in his throat. She was deep in a healing.

All by itself, my back hunched up and my eyes filled with tears. Grief, black and viscous as tar, cold as glacier ice, flowed through me. Over the pain rode a wave of lesser emotion; a spear of jealousy lanced through me, jealousy not my own, but my cat's. Deep inside, Beast whispered, *Mine!* And wanted to growl. As soundless as possible, I moved on down the hallway, boots in the deep butter-colored carpet, though, if a herd of moose had charged through the house, I doubted the priestess would have known it. And Bruiser, well, he was dead.

I lifted a hand to Deon in the kitchen; the three-star chef from one of the Caribbean islands was loading a tray with sushi, and he waved back. There was sushi rice on his fingers, and despite my warring grief and jealousy, it made my mouth water. I wasn't sure when I'd last eaten a real meal.

It might be the steak in the Lear. *Two days ago?* My stomach rumbled. I was ashamed that I could feel hunger when Bruiser was in such danger.

In the shadows of the servant's entrance to the parlor, I stood silently and studied the core of Leo's gathered scions and blood-servants. There were five vamps in the room, five blood-servants, and seven humans in night camo. I knew them all. And one of them might be a traitor. I just had to figure out which one. When I got the chance. Currently, my money was on Sneak Cheek, who had pummeled a vamp after the battle, but what did I know? Maybe the vamp had tried to coerce a drink, or worse, mesmerize dinner for himself, and the marine had refused. Aggressively. I had done the same thing myself a time or two. Judgment without sufficient data is stupid, and I was withholding mine.

The parlor was too fancy to call a living room, and too bawdy to call a gathering room. Parlor fit, from the upholstery in shades of gold silk to the bigger-than-life artwork of a nude Katie herself, to the polar bear rug on the Italian marble floor. A real skin, according to Beast, who had wanted to hunt one ever since she first got a sniff of the bear's white fur and a look at his huge white teeth. Polar bears are predators and prey, taking down seals for food and becoming food for killer whales and sharks. I didn't know where Katie's decorator had gotten the hide, but it wasn't old. It still smelled faintly of modern taxidermy chemicals and oils. It was missing a foot as if a bigger predator had taken off a hunk and the bear had died.

The blood-servants and humans had pushed the furniture against the walls, and two cube-shaped, six-foot, tarnished silver cages took up the floor space, gleaming blackly in the light of a chandelier. Beast reared up and I fell back a step as terror slammed through me, intense and hot as a heated blade. *Danger,* she thought. *Run!* And I had an instant vision of steel mesh and a room beyond, gray and dim with night. *Cage! Run!* Fear spiraled through me, slamming my heart into my ribs. I could feel the cage beneath my paws, metal cold and unyielding. Feel the place in my hip, sore, where white-men-with-guns had shot me. *Made me go to sleep. RUN!*

I caught the doorway with both hands, forcing myself up

from my Beast-mind, shoving away the memory, one we had never shared, tamping down the fear-stink, knowing that only an idiot entered a roomful of angry, tired, hungry vamps smelling like terror—like dinner. Idiots who wanted to come out on a slab, drained. I held my breath, forcing it out slowly, slowly. Took another. Beast retreated far into the dark, watching, claws working in and out, piercing my mind with pain. Big-cats purr when they are happy and they mutter a low growl when they are not happy. Beast was growling with each of my breaths, hyperalert, watchful. Worried.

The vamps would have heard the soft growl, except that the vamp in the cage closest started screaming. Derek was prodding the half-naked vamp with a long stick. On the end was a silver cross, and where the cross touched his skin, the vamp was burning. Smoke swirled up, contaminating the air like the stench of rotten meat on a hot grill. The prisoner carried the vamp disease, and it was heavy on the air with a ripe, sick stench.

The captive leaned as far from the cross stick as he could, his back only millimeters from the silver mesh; when he overbalanced, he fell into the cage walls, skin sizzling. His wail pierced the air, making my eardrums vibrate. The scream was nearly as earsplitting as a vamp's death wail. The vamp in the other cage was whimpering, his black pupils so wide they almost obscured the scarlet sclera. It was Corpse, who showed his own silver burns, and he knew he was next. I smelled scorched flesh and vamp blood, and at Derek's feet were vials of blood, labeled, dated, and timed. Someone had drawn the two vamps' blood for testing. I doubted it had been done with their approval or cooperation.

Angel Tit, Martini, and Chi-Chi, three of Derek's Vodka Boys, were watching the torture, faces in battle mode, unyielding and closed. Leo's vamps were standing apart from one another, vamped out as well, staring, mesmerized by the caged vamps' pain and fear. I could smell their arousal and bloodlust, hunting instincts quickened, even for the pain and blood of one of their own. The blood-servants were busy with handheld electronic devices, or looked bored, or stared at the portrait of Katie with rather more interest than the painting warranted, except that it was not in the line of sight of the cruelty.

"Your master's name," Derek said, his voice holding no inflection, no clue to his feelings. If I hadn't been able to smell his anger and self-loathing, I'd never have known how he felt about the job he was doing. "Your master's name." When the vamp shook his head and whimpered, Derek jabbed him again. The smoke was reddish, as if suffused with aspirated blood.

"Where is the master of New Orleans? Where is Leo Pellissier?"

The vamp shook his head violently. "I don't know. I saw him taken away. I don't know where. *I don't know!*" he screamed, when Derek touched him with the cross again.

"Ramondo Pitri," Derek said, changing the subject of the interrogation, pulling the cross away. A layer of skin clung to it, crinkled with heat.

"The Enforcer," the vamp shouted. "Pitri was my master's Enforcer." As if the admission had released a dam, he took a gasping breath, his ribs shivering oddly as they expanded, not a human breath at all, ribs moving snakelike. He kept speaking, the words gushing. "He was sent to reconnoiter and research Pellissier's Enforcer, in preparation to initiate a legal blood-challenge to her as laid out in the Vampira Carta."

I blinked. Stepped into the room. Leo's scions turned as one to me, staring, still as death, still as vamps. A laugh wanted to titter up in my throat. I'd killed Ramondo Pitri. I'd killed a man and started a vamp war.

"Ramondo was trying to discover information," he continued, "to find out why Jane Yellowrock was so special."

"Shut up, Kleto. Shut up!" the other vamp whimpered. That gave us one name and one nickname, Kleto and Corpse. We were making progress.

Kleto ignored him. "He wanted to learn how Leo's Enforcer made her way up the ranks so quickly, before he challenged the stranger to draw first blood."

Katie stepped toward me, her blond hair falling forward in a wave that swished like silk as it moved. Her interest pricked my predatory and territorial instincts; I almost reached for a blade but stopped myself before I could complete the move, which would have been taken as the gravest insult. A smile answered my abortive attempt, and it was like being studied by a hungry predator, daring me to try and take her down. It all happened inside of three heartbeats, banging against my ribs.

And the caged bird kept singing, as if having something he could say were a lifeline. "He was supposed to issue a Blood Challenge to Yellowrock according to the Carta, but he was worried that she was some kind of supernat, a were or something, so he went to her hotel room."

"A blood-challenge, Enforcer to Enforcer, for first blood," Katie said, her eyes holding me, unblinking, black and bloody, "is one acceptable first step to one master issuing a Blood Challenge to another—mortal combat for his position."

"But Leo's Enforcer killed him. Without provocation."

I didn't think shooting an armed man in my hotel room, one carrying multiple weapons, including the gun he had drawn—the gun with an illegal suppressor—was exactly without provocation, but I kept my mouth shut. Or Katie stared me down, which was not something I was willing to consider. Once again, flying by the seat of my pants and without enough info to do my job had caused problems—this time, big problems—and had resulted in a ticked-off, vamped-out vampire holding me within her sights. I could feel her compulsion wrap around me like electric razor wire, cutting and burning.

She took a breath, and I forced myself not to take one with her. Katie tilted her head to the side, that snakelike movement they do when they forget to act human. "You killed an Enforcer before he could issue challenge to you. This is not allowed under our law. You are permitted to take a life only in self-defense, official challenge, or mortal combat. As an Enforcer without a blood-bond, you are a danger to us all."

"Leo got a copy of the police reports. It was good enough for him."

Her shoulders lifted and her fingers opened out, claws dropping down and spreading. Her fangs clicked down, not instinct, but a carefully controlled action, something she did with purpose, a control only the very old ones, and very powerful ones, have. "Leo is not here," she said. "He has been taken by an enemy. For now, perhaps forever, I am master." Which made little lizards rush up and down my spine on cold, sticky feet. "This war appears to be, technically, legally, your fault. Now the rival Mithran may do anything he wants."

"Not Jane's fault," a voice croaked behind me.

I whirled and caught the naked man before he hit the floor. "Bruiser," I whispered.

His skin felt colder than a cadaver's. He was sweat-slicked and ashy and he stank like a three-day-old grave. But he took a breath and I felt his heart against my chest, beating like a wounded kitten's, fast and weak. Not concerned about what I was giving away by a show of strength, I lifted him up and over my shoulder in a fireman's carry, steadying his bare lower back and his thighs, his arms dangling over my shoulder; Bruiser was too big to cart any other way without dragging his feet or banging his head on the floor. I carried him back down the twisty hallway into the office and set him down gently on the leather sofa, found a throw, and wrapped it around him. It was teal cashmere with aqua silk tassels and fringe, the soft textures sharp as nails on my fingers, the colors overbright, almost harsh. Shock. I was in shock.

The priestess was nowhere in sight, but Katie knelt at his side and stroked his temples, her claws scraping his skin. She focused on him as if she could read his state of being through his skin. And maybe she could. What did I know? "George," she murmured. "You will live. And still mostly human. Do not despair. Do not despair."

Mostly human? What did *that* mean?

CHAPTER EIGHT

Your Security Sucks

The heir of the Master of the City—and most of the South-eastern United States—looked up from Bruiser's face, her eyes gathering up my consciousness like a spider weaving a silk grave for its dinner. My mind struggled in her grip, kicking. "You claimed the position of Enforcer. Leo did not refute you. Yet you did not drink from him? And he permitted this?"

My mouth went dry. When I didn't reply, she went on. "An Enforcer must be bound by the Master of the City, bound body and soul by blood and . . . *Pourtant, vous n'avez pas fait l'amour.*"

I had an idea what she had said, and, *no way, José,* but I settled for a succinct "Uhhhh."

"You claimed a right that you did not understand. I did the same once, when I was offered the life of the immortal night. I was young and beautiful and so very sure of myself, and foolish beyond understanding.

"As I did, you claimed the honor, not knowing what was required. No, you are not bound. I do not smell his blood in you. You are without the protection of the Master of the City."

That part felt like a threat, and Beast thought so too. She bit down into my mind and shook it like prey, her canines like ice picks in my soul. The action and the pain brought me to high alert. I took a deep breath and blew it out. Put a hand on my new vamp-killer. Slowly. Deliberately.

Katie's eyelids widened, pupils constricting in surprise. Her mouth made a pretty little O, distorted by fangs worthy of an African lioness.

And I grinned, showing my blunt human teeth and my beast-soul. Feeling Beast rise in me, knowing my eyes were glowing golden, like my Cherokee name. Golden Eyes. "Leo could have taken me at any time," I said, "and forced me into submission." I realized how true it was as soon as I said it.

We would have resisted, Beast murmured; I ignored her.

"So Leo *wanted* me unbound. He wanted me unbound, uncompliant, and unsubmissive. Free. Unlike the rest of you."

"He wanted your love, free and willing."

"Maybe that was part of it." *Most certainly that was part of it, but we don't always get what we want,* I thought. "But he left me free, for his own reasons. I'm guessing one reason is that some enemies require a clear mind. Some ..." I cocked my head and let my eyes take in the vamps between me and the way out, the only door. Old vamps, all of them. Not one younger than early nineteenth century. "... some youth. Some creativity." With my left hand, I pulled the brand-new cell from a pocket and tossed it to Katie, only feet away. With animal reflexes she caught it. "Call him. Maybe he has his cell with him, wherever he is, and assuming he isn't true-dead. Maybe he'll tell us where he is and to come rescue him. And while you have him on the phone, ask Leo why he left me unbound." Katie looked from me to the thing in her hands. Someone would have tried to reach Leo already, but I knew from experience she had no idea how to use a cell phone, and only with reluctance would dial the old-fashioned landline on her desk. I let my smile widen. "Yeah." I glanced at Bruiser, lying pale and broken. He had two scars on his chest, bullet wounds. His chest moved with a breath, faint and shallow. Abruptly I remembered the tearing sound when something deep inside him gave way and he bled to death. *He had died. Right in front of me.* And he was alive again.

I looked back at Katie, keeping my feelings off my face.

"Keep him alive. Keep yourself safe. Leo values you both." I paused and tested the words on my tongue before I said them. They tasted of truth. "Leo loves you both. I'll be back soon." I walked past Katie, snagging my cell, giving her my back, just as an African lion would give his pride his back, knowing he was bigger, badder than the others. I pushed through the vamps at the door.

I stopped midway and took Koun's wrist in my hand. He was still cold, pale, and shaky. "Thank you. Leo will be proud of you for saving his primo." Maybe it was my imagination, but he seemed to stand taller. "He is honored to have the great Koun as his warrior. But even more honored that Koun knows when to fight and when to heal." It wasn't a lie—or not exactly. Leo hadn't actually said the words, but he had chosen Koun as one of his four closest scions at a time when Katie was unavailable for duty. That was a lot of trust from a vamp as powerful as Leo Pellissier, Master of the City of New Orleans and half of the Southeastern states.

There was a lot of divisiveness in Leo's closest scions, at a time when that seemed dangerous. Maybe I could heal that some. "Leo will grieve the loss of the vam—Mithrans," I corrected, "Louise and Peter and their blood-servants."

The Celt met my eyes, his own human blue in white orbs. He turned his wrist to grip mine, his fingers and palm calloused and stronger than mine would ever be. He nodded and let me go.

In the hallway, I met Derek's eyes, dark and hostile. I opened my mouth to give him orders. Instead, I said, "You are the most brutal human being I have ever met." I hadn't intended to say the words, but they matched my thoughts. Deep inside, Beast huffed with amusement.

"Unlike humans, the vamps will heal," he said shortly, lip curling. "It's war."

"The excuse of soldiers for millennia."

He didn't react. I didn't expect him to. "The blood you sent was lost in the fire," he said. "We got some from them"—he canted his head down the hallway toward the parlor and the cages—"but we need some from the others to compare."

"I have some in my house from the Seattle clan's humans."

"Yeah? I'll send Chi-Chi for it."

"Sure. Whatever." I walked away from him, showing him my back too. I left the house, closing the front door behind me. And dropped against the red-painted door, heaving breaths. "Holy moly." I put a hand to my chest. "I'm not dead." And I fought laughter, knowing they might hear me inside. Or smell me. Sweat started to trickle down my sides, sticky and stinking of the aftereffects of fear.

When I had myself under control, I pushed away from the door and melted into the shadows. The night was warm and muggy, and the sweat wasn't likely to dry. So far, winter in the Deep South was a joke. I needed a shower, fighting leathers, and info. I needed food. I jumped the fence into the narrow alley separating Katie's from the building next door and walked down the narrow space, checking the cameras I had installed as I moved. Instinct. Habit, to check my security work for Leo's heir. It all seemed okay.

The brick fence behind Katie's was taller than I was by far, and I took advantage of the small hand- and footholds as I half climbed, half vaulted it, landing on the other side in the dark, and relaxed. I could tell by the smell that no one was here. I was alone. Safe. For now. Weird how a house that wasn't mine, and never would be, felt like home.

Inside, I stripped and showered, standing under the heated water, letting it pound my muscles, washing the smoke and blood off me. There was remarkably little blood, and almost none of it mine. I washed my hair, shaved my legs, all the girly things I do so seldom. When I shift and then shift back, the hair is always fully grown again, which, even with my Cherokee-lack-of-hairiness, is a pain to remove. But this time, it felt like therapy, like feeding my girl soul, which I so seldom did.

Afterward, standing in my bathroom in the steam, the exhaust fan going, I coated my skin with pure jojoba oil and plaited my wet hair into a tight French braid. It wouldn't dry quickly, but the damp didn't bother me. I dressed with care in my long silk underwear, and when I could put it off no longer, I dialed Leo. He didn't answer, and I closed the phone.

I opened the bathroom door, heard a click, and stopped in the doorway. Sniffing. *Someone was here.* I looked around, breathing in silently, slowly, thinking, analyzing the sound I had heard. The click was the kitchen door. I had changed the locks, but that didn't stop anyone really determined. I switched off the bathroom light, throwing the house into night shadows.

A man had been here. I sniffed again. Yeah, a he. Male. Sweaty. Nervous. A stranger. Just like the stranger in the hotel, the one I'd killed weeks ago. I sniffed again, mouth open. Gun oil. The stink of a gun, recently fired. Herbal shampoo. Not Chi-Chi, here to pick up the blood; not anyone I knew. But if I survived tonight, I'd recognize his scent again.

Soundless, eyes on the bedroom doorway, I stepped to the bed and felt around on the fighting leathers for the holstered Walther and a vamp-killer. I came up with the smallest one, six inches of silver-plated steel, crosshatched steel grip, and gripped it backhanded in my left. Safety'd off the gun, and stepped slowly, weight balanced evenly, into the foyer. Night sight kicked in, the shadows growing lighter, the light through the windows brighter.

By the scent traces, he hadn't come in through the front door. I stepped across the foyer, paused at the stairs. He hadn't gone up there, but he had paused here for a while. More nervous. Edgy. I followed his scent back to the kitchen, to the side door. He had come and gone through here. While I was in the shower. Weapons on the bed. Nothing with me but a hair stick I could use on a vamp as a stake. Nothing to defend against humans. Stupid! He could have opened the door and shot me. So why hadn't he? Because he had come in to kill me and heard the shower go off? Seen the weapons? Assumed I had a functioning brain cell and that I'd be armed, and had decided not to try to kill me. Instead, he had done ... what?

I moved through the dark house to the kitchen door leading to the ground-floor level of the long, two-story porch. The door was shut, but the wood jamb was splintered where it had been kicked open, light-colored wood splinters on the darker floor. So ...

I turned and studied the house, feeling, smelling, tasting the air. *The blood vials.* I raced back to the bedroom and bent over the shipping container. "Crap!" The bag holding the blood vials was gone. Rage boiled through me, Beast's fury. *Mine,* she thought at me. *Came into my den. Took what was mine. Thief of blood,* she thought. Beast was possessive of her belongings. Of my belongings, for that matter. But . . . The laptop was still on the bed, the tiny green light showing standby mode. So was my arsenal. The intruder stole only the blood.

That severely limited who the traitor in Leo's organization might be. Because only a very few vamps, blood-servants, and humans knew I had the blood, and even fewer might have guessed it was in my house. A human from Seattle might have figured it out, but more likely, the traitor had been in Katie's house only moments ago. And he or she called the enemy. Mentally, I listed the people in Katie's tonight. Derek and his boys: Angel Tit, Martini, and Chi-Chi. Katie. Koun. Alejandro and Estavan—vamps of Spanish descent who had been loyal to Leo for centuries. Girrard DiMercy, who had not always been loyal. Five blood-servants. Bruiser. The priestess. *Crap. The priestess?* She was loony tunes. Or so she appeared. Reach had included her in the list of possible bad guys, Leo's possible spy. Reach . . . *Crap. Reach.*

If *he* had access to the security, and I had to assume he did, then Reach knew a lot more about the internal workings of the whorehouse, and more about Katie's plans and thoughts, than I did. For all I knew, he had eyes in my house. I hadn't done a sweep for electronics since I first moved in. I put a search in the back of my mind for later.

There were an awful lot of choices to consider for the position of traitor. Anytime the number of possible suspects went above five, things got sticky, especially when one of them was my security expert. But what would be Reach's motivation? He didn't need money. He couldn't be forced to be a traitor, like somebody kidnapped his dog, like on a cheesy TV crime show. But then, everyone had a vulnerability somewhere.

Leo would know the hearts and intentions of any of his scions he fed from and shared blood with. Had he fed from all the vamps there? I had no idea. No one but Bruiser would know that, which meant that Bruiser might be in danger. Again.

Still in the dark, I dressed fast in fighting leathers and when the knock sounded, I was ready. I shoved the last blade firmly in place, gripped one of the Walthers as I walked to the front door. Drawing on Beast speed, I ripped open the door and grabbed Chi-Chi's shirt collar, yanked hard, pulling him across my leg. He overbalanced and I stepped back, letting him fall. But he was fast. He drew his sidearm as he fell, took the landing on his shoulder and rolled, the gun in a two-handed grip. He had me in his sights. I smiled as I stared him down the barrel of my own weapon. "My 380 will kill you just as dead as your nine-millimeter will me, and all we'll be is dead. Let's both just take a minute, okay?" I took a breath and blew it out to show him how to relax. "Did you send someone here to steal?"

"Huh?" Honest confusion leaked from his pores, but confusion from what? Landing in my foyer? My question? Or surprise that I had figured it out?

I sniffed, searching for anything that might suggest change in his pheromonal state. "Someone broke in here while I was in the shower and stole the blood I collected. That was too fast unless someone was dispatched here from Katie's. Maybe with orders to kill me if the opportunity arose. Who did you call?"

His aim steadied. His full lips firmed. His dark skin gleamed in the streetlight pouring in. "Legs, don't make me shoot you."

I detected no scent of deception on his body, heard none in his tone. Saw none in his body language. But I firmed my stance. "Who at Katie's used a cell after I left? Because someone called in a thief with a gun."

I could see thoughts processing, his eyes taking on a slightly unfocused state as he replayed the last half hour. "Five people that I know of, but we dispersed. Could have been more."

"Well, crap." Why couldn't it be just one? "If I stand down are you gonna shoot me?"

Chi-Chi barked a laugh, the humor not affecting his aim in the slightest. "I might."

Great. "I have a problem with trust when the other guy is armed."

"Don't we all?"

We could stand here all night. And Bruiser could die. Hoping I wasn't being stupid, I raised the weapon, removed the magazine, and unchambered the round. I stepped back. Chi-Chi shrugged, not easy to do while lying on the floor, and sat straight up. Still using mostly his abs, he rolled to his feet, proving he had stayed in top shape after finishing active duty with the marines. Lastly, he holstered his sidearm. "What entry?" he demanded. I pointed at the kitchen, and, keeping me in his field of vision, he walked through my house as I followed. He knelt and inspected the door, swinging it open and closed. He grunted, "One kick. Size eleven or twelve. Smooth soled, so not wearing boots. All our guys are in boots tonight."

"I knew it wasn't one of your guys." I almost added, *It was a stranger's smell,* but didn't. Go, me. I didn't respond to his odd look either, after my comment about trust problems. What else could I have meant, right? "There may be a security leak in Leo's chain of command, and it puts Bruiser in danger. He knows who drank from Leo, and therefore which vamps are loyal to Leo and can be eliminated from the short list of potential suspects. The ones who didn't drink from the MOC may be involved in the attack. Go keep the primo alive."

Chi-Chi raised a single brow. There were three shaved lines in it, giving the brow a jagged look, like a lightning strike. The look said that he wasn't in my chain of command and didn't take orders from me. I thought about that, and about the fact that one of Derek's men might be the traitor. But who better to guard Bruiser than someone who wanted to keep his lack of loyalty hidden? I pursed my lips and added, "Please."

Chi-Chi laughed again, the odd bark of sound. "You have trouble with that word."

"How long have you known the Vodka Boys and the new men in Derek's Tequila Posse?"

"Posse? Nobody says posse no more. We been together off and on for as much as nine years, most of us."

"Any of you have bad financial trouble?"

His face hardened in the moonlight. "You calling one of us a traitor?"

"Not beyond the realm of possibility. Is it." It wasn't a

question. The job market in New Orleans sucked. Chi-Chi walked back to the front of the house and out the open door. Without a reply, he disappeared into the shadows, silent as a cat. Drawing my gun, I reinserted the round from my pocket into the magazine, snapped it home, and chambered a round. I stepped into the shadow beside the door, feeling it close behind Chi-Chi.

"Your security sucks," a new voice said.

Lips tightly closed, I smiled and crouched low to the floor, pointed my weapon in the direction of the voice. I had smelled him as he entered, a clean but musky undertone that was natural to him. Not my thief. But maybe there was more than one. I could start firing and hope to hit him, or I could chat a bit. Chatting sounded safer. "Unscented deodorant, no cologne, unscented shampoo, and a body odor that says you shower often," I said. "You carry at least three weapons, all recently cleaned with an aerosol lubricant. Dry lubricant is better. It doesn't leave such a strong scent."

"Most people can't smell lubricants after an hour or so."

I adjusted my aim a fraction. "I'm not most people."

"Sergeant Lee said that much."

My insides clenched. *Derek sent him? To take me out?* "What else did he say?"

"You probably aren't human. You pay well. You need security experts—weapons, tactics, intelligence, and electronics. I'm looking for a crew to join, but if the security of this place is any indication, you aren't what I'm looking for."

"Not my house. You got a name?"

"Younger. Eli."

"Training?"

"Courtesy of the U.S. military."

"Ranger?"

"Is this a job interview?"

I thought about that. I had asked Derek for some guys of my own. He said he knew someone, but if he'd given me a name I didn't remember it. "Could be. How many knives do you carry? Silver blades? Stakes? Crosses?"

"In this town? Unknown territory, full of vamps? I opted for two of each. And I like steel—keeps an edge better than silver."

"Silver plating on the flat of a steel blade poisons vamps,

so if you didn't get them with the first cut, they get sick, sometimes fast. I usually carry thirteen stakes and at least one cross, silver, in a lead-lined pocket. That way if a vamp surprises me, it won't give away my location when it glows."

"Hmmm."

I had a feeling I had made a point, and that his cross was on his neck on a chain for all the world to see. "Silver is expensive," he said, sounding grudging.

"So is dying. You work for me, I'll supply the silver."

I could practically hear him thinking. Even more grudgingly, he asked, "About this place?"

"Looks like I'll be staying for a while." I surprised myself with the words. I hadn't intended to say them. Not ever. "You can handle the upgrade. Leo Pellissier or Katie Fonteneau can pay for it."

He named a price that made me wince. "That's for the first month, for two of us, my brother and me. Room and board is included in the price, along with a few upgrades on the house—easily secured windows, better doors, and a security system."

"I don't cook."

"I do. But you buy the food."

I took one hand off the weapon and reached up. Flipped on the light. Younger and I were aiming directly at each other, except his aim was a little high. Above my head. I chuckled softly. Eli frowned.

CHAPTER NINE

If I Lose, the Kid Eats Like a Soldier

Eli Younger was my height, give or take an inch, solid as an oak, fast on his feet, maybe mid-thirties, and not what I expected at all. All Derek's men were black and former marines. The Ranger was probably at least half white, and ... Different was too ordinary a word. He had dark gray eyes that might have a blue haze to them in direct sunlight, dark hair cut military short, skin as brown as mine, and a still-healing, jagged scar that started at his left jaw and ran down his neck to disappear into his shirt collar. It didn't look like a knife wound. Shrapnel, maybe. No tattoos that I could see.

I took a beer from the fridge and passed it across to him. Eli grinned at the fridge, twisted off the top, and drank. I was pretty sure he was smiling because the inside light no longer functioned. Security. Or maybe it was the stack of steaks inside. He seemed like a man who'd like steak.

I prepared tea for me, boiling water, pouring dried leaves into a strainer. Setting an antique pot in the sink and filling it with hot tap water to temper the old ceramic. We studied each other as we worked—him on his beer, me on my tea. I was tired, so I chose a strong Irish breakfast blend and got out the sugar. I worked in silence. It didn't seem to bother him, which was nice. I never knew what to say to men who needed chitchat. While the water heated, I sat and said, "Tell me about your brother."

His eyes shifted for a moment, and I figured I was about to get a portion of the truth. "Alex is my height, just turned eighteen, a graduate from MIT. He's on juvie probation, but if you hire me, you hire him. We're a team." I thought about that for a moment, then nodded, waiting for more. "He got caught hacking into the Pentagon." A smile pulled at my lips and about a hundred emotions flitted across Eli's face before he settled on wry. "Yeah. He wants to know what happened." Eli touched his scar. "He hates secrets. I wouldn't talk, so he tried hacking in, looking for my records. He's good. Arguably one of the top ten hackers in the country, not that they call it hacking anymore. But he made a rookie mistake, probably because he's worried."

I raised my brows. Eli went on. "Alex says I'm different since it happened. He doesn't like it."

"So different you can't do the job?"

"So different I wanted out. I was a career soldier. Then I wasn't."

Cub, Beast thought at me. It seemed like a good guess. I went with it. "Your parents are deceased." Eli's eyes dilated a bit in surprise. *Bingo.* "You nearly died, and Alex would have been alone. You quit for him, and if he knew that he'd be ticked off." Surprise and irritation leaked from Eli's skin. He'd not be happy to know he was giving away the good parts of his personal story by his olfactory tells, but I wasn't sharing that. Let him think I was just that smart, or that Derek had told me all. "So, with your injury, whatever the service gives you to retire early, good contacts, and a pocketful of medals, you hope to start a business—one where you can keep an eye on your brother—with your hard-won skills and your brother's genius IQ and computer flair." I nodded slowly at what I was reading in the tension of his jaw. Yeah. I was betting I had it all straight. "But you have to stay in Louisiana until his probation is over, and I'm the fastest job possibility you have. I have a big house at my disposal and you think you can bunk in here for a month or two, make good cash, and look around for better things. Anything I get wrong? Anything I need to know different?"

"No. And?"

"I'll think about it." I took the simmering kettle off the fire. Emptied the pot and set the strainer inside. Poured the steaming water over the leaves and set the top on with a little *clink*. I swathed the teapot in a towel and left it to steep. I walked into my bedroom and right back out with the sheaf of papers and the Apple I had taken from Seattle. "Small test to see if you are what you say you are. Get your brother to see what's on this computer. I want a list and summary of all files. I want the e-mail address book. I want to read every e-mail sent in the last month. I'm looking—"

Eli held up a hand, pulled out a cell, and hit a button. We both heard it ring. Right outside. "I told you to stay put. Get your sorry ass in here." He closed the cell. I laughed. Eli shook his head and sighed. "Crazy kid. He was supposed to stay in the truck."

A knock sounded at the front door. Eli got up and stood to the side of the door, checking out the window before opening it. A kid came in, looking much younger than eighteen, gangly, gawky, and carrying a slim electronic device about the size of two hands, and at least three electronic devices under one arm—an e-reader, a tablet, whatever. Eli pointed to a chair at the table. The kid seemed to melt into it, the electronics in his lap. He wouldn't meet my eyes.

Thief, Beast whispered to me.

What did he take of mine? He didn't have time to steal. I turned my back on the pair. Not a dominance action this time, but a chance to think. I got out two mugs and spoons and poured tea. Added sugar to both and stirred, putting two and two together.

I walked around the table and put one cup in front of the kid. Beast-fast, I yanked the electronic tablets off his lap and put the table between us again. I set the fancy electronics on the table just out of his reach. Eli started to react and stopped himself with a jerk, only his eyes showing a reaction to my speed and my thievery. "Are my financials okay, kid? My background check out? Did Reach burn your little butt for going deep into my life?"

The kid looked up at that. He was going to be a lot prettier than his brother, if he ever got over the sullen glint in his eyes and the stubborn grinding of his teeth. Then his mouth dropped slowly open. "That was Reach? *The* Reach?

Like *Reacher* Reach?" He looked at the small e-tablet and cussed softly.

His brother slapped the back of his head. "Lady here."

Alex rubbed his head, looking at me under too-long bangs. "Bugger's not a bad word, and she's no lady. She's a rogue-vampire killer. She's got more kills under her belt than any other licensed hunter in the business. She's also the Enforcer for Leo Pellissier, and no one knows how she got the position. Half of the fanghead hunters think she's his blood-servant. The other half think she's got a legal writ on him and is getting into position to take him out. She's got more money than Midas."

Eli rumpled his brow, and I knew he was thinking about the muffler company rather than the mythical king. I laughed, half wondering how I could read the man so well. It had to be more than his musky undertone. He was like a pheromone factory, every emotion immediately available to my nose, but even that shouldn't make him so transparent. "And Reach burned a hole in your system for looking?"

"Fried my ass. Fried my Teckton."

I didn't know what a Teckton was, but it sounded expensive. After checking to make sure his devices were all off, I pulled my cell and hit Reach's speed dial. "Evening, Money Honey," he said.

I snorted. "The kid you just burned getting into my records. Is he dangerous? And can he be trusted as an employee?"

"Yes and yes. Him and his Ranger brother. And for that and for taking care of you when you weren't looking, I just earned a crisp five hundred of your money."

I didn't bother to reply. I ended the call. Looked between Eli and Alex, and left my gaze on the kid. "I'm thinking about hiring your brother. I understand you come as part of the package deal. So, a test. You have one hour to get everything off that laptop." I pointed to the Seattle Apple. "I want a list and summary of all files. I want the e-mail address book. I want to read every nonpersonal, business-type e-mail sent in the last month. I'm looking for a challenge from one vamp to another. Travel discussions. Anything about doctors and research, about vamps getting sick." I tossed the Blood-Call business card on the desk too. "It's probably nothing, but that was at a . . ." I hesitated, trying to decide how to describe the Seattle Clan Home. "A crime scene. I want everything you can find on it. One hour."

"Are you nuts? One hour?" I raised my brows at his tone and he said, "I haven't had any sleep. I'll need coffee."

"You'll drink tea and like it. Your brother can cook you some dinner. If I like your work and his cooking, you're hired."

"You're hiring us on *his* work? Not what *I* can do?" Eli asked.

"You're the brawn. You can supplement my own skills and maybe teach me a thing or two. The kid, if he's any good, can take me and my business all kids of places. *He's* valuable." I looked Eli over, smelling his shock, and I grinned, knowing I had just verbally socked him in the gut. Men are so easy. After a moment I tossed him a bone. "I need a secure room in this house, one with egress in case of fire. I was nearly burned out not that long ago. Updated windows and doors. My vampire landlady and employer"— I pointed out the back of the house—"needs a safe room too. I started one. Got as far as installing a sprinkler system and dedicated communication devices. You can take that over too. Assuming your brother is as good as he thinks he is." The kid snorted and said something my house mother in the children's home would have washed out my mouth for saying.

"Alex?" He looked up from the screen to me. "You ever say that in my house again, or any other curse or swearword or phrase, in English or any other language, and I'll wash out your mouth with soap, something antibacterial, with a real slimy degreaser." His eyes sparked sullen again. "My house, my rules. Are we clear?" He looked at his bother and nodded, lank hair falling forward. "And if you get the job, you'll shower every day, and you'll do your own laundry and pick up after yourself. Your brother cooks, so you'll wash dishes and keep the entire house swept. I am not your mother. And if I was, I'd be twice as hard on you for showing disrespect to me and to your brother. Nod if you understand and agree." A long moment later, the kid nodded, but I could see the anger and a blue screen, both reflected in his eyes.

My cell rang and I opened it without taking my eyes off my current guests and potential employees. "Yeah."

Derek said, "We got a route for Leo. According to the crispy vamp, he was drained in what sounds like a gang-feeding, and then whisked away by two vamps and two blood-servants. Angel hacked the GPS of the car they were in and Chi-Chi, Lime Rickey, and Hi-Fi are heading to observe and gather intel. I assume you want to be there, so I've sent the coordinates to your cell."

I inhaled slowly, letting the shock settle. I could think later about what the gang-feeding analogy might mean to Leo, and moved to my bedroom to weapon up as I checked Derek's GPS info, merging it into a map and then taking a look at it on webcam pics. The car was on the far side of Highway 10, parked at a one-story house on Ursulines Ave. According to Google, there was a high school nearby, but not much else. Of course, Google was not something I wanted to depend on when planning an op.

"Trap for us?" I asked, sliding into my M4 harness and the holsters for the nine-mils.

"Could be."

"Okay. I'll meet them there." Behind me, I heard the familiar clicks and metal-against-metal of guns being checked and glanced back to see Eli Younger weaponing up as well. I watched to see what he carried and it was pretty much standard, the kind of stuff I had utilized when I first started out.

"If it looks reliable," Derek said, "we'll send Leo's blood-servants to be available."

Leo was drained. Drained vamps are dangerous. Very. "Okay. I'll get back to you."

From my closet floor I lifted the boot box I use for a jewelry box and set it on the bed. Inside were the few pieces I owned, each stuffed inside athletic socks to keep them from rattling around. And to keep my socks all in one place. I placed the black velvet gift box on the bed and lifted out my silver and titanium vamp-hunting collar. Underneath it was the coyote earring that had appeared in the box following a particularly horrible nightmare one night. I paused at the sight. I didn't have nightmares often, but this one had stuck with me. So had the earring, which was weird, but no weirder than the fact that the pocket watch had somehow gotten into the black velvet box with it. I distinctly remembered dropping the watch-amulet into the box, on top of the socks. The amulet's magic still smelled like meat. Like blood. Good thing Beast wasn't hanging around too much. She would want to taste it. Along with the watch, I stuffed the earring in a sock, wondering if they would both reappear, in a different spot in the box the next time I opened it. I removed the collar and put the box back on the floor of the closet.

"You going somewhere?" I asked Eli, questioning his weapons with lifted brows.

He shrugged. "Consider it a job interview for the brawn half of the Younger team."

"Suit yourself," I said. "We're going to rescue a starving master vamp from some kidnappers and torturers. Try not to get your throat torn out." That made Eli pause half a second in his prep work. He looked over my necklace collar, considering the implications. "No. I don't have another one," I said. "If I keep you around—"

"Yeah, yeah. You'll spring for one."

"Heck no. These suckers are expensive. I'll send you to a supplier and you can buy your own."

"Sweet lady."

"Your brother had it right. I'm no lady. We'll take your vehicle."

Eli shrugged and we were out the door and heading toward Highway 10, Eli driving, me reading out directions on my cell.

The house was in need of a paint job, but it had a newish, post-Katrina roof. It was deep but narrow on the front, with steps up to a porch and working shutters closed over all the windows. In the Deep South, shutters are for hurricane protection, not just looks. Unlike most of the duplexes around it, this was a single-family house, up on seven-foot stilts, with the lower area used for low-head parking and storage. We pulled down the block, behind the SUV, and parked, trees between us and the house.

Chi-Chi climbed into the backseat and closed the door softly, handing us com units. "Lime Rickey and Hi-Fi have reconnoitered and are in position," he said as we slid into the units and tested functionality. "The front door is six, and Lime is at two, Hi is at seven. We have a single-family dwelling with six-foot alleys to either side and a small backyard, fenced, with a couple of pit bulls, unchained. We have tranks and Lime can take out both dogs safely. What we don't know is if Leo is inside."

"Give me a minute," I said, and slipped out. Eli had rigged his vehicle to be able to turn off all the interior lights, which made it easy to come and go without being seen by neighbors, not that many were up at this hour. I moved through the night, my nose to the wind.

And I smelled blood. A lot of it, which made sense of this whole kidnapping. Leo's enemy had kidnapped him, drained him, and placed dinner before him. If what I was guessing about the transmission of the vampire plague was correct, it was probably someone who had the vamp disease. If Leo had drunk, it was likely that he was sick now, just like his old lover Rosanne Romanello. *Crap.* "Boys, I'm circling the house," I said. "Don't trank or shoot me, okay?"

"Copy." "Copy that." And a snort of laughter from Chi-Chi.

Listening, sniffing, I moved around the house, drawing on my Beast senses. At one window I heard voices. Panting. It was the sound of pain, when one has been so damaged that one can no longer even scream. *Crap. Leo.*

I tapped my mic. "Leo is in a room at nine o'clock. He's hurt. Where are the blood-servants?"

"Pulling up now," Chi-Chi said.

"When we go in, have them slit their wrists and follow close."

"Say again?" Chi-Chi said, startled.

I chuckled, no humor in the sound at all. "Leo will attack any human who gets near. If he scents blood, he'll likely go for that site rather than rip out their throats. I'm guessing that they know all this, but just in case, remind them. The wound doesn't have to be deep, but it has to be actively bleeding. It might save their lives."

"Son of a— Copy," Chi-Chi said. "Why don't you take point?"

In this case, point wasn't a position of honor for the best

warrior in the bunch, but the most dangerous position for the one they liked least. "Gee thanks, Chi-Chi."

"Anytime, Legs."

At least there was amusement in his tone. I heard a car brake out front and I pulled my shotgun from its spine sheath. Chi-Chi said, "Takeout is here. Trank the dogs." From the backyard I heard spats of sound and yelps as an air gun fired. The dogs went quickly silent.

"Dogs out," Lime whispered. "Moving to the back door."

A moment later Chi-Chi said, "Blood meals are appropriately bleeding."

I raced around the house to the front door and up the steps, hearing the sound of untrained feet running noisily behind me. The door was steel. Fortunately, when I turned the knob, it clicked open. It wasn't locked. Which meant very sloppy vamps or a trap. I said a small prayer and pulled on Beast-speed as I pushed open the door and raced inside. The place was unlit and unfurnished, all the rooms I could see were empty, but the smell of blood was everywhere.

Eli moved to my left and just behind: Chi-Chi and Hi-Fi were behind him. We checked each room, though the scents told me everyone was in the room with Leo. From the back of the house, I heard Lime Rickey enter.

I lifted my nose and followed the scent to the room on the left in the middle of the house. A light was on inside. Beast pounded her strength and speed into my bloodstream. I caught a breath and whispered, "On three." I turned the knob. "One, two, three." And slammed open the door.

In the space of a single heartbeat, light stabbed my eyes, and the smell of sickness assaulted my nose as I took in the room. It was a bloodbath. There were two bleeding bloodservants standing beside the back wall, and two bleeding vamps, sitting on a blood-drenched sofa. The strangers were sick, all of them.

Shackled to the far wall was what had once been Leo. Silver cuffs burned into his flesh at wrists and ankles. He was vamped out, his jaw dropped and thrust forward, looking as if it was unhinged—three-inch fangs out and glistening. His hair clung to his gore-smeared, sweaty skin in wild, bloody strands. His clothes were mostly torn off. Or bitten off. Fang marks were all over him, at knees, crotch, and elbows mostly, all places away from the defensive weapons of his own fangs and claws. His skin was palepalepale, ashen, dead-looking. His eyes were wild. Insane. His fangs were pearl white, no blood was smeared at his mouth. He hadn't fed from the infected offerings.

Before the vamps could move, I fired the M4, taking down the vamp on the left, then the one on the right as he stood. Nonlethal, standard ammo, midcenter, abdominal shot placement. Eli and Chi-Chi were standing over the humans, weapons aimed down at them. I hadn't seen or heard them taken down, but I had felt the thuds under my feet as they hit the floor, forcefully. I couldn't hear myself ready the shotgun for another round, nor my voice over the concussion in my ears, but I knew the vamps heard when I shouted. "You move, you die true-dead." One sank back on the sofa, clutching at her belly. The other one rushed me.

I reacted without thinking, dropped to one knee, and fired again, this time a head shot. The vamp dropped like a thrown rock—with momentum. I dodged left, out of the way of the falling body and bloody bits. So much for keeping them all alive.

Leo threw himself against the shackles at the smell of more fresh blood. It was the final proof that he hadn't fed off the infected blood offerings; he'd not still be this ravenously hungry. A weight fell from my shoulders at the thought. His blood-servants entered, hesitating a moment before converging on Leo. I didn't watch as the first one lifted his wrist to his master.

Sixty minutes after we had left, Eli and I were back at my house. Half an hour later, we were each eating a very good, very rare steak and sharing the events with Alex. When we were sated and the adrenaline had been burned off with several beers, Eli said, "So. Are we hired?"

He looked cocky and amused, and I tilted my head. "Ehhhh." I looked at his brother. "Your brother can follow orders and take down a house. How about you? You got info for me?"

"Yeah," Alex said. "I sent you some stuff."

I opened my own laptop, which felt increasingly out of

date after seeing the kid's electronics. The folders he sent were neat and orderly, the files organized under headings that were easy to follow, easy to read, and comprehend. I hit PRINT and added paper to the printer. I e-mailed the entire batch to Reach and dialed his number. When the line opened, he said, "Nice work. Leo is saved by the famed vampire-killer." I heard the sarcasm and him clapping in the background.

I didn't reply or rise to the bait. Instead, I said, "This one is for our old fees, not the exorbitant prices you've been charging me."

"And if I disagree?" When I didn't reply, he sighed and said, "Fine. What?"

"I just sent you a file. I want to know how it's organized. I want you to run a search through it for anything with the name of the Enforcer in Asheville. See who it ties into. See what you can dig up." I hung up and turned to Alex. "The name of the Enforcer in Asheville was Ramondo Pitri. You do the same assignment. We'll see how your skills stand up to Reach's."

The kid's eyes glowed. "Sweeeet." He went to work, fingers clacking on the Seattle vamps' Apple, his own laptop, and the two electronic tablets that still functioned, all four devices at once. Eli stared at his brother, then at me, and shook his head. Despite my demand that Alex had kitchen duty, he started cleaning up my kitchen. I liked that in a man.

Fifty-two minutes later my cell rang. At the same moment, Alex hit SEND. "Done," he said.

I opened my cell and said, "Thanks, Reach."

"I'll e-mail the info to you," he said.

I opened Alex's new file and smiled. I had a new name to work with, a vamp named Hieronymus, which I couldn't even pronounce. It seemed that Big H was mentioned in dozens of the files, as the next vamp-master to be challenged and attacked by the mystery vamp. At last I had a name and place to start. I compared and the same name popped up on Reach's search too. I looked at the two men sitting in my kitchen. "You're hired. Dawn is close. You start at noon. There are four bedrooms upstairs. Don't take the one over my bedroom. Don't play loud music. Get some sleep."

"I've got some ordnance in the truck," Eli said.

"As long as it isn't combustible or fragmentary explosives, you can bring it inside."

From his expression I could tell he was trying to figure out what to do with the explosives. I shook my head. Soldiers and their toys. With a full stomach and as much security in place as I could manage, I went to my room, stripped, and fell into bed next to my own *ordnance*.

My official phone informed me that I had a text from Adelaide. "Mom is dying. They all are. Maybe three more days, if we bleed the blood-servants dry. Please help."

I texted back "OK. Two days. I'll find something for her in two days."

I hoped. I pulled a pillow over my head and was asleep instantly.

I woke with my hands pulling a weapon from a shoulder holster tangled on the bed. There were people in my house and it sounded like they were tearing down the walls. Then I remembered the two men I had let into my home the night before. Derek had vouched for them, but . . . Really, could I get any more stupid?

I rose, brushed my teeth, swiped a hand along my braided hair in lieu of combing it out and rebraiding it, and dressed in a pair of wrinkled cotton pants and a T-shirt. I stuck three stakes in my hair and strapped a holstered .32 on my ankle—hopefully overkill, but making up for possible stupidity earlier. I unlocked my bedroom door, glad that I had at least turned the small thumb latch.

There were boiled eggs in a pot on the stove and I cracked and ate three for breakfast, watching the current changes in my world. Alex had taken over my kitchen table with his laptop and e-whatchamathingy tablets, the Seattle laptop, and my laptop. Cheeky kid. I sniffed him as I passed and said, "Take a shower. You stink." He grunted, which was no surprise.

On a scratch piece of paper, I wrote out the names I wanted researched, starting with Hieronymus, and ending with all of Derek Lee's men, including the ten New Guys. "These guys? Their names are on my laptop under a file named Derek Lee. Reach and I did deep background on

Derek's Vodka Boys prior to the Asheville gig, and the new Tequila Boys just last month. Maybe you can come up with something new."

"Sure. Okay. Do I have to be legal?"

"Yes." I slapped the back of his head. "Totally legal. You're on parole, remember? But you can be creative." At which the kid grinned like I had offered him an "all you can eat" dinner at a pizza joint. "Main thing I need first," I said, "is for you to find out where this Big H vamp is located and anything you can about his organization. You can use the Internet, access my own files, and the files from the NOPD's woo-woo room." I added a request for him to look over all building renovation permits requested within fifty miles of New Orleans. After the events of yesterday, it was clear the mystery master vamp was bringing his fight to Leo's home turf. If a vamp was moving in, he'd need real estate with vamp-requirements: steel-protected windows and reinforced doors, a room with easy exit via a hidden passageway, and updated electronics. There wasn't time to build from the ground up, but I added a request for an expanded search, starting over the last six months, for new buildings that might work for a vamp. I tapped the table. "No huge hurry. Tomorrow would be nice."

"Tomorrow?" His voice squeaked, that teenaged thing they do when their voices change at puberty. He blushed, half in anger.

"Kidding. Just kidding. Start on Big H info and the backgrounds on Derek's men first. I need them by sunset. Two days will be fine for the permit stuff." He shook his head at me with something like a horrified exasperation. "Hey, I'm used to Reach's timeliness," I said. "If you can't cut it—"

"I can do it," he said, sounding surly.

I turned away before he could see my amusement and went on into the living room. I stopped in the middle of the room, bare feet on the cool hardwood floor, chewing egg, and stared. There was a hole in the wall. It opened up under the stairs to reveal a little room with a slanted ceiling and another hole in the floor. The room's walls were lined in stone—slate, maybe—and there was a bed with a lumpy mattress and tousled sheets under the most sloped part of the ceiling. Across from the bed was a small stand with a pitcher and bowl, a ewer, I guessed. There was very little dust and no mold, which I thought was interesting, except for wallboard dust, which now was everywhere, including on the man kneeling in the corner, holding a measuring tape. He was making the safe room I'd asked for, but it looked like I had a hidden one already, one I hadn't known about.

Eli didn't look around before he said, "You didn't know this room was here?"

"I noticed the space my first night here, when I tore up the digital video equipment." I toed the broken electronics he had left in a pile. I thought about the lack of dust and walked over to the sheets. Fingered them. Fancy sheets were something I had learned about since coming to work for Leo. These weren't rotten, limp, or even old; they were *new* linens, 600 or better thread count, in a hidden room in my freebie house. I sniffed, several short inhalations, and recognized Leo and Katie. *Well, crap.* Most vamps had several lairs, which explained why this hidey-hole room was so dust free. One or the other—or both—had been sleeping here. Recently.

"There's another hidden space in a closet upstairs," I said. "But it isn't my house and I wasn't into vandalism. At the time." I didn't feel so bad about it now, however, knowing that I'd shared my house with the MOC and/or his heir when it was convenient for him.

"You need a safe room, you got a safe room," Eli said, looking around, following the geometry of the small space, "one supported by cypress timbers and lined with stone and poured cement, in case of fire. All I have to do is repair the wall and hide the opening with that steel door." He pointed out into the main room, and I saw a steel door in cardboard and shrink-wrap leaning against the wall. I hadn't even noticed it until he pointed it out—there was too much other destruction. "Then I cover it with a hinged bookcase. It'll do in a pinch, especially as it has an escape hatch." He peered into the hole in the floor. It was framed with wood and was wide enough to admit a skinny person. Me. Or a vamp. They were always skinny.

I evaluated the Ranger. He would have a harder time fitting through unless he could knock a shoulder out of joint.

Some people could, but it hurt for a long time after. His clothes were tighter today, revealing broad shoulders and a tapering waist, narrow hips and sleek butt in jeans and army-beige tee. Likely six-pack abs if he took off his shirt. I shook my head and then chuckled at the thought of Leo's face if I barged into his lair in the middle of the day. Or if I had survived his aborted attempt to burn me out by hiding in his own lair. The MOC would not have been amused.

Eli asked, "Something funny?" I shook my head but let my grin stay in place as I moved farther into the safe room to peer over his shoulder, licking egg off my fingers. Below the opening in the floor was damp earth covered with water-beaded plastic. "The passageway comes out in two places," he said, "under the side porch, and at the back of the house. I've already been to Katie's to check out the hidden room under her stairs and start renovating, but Tom suggested that I not work on it today. It might be *inhabited*."

I nodded. *Inhabited*. *Right*. Multiple vamps had been at Katie's and they would need a safe place to sleep by day.

"I'll check it out tonight," he said. "For now, I'll finish off the wall repairs and buy a hinged bookcase. We can store the ordnance here. You got any books to put on the shelves?" I figured he meant something other than *Tactical Weapons Magazine* and *Gun Digest*, and shook my head again. "You don't talk much, do you?" He was turned away, but I could hear the laughter in his voice when he added, "I like that in a woman." Before I could think of a snarky reply he added, "I'll pick up some books at a secondhand bookstore today."

Since I had been identified as a woman of few words, I just shrugged and went back to the eggs. They were pretty good with salt. I put on tea, and was cracking and salting my fourth when Stinky-Boy said, "I got something." He looked up, and when I didn't look impressed, he grinned. "I got you a *history*, and I found it before Reach did."

I dropped the shell into the garbage and leaned over his shoulder, reading the file as I chewed and swallowed the egg. "What is Greyson Labs?"

The kid grinned up at me. "It's the company that paid the salary of Ramondo Pitri, the man you killed in Asheville."

I stopped chewing, and said, "And you figured this out how?"

"I tracked down Pitri's bank records and got a look at his pay stubs. Greyson designs cancer-fighting drugs." He was grinning ear to ear and it was an amazing piece of detective work, but it wasn't much on its own.

"So, is this laboratory tied in to the mob?" Pitri had known New York mob affiliations, with one of the major families there. "Or into the vamps in some way? And how did you . . . You didn't hack into a bank, did you?"

Eli went nearly as still as a vamp. The kid just grinned, and I felt a rubbery dismay waggle down my neck. When he saw our reactions, he laughed. "No. I didn't hack a bank. I could if I wanted to, but it was a lot easier than that." Eli remembered to breathe and I shook my head. "Pitri had a few contacts on social media," Alex said, "and I tracked him through them. I'm tracking Greyson on the international financial markets now, but it's a little slippery. If we can find the top shareholder or owner of the company, we might have your big, bad disease-producing vamp."

"I'll need more than a possibility and a name to take to Leo, and way more than a possibility to act," I said.

"I'll get more and put all current info into a report for you. It'll be ready by lunch and I'll update it as I find new intel." He looked at his brother. "There will be lunch, right? Not just eggs?"

"Protein," Eli grunted. When he did, the iron-hard six-pack abs flexed, visible behind the sweaty tee. Wall dust filtered off him. I considered whether he'd end up with a nickname. Most people of my acquaintance got nicknames, but nothing fit yet. Alex was still in contention for Stinky-Boy, but Kid was slowly migrating to the top of the list.

"I'll pick up steak," I said.

Eli grunted approval, and I figured that grunts made up about seventy percent of the brothers' communication skills. The Kid shook his head. "Pizza? Pasta? A can of Chef Boyardee ravioli?" he asked. When neither of us bit, he sighed and went back to his electronic search. Moments later the printer started. I left the house on my bastard Harley, Bitsa, and picked up groceries. Steak, salad stuff, oatmeal, beer, milk, picked out a national brand of coffee, and a couple of cans of ravioli for the Kid. If he took a shower without me asking again, he got a treat. I figured it might be a lot like training a dog, but I knew next to nothing about raising boys, and what scant knowledge I did have was gleaned from children's home kids who thrived on rebellion, so maybe I was oversimplifying. I tucked the food into the saddlebags and bungee-corded the beer to the seat for the ride back to the house.

Riding slowly, I rested my bones and my mind, feeling the stress of the last few days in the tightness of my muscles and knowing the next few days might get worse. We had a company name that might—*might*—be connected to the attacks.

Which made me think of Bruiser. No one had called to tell me how he was. Worried about him, about his *humanity*, I dialed his number, and was shunted to voice mail. "Hey, uh, you know. Um. If you're alive, uh, call me." I looked at the screen and said, "It's Jane." I closed the phone, thinking, *Lame. I am so lame.*

It was four p.m. when I got back to the house, and upper-eighties, but it's always hot in New Orleans. It was November and it still felt like summer. Though locals had assured me that it gets cold in the winter, I'd yet to see any season but hot, so I didn't really believe it. Muggy, damp, and miserable, yes; cold, no. I kicked off my shoes and unpacked the groceries, to the happy sound of shower water running upstairs. When the water went off, I nuked a bowl of ravioli and met the Kid at the bottom of the stairs with the food and an ice-cold Coke. His hair was dripping, he smelled like fruity shampoo, and his clothes were clean. From the crushed-in wrinkles, I was sure they had been balled up in the bottom of a rucksack, not folded. Not ever. He took the bowl of tomatoey pasta with the kind of awe and half fear boys usually reserve for the latest video game or smuggled-in porn. He held the warm bowl in both hands, looking around for his brother, pure guilt on his face.

"Here's the deal," I said softly. "You take a shower every day, you get treats. I'll deal with your bother on the fallout. But if you stink, I'll call you Stinky-Boy to your face and let your brother feed you."

"His welfare is my responsibility," a voice said from upstairs.

I pulled a spoon from my pocket, shoved it into the ravioli, and jerked my head to the kitchen. The Kid took off like he'd been spanked and I looked up the stairs to the man at the top. Eli had showered too, and he was barechested. His scar went from his jaw, down his neck, across his collarbone in a starburst pattern that looked like it had shattered the bone, and down to his pec. He was wearing five-button jeans so worn that I could see the sheen of skin through the faded cloth. No shirt. He was ripped, arms like steel cables and a stomach I could have danced on. I managed to swallow, hid my appreciation, and leaned a hip against the banister to watch him. He watched back. But he didn't like it that I didn't talk much, so I let the silence build. When his jaw gave a frustrated twitch I said, "He's eighteen."

"He's on probation. Under my supervision."

I thought about that for a moment while he watched me. "My sensei's dojo is a few streets over," I said. "Let's go. We'll spar. Winner decides if the Kid gets ravioli and other treats for keeping clean."

Eli laughed, an amused-at-the-little-woman, self-satisfied huff that said volumes. I let a smile lift one corner of my lips. He disappeared and was back in half a breath, pulling on a T-shirt and flip-flops. My clothes were loose enough, so I just grabbed sandals and led the way out into the heat while braiding my hair fighting tight, twisting it into a queue that would be hard to grab. Eli watched my motions from the corner of his eye as I removed a handle he might have levered to bring me down.

My sensei was a hapkido black belt, second dan, with a black belt in tae kwon do and a third black belt in combat tai chi, though he hadn't competed in years. He thought competition was for sissies and martial arts were for fighting and killing. His style was perfect for me, because I studied mixed disciplines and had never gone for any belt. I trained to stay alive, an aggressive amalgam of styles, geared to the fast and total annihilation of an attacker, and my style had best been described as dirty.

The dojo was in the back room of a jewelry store on St.

Louis, open to the public only after store hours, but I was one of a select few students Daniel would see during the day. I had my own key. The dojo wasn't far and the jog got us both warmed up. I could smell the clean sweat on Eli as we turned down a narrow service alley, thirty inches wide, damp, and dim.

I keyed us in through the small door of the dojo and locked it, watching Eli check the place out. He scanned it like a combat veteran with close-quarters, urban training. The long room had hardwood floors, two white-painted walls, one mirrored wall, and one wall of French doors that looked out over a lush, enclosed garden planted with tropical and semitropical plants. Eli moved to the doors and scoped out the garden. The cats who usually sunned themselves there were gone today, their bowls empty, the large fountain shaped like a mountain stream splashing in one corner, the small pool at the bottom filled with plants. The garden was surrounded by two- and three-storied buildings and was overlooked by porches dripping with vines and flowering potted plants. Sensei lived upstairs in one of the apartments.

I punched the button that told Sensei he had a student, unrolled the practice mats, and started stretching. Five minutes later, he showed up, dropping into the garden from his apartment above. Most of his students weren't able to tell when the man literally dropped in, but with Beast's acute hearing and sense of smell, I always knew. The smell of Korean cabbage he loved so much was a dead giveaway. Eli knew too, which was impressive.

Daniel walked in, limbs loose and ready. He often leaped through the open doors and engaged me instantly, but today he seemed to sense something different. Silent, he walked around the room, bare feet solid, body balanced as a walking tree, looking Eli and me over, considering. Daniel was average height, had muscles like rolls of barbed wire, and a face no one would remember for two seconds. Mr. Average Man. To irritate him, I called him Danny Boy, but not today. Not taking my eyes off him, I gave a half bow. "Daniel, this man is a guest in my house. We have a disagreement and have agreed to settle it on the mats."

"And you want me to referee?"

"No, Sensei." I studied their reactions as I finished with "I want you to keep me from hurting him too much." Daniel laughed, surprised. Eli's brows went up. Even with Daniel, and all his training and speed, I held back a lot. If I let go with Beast-strength and speed, I could do some damage. But even I knew that the sparring over ravioli was just an excuse to prove who was the big dog in Eli's and my relationship. He was . . . aware, maybe. Aware that I was something other than a tall, skinny girl with guns. When I didn't laugh with my sensei, the room went silent. I could hear the fountain tinkling in the enclosed courtyard. I could hear the air through the air-conditioner vents. And I heard the slight hitch when Eli took a preparatory breath.

CHAPTER TEN

Worthy Prey. Will Not Hurt Him *Too* Bad

Eli's right foot shot out, heel first, leg going level and straight, balance shifting as he moved, weight sliding. Faster than human, I stepped aside. With an almost uncanny awareness, he seemed to expect my body shift and followed the kick with a sweep of his leg. His heel impacted my side, but I was moving as fast as the kick. With an elbow, I clamped his foot against me and ducked under his leg, twisting, forcing him to follow or wrench his knee. In midair, he spun with me. Yanked his foot free and landed, cat-footed and sure. Eli bounced back from me.

Fun, Beast thought at me. *Play with worthy prey.*

I stood still, letting my little half smile and my silence work for me. I didn't look at Daniel, but I could smell his surprise. Now he knew I'd been holding back. I wondered how that might affect our training and sparring sessions in the future. Eli stepped in, closer, studying my body language, which was almost lazy. He rolled his head on his shoulders, letting the action camouflage his next move. Just before he punched out, my knees bent; I leaped. His fists were a fast one-two-three, into the space where I had been. I was three feet back, my breathing slow and steady.

Something in his face shifted into a cool, neutral expression. The fighting man was no longer playing. I let my half smile spread and gave a little *bring it on* gesture with my left fingers. Eli moved left, placing each foot with precision, letting his balance shift and roll. I let him lead our little dance, following his movement.

Worthy prey. Will not hurt him too *bad,* Beast thought. I felt her eagerness rush through me, hot and sweet. *Hunt,* she thought.

Eli swept out with his leg. I leaped, kicked with the heel of my foot, straight for his solar plexus, holding back enough to keep it from a killing strike. Too fast for his human reactions, my kick landed. He fell back, grunting with the aftershock. Reached for my leg. But it wasn't there anymore as I landed, cat-footed. I circled him. He swiveled with me and punched with his right. And the fight was on.

Eli was faster than any human I'd ever fought. Had more muscle mass. Knew some dirty moves I wanted to learn, even as they landed and bruised and the breath huffed and hissed out of me. But I was faster and way stronger than I looked. Eli started to sweat one minute into the fight. At two minutes he was breathing hard. I was grinning. And Beast was landing some moves of her own, one a cat-clawing strike that I had seen alley cats do, right claw going for the face, body shooting back, and back claw spinning up and going for the abdominals. Nasty move.

I was no longer hiding that I wasn't human, or at least not fully human, not pulling my punches and kicks, and I was faster and stronger with Beast participating. At twelve minutes, by the clock on the dojo wall, I had broken a sweat, but Eli was dripping, stinky, breathing hard, and his cockiness had disappeared. He had a few scratches, maybe a bruised rib or three.

I leaped back and let my hands drop slightly—only slightly—I wasn't stupid. "Yield." The word was a growl, low and snarled, and I could feel that my eyes were glowing faintly gold. Grudgingly, Eli nodded once, a downward jut of his chin. "Ravioli?" I asked.

The combo of Italian food and an animal growl must have tickled Eli's funny bone because his mouth twitched down slightly and then up. He laughed, a soft huff. "One serving of pasta or one *small* pizza. Per shower."

There was too much wiggle room in the statement. I

clarified, "One fourteen- or fifteen-ounce can of Italian, pasta-based, prepackaged food, or one twelve-inch or smaller pizza from the restaurant or frozen brand of Alex's choice, or one fast-food meal of his choice, not supersized, to be given for every shower he takes with soap and shampoo, but limited to one food item per day. And for every day he skips a shower, he misses two days' worth of food."

Eli thought about that, weighing fast food against his brother's body odor. "Done."

"Pizza? This was about *pizza*?" We both glanced to Daniel, standing with his arms loose and ready and an incredulous look on his face.

In unison, we said, "Yeah."

Daniel shook his head, but he had a speculative look on his face that boded poorly for our next private sparring session. Daniel wanted to take on the fighter he had seen on the mats today, not the girl he had been working with for several months. Sensei might not want to compete, but that didn't make him want to fight or win any less.

We walked back to my house, Eli ruminating silently, me enjoying the feel of the late afternoon sun beating down on my shoulders. I felt, more than heard, when he had his questions all in order. "No. I'm not. And no. I won't."

He laughed again, that soft huffing breath that must have worked well in Ranger recon. "Say what?"

"No, I'm not human. No, I won't tell you what I am. And while I'm at it, yes." I let my half smile lift, feeling his eyes on me. "You were more fun than anyone I've sparred with in a long time. Even if I *did* have to hold back some."

"Hold back?" His voice rose a hair in surprise.

I slanted my eyes at him. "You're still alive."

Eli cursed under his breath and put one hand to his solar plexus where my first kick had landed. "Hold back, my as— my backside."

I just grinned.

Inside my house, the kitchen was clean, the dishes— including the ravioli bowl—were washed and left to dry on a towel by the sink, and Alex was hooking something up to the back of the television in the living room. Only it wasn't my TV, but a large, flat screen that hadn't been there before.

It was perched on a drop-leaf table I vaguely remembered seeing upstairs, and electronics were scattered across its top: black, gray, and silver boxes, wires, an ergonomic keyboard, and squares of tightly folded paper instructions, which the Kid hadn't needed to read.

"How much?" Eli demanded.

The Kid glanced up, just now seeing us. He had no security consciousness about him at all. We could have been two ninja attackers or even a couple of Angus steers, and I didn't think he'd have noticed us enter. "Less than two grand."

Eli took a breath to yell, I took one to laugh, and the Kid forestalled us both by adding, "I called George Dumas." He went back to work, his attention on the spiderweb of cables he was constructing.

My stomach took a rolling tumble and I managed to inhale. George was well enough to be taking calls. "And?" I said, sounding almost normal.

"Mr. Dumas approved the preliminary estimate as a start-up to replacing the security system lost by the Master of the City in the fire that took out his house. He gave me all the necessary passwords and I'll rebuild it from here, tie it in to the system at the Vampire Council Building, the system at the heir's home out back, and eventually move the operating system to the Pellissier Clan Home when it's reconstructed." He glanced up. "Oh. I e-mailed him the prelim estimate on your company's letterhead. You know, since we work for you now. Not trying to undercut you or anything."

Eli and I had both stopped speaking, watching the brainiac work. I looked at Eli. Several things to say flashed through my head and I settled on "I don't have a letterhead." Which was stupid but better than some other options.

The Kid opened a new coil of cable, watching us from beneath his too-long bangs. "You do now. Your business name's not real catchy, but the blurb line is. Yellowrock Security. Protecting and staking vamps—we do it all. Have Stakes, Will Travel."

I laughed out loud. Eli did his soft chuckle. "I just *know* I'm going to regret this, but I like it. But I don't think we're exactly going into business together."

"Sure we are. The three of us." He looked back and forth between us, suddenly confused at our reactions. "We make a great team," he insisted. He pointed at me. "You can't construct an extensive security system all by yourself. You'd have to hire help. Me. You need someone to handle the recon and work with extra security personnel, someone who can do everything from general construction to electrical work, to defusing a bomb. There he is. You've got the cash and connections we need to get started, only my brother's too ethical to steal your business out from under you. You're also more than human and are reported to heal fast, move fast, and fight like a demon. Perfect team.

"Oh. All that research on your security team and vamps is printed out, collated, and stacked at your door, as well as e-mailed." As if dismissing us, the kid bent over and started moving the electronic thingamajig boxes around on the old table. Eli watched, his lips pursed, mild confusion on his face.

Alex looked up at us again. "Hey. That company, Greyson Labs? I found a tie-in to vamps. It's not a huge tie-in, but it's there."

I couldn't help my smile. The kid was good. Arguably better than Reach, and even paying the outrageous fees Eli was charging me, he was cheaper than Reach. "Yeah?"

Alex stepped over and dropped to my feet, which I did not expect, and started talking. "There's this boutique pharmaceutical company called DeAli. It, in turn, is wholly owned by a company called Allyon Enterprises, which is wholly owned by Vazquez International. Vazquez Int. also owns Greyson Labs." His grin grew. "Greyson is the company that employed Ramondo Pitri. Greyson is also the owner of Blood-Call Inc. I traced the money up in a line, then across, and down to find it."

I dropped slowly to the floor, bringing my face even with the Kid's. "Blood-Call was the name on the business cards in Seattle."

"Bingo. And Blood-Call? It's like a—" He shot a look at his brother and changed whatever he was about to say into "Like, you know, an escort service for vamps." At my expression, he ducked his head to hide his gratified smile. He'd discovered something important and he knew it.

"Escort service. Meaning blood-meals and dates," I said. That seemed important, and I tried to put it all together, but there was too much going on in my brain to isolate it.

"Dates. Yeah. Riiight," the Kid said.

"How did you figure all that out?" I asked.

"Financial market info is pretty easy to come by on publicly held companies. I'm doing a search to see if any board members in any of the companies are suckheads."

"Publicly held companies?" Eli barked. "Government companies?"

Kid rolled his eyes. "I'm not hacking. 'Publicly held companies' means the general public invests in them and owns stock. They're traded on the stock exchange and stuff. Like that. A lot of info on publicly held companies has to be freely available, if you know where and how to look."

"And Ramondo Pitri is now tied in to Blood-Call, which caters to vamps," I said, "and to Greyson Labs, which has something to do with medicine. And disease."

Yeah. That was it. It was tenuous, but it felt right, the way a puzzle piece feels when you slide it into a hole shaped just for it. "If someone wanted to infect a vamp, giving him a disease through sex and dinner would be a good way, but I don't see how a company that makes cancer drugs would also develop a disease." I thought about that for a moment, seeing if the puzzle piece still felt right, and oddly it did.

"There are Blood-Call businesses in Seattle and Sedona and Boston," I guessed.

"Yes, ma'am, there are. Of course there are Blood-Calls in lots of cities in the U.S., and there haven't been takeovers in them. Yet. So I haven't proved a tie-in."

"Huh. I don't know how or if it ties in either, but as a pal of mine says, I stopped believing in coincidences when I stopped believing in Santa. Not bad work, kid. Not bad at all," I said.

I went to my room, picking up the pages as I went. *Business partners? Not gonna happen.* But temporary contract employees *this* good, I could live with.

I stepped into my room and stopped. Someone had been in here. I smelled a male and a female, raw fish, tea, powdered sugar, and perfume, something expensive and light. I sniffed, parsing the scent-signatures. Deon, Katie's three-star chef, a friend of sorts, and gayer than an entire line of chorus dancers, *had been in my bedroom?* Yeah, he had. With him was Christie, one of the girls who worked at Katie's Ladies. I did not want Christie, with her piercings and chains and tats and general air of disdain, in *my* room. But—

The place had been dusted. The bed was made up. The cobwebs hanging from the ceiling were gone. I walked in and lifted the coverlet. Clean sheets. I bent and sniffed. The corners smelled of Deon and Christie—only the corners, which was a happy discovery. It meant they had handled my sheets, not rolled around on them, which was a mental image I really didn't want to intrude in my psychological space. But there was a major problem. My weapons were gone.

A slow boil started somewhere in my gut, and I dropped the collated pages on the bed, walked out of bedroom, across the foyer, and into the living room. Before I could open my mouth, the Kid said, "In the ordnance room," and pointed at the hole in the wall. I narrowed my eyes and ducked into the hollow space under the stairs. My weapons and Eli's were laid out on the striped mattress, hung on spikes in the mortar of the rock walls, stretched out on trays on a battered bookshelf and on another table, both from upstairs. There wasn't much room to walk, but it was . . . organized. My blades were on the new table in sheaths or laid out by blade length. The stakes were on one end, the silver-tipped ones, then the ones made of ash wood. The vial of holy water was hanging above the table surface. My guns were on the bed by size, from the M4 shotgun to the tiny derringer. Eli's weapons and ordnance, including flashbangs and what looked suspiciously like C4 explosives, were on the other side of the bed and on the bookcase. And there was a lot of it. My hands itched to try out a garrote made to look like a bracelet. *Niiice.*

I went back into the living room, leaving Eli inspecting his own weapons, his face like a thunderhead. Once the swinging shelving in the main room was in place, the weapons would be better hidden than when they had been kept in the small locked gun safe in my closet. Here, they were safe from children, not that any lived with me any longer. And that was a pain I had no intention of dealing with just now.

Saying nothing, but smelling Eli's irritation, I went back to my room, let my hair down, and showered off before plopping down on the corner chair to read. It was boring stuff, the financial pages of a publicly held company. I was much more interested in the drugs Greyson Labs made, but I couldn't make heads or tales of that part either. Having taken an emergency medical technician course after high school didn't prepare me to understand the making of drugs I couldn't even pronounce. To stay awake, I got out my gun cleaning supplies and started to clean my .380s and nine-mils. It quickly became read a paragraph, work on a gun, read a paragraph, work on a gun.

Even with the necessary chore, I was about to nod off in boredom when the Kid knocked on my bedroom door. I set the weapon to the side and called for him to come in. Alex pushed in the door, his left leg shaking uncontrollably, his eyes wide, and his scent full of the adrenaline of excitement—which smelled a lot better than the kind of adrenaline that comes from fear or shock. Instantly, I knew he had found something, and the breath I took felt icy as it scored through my lungs. "What?"

"A vamp owns Greyson Labs. And Blood-Call. And all the other interconnected companies."

I got up and walked into the living room. "You might want to hear this," I said to Eli. "Did you know your brother is a genius?"

"Yeah. The court system said so," he said wryly.

"Spill it," I said to the Kid.

"His name is Lucas Vazquez de Allyon. The dude is a twelve-hundred-year-old, suckhead creeper, who fell off his rocker, like, five hundred years ago. He's seriously whacked." When I looked confused about the rocker part, he added, "A perv. A freak. A crazy-ass crackhead. An old dude who—"

"Alex!" Eli said. It was a military-grade reprimand in two syllables.

Alex's mouth slapped shut. I wondered what the Kid had wanted to say, and figured my cussing ban had been about to be abused. Instead, after a moment's hesitation, the Kid said, "He owns the company Ramondo Pitri worked for, though Pitri was way down the line. And de Allyon is a violent, narcissistic pervert, even for a suckhead." The Kid handed us each a sheaf of papers and, by unspoken agreement, we all went to the kitchen, Eli to make a pot of black glue he called coffee in an old percolator he'd found in the small butler's pantry where the tea things were kept, and me to start a pot of water for tea.

Lucas de Allyon had been around a long time, making a place now and then in history. He had lived in Spain about the time that Leo had been turned, and became a conquistador in search of gold, sailing to the Americas. A vamp on a ship at sea. I wondered how many of the sailors made it alive to the new world. Once here, he seemed to have reverted to the practice of Naturaleza.

Vamps and their killing bloodlust were kept in check by adherence to the Vampira Carta, which governed everything in their lives from how to care for their young scions while they went through the curing process, to how to address the need for territory and hunting grounds. Vamps who believed in the Naturaleza refused to be bound by the constraints of the Carta; they hunted and drained humans and killed without remorse or pity. Lucas's history was well documented. He had killed and enslaved hundreds, maybe thousands, of American Indians, putting them to work and to death as he saw fit. He had created himself a little kingdom and killed and drunk his way through his slaves: Choctaw, Cherokee, Natchez, and maybe even Mississippi Indian tribes.

I dropped the pages on the table, stood, and poured hot water over the tea leaves in a green ceramic pot. Moving by muscle memory and instinct, I got out a mug, Cool Whip, and sugar, and prepared a cup. Thinking. Remembering a painting of a Cherokee slave on the wall of an old vamp's house. She had yellow eyes like mine, and had probably been a skinwalker like me, but she couldn't have been trained, or she would have fought her way free of her slavery. She was dead now. Another of my kind I had found and lost without ever meeting her. I put my own failed hopes of finding another like me aside and carried my mug back to the table and pages Alex had prepared.

Not only had de Allyon enslaved the Cherokee. According to historians, he was also the first man to own African slaves on land in what was now South Carolina. He was bloodthirsty in every way an undead nonhuman could be. The accounts, even couched in terms acceptable by the Europeans of that time period, were gruesome. He supposedly died of a fever in October 1526, disappearing and reappearing in Charleston in the early sixteen hundreds. He stayed there for fifty years, and disappeared again. He later terrorized Boston for a few years before the tea party of 1773. De Allyon resurfaced in Atlanta during the Reconstruction Period after the Civil War, eventually buying old plantation land and setting up a sharecropper system that "employed" nearly a thousand freed slaves.

Quickly thereafter, Lucas claimed most of the state of Georgia as Blood Master of Atlanta—all the Southeastern territory, excluding Florida, that was not claimed by Amaury Pellissier, Leo's uncle. Now, it was possible that Lucas wanted Leo's territory and figured he was the undead man to take it.

I flipped through the pages. There was still no financial trail to prove that Lucas wanted Leo's territory. No proof that he had taken over Seattle and Sedona and Boston. No proof that he had sent his vamps to attack Leo in Asheville weeks ago or again at his clan home last night. No clues to where he was staying, or if he was even in the state. No nothing, except that he was powerful and a lot older and more vicious than Leo. And might be dominant enough to take what he wanted. I flipped back to the file on Blood-Call. It had businesses in Sedona, Seattle, Asheville, and Boston, with one slated to open in New Orleans in the next few months. Of course Blood-Call was also open in New York, San Francisco, L.A., Vegas, and a few other places, so it could be a coincidence, in which case I'd look stupid taking the information to Leo. Except for the fact that de Allyon owned Blood-Call, and had been Ramondo Pitri's up-line employer, there was nothing physical or financial or real that actually proved Lucas Vazquez de Allyon was the bad guy who had attacked Leo in Asheville or was making vamps sick and taking over their territories.

But my gut was saying our bad guy was de Allyon, and that Greyson Labs and Blood-Call were part of the attack on the vamps. Somehow. Even though all I had was a name from history, it was time to tell Leo.

I gathered up my laptop and retreated to my bedroom again. Copying and pasting, I prepared a report for Leo and Bruiser on Blood-Call, the lab, and de Allyon, making certain that they understood my concern was mostly conjecture at this point. With a single keystroke, I sent it off and then curled around the laptop to question myself and second-guess my research.

I must have fallen asleep because I woke before dusk to the smell of steak grilling and a dead laptop battery. Groggy, I freshened up and put on a clean bra and shirt. Having men in the house was going to seriously impact my comfort clothes. Before I left my room, I dialed Leo, but it was Bruiser who answered. "H-h-hello, Jane." His voice was low and warm and breathy, with a faint English accent and nearly a purr of sound. *Bruiser*. Who did *not* sound like himself.

"Bruiser. You sound . . . odd. Do you feel okay?"

"I discover that I quite like the way I feel."

"Uh-huh." Bruiser had been partially healed by Koun, a vamp who claimed to be pure Celt, and who would, if true, be much older than Leo. Then he'd been brought back from the dead, or near enough as not to matter, by an infusion of the blood of Bethany Salazar y Medina, a vamp who was nearly two thousand years old. And Katie had said, "*George. You will live. And still mostly human. Do not despair.*"

"Crap," I said softly.

Blood-servants were much faster and stronger than regular humans, because of the sips of vamp blood they regularly took in. They had better night vision, better hearing. I didn't know what Bruiser was now, but I had a bad feeling about it. "Have you heard from Leo?"

"I have spoken with my master," he said. "With your help, he escaped the Mithrans who held him for a time last night. But he was injured badly. I have sent the priestesses to his lair where he sleeps, to heal him, and his most loyal blood-servants, to feed him when he wakes and to complete his healing." He paused, then added slowly, "He brought a Mithran with him when he escaped, and will be interrogating her soon. I am driving there. Leo requests your presence as well."

Going to any vamp's lair when he was injured and bleed-

ing and had not been sent to earth to heal was not a smart
move. I thought about the vamp Leo had captured. I didn't
want to be part of that, not again, with the silver and the
questions and the stink of burning vamp-flesh, but I thought
it was more likely he'd let her live if I was there to temper
his mood. Assuming I didn't tick him off and make him kill
her outright.

Deep in my mind, Beast huffed. *We will see the vampire
in his den. We will know much, just as when we saw his hidden place in his Clan Den.* I had seen one of Leo's lairs, deep
beneath the clan home, which was now burned to the
ground and beneath it probably. And yes, I had learned a
lot.

And hey, Leo paid the bills. I'd probably suffer vamp-
consequences if I didn't go, once Leo was up to meting
them out.

I checked the time and said, "Okay." And I wondered if
I had just screwed up badly or made the smartest move a
vamp-hunter could make.

"I have sent the location to your cell phone. Meet me in
ninety minutes."

An hour later, after I had eaten a fabulous steak and a
mediocre salad, I dressed in the kind of clothes I wore when
I went to visit a vamp instead of to fight a vamp. No armored
jacket, no Benelli strapped to my back, no guns except the
one I tucked into a boot beside the hidden vamp-killer.
Thick denim jeans like bikers wear instead of armored
leather vamp-fighting pants. Only three vamp-killers. Hair
braided tight. Stakes in the loops at my belt, ready to be
tucked into my hair like ornaments when I unhelmeted. I
put on the silver choker to protect my neck from fangs. Leo
would have plenty of humans around to feed him, but that
was no reason to be provocative, and a bare throat was a
clear provocation to an injured vamp.

I pushed Bitsa into the street. I felt the eyes of the brothers on my back—and legs and other body parts—as I straddled the bike, rose, and kick-started my Harley. I could also
feel their misgivings, which did nothing to quell my own. I
checked the phone for the address and GPS directions
Bruiser had sent to it, before heading into the Warehouse
District of New Orleans.

The Warehouse District was just what it sounded like—
the centuries-old storage facilities of the New Orleans docks,
where indigo, rice, cotton, food crops, cloth, tobacco, and
other items had been shipped downriver and to Europe, in
return for silk, porcelain china, tea, and slaves. Later centuries had shipped cars, mechanical tools, raw and formed iron,
steel, coal, technology, imported illegal drugs, and exported
sexual slavery, cash, liquor, cigarettes. Everything, legal and
illegal, moral and immoral, had been stored, for a time, in the
warehouses. Now the old refurbished buildings housed art-
ists' lofts, cafés, exclusive restaurants, galleries, apartments,
spas, fitness centers, and all manner of upscale social businesses.

The address I turned in to was a recently rehabbed
warehouse, updated and secluded. There were bars on the
windows, the wrought-iron fleur-de-lis made so popular by
French immigrants, pretty as well as effective at keeping
out burglars. The building also had electronic security up
the wazoo: dynamic cameras with low-light and infrared
capability, keypunch locks; two armed guards with earpieces, bulges suggestive of guns, and the look of trained
soldiers patrolled the place. It was all stuff I had recommended to Leo for the Mithran council's headquarters and
his now-burned clan home. I'd have to remember to send
him a bill, now that he'd finally followed my advice.

Blinding-bright security lights brought tears to my eyes
and threw the place into sharp-angled shadows. I wheeled
into the parking area and Bitsa's roar went silent. I pulled
my riding gloves off. I didn't really need to, and didn't often
ride with gloves, but the finger-by-finger let me scope out
the place.

Sitting on the seat, I smelled seafood, hot grease, and
coffee—natch—and wine and beer—also natch—and the
scents of mold, hot tar, exhaust, stagnant and moving water,
and flowers—jasmine, I thought—that marked the city. I
saw the last traces of the sun on the horizon, bleeding reddish in the cerulean sky. I smelled humans I recognized.
Two of Derek Lee's Vodka Boys were among the security I
saw patrolling. I smelled Bruiser and Wrassler. I smelled
Leo's Mercy Blade, Gee DiMercy somewhere close by, and
I smelled several vamps too, which was a surprise. Sabina,

the oldest outclan priestess, had been in the parking lot before total dark set in. Day-walking, or dusk-walking, was something only the really old ones can do and live. I could think of no reason for any of them to be here unless they were here for Leo to drink from. Injured vamps needed a lot of blood to heal really bad injuries, even vamps as powerful as the Master of the City. Something tightened deep inside, though I refused to name it fear or worry for the MOC. I unhelmeted, strapped it to the back of the bike, and stuck the hair sticks into my bun, wishing I had brought more than six. I adjusted the vamp-killers so they were easy to hand.

Bruiser glided through the falling dark toward me as I tucked my gloves into a pocket. I studied him as he wove between cars. His dark hair fell over his forehead in a silken wave; his brown eyes were liquid and intent. He was the same, but better somehow, richer, more mesmeric. He moved differently too, smoother, catlike. Sleek. The breeze, hot and wet, shifted, bringing his scent to me. Vamp and human and . . . *vamp*. He smelled of mixed vamp odor, almost like a blood-slave, the herbal pong something they acquired as they were passed around. As he got closer, his eyes holding me still, I could see even more differences. Bruiser was so full of vamp blood that his eyes were half-vamped out, pupils huge in his brown irises, and not just because of the night. His eyes gleamed, cold and dark and empty, yet hot and speaking to me of sex even before he opened his mouth.

"My Jane. You have arrived."

I grunted and swung my leg over Bitsa. *His Jane. Yeah. Right.*

Bruiser reached me and slid an arm around my waist. His arm felt different, harder, stronger, like a steel band, as if he could lift me up and toss me into the air, a dance move to end all dance moves. He pulled me close and ducked his head, nuzzling my neck, his lips hot and softer than velvet and finding that place under my ear that sent shivers through my body, raising chill bumps on my skin—hard to do in the heat. I wasn't used to being smaller, shorter than anyone, and the sensation of feeling petite and weak against the taller man was oddly arousing. I let him lift me to my toes, breathed in the scent of his sweat on the warm night air. Almost with a will of their own, my fingers laced through his hair.

"I missed you," he whispered as his other arm went around me, pulling me close, close enough that I knew just *how* he had missed me. Bruiser was four inches taller than me, and was now clearly stronger too. I *knew* that, predator to predator. But the knowledge faded beneath the onslaught of his scent, the heat of his skin, and his arousal pressed against me. "I *missed you*," he repeated, the three words morphing into a growl.

Beast breathed in his scent with me, claws out but not yet pressing in. *Vampire. Much vampire blood,* she thought. *But still your Bruiser.*

He pulled me up, closer, my body crushed against his. I'd never been *the little woman* before. Ever. But I was now. Weirdly, I liked it. His mouth found mine, his lips hot and soft one moment, hard and demanding the next. My breath caught.

He broke the kiss before I was ready. "When this conflict is done"—his lips moved against my ear—"I'm taking you to my place, and we will not leave until long, *long* after dawn."

Heat shot out from the touch of his lips and settled deep in my belly. Spreading out in tendrils of desire and need and pure *want*. I had to lick my lips before I could answer, half gasping, "Okay. Fine. Sure."

Bruiser laughed into my hair and swung me to his side, effortlessly. I fell into step beside him. The warehouse had two heavy steel doors and, situated between them, one oversized delivery door. We made our way to it, Bruiser holding me so close my right arm was trapped under his shoulder. He pressed a button, and the delivery door began to slide up, revealing the darkness inside. Our shadows were long and thin across the charcoal-painted cement floor. The room inside was empty, all in gray, with a bar at the back. And doors leading off into the dark. "So, where is the lair?" I asked.

Then it all went to hell.

CHAPTER ELEVEN

But He Didn't Let Me Go

I smelled/heard/tasted the attack before it came, a single breath, pulled in over my tongue, the taste of betrayal. Scent-laden with pheromones: the clan's Mercy Blade, vamps; Sabina, the older priestess who lived in the vamp graveyard; Katie and Leo. Distinct pops of displaced air, vamp-speed. Blurs of motion.

My expectations ruined me. I expected Bruiser to release me and move two steps to my side. I expected him to draw a weapon. I did *not* expect him to freeze, my arm clamped to his side, stealing my single moment of reaction time. I did not expect his whispered "Leo. I—No!" I jerked my arm and twisted my body.

Bruiser held on to me. And my trust was shattered.

Katie caught my free arm, which was reaching for my ankle holster, in a vise. The Mercy Blade stepped on my foot, which was lifting to my hand, and forced it back to the cement floor. Sabina circled behind me and caught my head, twisting my chin up, stretching my neck, holding me still. I was immobilized. The electric door whirred down behind us, enclosing us in the dark. Leo walked out of the echoing shadows, footsteps measured and slow. He was vamped out, his fangs snapped down, eyes all black pupil in bloody, scarlet sclera. Sabina unlatched the clasp on my silver and titanium necklace.

Bruiser swallowed, the sound of his throat moving loud in the sudden silence. "I brought her to you. But . . . This is not what . . ." His voice sounded thick, confused, and trailed off into nothing, but my eyes were on Leo. I understood what was about to happen. My heart thumped hard once and raced to a limping beat. I wrenched my body, fighting for freedom. It was like wrestling shaped steel.

Beast is not prey! she raged inside me.

"George. Bruiser. Don't let him do this," I said, my words strangled from the angle of my neck.

"I . . . can't. I'm sorry," he said again, real regret clotting his voice, and maybe real pain.

Leo stepped up to me, like a dance step, measured, smooth, like the opening movement to a tango. He was slight but strong, shoulder-length black hair pulled back in a queue with a black ribbon, the end hanging over one shoulder. His eyes, Frenchy black; his face, usually so pale, was now suffused with blood. He looked well fleshed, as if he had been working out and had put on muscle. His usual scent, like pepper and papyrus, was different, with a hint of berries and oak and fermentation, like fine wine. I realized that Leo had fed long and deeply.

His fangs clicked down, three inches of glistening white, his jaw having to do something odd to allow the movement. My breath heaved and my heart raced, and Leo's eyes bled slowly black and scarlet, vamping out as he smelled my fear. "You, my new *Enforcer*, have equally served me well and caused me much grief," he said, the words sibilant and echoing in the empty space. "You found my enemy, which is a service to be well rewarded. But this trouble you have brought to me must end. I have taken council of my advisers and have discovered a way to reward you for both." He smiled, and my heart sped even faster. Leo chuckled softly and leaned in, breathing deeply of my panic. "Yessss," he whispered, his lips close to my ear. "And then you will be my new Enforcer indeed. You will be bound to me as the Carta rightly requires. You, rather than my George, will act as my second in the Blood Challenge I will issue to this enemy you have identified." He smiled and it was snakelike. "That is, *if* you survive your own duty and fate."

"Boss—Leo, don't—" Bruiser stopped as if his throat

was choked shut and buried his face in my hair, speaking now to me. "I'm sorry," Bruiser whispered, the word echoing exactly as Leo's had. "I can't stop him. I'm sorry. I'm so, so sorry." I could smell his misery, his self-disgust. *His compulsion.* He *was* sorry. But he didn't let me go. He couldn't. He was blood-trapped, blood-drunk. Compelled. Leo's slave. *This* was why vamps were evil. This stealing of will.

"I'm sorry for causing you trouble," I said, fear like lightning, my words gasping. "And I don't need any reward for discovering Lucas de Allyon. I haven't even proved he's your enemy. I said it's possible."

"Your analysis was exemplary and your conclusion valid," Gee said. "We concur with your hypothesis and analysis. My master's true-dead uncle had previous . . . rivalry with this Mithran regarding some small territorial disputes following the Civil War. Hence this necessity."

Leo lifted a hand to my face, calloused along the thumb side of his index finger, and warm from all the blood he had ingested. The Mercy Blade pressed against my knees and they buckled, the vamps riding me down until my knees hit the cool floor, a supplicant, as if begging. I might have thought that Gee DiMercy would save me as he did once before, would have compassion, but he wasn't human either. And he too was Leo's.

Bruiser fell to his knees beside me, still holding my arm. I started to threaten Leo, but Sabina yanked down on my bun so hard my hair tore and my scalp bled. I could smell it. I fought to inhale with my head at this angle, my breath sounding tortured. Leo bent over me, his black hair falling forward, to caress my cheeks. From the corner of my eye, I saw a flash of steel and smelled Leo's blood where he cut himself. One of Sabina's inhumanly strong hands held my head back; the other hand pinched my nose closed.

"Blood to blood," Leo murmured, "mind to mind. My power calling to your power." He bit into my throat. Electric pain cut through me. Magic slammed into me, hot and wet, raw and scarlet, heavy with semisolid *things* that flooded into my spirit cave and molded to my soul like clots.

Leo's wrist covered my mouth as I gasped. I breathed down the drops of blood and the magic, choking, feeling it hit my lungs and slam into my bloodstream, my jaws suddenly aching with heavy pressure, my fingertips burning, as Beast struggled to break free. There was nothing of compulsion in Leo, nothing of the painkilling laving of tongue that could have blunted the pain. Nothing of the mesmerizing ability that made the taking of blood pleasurable for the victim. This was control. This was dominance, not the reward he'd promised. If I fought, he'd rip out my throat.

As soon as I thought that, a wave of pleasure rippled through me, starting at my neck and following every nerve ending across my torso to settle low in my belly. Heat and desire coiled there, mating together. *No,* I thought. *No . . .*

Tears blurred my eyes, and my stomach roiled. My mouth filled with Leo's blood, almost human-warm, gelatinous, with a sharp, peppery, fermented flavor. I had no choice but to swallow. My gulps tore my throat where Leo's teeth pierced me, and more pain/pleasure flared out. My heart beat fast against my ribs as he drank, fangs buried deep, lips sealed tight. Sucking hard. And I swallowed as he swallowed, a dance of pleasure and agony. Two, three, six gulps. Need cascaded through me with each sip of his blood. If my hands had been free, I'd have clutched him to me, and I hated him for that control, for that want. This was what made blood-slaves willing to do anything to get their next high. Anything at all.

Leo's arm moved from my mouth and I finally got a breath, inhaling, the sound a hissing panic and a gasping desire, and Leo drank in my fear and craving. He slid his arms around me and pushed me flat to the floor, until I stared up at the shadows. Sabina released me, stepping away; the Mercy Blade followed her, leaving me on the floor with Leo and Bruiser. They held me between them, the two of them, as Leo's magic welled up, twining around me, sliding inside me, like electric vines. In the dark I could feel it, a prickling breeze over my exposed skin. Could see it, wisps and strands of pale gray light. Could smell it, like old parchment and pepper, Leo's personal scent. His magic flowed beneath my skin, pumped through my veins, mingled with my blood, and I sobbed once, only once, my flesh throbbing against his fangs. My heartbeat was a soft thump-thump, thump-thump, growing louder as the blood I'd breathed in and swallowed was carried with his magic

through my body, through my heart, and arteries and veins.
Changing me. Empowering me. Half a dozen gulps of my
blood. Stolen.

Thief of blood, Beast hissed.

Leo's fangs withdrew, the motion slow and cutting like
twin razors. I grunted with the pain. Bruiser was still whispering, his lips barely moving air, "I'm sorry, I'm sorry, I'm sorry."
Katie took Leo's place, standing over me, staring down, alpha
to my zeta. I curled back my lips and growled at her. She
chuckled at the sound, her own power flowing over me like
cold water, brown and teal and dark green. She held up her
arm and I smelled her blood. Three claw marks scored her
wrist, blood running down to her fingers and up to her elbow.
Beast had drawn blood. I snarled at her. I felt Beast's fangs
in my mouth, long and pointed and built for killing, for
shredding meat, not for draining the blood of prey.

"You are not human," she said. She licked her own blood,
staring down at me as her wrist healed. "We have always
known this. Your blood will taste sweet." She knelt and bent
over my elbow, rolling my sleeve up, lifting my arm to her
mouth, bending it at a painful angle. She bit me.

The pain this time nearly broke me, an electric shock
that froze my breath and darkened the edges of my vision.
I lay still, my body against the cool cement. She was lying
across me, her legs to the side, her weight far heavier than I
expected.

Leo's heir took only three deep gulps before withdraw-
ing her fangs. They clicked back into her mouth on the little
bone hinges and she slid her tongue along my arm, closing
the wounds before she wiped her lips with a finger, licking
off a drop of my blood. Bruiser was curled along my side,
still whispering his sorrow.

"Now you are mine," Leo said.

"Now I can bind you easily should Leo fall," Katie said.
"Our defenses will not be subsumed, nor will they fail
should the worst happen. The Vampira Carta is now our
defense."

As if they had rehearsed it, they stood and stepped away,
leaving Bruiser and me on the floor. Our hips touched, my
arm stretched around underneath him. I was gasping, trying
to catch my breath, trying to slow my heart. Not succeeding.

I pulled my arm from him. The simple movement sent jagged pain through my nerves from my neck to my fingertips. I wiped my tears away. I felt pelt on my cheeks and a misshapen jaw. My hand came away bloody with vamp-blood that had missed my mouth. I sat up, moving with pain. My hair had come down, and it slithered loose around me.

Leo, dressed all in black, was across the room, perched on a stool, one forearm on the bar. A candle burned near his elbow, and a dusty bottle of red wine with a curling, crinkled label sat near. He lifted the bottle and poured the wine into crystal goblets. Katie walked to him. She was wearing champagne-colored silk pants and a flowing vest; the cloth caught the light, glistening. Sabina, the priestess, dressed in her ubiquitous starched white robes, stepped close to them. Leo held out his hand. "George."

Bruiser pulled a leg under him and stood, leaving me there, going to his master, his eyes averted. Cold steel touched my throat from behind, the Mercy Blade's sword, his scent distinctive, and so I stayed on my butt, in submission. The three vamps drank the wine, like a toast or a pledge, as Bruiser stood there, looking away. I tried to slow my heart and find my breath, weight balanced on my hands, the floor cold beneath me.

This is a great gift I have given you, the sharing of my blood and favor, Leo said.

I started to reply when I realized that he hadn't spoken aloud. He was talking into my mind. *Well, crap.*

He smiled, just a bare curl of lips, his fangs hidden away. *Beware when you claim a position of power in my territory, little Enforcer. With power comes both responsibility and cost. And sometimes sacrifice. By your own works and your own choices, you are mine.*

Have you used the bones? another voice murmured into my head. I recognized the dulcet, accented tones of Sabina, speaking of the sabertooth lion bones hidden in my garden. I tried to shake my head, tried to lie, but the pain in my throat stopped me. *Your enemy will know you by your scent,* she thought. I had no idea what she meant.

"What is she?" Katie asked Leo. "She is delicious. I like it."

"Unknown. Something cat, of course, though not were-cat. They stink. She is elegant, like this wine"—he tilted the glass, and I could see the ruby fluid coat the crystal—"rich and earthy and heavy with the tannins of aged oak." I knew that Sabina could have answered Leo's question. Instead, she looked at me over her shoulder, no expression on her face.

I reached up and pushed away the sword at my throat. Gee DiMercy must have considered me no threat now, for he stepped back. Any movement hurt all over, and I thought I might fall, but I pulled myself to my feet, unsteady. Bruiser rushed back and reached out to stabilize me. I growled at him and he stopped as if a puppet master had wrenched his strings. When I spoke, the words were slurred, my cat-mouth not meant for speaking human sounds. "I' no' a vintage," I said, my vocal cords tight and aching, my voice rough with pain and with Beast's nearness. "This was no gift. It was my punishmen' for claiming to be your Enforcer."

"You transgressed," Leo said. "That transgression bent the law and forced us into this war. Now we can rectify the problems you have created and turn the balance of the war in our favor. You will assist us in this endeavor."

I felt the pull of his will, his pressure of his commands, and I said, "I'll fulfill my . . . responsibilities."

Leo's brows went up in surprise. "Of course you will." And I felt his compulsion caress me like a huge hand smoothing my pelt.

"I would have fulfilled them anyway. Without . . . this." My voice broke and I struggled to find my breath. "I'll do my duty. But if you ever t-t-t-try to drink me down again, I'll shhtake you and cut off your head." *And eat his heart,* Beast added. Leo went still at that, as if he could hear her promise.

I turned and walked to the sliding door and extended my hand. At the end of the palm was a golden-furred paw/ finger, human shaped, but bigger, knobbier, with a retractable claw at the tip. My index finger found the button that made the door rise. It whirred up and I walked under it and into the night. It closed behind me. I made it to my bike. Pulled my sleeve down over my aching inner elbow. Straddled Bitsa. On the third try, my fingers folded around the handlebars, mostly human-shaped again. I managed to kick-start her. And I rode away.

Tears flew from my eyes, snaking with the wind across

my face, into my hairline. I wasn't wearing my helmet. My loose hair blew out behind me as if the wind ran fingers through it, unbraiding it, tangling. I could still feel Leo's fangs at my throat. Katie's against my arm. Still feel my own fangs in my mouth, sharp against my tongue, and knew my jaw and lower face were still misshapen. If a cop stopped me for riding without a helmet, I'd scare the crap outta him.

I sobbed with misery and what might have been despairing laughter. I had been delusional, thinking I could work for vamps and not get bitten, not be forced to drink from them. Delusional and stupid. *Stupid, stupid, stupid.*

I dropped the bike on the far side of the Mississippi. Just pulled off the narrow, unmarked road into nowhere, into the brush beside the road, and propped her against a tree. I stripped off my shirt, the stench of vamp and my own blood strong in my nose. So much had happened in the converted warehouse. I had learned so much. And lost so much.

Have you used the bones? Sabina knew what I was. She knew I was a skinwalker.

"What is she?" Katie had asked Leo. He had replied, *"Unknown."* I hadn't realized it at that time, but he had scented of the truth. So Sabina hadn't told the Master of the City about me. Why not?

I stepped away from the bike into the woods. Briars tore at me. As I walked, I dropped my clothes and boots, leaving them where they fell.

I had clawed Katie. My face had transformed. They knew I was *something.* Something cat. Leo and Sabina had talked into my brain, something gained from the magic ceremony, the taking of my blood, and force feeding. Compulsion that bound me to Leo. Even here, out of the city, miles away, I could feel him inside me like a ghost crouching in the corner of my brain, like a demon's dark shadow, waiting to command me.

Something splashed my legs, wet and cool. I stopped. I had walked a long way into the woods. Yet I knew where I was, at Beast's hunting grounds, the swampy water where deer and other prey came to drink, where gators slept in the heat and hunted in the night. Something splashed nearby, landing heavily in the water. Mosquitoes buzzed me, biting. Sweat was slick on my body. The water moved slowly, stirred from beneath, the moonlight rippling on the surface. I touched my neck, the tissue swollen and tacky with half-dried blood. Time seemed to bend around me, a languorous pain.

I sobbed into the night, the sound raucous, ripping from me like a scream of torture. I had been . . . dominated. Controlled. *Beaten.* I wrapped my misshapen hands around my aching throat, the gold necklace I always wore now crusted with my blood, and let the tears fall. *Ten minutes,* I thought. I'd allow myself to grieve for ten minutes. The tears fell, scalding across my cheeks, through my pelt and dripping onto my hands. I had been prey. *Bruiser had betrayed me.* Another sob ripped from my injured throat, the sound spreading out over the water, settling into the swampy ground. *Ten minutes.* Then I'd get on with living.

Beast rose, fast, powerful, and demanded, *Shift. Now! Beast is not beaten. Beast is not prey!*

I let my half-human-shaped hands fall away from my throat, closed my eyes on the moonlit water. Pain, physical pain swatted me down. I fell forward, toward the water. Cutting, burning, slicing pain. Gray light filled with black motes of energy shot into the darkness. I screamed.

I leaped onto the shore. Shook swamp water from my pelt. Screamed into the night. *I am Beast! This is my land. My territory. I hunt. I am not beaten!* In the water, something long and dark moved. Alligators. Worthy prey. But not in water. Would hunt gator someday, on land. I screamed challenge again. Things in swamp sank into deeps and water went still. Moon and stars were caught in water, trapped.

I shook again, flinging stinky water. Walked into the night. Inside mind, I found Jane. She still grieved, her mind curled tight, sleeping like kit. Near her in mind was dark thing, like mist and marshmallows, like shadow and sponge. From the dark thing a chain ran, to curl around Jane's neck. I pushed on dark thing with paw. It moved. It stank of Leo.

I studied it, thinking, thinking like Jane.

This chain was a new thing. It had not been here in mind before, and now it was here. It stretched to Jane like leash. I understood. Dark thing was the creation of alpha vampire, magic of Leo. His ownership was like collar of metal, spikes poking Jane's neck. Was like cage, holding Jane. Dark thing was binding of Leo. I growled. Put claws on binding, testing. Cutting down with sharp claw edges. Binding was not tight. Not strong. Could shift and shift and shift, maybe only five times, and poking collar of binding would be gone. Jane was not human to be bound. Beast was better than Jane alone and better than big-cat alone. Jane should not grieve. Leo hurt her, but did not defeat her. We would still be free.

I walked through woods, night like a gift of hiding. Black panther, black leopard, black big-cats liked night best, but Beast was good hunter by day or night. Could hunt in tall grass under sun, or at night under no moon. I tracked by smell moving on air, going to place Jane needed to see. Following stink of old meat, spoiled long ago under hot summer sky. I sat at edge of killing place, looking, seeing many bones. Many more than five deer had been killed here, stolen from Beast. Winter food, killed by thieves of meat, by pack hunter. Deer bones mostly gone now. Bones scattered. Wolves had taken food in bloodlust. In killing spree. Jane needed to see. To understand.

She stirred, eyes still leaking. Sad for being prey. Sad for Bruiser who was not Bruiser tonight. She did not understand that Bruiser would grieve too. *Beast?* she called. I huffed. She stared out at night through Beast eyes. Night was sharp with greens and blues and silver tones, everything bright and clear. Bones stood out in grasses and on top of pine needles. *Bones?* she asked.

Deer bones. Killed by wolves, by pack. Stolen from Beast. Thieves of meat, like in Hunger Times. Pack thinks like strongest, like alpha. Pack thinks like pack. Not like one. Not like two. Like pack.

Jane sighed, breath in mind tired and sad. Not understanding. *Yeah, yeah. Got that. Sorry, but . . . I don't get why we came here.*

I growled, sound vibrating into night. *Beast lost much here. Beast lost winter food. Beast lost meat.* Hissed thought, *Lost* to pack. *Tonight Jane lost to pack. Bruiser lost to pack. But Jane is not pack. Bruiser is not pack. Jane is Jane and Bruiser is Bruiser.* I batted a rib bone hard with paw. It spun into dark and landed in brush. *There is no shame in losing to pack with strong alpha. Shame is from not fighting again when pack is smaller, when pack-alpha is not expecting at-tack. Only shame is giving up.*

Jane made strange sound, air and laughter like bubbles in mind. But when she thought, anger and joy thrummed in words. *Like taking a pair of brass knuckles to a half-awake werewolf and knocking his butt into never-never land. Like sitting on a nice tree limb and dropping down on unwary prey. Patience. Yeah. Okay. I can wait to get Leo back for this.* Her tears began to dry.

And Bruiser? I thought to Jane. *He was prey tonight too, caught in alpha's mind. In Leo's pack. He smelled of griev-ing, like Jane smelled of grieving. Like Beast smelled of grieving when I killed injured fawn here, fawn left by pack to die slow death. Did not want to kill. Did not. But must. Forced by pack. Like Bruiser.*

Jane made sound in mind. Like snort. Like disbelief. Like acceptance too. *Yeah, yeah, okay. Bruiser is all innocent. When did you get so wise?*

Beast is good hunter. Beast is good mother of kits. Jane is not. Jane said nothing to that. *I hunt now. Go to sleep.* I put paw on her mind, pushing down, forcing her to rest. I walked into forest.

I woke up at dawn, naked on a bed of pine needles, which Beast seemed to do to me as often as possible, knowing that needles hurt in places that tender skin should never be ex-posed to. I always figured it was a joke of sorts, reminding me who was really boss. But at least she had brought me back close to my clothes and my bike and I didn't have to hike barefoot through the woods. I gathered up my undies, jeans, and boots, shook them free of bugs, and dressed. Col-lected my weapons where they had fallen and stuck them into their various sheaths and holsters. Braided my hair. And thought.

I was feeling calm, steady, clearheaded, seeing the world and my place in it with clarity. Without excess emotion. En-visioning what had happened the night before and my fu-ture options as if everything were laid out on a table for my consideration.

Beast was right. Bruiser had little responsibility for what had happened last night. He was blood-drunk and recently risen from the dead, or near dead. He wasn't a vamp, so he was something else, though I had no idea what he was now.

Leo . . . Leo was a master of a city, a powerful vampire, politically and personally. That excused him nothing, but it explained a lot. Like kings and monarchs throughout history, the powerful did bad things to cement and keep their power. Leo believed that his taking of my blood helped him in some way. Weird as it was, Leo really believed that giving me his blood and binding me to him was a gift.

And as for me . . . I didn't know what I was feeling, but I was done with grief. Though I was temporarily bound, it was an imperfect binding. I had options Leo didn't know about. I could get on Bitsa and take off and never come back. I could claim my freedom. Or I could stay and put to rights what I had made wrong by killing Ramondo Pitri, even though that death was purely self-defense. I could maybe even save Bruiser from whatever fate now awaited him. I could still do my job. If I wanted. If I could face Leo without killing him.

I let that thought settle. I could leave. Or I could stay. I twirled the tip of my braid and tied it off with a thread ripped from the inside of my pocket.

I'd been hurt, but I wasn't beaten. I could still work, could still be there for the friends I had in this city. I smiled slowly. I could get Leo back for the forced feeding and binding later.

Which led me to Leo's own gang-feeding. A forced or coerced feeding from a human was a vamp's version of takeout, though from the victim's point of view it was an assault. It took away a person's will and rights and it hurt. It hurt bad. What was it like when a powerful vamp was drained? What had Leo's forced feeding been like, and how had it changed him? And how much of my internal debate was the binding? How much of my willingness to stay was Leo's draw on my soul?

Holding my hair in one hand, I touched my throat, feeling again the slice of fangs going in. The electric shock as they sliced through me. I should want to kill Leo, tear him limb from limb, but I didn't. I didn't know what I was going to do about it. Not yet.

I rode at a leisurely pace, the sun rising gray and brown

through a haze of pollution. My clothes were bloody, and if I got stopped I'd have a lot of explaining to do, but I needed some time to assimilate everything that had happened, everything I had learned. Hunger twisted my insides, the hunger of the shift that needed calories for fuel. But I didn't stop for food. I needed to be fasting. I took the roads, heading for Aggie One Feather's, the one place I might find a measure of peace.

Aggie was standing in the yard when I rode up, Bitsa puttering along with that signature Harley roar. The elder of The People was wearing jeans, a long-sleeved T-shirt, and gardening gloves, holding a pair of clippers in one hand and a dozen sprigs of rosemary in the other. A basket lay at her feet, full of fall herbs, heated by the warm, late fall air. Fall, assuming there is such a thing here, lasts a long time in the Deep South. There would likely have been a frosting of snow in the mountains of home already. Tree limbs would be bare. Here it was still warm, even at dawn, and half the trees were still bright with fall color.

I parked in the shell drive, turned off the growling bike, and unhelmeted. As Aggie watched, I began removing my weapons, stashing them in Bitsa's bags. Guns, blades, stakes. The cross in the lead-lined pouch. Everything. Nothing that might be considered a weapon could be brought into an elder's house. I filled up one saddlebag and started on the other.

Paper crinkled in the bottom and I dug out a white paper bag. I had bought Aggie and her mother gifts while I was in the mountains, and left them in the bag in my bike. I closed the lid of the saddlebag, feeling the witchy-lock tingle under my fingertips as it activated. A thief would get a nasty shock if he tried to steal Bitsa. Carrying the small white paper bag, I crunched across the shells, my boots falling silent on the grass. I smiled down at Aggie, her face unlined, her black hair pushed back behind her ears. She had cut it into a pageboy that just brushed her shoulders, and it glistened like liquid onyx in the sun.

Aggie wasn't surprised to see me. But then, little really surprises Aggie. She's like a leaf on the surface of a stream, floating along in the eddies, sliding across rapids, untouched by it all, and serene. "I have no idea what that kind of serenity might feel like, *Lisi.*" It wasn't what I had planned to come out of my mouth, and I rattled the bag to take attention away from my words. "I come bearing gifts."

"You are covered in dried blood. Are you injured?" she asked.

I touched my shirt, crusted through with blood. "No. Not mine. And no one else is hurt either." At her disbelieving expression, I added, "Some vamps tried to bite me last night." Which was true. I just didn't add the part about them being successful.

"Are they dead?" she asked.

"Not any more than they were before they tried."

Aggie's mouth twisted into what might be the start of a smile or a grimace, and tilted her head in acceptance. "Come inside. My mother asked to see you this morning when she woke."

"Uh. Sure." But Aggie's mother scared me witless. *Uni Lisi,* grandmother of many children, a term of respect, was an old woman who saw too much sometimes. I followed Aggie into the house, feeling like a lumbering giant next to her petite grace. "Wait here," she said, pointing to the living room. Inside, the windows were thrown open and bees bounced at the screens. The small living room was spotless, floral fabric on the sofa and chair, a brown recliner, a new wide-screen TV, a rug I hadn't seen before on the floor, and on a side table, a bowl of potpourri flavored the air with dried herbs and synthetic scent. A feral hiss brought me up short. A huge tabby cat lay curled on the cushions of a well-used old rocker. She stared at me with wide green eyes. I stared back, Beast rising inside. The cat drew her paws beneath her, the body language saying she was ready to run or fight. Her hair bristled and she showed me her teeth. Cats don't like me. Never have.

I dropped my eyes, though Beast pressed her claws into me, painfully. She didn't like showing submission to anyone, but this was the tabby's den, the cat a new addition since the last time I'd been inside the house. I smelled her now, over the potpourri. I didn't enter the room, but stood at the entrance, eyes down. The cat settled slightly, uneasy, and kept her eyes on me.

Aggie stuck her head in from the kitchen. "I see you met

the queen. She showed up here a few weeks ago and moved in. Sweetest cat I ever saw. 'Til now."

"Cats don't like me," I said.

Aggie looked at me strangely. "Queenie likes everyone. Even the dogs." I grunted as Queenie showed me her teeth again. Aggie's brows went up at the threat from the house cat. "Hmm. My mother is out back on the porch. Come."

I trailed Aggie, and Queenie dropped heavily to the floor, following us through the house with regal disdain. Her scent came strongly then, heavy with hormones and faintly with blood. I said, "You know she's pregnant, right?"

Aggie turned back and stared at the cat. "Well, darn. I knew she was getting fat."

"She's due soon." Like today, but I didn't say that. Queenie was already in early labor, but since I had no way of knowing that, except my extra-good nose, I didn't say that either.

Aggie made a long-suffering sound, half sigh, half snort, something I remembered from The People, the *Tsalagiyi*, a sound that was pure Cherokee, and I smiled, relaxing at the familiar noise. On the back porch *Uni Lisi* was sitting on a deeply upholstered chair, a bowl of bean pods on the table in front of her, shelling them fast, her knobby hands flying through the beans, pinching off the ends and stripping the string down the side of the pods, exposing the plump beans inside, tossing them into a bowl, and dropping the empty shells on the table. It seemed like a lot of work when they could buy beans in a can, but I didn't say that either. She paused in her shelling and gestured me to the table. "Come. Come, Jane. Sit." I sat across from her, my little paper bag on my lap.

Aggie placed a glass of sweating tea in front of her mother, a single mint leaf in the bottom; two identical glasses went to the side. One was clearly mine. "Jane says Queenie is going to give us kittens soon."

"Oh?" *Uni Lisi* leaned over and studied the cat. "We have to get her a basket and a blanket. That big pink one in the corner of my room. Make her a place on the porch so she doesn't take the babies off. Good to see you, Jane. Go get the basket, Aggie." *Uni Lisi* drank her tea and smacked her lips. I had never heard the old woman so chatty. "Drink," she commanded. At her gesture I drank too, the tea so sweet it coated the inside of my mouth, good Southern tea, one-third sugar, the rest tea so dark it looked like bayou water. It was delicious. I tried to think of something to say, as the old woman went back to shelling beans. "We gonna have some kittens," the old woman said, as if I didn't already know. "You want a kitten?"

"Um, thank you, no," I said, with my best Christian children's home manners.

Aggie carried the pink basket back onto the porch. It was really pink—flamingo—with a pink bow on top. The basket was about three feet wide, with a huge hoop handle, the biggest basket I had ever seen, and Aggie placed it at *Uni Lisi*'s feet. The blanket Aggie set inside was fleece, yellow with red and green polka dots all over it, a color combo that was ... interesting at best. Queenie walked past, her tail high, and hissed at me, warning me to stay away. She leaped gracefully into the basket and began pawing the blanket into submission, ignoring me totally now. Aggie sat beside me and drank her tea, sighing once as she eyed the cat. "Kittens," she murmured with disgust.

"I brought you gifts," I said. I tilted up the paper bag, and two small foil-wrapped packages fell into my hand, each one tied with hemp string. I placed the silver foil–wrapped one in front of Aggie, and the gold foil–wrapped one in front of *Uni Lisi*. The old woman clapped her hands together like a child and began tearing at the paper. Aggie took hers and untied the string. They both got them open at the same time. Both women made little oohing and aahing sounds as they lifted their necklaces to the light.

"I'd have brought them to you on my last visit, but I didn't come inside."

Uni Lisi swatted her daughter's hand. "You should have brought her inside. She had presents." Aggie looked at me under her brows and I stifled a grin.

"The amethyst came from a small mine near the Nantahala River," I said, "on Cherokee land. A Cherokee silver artist named Daniel Running Bear did the silver work. Daniel *Yonv Adisi*. I found the silver chains online and they probably came from China. They should be long enough to just put over your head," I finished. I had planned that part carefully, remembering the older woman's knobby hands, but if I had seen her shelling beans, I'd have just bought her a short chain and let her use the clasp.

Aggie and her mother draped their necklaces over their heads in gestures that looked choreographed, the twin actions of people who had lived together for many years. Aggie looked at me with a smile, the first one I had seen on her face today. "They are beautiful. Thank you, *Dalonige i Digadoli*."

"Oh yes. This is pretty. Pretty, pretty!" *Uni Lisi* patted her amethyst between her shrunken breasts. "I like purple."

I nodded formally to each of them. "You are welcome, *Egini Agayvlge i, Uni Lisi*."

"Mama, you wanted to tell Jane about your dream."

"Yes." The old woman nodded, her hands busy once again with the beans. "I have many dreams as I get older. Some are nothing. Some are something. This one was something." A prickling ran up the back of my neck, as if cobwebs trailed across me. I placed the tea glass on the table, my hands curled around it, wet with condensation, cold from the ice. *Uni Lisi* drank again, her lips making that smacking sound when she was done. She reached down and stroked the cat, feeling along her belly. Queenie rolled over and let the old woman feel of her stomach. "Fat kittens. I count four. Maybe more." She looked at me again. "You sure you don't want a kitten?"

I shook my head, waiting on the dream. The dreams of the elders were important, not to be ignored.

"This dream was strange, even for me. It was about a man hanging over a fire."

I stilled, slowly dropping my hands into my lap, my tea glass forgotten. "A white man?"

She nodded, returning to the beans. "Dirty. Naked. He had a beard, like he needed to shave. His mustache was longer, like he had it first. Brown hair. Brown hands. He was dead. He had been cooked over a slow fire for many hours." She looked at me from under her brows. "This was not the way of *Tsalagiyi*. Not the way of The People. This was the way of the Mohicans, maybe. Or the Creek. Savages. Not *Tsalagiyi*." She nodded once, firmly, her hands flying through the beans. "Not *Tsalagiyi*."

If I thought it was strange for a member of one tribe to call another tribe savages, I didn't show it. I kept still, waiting on the rest of the dream. *Uni Lisi* drank again, smacked again, and said, "There was an old woman standing beside the fire. She was wearing a long dress, blue or gray, and her hair was in braids down her back. She was holding a stick, the end sharpened and black from the fire. She poked the body and it didn't bleed." She pointed one knobby finger at me, her black eyes throwing back the light, like faceted stones. "When Aggie takes you to sweat, you will think on this." She looked at her daughter. "Take her now. I'll finish the beans and take a nap on the couch with Queenie. We gonna have us some kittens tonight, I think. Go, go." She shooed us with her hands.

I stood, my knees feeling weak at the vision *Uni Lisi* had seen. Aggie made the sighing-snorting sound again and said, "Go to the sweathouse. I'll be there shortly."

CHAPTER TWELVE

Bitsa Alone Could Wake the Undead

Once again I was sitting in the sweathouse, feeding kindling to the fire. The coals had been smoldering beneath a heavy layer of ash when I entered, and I had uncovered them, fed them twigs, then larger pieces. The rocks were heated, and the smudge basket was full of smudge sticks. It was as if they had known I was coming. Considering the dream, they probably had. I had started to sweat long minutes past, and had a steady trickle going when Aggie entered and closed the door on the rest of the world. She sat beside me, and I could feel her eyes on me. I kept mine on the fire, letting the flames steal my vision in the dark hut. More minutes passed. I was sweating freely and stewing in my own irritation when Aggie finally spoke.

"We have spoken of your soul house, of the cavern that drips with moisture, lit by flickering firelight, the place of your earliest memories."

I nodded to show I knew what she was talking about. It was the cavern where I made my first shift into *we sa*, the bobcat, when I was a child of maybe five. When Aggie took me back into my own memories it was to this place I most often went.

"You carry anger around in your soul home like a trapped storm cloud full of thunder and lightning and heavy rain," she said, her voice a murmur. "Your spirit overflows with that anger. This anger is too large for you to contain, and it is compressed within you."

She fell silent while I envisioned the darkness within me, and the storm she could see there. She was right. It was a raging storm, bigger than Katrina, more destructive than Hurricane Andrew, trapped there, inside me.

In the sweathouse, the fire crackled and spat, stealing energy from the wood with a soft hiss. "Do you want to tell me about the anger?" she asked.

I opened my mouth. Closed it. Fed the fire. Aggie waited. I had the feeling that she would wait until nightfall and say nothing else. She had given me an opening and now it was my turn, to take or not. "I killed a man in my hotel room in Asheville. I didn't see a gun—it was down at his side—but I reacted to the threat I sensed, the fear I felt, and I shot him. He died. Only after he fell did I see that he was carrying a gun with a sound suppresser on it." Aggie's expression didn't change; even her scent stayed the same, calm and waiting. "I found out later that he was only there to look me over in preparation to challenging me to a fight of some sort. And now all the vamps and blood-servants in the Southeast are in danger. Because I killed a man."

After a long moment, during which Aggie added a log to the fire, she said, "He was only there to look at you? He could have done that in a restaurant. On the street. Anywhere. He came into your hotel room? With a gun in his hand?" I nodded. "Then perhaps he was going to kill you and slip away, so he didn't *have* to challenge you."

My head snapped up. I met Aggie's eyes and she laughed at whatever was on my face. She shrugged, as if to say, "It's just a thought," but she said nothing.

Some of the shadow I carried fell away from my shoulders. "Thank you," I said. Aggie shrugged again. "In your heart, you knew this. It is only part of your darkness."

"Last night, Leo Pellissier and his heir forced a feeding on me. To bind me to them."

Aggie didn't flinch, but I smelled her reaction: surprise, anger, and something deeper. *She was protective of me.* That lifted my hurt even more, and the darkness was no longer so heavy. I took a breath and it felt clean and fresh, like the way air felt coming out of a cavern. The breath of the earth.

The breath of my soul house, my spirit place, moving again, no longer blocked.

"I had stupidly claimed to be Leo's Enforcer, a position that requires sharing of blood, and sometimes sex, in a binding ceremony. When I made the claim, it was to protect myself and others, and I had no idea it involved any kind of sharing. When it first happened, I wouldn't let him bind me, but now that he's facing a new threat, a bigger threat, he took what I'd verbally given him."

"And are you bound by this vampire?"

"Not so much. It isn't permanent." *But it should be.* I didn't say that part. "I'm angry. He had no right. It was an assault. And I have no legal recourse."

"Because under this Vampira Carta you have told me of, you gave him certain rights over you when you came into his employ." I nodded. "Rights you did not understand." I nodded again. "But once you knew of these rights, you still remained in his employ."

I didn't nod this time. Aggie had hit the nail on the head. I had known a forced feeding could happen. I stayed because the money was good. Because I was curious about vamps, and had allowed myself to get caught up in their lives and society. And maybe for other reasons I didn't yet understand, reasons that had to do with my own forgotten past. "I was stupid," I said, now hearing my bitterness.

Aggie cocked her head, letting me think it through. She shifted and resettled her legs. "And now you are conflicted, because you gave him the rights over your body and blood, but you never expected him to take them."

"Yeah. That about covers it. It proves I'm pretty stupid, doesn't it?"

"A scorpion's nature is to sting. A raptor's nature is to rend and tear flesh. Did he do that which was normal and right according to his nature?"

"Yes," I whispered.

"And your nature is to protect and to serve. Did you do that which was normal and right according to your nature?"

"Yes," I said again, my brows coming together. There was so much wrong with that line of thought. It's the nature of a serial killer to trap and torture humans. It's the nature of a pedophile to touch children. But nature doesn't make everything right. It's often just an excuse. Yet understanding one's own nature is often a first step to personal growth. All this psychological crap was making me irritable.

As if she sensed my irritation, Aggie changed course. "Will you leave his employ?"

I thought about Leo. And Bruiser. And the other humans I had met and liked. "I should. I don't know. I have to think about that."

"If you stay, it will be with eyes wide open now. Fully adult and fully informed."

"Yes. I understand." I shook my head and started to rise.

"There is still an angry darkness inside you." Aggie leaned back and relaxed, her eyes serene, like a nun's, like a woman who had made her choices and was okay with them. Not anything like me. "This anger is perhaps the core of who you are. It storms in the very center of your being, and it forms the basis of every decision you have ever made. We should look at this anger."

After a moment I said, "I made a vow when I was five years old." Aggie waited, implacable, resting in that enveloping sense of peace. "I made a vow to kill the men who murdered my father and raped my mother." To give her credit, Aggie didn't flinch at the bald statement. I eased back to the floor, my heels and butt on the cool clay. "I put my hands in my father's cooling blood." I put out my left hand as I had done as a child, to show her. "And I wiped it down my face." I lifted my hand, palm facing me, and dragged it down my face, slowly, feeling again my father's blood, sticky. The air cool as it hit the streaks of blood on my cheeks and forehead. "And I promised to kill them. I looked them in the face, silently, but promising that they would die. I was only five. I thought I hadn't succeeded. Until I remembered the bearded man hanging over a fire circle." This time, Aggie sat forward, her pupils wide in the firelight, her mouth opening slightly. "He was the *yunega* in my memory. There was an old woman, my grandmother. She poked him with a stick. I want to remember that. All of it. I think that is part of the dark, angry place inside."

"Anger, building and storming," Aggie said. I nodded. "Okay." She put on the music, a wood flute, playing a haunting melody. She lifted a heavy, earthen pitcher and dripped water over the hot rocks with a ladle. It hissed and spat. Steam rose, the air growing close and humid. My sweating increased instantly. Aggie passed me a bottle of water and I opened the top and drank. The water tasted bitter, and I stopped midswallow, watching her. "It's got a little something in it to help you remember," she said. I grunted and finished the bottle, draining it.

Aggie took the empty and chose a smudge stick from the basket. She lit the end. A bitter, acrid smell filled the steamy room. I breathed in. Closed my eyes. Time passed.

The room grew much lighter, as if the door was open. I turned to it, and saw an old woman enter. She was wearing a shift, coarsely woven cotton over her naked body, bony legs showing beneath, her feet bare. "The *yunega* is dead," she said. "Come."

I stood, the clay floor chilling the soles of my bare feet. I was wearing a blue dress, which I saw in glimpses as I walked out of the house, down the trail to the small clearing. I kept my eyes low as we entered the open space. In the center of it was a circle of white quartz stones, with gray rocks inside and the remains of a fire—ashes and one blackened log. Something black hung above the cold fire. It dripped once, a drop of reddish water trickling down and falling into the ashes. I let my eyes rise to the blackened stumps. They had once been feet. Now they were scorched meat, with blisters above in the scarlet flesh. The skin had split and wept. I let my eyes rise up the man's body.

His upper thighs were red and covered with dried blood. I smelled burned hair, and saw little blackened curls of hair on his skin. His manhood was gone, leaving only a patch of raw meat. I remembered his scream when it was removed— a long ululating wail. Above the wound was a white belly, hanging and slack, like a fish belly. His chest had brown nipples and hair, like the stomach of a dog. Men of *Tsalagiyi* did not have so much hair on their chests. Only the *yunega* had hair all over their bodies, like dogs or rats. My father's chest had been smooth when I dipped my hand into his blood.

The white man who raped my mother hung from sharpened deer antlers that had been shoved through his shoulders. His hands were tied behind his back with rope. Lank hair, the color of acorns, fell forward, half hiding his bearded face. He had had no beard, only the mustache when *Uni Lisi* captured him. Now his face was scruffy, like a bear, with hair. His blue eyes were open and dry, staring down at his body. His mouth was open in a silent scream. With my skin-walker nose, I could smell his blood and the stink of rot, but white men always smelled of rot and unwashed bodies. "Are you sure he is dead, *Elisi*?" I asked.

Elisi picked up a stick from the fire and stabbed him. "He no longer bleeds."

"Do we eat him?"

"No. Skinwalkers do not eat the bodies of our enemies. It is forbidden. It makes us sick."

I nodded and turned away. "Good," I said. I looked up at the leaves in the trees. They were golden and scarlet, with patches of blue sky showing through. "And the other one?" I asked.

"He is next."

I swam back up from the vision of fall leaves and blue sky. I was gasping and wet with sweat. The thin cloth tied above my breasts and hanging to my knees was soaked and limp as I shoved up with my elbows against the clay floor. "*Elis—*" I stopped, my throat so dry I couldn't speak. Aggie handed me another bottle of water. I opened it and drank it down, and nothing had ever tasked so good.

A demon had told me recently that I had never taken vengeance on my enemies. That *he* had killed my grand-mother in the snow, as he had killed many of the Cherokee on the Trail of Tears. The demon had lied. A laugh escaped my mouth, half hysterical with shock. The demon had lied. Fierce joy threaded through me, weaving into my soul. "*Elisi* killed him. My grandmother killed him."

Aggie nodded slowly. "Your grandmother was a warrior woman, like those of old." There was no condemnation in the tones. "Did you see it? Did she make you watch his death?"

I started to shake my head and stopped. I had a quick image of leaves, dark and thick, over my face. Beyond them was fire, a man hanging over it, screaming. Three women worked over him, mostly naked, wearing only thin shifts, their clothes draped across nearby bushes. The women were

Etsa, my mother, and her sister, and *Elisi*. "I wasn't supposed to see it," I whispered. "But I hid. I watched. Until he started screaming so bad. When they cut him."

I looked at Aggie. "I led my grandmother to him. To them. I caused their deaths."

"And is that part of the storm inside you, child?"

I shook my head, stopped, and nodded, uncertain. "I think that there's more. I need to remember the rest."

Aggie looked as if she would disagree, but after a long indecisive moment, she passed me another bottle of water. "One bottle should have kept you in the dream place for many hours. No one has ever needed two."

I stopped with the bottle halfway to my mouth, watching her.

"Did your grandmother have yellow eyes like you?" she asked

Holding her gaze, I drank the drugged water down. Recapped the bottle. Handed it back to her. "Yes. So did my father."

"I see." And I was afraid that she did indeed see. Before I could comment, the dreams took me again.

The *yunega* was in a cave up the hill beyond *Elisi*'s house, bound and naked. I squatted before him, bare feet on the smooth clay floor, my hands clasped between my knees. "Did you see what they did to him, to your friend?" I asked. "They will do much worse to you." The man looked at me. He was *yunega*. He did not understand the speech of *Tsalagiyi*. He was staring at my face. It was still crusty with the traces of the blood of my father. I wouldn't wash it until my vengeance was done. I smiled. He shrank back against the cave wall.

The night was cold and wind blew through the trees, whispering and sighing, and golden leaves swirled on the night air. But I was warm in the coat that had once belonged to the killer of my father. It had been in the saddlebags of his horse, wrapped up in brown paper and twine. It was too big, but it was warm and red, the color of blood.

The last *yunega* had been brought to the clearing. He was gagged. Naked. Tied. He was lying on his stomach, screaming into the dirt as *Elisi* pounded deer antlers through his shoul-

ders with a huge piece of white quartz the size of a human
head. I was with the women this time, sitting on a log at the
fire, not hiding. The wind skirled through the clearing, setting
the leaves dancing. I pulled my new coat closer and the
women hauled on ropes, lifting the man into the air and over
the fire circle. There was no fire tonight. Tonight the women
each held knives. I too had a knife, my first blade. It felt
strange in my hand, cold as the winter wind, sharp as the
pain in my heart at the death of my father. We gathered
close. *Etsa*, my mother, made the first cut.

When I woke much later, it was night, and the sweathouse
was cool and empty, the fire out, Aggie One Feather gone. I
was alone. And I knew why Aggie One Feather thought me
angry and full of storms. I *knew*. Slowly I stood and went
outside into the night. Winter had come in the past hours. It
was cool, with a north wind blowing. I removed my cloth
covering and placed it in the basket for used sweat clothes.
Turning the faucet on, I washed the smoke and sweat from
me, the cool well water sluicing me clean—the washing part
of the ritual—a cleansing after the pain of old memories.
On the narrow shelf high above the faucet, there was a
scrub brush, new, still in its plastic wrap, a new bar of soap,
and shampoo in a small bottle like the kind hotels leave on
the counters for the forgetful patron. They were gifts from
Aggie. I opened them all and applied them to my body to
remove the stink of fear-sweat and the stubborn reek of
smoke. Afterward, I dried off, braided my hair, and dressed.
The house was dark and silent as I walked to Bitsa. I hel-
meted up, kick-started her, and drove into the night.

The ride over the river and back into the French Quarter
was fast, but less furious than the one this morning. My
mind was quiet, my spirit was quiet, and even my emotions
were quiet. I was quietness all inside me. I had found a part
of me that I had lost. It wasn't a pretty part, but it tied the
lost pieces together. I was born of a war clan. Of a skinwalker clan. We led our people into battle, tribe against
tribe, tribe against the white man. When there was no war,
we were the executioners.

I remembered the vision of one of the men who had
raped my mother, hanging, bucking his body, fighting to get

free as the women took their time with him. I blinked the image away, but it was burned into my mind, the memory, once found, now a part of me.

My grandmother had not let evil lie. She had searched the evil ones out, had hunted them down, and killed them in the worst way possible, which was the ancient, long-forgotten way of her skinwalker culture. She had brought justice to the people who depended on her. But there was a narrow, thin line between justice and sadism. Between justice and evil. My grandmother had surely crossed that line, had dumped gallons of blood onto it, obscuring it totally. I wasn't sure she was any better than the men who had killed my father.

No wonder skinwalkers went crazy when we got old, if we carried that kind of thing with us, inside us. Vengeance and justice were what we did. It was what I was. That spiritual constraint and demand for justice was why I had become a rogue-vamp hunter. Was why I was so good at killing. Living with it had never been easy, but at least I understood more of who I was now, more of why I made the choices I made. And more of the guilt that rested in my heart, a guilt that was trying to reconcile the duties of the skinwalker with the rules of the Christian God. *Thou shalt not kill. Turn the other cheek. Pray for those that despitefully use you. Vengeance is mine, sayeth the Lord.* The rules were supposed to uplift the human spirit and make us better people and help take us to a better place within our own hearts here on earth and after death. I had helped torture a man to death, and then buried the memory.

Now I remembered it. I remembered it all, every cut, every scream, and the joyful rage that rose in me when he died at my hand. I was five years old.

And now I could chose who I would be in the face of evil, in the face of life's problems, in the face of a vampire who had taken what I stupidly offered him. In the face of who I could become. If I lived long enough, I could decide — rationally and without emotion — how I would deal with Leo's blood theft. Leo, who was a scorpion with a stinger, and who acted only according to his nature, just as I had, when I was a five-year-old skinwalker, only recently awakened to my shape-changing gifts.

I pulled into the side yard of my freebie house and

locked the gate behind me. I lifted Bitsa to the porch and leaned her against the house wall, leaving the helmet on Bitsa's seat. As I gathered my weapons, I smelled steaks on the grill in the backyard, and my stomach growled like a wild animal. I entered my house, smelling Kid—freshly showered—and Eli, and beer, and potatoes, and . . . Bruiser.

I stopped in the kitchen, placing my guests. They were sitting in the living room, a football game on the TV, and they were talking beer—brands, hops, distilleries. Guy talk. The kitchen table was set for four. I pushed a plate over and placed my weapons with a clatter in the cleared spot, knowing the men had to have heard me—Bitsa alone could wake the undead. I took a beer from the fridge and twisted off the top, drinking it down fast. The alcohol hit my system like a bomb, even with my skinwalker metabolism. I was dry as a bone and the sudden rush felt wonderful. I finished the beer and picked the weapons back up.

I walked silently through the house, avoiding the men, and into my room. I stopped, placed the weapons on the bed, and dropped my blood-stiff clothes to the floor. I dressed in black jeans and a yellow, long-sleeved T-shirt, smoothed and braided my hair, the long plait hanging down my back, still wet. I shoved stakes in, scraping them against my scalp. I strapped one blade to my thigh in plain sight. I didn't bother with shoes.

Back in the kitchen, the smell of cooking meat blowing in from outside made me salivate. The hunger that had been quiescent all day rose, clawing my stomach like a taloned hand. I hadn't eaten after the shift. I was starving. But there were things I needed to face before I ate. I opened another beer, the alcohol potent in my blood.

Sipping my beer, I walked into the living room and stood in the opening, my feet apart, one hand loose at my side near the knife. The swinging shelves were in place over the safe room, no hinges showing. If I hadn't seen the mess earlier, I'd never have known the hidden room was there. The living room looked as if nothing had been done to it; even the construction dust was cleaned up, the room spotless.

The men finally saw me, and the TV went mute, leaving the room in silence. I turned my gaze slowly to the men, the Kid first, then Eli, then Bruiser, and his gaze I held. The tension in the air rose, electric, as if Bruiser were sitting on a live wire. Eli and Alex were watching him, watching me, uncertain, knowing that something was up, but clearly not knowing what.

"Good evening, Jane," Bruiser said, after an eternity.

I didn't reply. Just took another sip, waiting.

He stood, and took two steps, as if he thought he might cross to me, and then stopped, a yard from his chair, in the middle of the room. "I'm sorry. I didn't . . ." He stopped and drew in a breath as if air-starved. "I couldn't stop them. When they forced you."

Eli came to his feet in a single rolling motion, as if he were all muscle, no bone. He stood between us, but back, so that we formed a tripod with me at the apex. His body was loose in that precombat tension of the best fighting men, and his eyes shifted back and forth between us. The Kid rolled the other way, all elbows and knobby knees, and stood behind the couch, out of the way. I let one side of my mouth rise, just slightly. Eli didn't know what had happened, but he was ready for anything.

"Jane?" Bruiser held out his hand. It was bruised, purpled, and swollen, as if it had been broken. So was the side of his face. Bruiser had been hit. Hard. It was difficult to injure a blood-servant. It took a vamp.

I indicated his hand with the beer bottle. "Leo do that?"

He looked down and turned his hand over and back, as if seeing the injury for the first time. "Yes. When I disagreed with his tactics." He looked back at me, his brown eyes catching the lamplight. He raised the hand and shoved it through his hair, sending the brown strands askew. "I thought it was simply a planning session. That was how Leo phrased it when he asked me to bring you. I didn't know they were planning to force a feeding and binding on you."

"And when they forced me? And you were holding me on the floor? What then?" As I said those words I could see Eli tense, shifting one pace in for better positioning. I lifted a finger from the beer, stopping him. I wanted to hear this.

Bruiser stood straight, dropping his hands to his sides. He blew out a breath, his face going from supplication to something colder, harder. I liked this Bruiser better. It was more honest. He was Leo's plaything and blood meal, Leo's right-hand man, and he always had been. It should have hurt, but the hunger growing inside me and the emptiness that Aggie had exposed when the trapped anger stormed away stopped my pain.

"I was blood-drunk, Jane. I wasn't able to move, wasn't able to fight, wasn't able to stop them. I held you down and they hurt you. They forced me. I want you to know that. It was against my will."

I didn't say anything and he added, "When you left, I attacked Leo. He *stopped* me." Bruiser held up the hand as explanation. "He backhanded me into a wall. Broke my hand and jaw. It was bad enough that I didn't heal instantly even with all the Mithran blood in me." Bruiser dropped the hand. "Leo needed your cooperation once he read your report and saw the name de Allyon. He remembered the problems his uncle Amaury had not so long ago, and he thought you wouldn't agree with his plans. So he used me to get you. I'm sorry, Jane."

Not so long ago. Only a man who had already lived more than a hundred years would think two centuries was *not so long ago.* I understood what had happened. I even understood my own stupidity in being part of it. But I was not ready to forgive. "And you defend him?"

"No. I explain him," he growled. "And I apologize for myself. It's what a primo does."

It's what a primo does. Yeah. Got that. "Get out, George. Now. Before I decide to let my Eli here hurt you."

He heard his given name and he put it together, understanding that my calling him George and not Bruiser was important on many levels. And he processed the "my Eli." George swiveled his head to the man standing one pace away. He considered Eli's positioning, the placement of his feet, the relaxed posture. The two men, who had just been talking beer and sports, studied each other now like potential combatants, one trained by Uncle Sam to kill, the other still so full of vamp blood he was nearly healed in one day from wounds that would have incapacitated a human for weeks.

George turned his head to me, dismissing the soldier as if he posed no challenge. From the corner of my eye, I saw Eli's mouth curl up in a smile. Without looking at him, I smiled too. It was one of those perfect agreement things that happens sometimes when two people understand each other on an instinctive level, on a snake-brain level. Eli and I had fought. We knew what moves we'd make and how fast. If it was needed. I saw his fingers curl in slightly.

I tucked the thumb of my free hand into my jeans at my waist, to indicate action wasn't necessary. Yet. "I'll do my job for Leo," I said to George, "but not because of his forced blood-bond. I'll do my job because I killed a man in Asheville. Because humans were killed there and here on my watch. You tell that blood-sucking fiend I said that.

"If there was a dinner invitation, it's rescinded. Get out of my house. You know where the door is." I stepped out of the way and gestured with the bottle at the door.

George's mouth firmed, an obstinate gesture that said he was going to disagree. But he didn't. He walked past me out the door and closed it behind him with a firm snap. That sound said something important, but I didn't want to deal with it, not now. I followed and keyed the dead bolt, then went back to the living room. Eli and Alex hadn't moved. I leaned against the wall and finished my beer, watching them.

"Are you okay?" Alex asked.

"Just ducky. But if your brother doesn't feed me I may eat him."

Eli laughed at the double entendre, but he went outside to the grill and came back in with four steaks. The Kid cleaned off a place and put away the unused dishes. We ate in silence at the kitchen table, companionable silence. I liked it. And I got the extra steak.

After dinner, while not-so-Stinky Alex cleaned up the dishes and griped about not having a dishwasher, Eli and I stayed at the table, going over the day's intel. "There might be a correlation we haven't considered, between the Blood-Call businesses and the cities where de Allyon has taken over," Eli said, passing a printout to me.

"I'm listening."

"De Allyon was making vamps sick. What better way than to have them drink from sick humans at Blood-Call?"

I remembered thinking at one time, in the last hectic days, that vamps were being made sick by drinking diseased blood, but that had seemed impossible unless a normal, natural plague had entered the human population. There had been no reports of horrific human illness in the media, and no way could that have been kept quiet.

There were also so many cities where Blood-Call was operating, cities that had no sign of sickness. The lack of plague and the specificity of attack had made me put the idea on the back burner. But then, there were the sick humans in Seattle who had claimed they were getting better. They weren't Blood-Call employees, they were blood-servants who lived and worked at the Seattle Clan Home. Without explaining, I pulled my cell and dialed the Seattle Clan Home. When a woman answered, I said, "This is Jane Yellowrock. I was there a few days ago, and took some blood from some blood-servants who were left on the premises after the revolt staged by the Mercy Blade failed. Are they still alive? Did they get well?"

The woman said stiffly, "Yes and yes. And then our new master removed them. Don't call again." There was a click and the call ended.

I stared at the cell and smiled. "Of course he did." I looked up at the brothers and said, "Alex, how certain are you about the money trail of the corporations that own Blood-Call?"

He was standing at the sink, drying his hands; he pushed a tiny laptop to the center of the table and opened it. It must have been sleeping because it opened to a company Web page instantly. Blood-Call's graphics were red and black with two beautiful, scantily clad couples on the front. One partner of each couple was a vamp, and the other was being a meal. It was clear that sex was on the menu as well as blood. Eli scooted his chair closer to me and we both leaned in, studying the screen, arms almost touching.

"I've traced it back through several shell corporations to an offshore account," Alex said. "The mailing address is a PO box on the main island. The shipping address is here." He pointed to the screen. "I have a *World of Warcraft* buddy on the island and he's doing some footwork to see what's at the address. I'm betting it's a café or an empty lot. The finances trace back through four shells to a numbered account. There's no way to find out anything further. No way to see if it ties to Lucas Vazquez de Allyon."

"Why not?" I asked. "Someone has to come in from time to time and deal with the accounts."

"Not offshore accounts. Not if they have the numbers and the passwords. Back in the day, someone had to show up in person and open an account. Now it can be done electronically and no one at the bank ever sees the client. I tried tracking the money back, but I couldn't get through."

He looked at his brother with a sly grin. "Offshore banks have better security than the Pentagon." Eli raised his eyes without lifting his head, and Alex laughed at whatever he saw on his brother's face. He looked back and forth between us, his expression changing to speculation. He grinned at his brother and went back to the dishes.

That speculative look suddenly made me aware that I was sitting close enough to feel Eli's body heat, close enough to feel the fine hairs on his arm graze mine when he moved. My limbs went heavy. A slow warmth settled deep inside me. I felt Beast start to purr.

I kept my eyes on the screen as Eli sat back. When I could trust myself to speak casually, I stood and said, "I'm beat. I'm heading for bed." Beast hacked deep inside and Alex looked over his shoulder again at his brother, then at me, and he grinned. *Crap.* I turned and went to my room without another word. And I slept in boy shorts and a tank instead of naked. *Men.*

The phone rang, waking me before dawn. I knew without looking that it was Leo—I could feel him pulling on the blood-bond. I wanted to ignore the cell's insistent ringing, but my hand went out all its own and I picked up the phone, hit the TALK button. "What?"

Bruiser said, "At sunset yesterday, Lucas Vazquez de Allyon, Blood Master of Atlanta, Sedona, Seattle, and Boston, claimed blood-feud with Leonard Eugène Zacharie Pellissier, Blood Master of the southeastern states, in direct contradiction of the Vampira Carta." His tone was stiff and formal, and I knew that Leo was right there, listening, exerting all sorts of emotional overtones to the conversation.

For a moment, I froze, that electric stillness of remembered fear and pain, Leo's fangs buried in my throat. Beast placed a paw on my mind, all claw and spiking demand. *We are not prey.*

I sucked in a breath that sounded of sorrow as much as remembered agony, and shoved down on my fear, letting Beast trap it beneath her claws as if it were her dinner. The memory of the feeding eased. Beast was right. *We are not prey.*

His voice even more unyielding, Bruiser said, "We believe that somehow he knows we discovered who he is, and this forced his hand."

Somehow. Yeah. Like the leak I warned you about that you can't find. All I had to do was send you a report on Blood-Call and Lucas, and everything changed. But I didn't say it. I didn't rub salt in the wound. Go, me. "Okay," I said to Bruiser and to Beast. "Why blood-feud and not a Blood Challenge? What's the difference between the two?" I asked, rolling up to my butt, sitting in the middle of the bed, the covers wrapped around me in the chill. I was facing the windows at the front and side of the house, seeing car lights move past one, seeing the bushes move with a slight wind in the other.

"A challenge follows the protocol of the Vampira Carta, all the rules and regulations set therein. A blood-feud is a much older contest, one from before the Carta was written, and it puts aside the Mithrans' most important legal document. According to historical precedent, there are no established protocols for the feud. Because you killed his Enforcer, Ramondo Pitri, unprovoked, de Allyon can declare blood-feud, according to the old ways."

It always came back to the man I had killed in Asheville. But I remembered what Aggie had said yesterday morning. "His Enforcer was in Asheville to check me out, to see why I had moved ahead of all of Leo's people into the rank of Enforcer, cutting you out of the position too. He could have looked me over on the street, in a restaurant, anywhere. Yet he was in my room, his gun drawn, with an illegal suppressor on it. Seems to me he was going off the reservation, hoping to take me out first. Seems to me that I'm lucky to be alive."

I heard background noises and then Leo said into the phone, "Unfortunately, my Enforcer, we have no evidence of that. When my George suggested that very scenario to de Allyon's messenger, he asked for proof. We had none to of-

fer, except for the human police reports, which are not sufficient in a Mithran court. Only a Mithran eyewitness would
be acceptable to others of my kind."

"Right," I said, and though I knew he could hear the
sarcasm, he went on, unperturbed.

"Therefore, the demand for blood-feud remains. I have
petitioned to the Outclan Council of Mithrans for a ruling
on the matter, and they have put it on the agenda for when
they meet again in the new year."

"Meantime we're all in the crosshairs," I said.

"Precisely. My George will send you the information we
have on the methodologies of blood-feuds."

I heard background noises again, thinking over the "my
Enforcer" and "my George" phrases as the cell was passed
around. Leo was staking claims—pun intended—as I had
done with my use of the words "my Eli" last night.

George said, "You need to know that de Allyon offered
another way out of this. Leo could turn himself and you
over and de Allyon would let all the others live. Leo turned
him down."

Yeah. I bet he did. "Wait." The winter chill of the room
made goose bumps rise on my arms. "Let all the others live?
Does the blood-feud mean he can kill everyone?"

Bruiser made a sound, very British, all nose and curled
lip. "Historically, all of one side or the other died in a blood-
feud, all the Mithrans, all the servants, all the slaves. Everyone."

At last I understood, and lots of things fell into place,
including Leo binding me—just after sunset, yesterday.
"Well, crap."

"I'll send you all the information I have on the prece-
dents and the histories. Most of it isn't electronic. Most is in
the form of letters and reports, so it'll be photocopied and
messengered over later today.

"My master will agree."

I hated that "my master" crap and wanted to hurt Leo
for trying to bind me to him, and for tying Bruiser to him so
tightly, even if it did save his life. I felt something pull again
in my mind, a compulsion to help Leo, a *need* to help him,
and my anger at Leo flamed out. Leo needed a huge take-
down or maybe some sensitivity training, delivered with the

pointy end of a stake. I smiled grimly at the thought. My grandmother had been very adept with sharp pointy things. "Later," I said, and ended the connection.

"What?"

I turned and found Eli in my bedroom, standing in the dark with his back to my wall, the door open beside him. I eyed the door. Then Eli. He was in boxers and a tee. His arms and legs were corded with muscle, his eyes dark in the shadows. He was holding a weapon in each hand, both semiautomatics. "When I lock my door, it's to stay locked," I said.

"Not when the house is under surveillance."

"You mean the guy who appears to be sleeping in the alcove across the street? Small guy, dressed like he has money, but no place to crash?" It was a guess, but Leo's Mercy Blade had used that doorway to watch my house before. So had Leo.

"You knew?"

"I'm not surprised. Next time, knock."

"Next time, tell me when we're being watched."

I lifted my hand to show that I was prepared. I was holding one of the twin Walthers, the grip bloodred. Eli gave me one of his lopsided smiles. "You look good curled up in that bed, wearing a thin tank and not much else but a gun." I didn't reply except for a faint flush he couldn't see in the dim room. He moved out of my room and pulled my door closed behind him. I flopped back on the bed. "Crap. Crap, crap, *crap*," I whispered to the ceiling.

Seconds later the cell rang again. "What do you want, Bruiser?"

I could have kicked myself when I realized what I'd said, and there was a smile in his voice when he said, "Callan was sick, and Sabina has healed him."

I ignored both my gaff and his tone. "Who is Callan?"

"One of the vampires in a cage at Katie's. He says he served de Allyon only because his master kept him alive. He has asked to join Leo's power base and it's being considered. Leo would like you to speak to him before dawn, find out, if you can, what de Allyon's plans are."

"Yeah. Fine. I don't need to sleep anyway," I said crossly. I threw the covers away and hung up on Bruiser.

CHAPTER THIRTEEN

Free Đick Đot Come

I took the back way to Katie's Ladies—over the back brick wall. Troll opened the door for me before I knocked, as if expecting me. "Little Janie," he said, his voice like two rocks grinding together.

"Morning, Troll," I said as I passed him. "Your scalp needs shaving."

He rubbed his hand over the pale dome as he closed the door on the morning's predawn light. "When I get time. George said you wanted to talk to the new guest."

"Yeah. It's all my idea. Where is he?"

"Upstairs with Christie."

I stopped and looked back. "Not . . ."

"Not. Christie came home this morning and took a liking to the newcomer. He needed to be fed and she was willing, but that's over with now." He grinned at me. "You won't walk in on anything."

I shook my head and went through the twisting hallways to the back stairs and up. Walking in on something with Christie could be detrimental to my sexual well-being. Christie was the resident S&M practitioner, with a penchant for whips, chains, and pain, able to play the part of top or bottom in BDSM games. The fact that I now understood what that meant was kinda scary. Not my thing. I knocked on her door and entered when she called out.

The inside of Christie's room was decorated like a gym, but without the charm. Bare mattress on a plain, steel bed, the four corners and headboard adorned with flex-straps and chains and cuffs. Bare white walls, bare wood floor, plastic rolled up in the corners. I didn't want to know what *that* was used for. Steel shutters and padded blinds were over the windows, blocking out the coming dawn, the latest vamp fad.

Christie was lying on the mattress with a dark blond vamp curled around her. Both were dressed, but only barely, Christie in a sheer top that exposed steel chains through her nipple rings—ouch—and the vamp in black silk pajama shorts. Seemed that Corpse had a name after all. The vamp looked vastly different from the way he had looked the last time I saw him, covered in blood and burns. Now he was clean, his hair combed, and his face stretched in a contented, well-fed smile as I looked him over. His silver cross burns were healed, and that kind of burn usually took a long time to heal. I'd burned Leo with one once and really ticked him off.

"Christie. Callan," I said.

Callan roused enough to lift his head from Christie's shoulder and I could see the tiny pinpricks on her throat that marked the constricted vamp bite marks. "You're my new master's Enforcer," he stated, his accent Southern, maybe a mill-town accent from the piedmont of South Carolina. He climbed slowly from the bed, moving like a feral animal, all smooth muscle and grace. Callan stood in front of me and slung the hair back from his face, holding my gaze, letting me look my fill. He was pretty. Dang pretty. And he knew it. Like a lot of vamps, he'd been turned for his looks, no doubt about that. He had a boxer's shoulders, a cyclist's thighs, and a painter's long, slender fingers, with an angel's face on top. But something about him made me think he wasn't the brightest bulb in the chandelier—maybe the fact that he was posing. He held the pose a moment longer and then dropped slowly to one knee, like an old-fashioned bow, but with a dancer's sense of balance. He bent forward, curling his spine so his hands and his hair fell forward to the floor, exposing his back, which was a swimmer's back, tapering to a tiny waist.

"Get up," I said. Before he could rise, I asked, "How did your former master infect you with the disease?" I expected him to say that he had dated a sick human at Blood-Call.

Callan stood, his shoulders back, a sculptor's model on display. I held in an exasperated sigh. "My former master fed me a woman. He feeds her to lots of us."

"*One* woman?" I said, not sure I heard correctly.

"Yes, ma'am."

My amusement vanished. A Typhoid Mary? A human with a disease that infects vamps? A prisoner, kept to be fed upon? *Like a slave?* I thought I had it all figured out, that sick humans were being passed around. I wasn't sure how a single sick human connected. Not sure at all.

"Against her will?"

"She's his prisoner. We all were."

"Crap." So what *now*? I'd have to kill de Allyon *and* rescue all the vamps and the blood-servants? I didn't say it, but I could feel the need burrowing under my skin. Saving people, fighting for people, is what skinwalkers do, when we aren't torturing them. "Is she here in Louisiana?"

"No. She is in Atlanta, in my mas—my former master's lair."

"So how did de Allyon infect all the vamps in Sedona, Seattle, and other places? Does he fly her around?"

"Lady, I got no idea how he did his thing. It ain't like I was up high in the pecking order or nothing. But I will say that he never let that woman out of his compound. Like not never."

I felt my hope deflate. "Is de Allyon in Louisiana?"

"Yes."

"Do you know where?"

"No. Somewhere north, and maybe west. In a little town on a river. I'm not good with directions."

The comment was so unexpected I almost laughed. Was the guy really dumber than a box of rocks, or was he dissembling, somehow hiding his true mind even from whichever old master vamp had fed him to heal him? That would have made Callan the best spy in history. Nope. He was no spy; Callan smelled of truth. And Callan was intellectually challenged—pretty, but dumb. Nearly every place in the state was north and west of New Orleans. "How did de Allyon know about me? How did he know I was Leo's Enforcer?"

Callan shrugged. "I don't know. Somebody tells him things."

"Yeah. I was afraid of that." A few more questions convinced me that I had discovered everything that Callan knew. Which was sad in all sorts of ways. Leo had a mole, a dissenter, a spy in his camp. I wanted it to be someone who recently joined the ranks, but it had to be someone who was in Asheville with the parley there, which limited the number of people involved. I had to study the Kid's deep background search info on the Vodka Boys and the Tequila Boys. I had to unearth the mole. Unfortunately, Callan would be no help at all.

It was nine a.m. when I got back to the freebie house. I'd stayed and eaten breakfast with Deon. My meal had consisted of eggs Benedict, Caribbean-style, with spices and peppers and some really melty, gooey, fabulous Hollandaise sauce. Totally delicious and totally sinful. Eli would have turned up his nose at the fats. I scraped my plate clean.

Back at my house, I found a postal box on the front porch, filled with the CS canisters. They were plain metal canisters, like spray paint cans, but with a lever system on top to lock them on, so they could spray until empty or be stopped at will by the wielder. "Cool," I said, and packed them away.

Sitting on the couch, I booted up my laptop and opened the file containing the English translation of the Vampira Carta. I scrolled down to the part about the Blood Challenge between masters and checked the footnotes for other info. There were four codicils to the challenge and three histories, none of which were in English. It looked like Latin, probably from a millennia ago. "Crap," I muttered.

"Anything I can help you with?" Eli asked.

Instantly, I remembered his predawn comment about how I looked in bed. I was pretty sure I blushed and didn't raise my head for him to see. "Not unless you speak Latin from the tenth century."

"Free dick dot come."

I lifted my eyes. "I beg your pardon?"

He laughed and bent over the laptop, typing "www.free dict.com" in my browser. I'm pretty sure my blush was visible even through my Cherokee coloring. He smelled good, all pheromones and self-confidence and man. "Oh. Thanks," I muttered. Still grinning, he wandered away, leaving behind his scent and the echo of his laughter.

I went to that site and three others, subscribing to two that looked reasonable. I typed out the Latin info and started getting translations, none of which matched exactly. To be on the safe side, I sent snippets to all four sites and compared and contrasted the translations, taking the ones that seemed to match best. I quickly discovered that the VC's Blood Challenge was instituted in direct response to a blood-feud that took out nearly two thousand humans and vamps in southern Italy in the mid-tenth century. The descriptions of the dead in that history were horrible, humans and vamps drained, torn apart, discarded, their bodies left to see the dawn. It was wanton destruction, leaving even the children of blood-slaves drained and dead in the streets. And a blood-feud was what we had here, what had been staring us in the face all this time, and I hadn't really understood.

I went back to the date. If the history of Lucas Vazquez de Allyon was correct, he would have been alive back then. Just because his name was Spanish now didn't mean he hadn't traveled, or even been Italian—Roman—originally. As I worked, the smell of coffee filled the house, rich, dark, and wonderful. Too bad that coffee smelled so much better than it tasted to me.

Trying to block out smells and the small sounds made by men moving around in my house, I translated segments on blood-feuds, spending two hours before I realized that, basically, a blood-feud was a no-holds-barred free-for-all with winner take all. This one would be blamed on me for killing a man who had likely been intending to murder me the first chance he got.

"Jane," Alex called from the kitchen. "I got something."

I put the laptop to sleep and went to the kitchen, stretching on the way in. In the kitchen, I discovered where the coffee smell originated. The men taking over my life had purchased an espresso coffeemaker, a fancy stainless steel

version by DeLonghi. According to the box at the back
door, the thing cost nearly a thousand bucks. I hoped I
hadn't paid for that.

Before I studied the info Alex had, I put tea together.
While the tea water sizzled on the stove top, I pulled up a
chair near Stinky. Who definitely was not getting any fast
food today. "Show me," I said.

"Lucas Vazquez de Allyon purchased property in several
states, including Louisiana last year. He has property in
New Orleans, in Lafayette, and in some little towns between
Lafayette and here. I put them on a map."

It was a melded map, showing topo, streets and street
names, bayous, rivers, airports, bus stations, and a lot of
other stuff I would need if I had to go to each of them hunting him. "Have you found de Allyon yet?"

"No, but I'm close."

"Good. Now go take a shower. You're living up to your
nickname." At his puzzled look, I said. "Stinky. I've named
you Stinky and it'll stay Stinky until you remember to
shower every day."

"And when I remember?" he asked, sounding belliger-
ent.

"Then it'll be Kid."

"Like Kid Rock?"

"More like Billy the Kid, Cisco Kid, the Durango Kid."
When he still looked puzzled, I said, "Do an Internet search.
And it's a crying shame when an American teenage boy
doesn't know his gunslingers." I slapped him on the back of
the head. "Good work, Stinky."

I finished making my tea and went back to my laptop.
Shortly, I heard footsteps up the stairs and then shower water going. "The Durango Kid? He's a modern-day shooter."

I looked up to see Eli standing in front of the open bookcase. He had a habit of standing with his arms loose, one
hand near the spot where a military sidearm might go, the
other on his thigh where he might wear a military knife.
"Yeah. A cowboy six-shooter. There was an old black-and-
white film about the Durango Kid."

"You watch old black-and-white cowboy films." It was
said with a hint of disbelief.

"Yeah. The kind where your people kill off my people

and steal our land, and somehow make murder and theft seem heroic."

A hint of amusement twinkled into Eli's eyes in response to my sarcasm. He said, "My people? You mean the mongrels of society? I have ancestors who *were* slaves and ancestors who *owned* slaves."

He was of mixed blood, mixed race, which I had suspected from his skin tone. Alex was much paler than Eli. Maybe they were half brothers? I brought my mind back to the conversation and tilted my head to show he had made his point.

"You're good with Alex," he said. "We were doing nothing but fighting about him showering." The twinkle bled away. After a moment he said, "We were fighting about everything, actually."

"Yeah. You treat him like a son or a soldier, instead of like a brother. He wants you to like him and admire him and love him. Maybe in that order."

"Hmmph," Eli said. "And you know this about families when you were raised in a children's home?"

That could have been intended to be snide or even hurtful, but the look on his face was simply puzzled. I squelched the retort budding on my lips. I didn't explain about my early years very often, mainly because it sometimes brought the memories back, like a tsunami, overwhelming, overpowering, visceral, and intense. With Alex's ability to ferret out info on the Web, it wasn't a surprise that the brothers knew about my history. "I came out of the woods at age twelve, give or take, with no language, no social skills, no nothing. I watched the body language and interactions between the kids and the adults in the home long before I could understand what they were saying. Tone and intent were clear enough even to the outsider. Your tone and body language say you don't trust him. Your tone and body language say you are the boss and he better listen to you or else."

"Yeah? So?"

"What do you mean *So*?" Men can be so obtuse sometimes. "He's not a soldier under your command. This is family, not the army. And Alex doesn't understand that you love him and want to protect him and that's why you are all over him like white on rice. Tell him you like him. Tell him you admire what he can do. And back off and let him make mistakes. He'll respect you more for it. Sheesh." I went back to my research. Eli tucked his thumbs in his pockets and meandered up the stairs, I hoped to play nice-nice with his baby brother.

Before dark, Alex sent me an e-mail with an attachment, and stood over me with a half-proud, half-sheepish grin as I opened the document he'd sent. As I studied the file, he fidgeted, sitting down, standing up, roaming around and around the room. Without looking up, I said, "Stop. Light somewhere. Explain this to me."

"It's how Lucas Vazquez de Allyon is making some vamps sick when they to go Blood-Call for a date, without letting his Typhoid Mary out of his sight."

I felt lighter, as if someone had just taken a lead overcoat off me. "Yeah?"

"Yeah. Proof that Blood-Call has everything to do with the sick master vamps."

I leaned back in my chair and said, "Okay. Shoot. Convince me."

An hour later, I realized that the Kid had hacked into another government agency and found something in the CDC's employee files that might help lead us to someone who could heal all the sick vamps in the nation—proof of what the plague really was, and how it had been developed—because it wasn't something that had appeared naturally. Alex was grinning like a trained monkey, and I smiled back. "Not bad. Not bad at all."

"So, do I rate a Big Mac?"

"Nope. The lady had to tell you to shower," Eli said from the opening to the safe room. "But you did good, kid. Real good. I'm proud of you." Eli turned back without waiting to see what effect his words had on Alex. The Kid glowed pink from his palms to his ear tips. I managed not to grin, which might have spoiled it for him, and nodded instead, my eyes on the screen. "What he said. Good work."

"Okay. Okay, then." Alex stood, bristling with energy, with purpose, with poorly concealed delight. "I'll have a cup of coffee. You want one, Eli? Jane, you want tea?"

"Sure," we both said at the same time. Eli tipped his head around the door just enough to see his brother go into the kitchen. When the Kid was gone, Eli tilted his head at me in thanks. And I realized that, maybe, we had just become a team. Turning away, I called a high-level parley at Katie's.

Alex, showing his nerves by the way one knee jerked spasmodically, stood in front of a specially picked small group of vamps and humans. I stood over to the side, where I had a good view of every person in the group. Leo, who I wanted to stake on sight or curl up at his feet, sat front and center in a padded chair that looked like a throne. Katie, his heir, Grégoire, his second heir should Katie predecease him, Troll, Grégoire's B-twins, Brandon and Brian, all the clan heads still alive after the battle, and a smattering of humans and servants sat or stood around the walls. The room was crowded, even with the silver cages removed and the furniture back in place, and over it all rode the half-muted tingle of power and the scent of Leo Pellissier, peppery parchment, still tainted with the faint, fermented hint of too much blood. It made me grind my teeth, and I had to breathe slowly to keep my heart rate from speeding and betraying my emotional state. The MOC didn't look my way, to see if I was okay, or still hurt from his attack.

The room fell silent for long, awkward seconds and finally Leo turned his head and met my eyes, his own guileless and superior. Even though my brain said to ram a silver stake through his black heart, I still wanted to fulfill his wishes, the result of the dregs of the binding that still trapped me. I wondered fleetingly how bad it would be if I had no way to resist, if the binding was permanent, and not something that Beast and I could destroy eventually. I didn't want to think about what a person would do or become if she had no will at all. Rather than do what I wanted most, I broke the master's gaze and nodded to Alex.

He cleared his throat. "Hi. I'm Alex." He wiped his sweating palms on his pants. "Okay. Well. Yeah. Okay." He took a breath and launched into his spiel. "The disease is from a mutated strain of the *Filoviridae ebola* virus, one that can be safely carried by humans," Alex said, opening with a bang. It was clear from Leo's reaction that even old vamps knew of the Ebola virus. The MOC sat back in his chair slowly, as if putting distance between himself and Alex. The other vamps took a collective half step back.

"The only human known to have contracted the virus," Alex said, oblivious of the vamps' reactions, "was one Tanya Petrov, a virologist who worked at Greyson Labs. Two weeks after she contracted the virus, the lab was purchased by de Allyon's company, and the victim vanished from a level-four containment facility, while under lockdown, something that was not supposed to be able to happen. Subsequent electronic forensics showed the disappearance took place between four a.m. and four-ten a.m., when there was a disruption in the digital security system.

"A few years earlier, a boutique pharmaceutical company called DeAli, owned by our head evil dude, announced trials for a new drug that was supposed to help an existing cancer chemotherapy drug locate and penetrate cancer cells with the help of a deactivated virus. This drug was never released to the general market, though it went through all the trials with excellent results and has been in production for months in small batches. The drug never got a market name, and goes by the moniker VR1389. For the purposes of this discussion, we'll call it VR." Alex grinned when he looked up, seeing all the vamps concentrated on him. To me it looked like a pride of African lions fixated on prey, but the Kid seemed immune to that imagery.

"This part is guesswork, but what I think happened is that de Allyon—whose base is the same city as the CDC, by the way—wooed some top people from them. A virologist, a microbiologist, and a couple of people who specialize in genetic recombinant studies left within the last couple of years." He looked at me quickly and back to the room before adding, "They all disappeared, like totally, literally." He wiped his hands down his pants again. "I think that one of de Allyon's pet virologists or microbiologists discovered that the new cancer drug, VR, worked like cocaine on vamps, making them all mellow and buzzed. I think that after he got all his medical team together, they discovered that it also would bond with the new strain of Ebola. De Allyon kidnapped Tanya Petrov, injected her with VR, and made a vamp . . . ire," he added, "drink from her.

"The combo of the virus and the drug seem to work like

a highly addictive narcotic on vampires. They are both sick and stoned. They need more of the drug, which is available only in a virus combo cocktail. And they eventually die. Meanwhile, it looks like de Allyon discovered that a very few of his humans, who had been dinner to vampires infected with the VR combo, were able to pass along the disease *and* the addiction for several days before falling really sick themselves and developing antibodies to the virus. If what I think is true, de Allyon now had a disease *and* a treatment. If the sick vampires drank from these humans, and no longer drank from a recently infected host, the vampire would survive."

It was a lot to take in, and I had heard it already once. The small crowd in Katie's sat in silence. A lot of what Alex had pitched to the vamps had started out as thinly supported conjecture on our part, but Reach had contacted a researcher at CDC and managed to confirm most of it. This scenario was the only thing that explained why the Seattle humans had gotten sick, then better, and then been taken away. It also explained why the new MOC had left only one human antibiotic factory in Sedona for Ro to drink from.

Alex looked at me for his cue. We had planned the timing of this part of the lecture carefully, to allow the vamps and humans time to take it all in without panic, and for me to study them all while they did. When I thought there had been enough time, I lifted a finger to Alex.

"There is also a new nationwide corporation called Blood-Call," he said. The attention of several vamps sharpened at the name. "VR," Alex said, "may be administered to unsuspecting vampires on a Blood-Call appointment. A vampire drinks from a Blood-Call lady or man of the evening, one who is freshly injected with the drug and virus combo. The vampires who drink from the infected humans get a feeling of euphoria, driving them back again and again. After a few visits, they begin to bleed internally. They need more drug *and* they need the treatment, and they'll give anything to get it."

I figured that VR was the metallic scent I had detected early on, in victims of the disease, but saw no point in saying so. I could identify the drug by its smell. Not that it would ever do me any good.

A vamp raised his hand, and I covered a snort with a fake cough at the sight of an elegant undead requesting permission to speak, like a kid in class. Grégoire asked, "Are all of the blood-meals offered by Blood-Call infected?"

"No. Most of the humans are healthy," Alex said. "I've traced indications that special transportation is arranged to the city of choice when de Allyon is ready to make a move on it. He uses a charter company based in Atlanta, and flies his infected humans into the city for dinner."

Grégoire, Leo's *secundo* and heirs' heir, nodded, one finger in the air. "So, perhaps we can trace the location of the next attack by the movements of this special charter service, *oui*?"

"Good idea," Alex said, typing into his little electronic tablet thingy. "I'll see if I can get into the system and trace down the accounting. That way we can tell when a flight is being activated by de Allyon. In fact, I can take a look-see and find out how many have been sent here." The silence in the room was intense at that, as the vamps all considered who they had sipped from recently who might not be in their own personal menagerie.

Into the worried silence, Katie said, "Leo owns two small research laboratories, one in Arizona, one in Houston. They are currently working on a cure to the disease and an antidote to this drug. We have Sabina and Bethany, two of very few priestesses in his land, both of whom have the power to heal, even to cure this disease. Few masters of the city have such outclan at their disposal. We also have the Mercy Blade, with the power to heal. This new information will accelerate the process of finding a cure. Our people need not worry, should any become ill with this plague. We will care for our own."

Alex looked up from his keying. "Sorry. Okay. So. How does the virus work? The vampire immune system is attacked by the Ebola variant and VR combo, and other bacteria quickly take over," Alex went on, "the same way that bacteria would break down any dead body."

I almost groaned. He had just called some of the most powerful vamps in the nation dead. Which they were, but still. I glanced around, gratified that none of them seemed to be taking offense. I'd hate to have to stake someone for hurting Stinky, and I was already in enough trouble with the vamps.

"It makes the victims look like plague victims. The important thing to remember is that the vamps are addicted *and* sick. That's why the masters of the city in Sedona, Seattle, and Boston gave up without a fight. De Allyon owns them undead body and soul."

I spoke up. "And do we know who from Asheville, um . . . *dated* a Blood-Call escort?" All the vamps in the room turned as one to me and stared.

Finally Leo said, his voice all Frenchy and stilted, "An internal investigation will take place. Those who need to be notified of the results will be informed. Please continue, young man."

Ah, I thought. *As in "not me." Gotcha.*

CHAPTER FOURTEEN

Vampires Are Like Boars. And Like Kits

An hour into the meeting, my phone vibrated in my jeans pocket. I stood to slip out of the room. So did Bruiser, holding his own cell. We met in the hallway and both of us took the calls.

"Jane. Derek here. I just got word that Sabina is sick. The crazy nutso priestess, the one with loose marbles, that Bethany chick, wants to go to her, but I'm not risking one of my men to take her."

"Wait, wait. Sick? How sick?"

"She woke up this evening and she was bleeding. She called in, but my men are *not* driving Bethany. And Leo's cars all got torched along with the house."

"Bleeding," I whispered. Sabina had healed the once-sick vamp Callan. Now she was sick. "I'll make sure that Bethany is taken to Sabina. Thanks."

"Copy." The call-ended light appeared on my cell.

Bruiser was hanging up too. "Bethany wants a ride to the Mithran graveyard," he said.

"Yeah. Sabina is sick." My mouth turned down. "She probably has the illness she healed Callan from, and if Bethany sips from her while trying to heal her, Bethany will be sick too."

"Understood," Bruiser said. "I'll handle it." But he didn't

hurry away, instead, standing apart from me in the narrow hall, watching me, giving me space. Giving me time.

I remembered the way Bethany had healed Bruiser from the dead. She had been more than half naked, sitting on top of him in Katie's office, giving him her blood, her essence, to bring him back from the dead. I wanted to be angry at him for his subsequent betrayal—okay, I wanted to hit him so hard my fist would pop out his back—but I knew what vamp blood, especially large amounts of vamp blood, could do to a human. "You know, if the vamps and their pals would tell me what was going on and I didn't have to fly by the seat of my pants all the time, I'd make fewer mistakes. Like maybe I'd have carried the Enforcer I shot into Grégoire's room and made him heal him. Instead, he's dead."

"Had Grégoire's blood-servants known the man you shot was going to die, and had we known he was a valuable blood-servant, and had we known his master was going to attack so many other masters, the man would still be alive." Bruiser's face softened and something odd sifted through me. He was being kind. "You did the best you could with the information you had, Jane. So did we. No one knew that you had hit an artery with your second shot. No one knew he would bleed internally. None of us could read the future or delve into the heart of an enemy. Don't carry guilt that isn't yours."

I stared up into his eyes as he spoke, trying to remember to be angry at him, unsettled by his kindness. But after all the events and memories of my own, that was hard. Instead I just felt . . . more empty, if that was possible. Bruiser cocked his head at me, as if trying to read my thoughts. He looked younger, leaner than only a few days past, and his skin glowed with health. The amount of vamp blood he had ingested had given him back ten years. I wanted to smooth my hand along his cheek, just to see if his skin really was as velvety as it looked. I also still wanted to belt him a good one. I curled my fingers around my cell and shook my head. "None of you ever leads a normal life, do you?"

"I bloody well hope not," Bruiser chuckled, his British tones leaking through. "Normal is short, painful, and boring."

"But if you were normal—" I stopped, having almost

said, *If you were normal you wouldn't have had to watch me being forcefully fed on.* But I had been normal once, and I'd watched my father killed and my mother raped. Being normal was no proof against horror.

Bruiser reached out a hand and touched my face. "If I were normal, I'd be dead by now, love. I'd likely have never lived to see a moon landing or an intercontinental flight, never had the chance to see the Russian ballet, or hear Pavarotti in his prime, never lived to see the advent of the electronic age. I'd trade normal for that any day." His smile widened. "And even if I'd lived as a *normal* man, I'd have been very, very old by now, and you'd have thought I was cheeky at best, not charming and debonair." I raised my brows as if challenging his self-description. "You might have seen an old photograph of me and thought, 'He was a good-looking chap when he was young.' But you'd never have let me kiss you, which I full well intend to do again, just as soon as we get past this.

"But for now, I have work to do." He kissed the tips of his fingers and pressed them to my cheek. "Later, love." Bruiser turned and moved away from me, tapping on his cell as he moved. I watched him go, my eyes moving down his body. He had a very nice body and a perfect butt. It was one of his best attributes. And he was right: he wouldn't have been even slightly attractive to me if he was wearing dentures, a lifetime of wrinkled skin, adult diapers, and was perched on an adjustable bed. He'd have been a horny old man at best.

Love. He'd called me love. Twice. And then there was Eli, perfectly human and perfectly delightful, with a nature that matched mine, and a set of abs that would make the Madonna—the original Madonna—lust. And Rick. My heart twisted at that thought. Yeah. Rick. I was so screwed up.

Leaving the guys to work and the vamps to worry, I climbed on Bitsa and headed across the river and into the woods and wetlands. I pulled the bike off the road and hid her in the brush. Bending over the front tire, I raked the gold nugget necklace across the sidewall in lieu of a rock, and hoped it would work as well as a homing beacon in case I got lost. I stripped, folded my clothes on the bike seat, grabbed my large winter go-bag, my emergency mountain lion tooth, which I used to make shifting easier and less painful, and walked into the woods a short ways, the soles of my feet protesting.

Shifting in the sudden cool spell meant more clothes to leave with the bike and more clothes to carry with me, but I needed to get into my Beast. I was feeling uncertain and edgy and Beast, well, Beast never had those feelings. She was all about hunting and eating and sleeping. As long as there was food, she was happy. I needed some of that simplicity, even if it was a bloody simplicity.

I sat on a log at the edge of a bayou, with my go-bag on my neck, adjusted to allow for Beast's neck girth. I was shivering, my skin pebbled, and my breath was blowing white clouds. The waning moon was reflected in the black water.

I gripped the fetish tooth with both hands, and tried to find some sort of peaceful mind-set. I usually needed to meditate to have a less painful shift, though lately I wasn't as picky. In fact, I'd shifted in some really unusual places and emotional states.

Holding the tooth, I closed my eyes. Listened to the plink of water moving across the earth, the susurration of the wind, the beat of my own heart. Beast panted inside me, ready, eager to hunt, more eager than she had been since she came into contact with an angel. I still didn't know the outcome of that encounter and from her reticence about the subject, might never know. Beast wasn't talkative at the best of times, and had become downright closemouthed about Hayyel and what changes the angel had wrought in her.

I slowed my heart rate and let my muscles relax. I stretched out on the log, shivering. I sank deep inside, my consciousness falling away, remembering only the fetish tooth. The notes of a wood flute, soothing and mellow, like the one on the CD player in Aggie's sweathouse, filled my memory. I smelled the cleansing herbs of a smudge stick, and I dropped deeper, into the dark within. The place of the change within me seemed bigger inside than I remembered, more hollow, a large cavern branching off into other dark places. It had a sense of far-flung echoes and the resonant plink of distant water.

As I had been taught so long ago, I sought the inner

snake lying inside the tooth's root, the coiled, curled snake deep in the cells, in the remains of the marrow, the DNA peculiar to all animals on earth. For my people, for skin-walkers, it had always simply been the inner snake.

I dropped down into it, like water flowing through the bayou, like gators swimming in long, swirling water-glides. Grayness enveloped me, sparkling and cold; the world fell away.

My breathing deepened. My bones slid. Skin rippled. Pain, like a scalpel, slid between muscle and bone. My spine bowed hard.

My nostrils widened, drawing deep. I gathered paws under me, ear tabs flicking, listening, scenting. World was bright with greens and grays and silvers, the colors of night to big-cat eyes. Clear and sharp. I yawned widely and chuffed. Jane had left steaks back at dead, not-dead Bitsa. Jane was tricky. Wanted me to take tooth back.

I stood and stretched through belly and spine, back legs and front legs, paws flexing into old wood of log. I shook, pelt moving over body, loose. Predators had sunk claws into pelt, and found no vital organs beneath, pelt sliding across instead. Beast had killed other predators who thought they would win. Foolish predators. *Pack hunters*.

I lifted tooth in teeth and trotted back through pine trees to road and bushes where Jane had hidden Bitsa from any *thieves of Bitsa*. Did not know why thieves would steal Bitsa. Could not eat Bitsa. No blood, no bone. I did not understand. I dropped Jane's tooth on top of the pile of clothes and sank to ground beside cow meat. Sniffed. Meat smelled old and watery, not hot with blood and fresh with chase. I ate anyway. Cleaned up all blood with tongue and lay, belly to ground. Groomed mouth and paws, satisfied, listening to night. I heard something.

Tilted ears. Felt through ground on belly, heard through air. Stampstampstamp. Knew that sound. Stood slowly. Opened mouth and pulled in air over scent sacs in mouth, with long, soft *screeee* of sound. Smell came on wind, strong. Big prey. Much good meat.

Beast? Jane said, waking in mind.

I didn't answer. I padded into wind, testing, tasting, feel-

ing vibrations with paw pads on ground. Big prey. I found
good place to watch and leaped to tree limb hanging over
narrow path to water. Good place to hunt. *Ambush*.

Stampstampstamp, fastfastfast. Running, trotting, big
prey. Only one. But big.

Waited for prey to come, paws tight under belly. Eyes on
path. Small hooves got closer.

What is that thing? Jane thought.

Huge black creature trotted into view. Boar. Big boar.
Big teeth curling up from mouth. It raced under limb. *Ambush!*

Oh, crap, Jane thought. *That thing has tusks. It has to
weigh nearly a hundred pounds. You are* not *going t*—

I leaped. Landed on boar's back, claws gripping through
coarse hair of stubby mane. Killing teeth biting down at
base of skull. Found only hard fat and muscle. Boar stumbled with force of Beast, but did not fall. Screamed, pig
scream. Started running. Raced through scrub, Beast on
back. Branches hit Beast.

Beast bit down again and again, shaking hard, tearing
flesh. Spurt of blood. Hot. Tasty. Boar bucked like horse,
jumped high and twisted body. Beast held tight with claws
in boar haunches and shoulders. Bit down again. Boar ran,
fastfastfast through woods, screaming.

Boar ran under downed tree, resting across path. Log hit
Beast in head. Ripped Beast off boar. I fell. Boar spun.
Squeal changed to sound of anger. Boar attacked. Shaking
head, Beast raced back along path and leaped high to stump
of broken tree. Boar jumped. Teeth and tusks ripped at
Beast's paws and legs. Boar was too close. Beast was not
able to leap or fall onto boar.

Boar stood up on hind legs and jumped high, tusks stabbing. Beast spun in midair, long stubby tail spinning. Killing
teeth caught boar under chin. Deep in blood-rich flesh.
Blood spurted over Beast. Hothothot. *Good*. Beast clamped
down with jaws. Shook prey. Boar stopped squealing. Beast
had boar's air pipe in killing teeth. Crushed down. Crushing.
Crushing. Boar could not breathe. Fell to knees. Hard. Pulled
Beast off stump to ground. Beast stood over boar, could see
tusks near face. Smell of old blood and old vegetable. Rot-
ting human food from waste pile, grubs, and fungus. Pig food.

Boar fell back, belly to sky. Beast followed, holding, killing teeth clamped tight. Claws hooked in boar belly. Time passed. Beast shook boar many times. Boar died.

Son of a . . . Jane breathed hard in back of mind, thoughts full of fear. *You do know that if it ate you, there would be no way of coming back. I mean, it would have killed both of us.*

Beast did not reply. Beast tore into boar stomach and ate. Good tasty bloody hot meat. Good pig-boar. *Beast is good hunter.*

Later, Beast cleaned boar blood off pelt and out of claws with rough tongue. *Vampires are like boars. And like kits,* I thought.

Yeah? How's that? Jane thought, her fear gone, her thinking calm.

Bad vampires need to be killed. Have much blood. But vampires who are good are like kits. Need Jane.

Jane said nothing.

I stood and walked back to water, full belly heavy with meat. I drank at water's edge and stared at water, holding night sky in surface. I thought about Jane. Thought about Leo. *I see leash in den in mind. I see chain. Leash put onto Jane by Leo. Leash is not on Beast. I can break it.*

Can you? Jane sounded happy.

I walked to dark thing that was Leo's cage inside Jane. Extended claws. And swiped at chain of binding.

I found myself awake near the water, the sun's rays just peeking over the horizon. I felt . . . incredible. Leo's compulsion was nearly gone. I could still feel it, like a hard nut cocooned with spiderwebs in the back of my brain, but it was smaller, more compact, less diffuse. A couple more shifts, and it would be totally gone.

I reached up a hand to touch my neck, finding the gold nugget necklace I never took off. Unfortunately, the go-bag was gone. My clothes, my shoes, and my throwaway cell phone were no longer attached to me. The fight with the boar had ripped the go-bag off my neck. It was lost in the brush somewhere. I was a long way from Bitsa and my clothes, which meant I needed to find the gear.

I spent nearly an hour looking for the go-bag, and when

I finally found it, it was covered in boar blood. I rinsed the flip-flops off in a nearby bayou, hoping that the morning was too cool to attract alligators, wiped off the throwaway cell, and tossed the rest of clothes into the water. Naked and cold, I walked back to the bike, dressed, and kick-started Bitsa, riding into the city. I stopped at a tiny French Quarter restaurant and had a huge breakfast starting with a stack of pancakes, six eggs over easy, and a rasher of bacon. I'd eaten here before and the waiters knew I was a big eater. I'd overheard them making bets on me. It might be bets about when I'd balloon up with the pounds, or bets about whether I'd order blueberry pancakes or harvest grain. Whatever they were betting on, I always got great service, my teacup was always full, and my syrup was always warm. I tossed three tens on the table when I was done and went home. I needed sleep.

Just before I dozed off, my other throwaway rang. I reached off the mattress and opened my cell. It was Reach. I pursed my lips and said, "How did you get this number?"

"You're kidding, right?"

I sighed and said, "Yeah, I guess that was a stupid question. What do you want?"

"The Kid is okay. He's good and he's capable, and in about two hours, he's gonna knock on your door and tell you who your mole is."

"You want to tell me now?"

"Nah. Why spoil the Kid's fun?" The phone call ended.

"Well, crap." So much for sleep.

But I did sleep, a hard, deep nap. Two hours after the phone call from Reach, I heard a knock at my door. "Coming." I got up and shook out a pair of sweats that had been lying in the bottom of the closet. They didn't smell too bad, so I pulled them on and padded to the door. Opened it. Stinky, who smelled of herbal shampoo, was on the other side, his knee doing that shaking thing he did when he had too much nervous energy. He was holding a cup of very strong tea. "Yeah?" I said. I'm not my best on little sleep.

He handed me the tea, which was a nice surprise. I could get used to this. "I know who the traitor is. You are looking for a traitor, right? That's why the deep background on people you already work with? So I found him. I think. I'm pretty sure. I've checked it about a dozen times. So, yeah, I'm sure."

The Kid was smart. Way too smart for my own good. I sipped the tea, which was so strong it was bitter, the sharp taste only slightly masked by a lot of sugar. I'd have to teach him how to brew tea. I crossed my arms, sipped again, and waited.

"It's the intel guy. Corporal Joran Stevens. The ex-marine."

He was talking about Angel Tit. All the pleasure drained out of me, leaving my limbs feeling heavy as lead. "Former. Former marine," I murmured, thinking, trying to take it in. "There are no ex-marines." I'd had that "no ex-marines" thing made clear to me early on. Except this former marine had turned against his unit. Stupid, disconnected thoughts. Shock.

Angel Tit? I'd thought it would be one of the vamps. I'd hoped it would be a vamp. "Crap," I whispered. "Let me see what you have."

Alex had hacked Angel's e-mail and the evidence was clear, if cryptic. A few months back, Angel Tit had been approached in a Special Forces chat room. Angel had needed money fast. One of his sisters was in trouble with the law and he needed to hire a better lawyer for her than the wet-behind-the-ears public defender the court had assigned. In return for some much-needed cash, he had been asked to provide a bit of seemingly innocuous information about the blood-servants in Leo Pellissier's household. The information hadn't been secret, so he had complied. Later, the anonymous person from the chat room needed something else. Then something else. And suddenly Angel Tit was in so deep he couldn't get out.

The money he had earned hadn't been that great, but any money gathered by a traitor was enough to get him . . . what? Killed? Kicked out of Derek's unit? "Print it out," I said softly.

I turned away and called Derek on my official phone. "Whatchu want, Injun Princess?"

"We need to talk," I said. "Privately. Can you come to my place?"

"Sure. I'm at Katie's, watching your boy work on her safe room. Not bad skills for the army. I'll be there in ten."

"Fine." I closed the cell and turned back to Alex. "You did good work. Can you find out the ID of the person who contacted the corporal?"

Alex looked at the screen, pouching out his lips, and back to me. "Maybe. I'll try. You want everything on him?"

"Yes. I want to know name, banking, family, habits, hobbies, who his pals are, and where he eats breakfast." Which meant a very deep search indeed. "But for now, go upstairs and shut your door. I need some privacy." I went to my room and dressed in cleaner clothes. Put on some lipstick. Strapped on a Walther PK380 shoulder harness on top of my T-shirt. The weapon was snug under my arm, but not hidden. I didn't want Derek to think I was unarmed. I French-braided my hair and tied it with a scrunchy, which was so much better than a string torn from a pocket. I met Derek at the door and held out a hand. "Phone."

"Why?"

I didn't answer, my hand outstretched. He put his cell in my hand and I tossed it into my room onto the bed, next to mine, and shut the bedroom door. "We've been compromised," I said. "I want to make sure no one can listen in."

Derek stood at my table studying the printouts. His face was expressionless, his eyes scanning page after page. At one point, he leaned over the table, bracing himself on one hand. His breathing didn't alter, but his heart rate went up, the pulse in his neck starting to jump. When he reached the last page, he swiveled his head on his neck and looked at me. Took in the Walther and my stance, which was far too relaxed. "You thought I'd need to be shot, Legs?" I didn't reply. "I've seen you fight Grégoire's half-human goons. I know what you can do."

I still didn't reply, and Derek stood upright, his body at an angle to mine, perfect for drawing a weapon if he was wearing a shoulder holster. But he was wearing a low back holster. He'd have to reach behind and pull forward. I'd noticed his weapon was snapped in. Mine wasn't. I'd have plenty of time if needed. Beast rose in me, staring out through my eyes.

"You can take a lot of abuse," Derek said. His cheek started a tic and his pulse increased again. He looked at the gun under my arm, taking in the unsnapped safety strap. "You think you can take me?"

"Are you asking me to hurt you because your boy is a spy?"

"Angel's no boy. He's a man. He's faced combat. He's—" Derek stopped, his breath fast. Betrayal hurt. This betrayal more than most, because Angel had been in Iraq with him. They had been together for a long time.

"He's your friend," I said. "He's in trouble. He should have come to you for help. He didn't. He's not happy to be in the position he's in. He's hurting." That was me being compassionate. The next bit was me being me. "And he also has an in with the enemy."

Derek thought about that. "You want me to use my friend to get to the enemy vamp."

"If he's willing."

"And if he's not?"

"Then he gets put on ice until this is over with," I said. "And his sister's fancy new lawyer drops her case for non-payment. He'll deal. He has amends to make and trust to rebuild."

"You think I'll keep him around after this?"

I smiled, but it wasn't a pretty smile. "I hope you kick his ass and turn him over to the cops. People died on your watch, because of him. But I'll agree that it's your call."

Derek dropped his head, then looked up at me under his brows. "I was hoping you'd say something stupid so I could hit you."

I chuckled. "Sorry to disoblige. But I need you healthy and not laid up in the hospital."

An unwilling smiled pulled at his mouth. "Someday we're gonna fight, Princess. For real."

"Yeah, yeah, yeah. Big words from the tough guy. So, how do you want to play this?"

"Straight up," Derek said. "Him and me. We'll talk. Then I'll kick the crap outta him. And then we'll use his contacts to draw out our fanghead."

"Works for me. Do all the talking where there isn't any electronic surveillance that could be compromised. Let me know when you want me."

Later that afternoon, Derek called. "We're coming over, Injun Princess."

I was waiting in the kitchen when their car pulled up and they knocked on the front door. "Come in," I called. Angel and Derek walked in, Angel in front. He had a puffy lip and the beginnings of a black eye. Angel stood in front of me, not meeting my eyes. "Teeth?" I asked.

Angel touched his lip. "A few a little loose."

"You deserve that and more. People died because of you. But now you've got something we want. A connection. If you work with us, I'm happy to tell no one, even Leo, even your buddies, about your little indiscretion. You want to start on the road to recovery or be locked up?"

Angel glanced back at Derek, who looked none the worse for wear. Apparently Angel hadn't put up much of a fight. "Recovery." He shook his head, but not in disagreement, more like resignation, and drew to attention. "Hi. I'm Joran Stevens and I'm a fuckup."

Kid yelled from upstairs, "Watch your language. There's a lady present." Derek and Angel both laughed, whether at the timing or idea that I might be called a lady, I didn't know.

Alex and Angel were working out the basics of a scheme to draw out the unknown subject who had turned him. The condition of his face was the ace in the hole of the plan. Angel typed in a text on his phone, showed the text to us, and hit SEND. I took his cell back to my bedroom. There was no way to detect if someone was listening in through the phones, so we had to keep the cells we were known to use in one room together. Derek had purchased a dozen throwaways and some other low-tech electronics for us to use until this was all over. Luckily, I had five thousand in cash on hand—my runaway money, I hadn't used, so if someone was keeping tabs on credit usage, they couldn't see what we had bought or done.

"Now what?" Angel asked.

"Now we wait," Alex said.

"And eat," I said. "I've ordered pizza." Alex grinned like the teenaged boy he was.

Halfway through the pizza, we heard the tone Angel had assigned for the mystery man. The tone came over the baby monitor we had set up on the phones in my bedroom.

Derek raced in and grabbed the cell, showing Angel's text to the small group. The text said "Moonwalk bench 2pm."

Which made no sense to me whatsoever, but the others seemed to understand.

When he came back to the kitchen, after putting the phone back in my room, Derek said, "We're on." At my obvious confusion, he said, "The Moonwalk is the scenic boardwalk along the Mississippi." When my confusion didn't abate, he said, "It's called that after Moon Landrieu, a former mayor."

It was perhaps telling that my first thought was the Moonwalk was the place where I'd taken Rick down on our first sort-of date. "Ducky," I said. I hadn't been in New Orleans long, but it already had its share of painful memories. "Okay. Let's do this."

CHAPTER FIFTEEN

Landed on a Limo Floor

Angel asked his handler to meet him to pass along some hard copies of the location of the New Orleans vamps' lairs that Angel claimed he had stolen from me. He asked for five thousand dollars for the pages, not such a high number that the anonymous person might have to go to a higher-up for approval, and not so low that the handler would think the pages could wait. The handler took the bait, which told us something about him. He had some autonomy, he had ready access to funds, and, because it was still daylight, he wasn't a vamp, which made our plan much less dangerous and much more feasible. If he showed.

Minutes before we left the house, I dialed a number I hadn't called recently. "NOPD, Jodi Richoux," she answered.

Jodi was my contact with the New Orleans Police Department's supernatural crimes unit, in charge of all things paranormal and woo-woo. We were friends of a sort, but like most of my pals, we were going through a tough patch. My job was hard on friends. Or I was. "I might have a package for you soon."

"Jane Yellowrock. Why should I accept anything you throw my way?"

"Because you want to avert a vamp war in your town

and I don't have a place to store a high-ranking enemy blood-sucker."

"*War?*" she said, half question, half demand.

"Yeah."

I filled her in, and when I was done, Jodi said, "I wish I'd never laid eyes on you, Yellowrock," and hung up the phone.

We left the house at different times, took three separate vehicles, and arrived at the rendezvous site from different directions. I was the most conspicuous of us—six-foot-tall Cherokee women are not common even in a city where racial and ethnic markers were all over the place—so I stayed in the van that Derek and his crew used for security gigs. I didn't like being out of the action, but I knew the others could handle a human.

Only, the handler didn't show. A woman did. And Angel didn't know her. As she approached, his spine straightened and his fingers curled under, the telltale actions of a trained fighter facing the unknown. I watched through the smoked windows as she approached Angel Tit, who was sitting on a bench, away from the tourists, on the Moonwalk. She was tiny, efficient, and brisk: all of five feet, business suit, rapid walk, and when Derek and Eli—both wearing ball caps with the brims pulled down low—raced in to take her, she put up a serviceable fight, though her defensive measures were no match for two guys trained by Uncle Sam. They picked her up, whisked her to the van, dumped her inside, secured her limbs with zip strips, taped her mouth shut with clear surgical tape, and flipped her over, all in the seconds it took us to pull sedately away from the curb. The woman, who was maybe forty-five and matronly, inspected the blade held under her nose, which was sucking breath so hard it whistled.

"Any lookouts, any witnesses?" I asked into the mic.

The three lookouts responded, "Clear Alpha." "Clear Beta." "Clear Delta."

I opened the woman's pocketbook to find a .22 with an illegal suppressor. The end of the barrel was attached to the end of the purse with a swiveling coupler like nothing I'd ever seen before. I maneuvered the gun. It didn't come lose. The .22 was hooked in, but attached in such a way that she

couldn't have gotten her hand around the grip. Which was
just plain weird. The only other things in the bottom of the
purse were an extra magazine, a pair of reading glasses, and
a tube of L'Oréal lipstick. I twirled the lipstick up. "Coral.
An interesting shade. Sedate, maybe just a little bit saucy. A
good choice for a woman who's looking less and less like
Angel Tit's best pal."

I held the purse up, inspecting it closer, and accidentally
slid my fingers through the side panel. I pushed on the
panel and held it up to her. "Nice. Very nice. I like. You can
be walking along, an office clerk on her lunch hour, maybe
getting close to a guy on a park bench, shove your hand into
the purse through here"—I showed the guys the panel,
which was hinged with tiny brass jewelry hinges—"aim this
little gun, swiveling it in the coupler, give a two-tap through
this small hole on the other end"—I tapped my finger on
the barrel—"and walk on."

I looked at Derek and Angel. "The handler sent someone to take Angel out. Seems he's become a problem, somehow. Let's drive." I handed Derek the purse, turned off the
radio system, and took off the headpiece.

"You know who I am?" I asked the woman. She nodded
once, jerkily, angry eyes above the tape. "You know what
we'll do to you if you don't volunteer the info we want?"
Her pupils dilated and her sweat smelled of fear, but she
didn't look away or shrink back. She had moxie, I'd give her
that.

To Derek I asked, "Who is she?"

He was going through her bag now and held up a respi-
ratory rescue inhaler. "That's it. Except for—" He snapped
open a side pocket on the purse and pulled out a set of keys.
One was an electronic key with a remote engine start.
Derek grinned. It was a rookie mistake. "Circle the block,"
he instructed the driver. "Then if we don't find what we're
looking for, we'll widen the search perimeter." We circled
back and drove around for ten minutes, Derek pressing the
key, looking for lights blinking on parked cars. We found the
woman's car in a small private lot on a side street up from
Decatur.

Derek pulled off his T-shirt to reveal another one underneath and jumped out. I watched as he tossed the stoner

watching the lot a twenty, climbed into the running car, and drove it away. We followed. The stoner went back to sleep.

Derek wove slowly through the Quarter, through traffic, and pulled into a hotel on St. Charles Avenue. He tossed the keys to the valet and went into the hotel. Moments later he jogged around from the back and jumped into the van. He pulled on the original T-shirt and hat and grinned, handing me the contents of the car and its glove box in a grocery store plastic bag. Derek was having fun. The woman we had kidnapped, however, was not, and I could see why. There were three different .22 handguns in the bag—two pistols and one semiautomatic. Twenty-twos were the weapons of choice for made men and contract killers. I was betting on contract killer for our tiny, not-so-efficient hostage. Our enemy liked hit men. If he had sent a hit man to take out Angel, then we could no longer use the former marine to draw him out. Checkmate. Dang it. I'd never gone up against someone who was always one step ahead of me.

I gave the driver an address on South Broad Street, suggesting that he ride around some more and get there in fifteen minutes. He looked at me funny, but I ignored it and pulled on nitrile gloves to open the bag. "So. Sophia," I said, paging through the papers Derek had lifted from her car. "Sophia Gallaud."

"Guh-lode," Derek said, correcting my pronunciation.

"Gallaud. Sorry," I said. Seemed like Derek was going to be good cop to my bad. "Local address on a Louisiana driver's license, local dry cleaning stub." I held it up. "Local shooting range membership. I've been to that one. I like the black-painted floors. It's easy to police your brass. Goodness, congrats on the nephew's Catholic thingamajiggy." I passed the invitation to Derek.

"Confirmation," he said. "It's a Roman Catholic rite of passage. Like laying on of hands."

"Like a special Mass or something?" I asked.

"Seems so." To Sophia he said, "I was raised Baptist, myself. None of that Latin stuff or rolling in the aisles either. Now, Yellowrock, here, she's Cherokee. They practice blood rites. The Injuns ever use human sacrifice? Scalping or stuff?"

"We didn't scalp. That was a white man thing. And no

sacrifice in religious practices. Cherokees were known to use knives to great effect in other ways, however, like killing enemies. Yeah, we were real good at that." If I sounded bitter, no one called me on it. I handed him my biggest vampkiller, a new knife to replace the eighteen-inch blade destroyed in Asheville. "Like this one."

He took it gingerly. "You ever killed anyone with it?"

"Not yet." The words brought me up short. They said awful things about my job, but it was the truth. "But the blade that one replaced . . ." I looked away, unable to hide my reaction to the memory of the silvered blade sliding into Evangelina's belly. The feel of the hotter than human blood pulsing out. "That was a bad one," I said more softly.

"Anything else in there?" Derek passed the knife back.

I sheathed it. "Cell phone. Let's see." I paged through the text messages, and then through the received calls, jotting down numbers, names, times and frequency of calls onto a paper tablet with a regular pen. "Our Sophia has been a bad girl, as well as a stupid one," I said a moment later. "She took a gig from someone. They put five K into an account for her just two hours ago. She gets another five K when the gig is finished. Our Sophia is a hired killer. Which means she knows nothing. Now that we have the phone, we can dispose of her."

Sophia started to hyperventilate in earnest, her nostrils whistling high and fast. I smiled. I bent forward and peeled off the tape over her mouth. "You want to talk to us? Give us a reason to keep you alive?"

"You'll let me go? You'll leave my family alone?"

"Your family is safe. I won't kill you," I said. "Talk."

Sophia knew little except that she was between a very jagged rock and a very sharp blade. She told us everything. Sophia—if that was her real name—had been contacted two days ago to be available at a moment's notice to take care of three problems, two high-ticket problems—George Dumas and Jane Yellowrock—and one floater, fees to be discussed later. Unfortunately for her, she didn't have my freebie house address, and the address she had for George was now a lump of soggy charcoal briquettes. What she did have was Katie's address.

I glanced at Eli and he nodded once, his eyes hard. We

had to move the vamps, and safe houses were getting few and far between. I looked out the window, saw we were on South Broad Street, pulled my new throwaway cell, and hit REDIAL.

"NOPD, Jodi Richoux," she answered.

"That package I told you I might have for you?" I said. "It's a little different and it eats its dinner cooked, but it's still interesting. We'll be out front in a sec."

"This better be good."

"All I can do is deliver. It's up to you boys in blue to make good on the package." I ended the call.

Sophia closed her eyes. "Bitch," she said around the tape that dangled from her cheek.

I showed the hit woman my teeth. It wasn't a smile. "I promised to let you live and to leave your family alone. Free her hands and feet, Derek." To the driver, I said, "See that woman running out of NOPD up ahead? Pull over to her." I emptied the guns and as much info as I thought would help Jodi into a zip-lock baggie and sealed it.

When the van slowed enough, I slid open the side door and pushed the contract killer out into the street. She bounced twice and rolled a bit, probably scuffing her knees and elbows. I dropped the plastic baggie containing her little toy guns into the street next. They bounced too, but I had removed the magazines. Protecting the surfaces from my fingerprints, of course. We pulled away. My last sight was Jodi Richoux picking up the tiny woman and directing a uniformed guy to watch the guns. Oddly enough, Jodi looked irritated.

When we got back to the house, Alex was waiting, shaking like he had been mainlining espresso, like a bunny in the sights of a pit bull. "I think I found him. The fanghead you're looking for." He grabbed my arm and pulled me into the kitchen. A map was open on the laptop. "The problem is that we've been looking in all the wrong places. In Louisiana. But he's in Mississippi, in the territory of Hieronymus."

Big H was the vamp we had expected to be targeted next. Seems we were too late; he'd already been hit, long before our enemy targeted us. The upside? De Allyon had a power base only an hour away, and it was more than likely that he was making his forays from there. I nodded for Alex to continue.

"There's a business in Natchez, in the old downtown, near the main street, three stories, built in the eighteen thirties. The building changed hands two months ago, and has been under renovation, and it just passed a building code check and is ready for occupancy.

"The county requires all renovations of historic buildings to submit a floor plan, and this one fits what vamps are looking for. The building was originally a bank, and the vault is still there. The new owner ordered a safe room built, adjacent to and in front of the vault. No windows, no doors. All the internal rooms are no-window, no-door rooms too. Three stories' worth. And the reason the building was so hard to find? It was purchased by Ramondo Pitri a week before you shot him in your hotel room. It was listed under the name of a dead man. And it just went into probate—to the new owner, de Allyon."

Finally. We had the tie-in between Ramondo Pitri and Lucas Vazquez de Allyon. I took a breath and it filled my lungs with a fresh, blissful delight. "You, Kid, are good," I said. And then it hit me. We had to go after de Allyon, had to beard the lion in his den in a preemptive attack, which would be either the smartest thing we'd ever done or the dumbest.

The history of the Natureleza vamp suggested he didn't have both oars in the water, and the whacked-out old vamps were always the worst. Any vamp taking out masters of cities, infecting humans and vamps with a disease, and targeting Leo had to be crazy, meaning I'd need a plan that allowed me to take the attack to our antagonist before he got his forces realigned after the battle in Leo's fields. And I'd need lots of backup. And maybe a tank. And air support. Derek was put in charge of vamp security by day and ordered to move the blood-suckers somewhere safer before dawn. Katie's had been compromised. Eli was put to work gathering supplies, and I added my own gear to the equipment that would be delivered to Natchez via separate vehicle.

His work on the safe room would become a long-term project, not something to use for today's crisis. Leo and his vamps had other places they could hole up tomorrow, like the warehouse where Leo had attacked me. I still got an empty feeling at that thought, but Beast, the pragmatic one, simply yawned and milked my mind with her claws. *We are not dead. We are not caged. We will soon be free of him,* she thought. Which was the truth, as cats saw it, and would be something I could live with, eventually. *And if he needs to be staked,* she added, *we will stake him. And eat his heart.*

Which was a whole 'nother kettle of fish entirely.

Leo's old limo was a charred shell, and so we borrowed Grégoire's brand-new, heavily armored, slightly stretched Lincoln. I had helped design the bespoke limo from the ground up, taking ideas from a limo owned by one of Leo's scions, and from the latest defense industry specs. It had a three-quarter-inch steel plate underneath to protect the occupants from possible bombs, and dark, polycarbonate-armored glass windows to protect them from daylight and gunfire. The car had a special braking system and heavy-duty suspension to accommodate the weight.

Inside, it was a work of art, with a long U-shaped steel-construction seat covered with cream-colored, butter-soft leather, a bar, flat-screen TV, satellite phone and Internet uplink, and cool weaponry that would rival anything Q would have designed for James Bond, including a Mossberg 590 twelve-gauge shotgun mounted under the longest section of window seat that ran along the driver's side. There were three handguns on mounts near the bar, hidden along the passenger-side windows, all of them nine millimeter, with plenty of extra magazines secured in pockets along the sidewall.

The limo was black, low-slung, and totally cool. It only got about six miles to the gallon, but I hadn't been worried about being green; I had been worried about being alive. I also hadn't thought this through or I'd have ridden Bitsa. Or ridden in the gear truck that followed, just me and the driver. Instead, it was Eli and Alex. And Bruiser. And me. In a limo. Together. Driven by Wrassler.

Alex rode shotgun, occupied with video games and a music collection of head-banging rock, playing while search programs ran in the background on three laptops. I took the far backseat, facing forward, slouching, with my legs half on the seat, one foot on the floor. Studying the two men. They were as different as possible and all I could do was compare and contrast them.

Bruiser, on the long side seat, was wearing brown dress pants that had been made to order, polished Italian leather dress shoes, with a starched dress shirt, the sleeves rolled up to reveal tanned, corded arms. He was even wearing a tie, silk, of course, though it was loose at the neck. His legs were stretched out, crossed at the ankles, and he sat with his hands laced together across his lap. He was wearing a tiny gold pinky ring, and he was the picture of elegance, marred only by the compact handgun under his arm.

Eli took the seat facing backward, and was wearing button jeans, scuffed combat boots, and a skintight T, with a shoulder holster, an ankle holster, and probably three or four blades concealed on him somewhere. A wrinkled denim jacket lay on the seat near him. All in black. He looked dangerous and in control. Yet, in a hand-to-hand fight, Bruiser would win. Despite his casual and relaxed demeanor, he was full of vamp blood. He'd be faster, stronger, meaner, and though I'd never fought Bruiser—except the first time I ever saw him, when I'd gotten the drop on him—he'd had a hundred years to practice martial arts, and I was betting he fought like he danced. Perfectly balanced, and totally in control.

As we pulled away from the curb, Bruiser swiveled his head to me. And looked at the floor. Reminding me of the times we had landed on a limo floor. And almost done something I'd likely never regret. I tilted my head and slammed down hard on the blush that wanted to rise. Eli looked back and forth between us, taking in everything and drawing his own conclusions.

Fortunately, before I could feel too uncomfortable, Eli reached for the remote and turned on the television to Fox. The two men started into a discussion of politics and I closed my eyes and feigned sleep as we hit the road out of New Orleans.

The surfaces of most major highways in Louisiana are horrible, composed of concrete with expansion joints every ten feet or so. The joints rose in the heat of summer and stayed deformed forever, creating a rocking, bumpy ride, noisy and unpleasant even in the limo. But for me, it felt soothing, like a rocking chair, and my fake sleep quickly turned into real sleep. We were rolling into Natchez when I woke and I stretched, touching my mouth to make sure I hadn't drooled in my sleep.

I didn't know much about the town. Natchez, named after the tribe of Indians sold into slavery by the Europeans, was the first major Mississippi port city north of New Orleans, and had once been a major hub of steamboat travel and trade. It had been a bigger place before the war—the Civil War—and had struggled to hang on since. Union troops hadn't burned it to the ground, and after the war ended, Natchez had been left with swamp, forest, bayous, a checkered and notorious past—all set high upon a bluff above the Mississippi. It also had lots of fancy, prewar buildings, antebellum homes, churches, graveyards, and old live oak trees swathed in moss. After the war, the town also had hundreds of freed slaves needing work and carpetbaggers by the dozens bringing in an influx of cash. Its location and history allowed it to survive and thrive when most other towns around the South had suffered.

Natchez was rife with gossip. The locals knew everything. When we stopped for gas, Wrassler chatted up a local girl working inside behind the counter. In minutes, he'd learned most everything that had happened to the town in the last twenty years. Back in the limo, Wrassler moved his massive bulk into the car, shut the door, and said, "You were right, Kid." To the rest of us, he said, "De Allyon has been hiding in plain sight here, having taken over from the local MOC, Hieronymus—who owes Leo allegiance and loyalty and who did not call his boss to report the presence of an enemy." He started the limo and pulled into the street. "Funny how Leo's research guy didn't know any of this. Not you, Kid," he said to Alex, "but that other guy the master uses."

I laid my head back on the leather upholstery and thought about our leak. Leaks. Whatever. Not only was someone sharing info with our enemy, but our own intel sources had left us high and dry on what was happening in Leo's organization. That needed to be addressed, eventually, once this crisis was over. With vamps, there was always something.

*   *   *

As for this little out-of-town gig, the possibility that there was more than one leak—Angel Tit *and* a snitch in Leo's camp—came back and perched in the forefront of my brain, like a buzzard over roadkill. Was there a chance that the spy was Reach himself? Reach had electronic fingers in everything, and he was nearly paranoid about security. If he was the spy, he'd already have taken down Leo's security and finances and, well, just about everything. Reach had that kind of . . . reach. I let a bit of humor bubble up through my worries and forced my shoulders to relax. They had crawled up my neck to my ears with tension at the thought of Reach as a traitor.

"It isn't Reach," I said politely. "Go on, please?" Who said I didn't have class?

Wrassler met my eyes again in the rearview, and I couldn't see enough of his face to tell what he was thinking, but he went on. "According to my date, Hieronymus initially billed himself as a producer, which was a new one for vamps, but fit the town perfectly."

"How so?" Eli asked.

"Look around," Wrassler said, his eyes back on the road. "On the backs of slaves and then cheap manual labor, the town fathers kept the place looking both spiffy and old. To supplement tax revenues, the good-ol'-boy town fathers have always looked outside farming, shipping, and transportation. Mississippi might be rife with the usual blunders and nepotism and thievery of any bureaucratic government, but their film commission pushed the beauty of the town to the outside world."

My brows went up at his vocabulary. I'd had no idea Wrassler could pronounce the words, let alone use them right.

"Natchez made a name in Hollywood. Movies, TV, and documentaries have been made here and the politicians were hoping that the new residents would bring another— the new residents being the owners of a newly renovated three-story building in the middle of historic downtown. Or maybe they call it uptown here." He glanced up at me again and this time I could see his grin. "All that and I get to go dancing. I am a happy man."

Wrassler danced? Somehow the muscle-bound burly guy

't strike me as the dancing type. "Wrassler, you have a way with words and a way with women," I said.

rode toward town, past shacks, trailer parks, and advertisements for tours of plantation homes, and took in the sights. The place was like something out of a Civil War movie, and we spotted some magnificent antebellum homes between the huge trunks and trailing limbs of live oaks. Most of the old homes were the traditional, Tara-in-*Gone-with-the-Wind*–style of whiteboard with lots of pediments and architectural elements made out of marble and wood, and wraparound porches. Two-story, sometimes with fancy gabled windows in the roofline. Some of the sprawling monstrosities had iron or brick privacy walls, horses prancing in the whiteboarded fields out back, and multicar garages with living space—presumably for servants—overhead. Even in town we saw homes that belonged on the covers of magazines.

started at Canal Street and worked our way in. For blocks, the town had businesses in old buildings from the eighteen hundreds: art galleries, restaurants, grills, boutiques, a bookstore, and in the middle, we passed by the town's most recently refurbished three-story building, restored, revamped (pun intended), and once owned by Hieronymus, Blood Master of Clan Hieronymus, now owned by a dead man, and being refurbished by Lucas Vazquez de Allyon, who was soon to be a true-dead vamp.

we circled the block, Eli slid down the window and took dozens of shots of the building with a camera set on burst mode. The old windows on the ground floor were swathed in silver velvet draperies, hiding the building's interior. The windows in the two upper stories had functioning copper shutters, all closed. If not for the plans on file with the county, we'd have no idea what the interior was like.

circled back around and followed GPS instructions to the bed-and-breakfast we had rented on the outskirts of town. It was a huge, three-story place landscaped with the ubiquitous live oaks and magnolias, acres of pecan trees, azaleas, and even flowering trees, which was odd for this time of year. Bruiser leaned close to the dark-tinted windows and said, "Japanese apricot and Higan cherry. Lovely."

Eli grunted and said, "This place is gonna be a bugger to secure."

"Yeah," I said to them both. That's me, full of chatter.

I left the men to unload and I knocked on the door. I was let in by the owner, a skinny, wrinkled woman with shocking red hair and no fashion sense. She was wearing gray velour elastic-waist pants pulled up over her tiny, rounded belly, a purple shirt, yellow house shoes, and an olive green scarf printed with red and blue flowers. A string of pearls that had to be at least fifty inches long was wound around her neck and rested across her belly.

"You must be Esmee," Bruiser said from behind me. He leaned past to take her hand and insinuated himself into the foyer. "I'm George Dumas."

"Ohhhh, Mr. Dumas," she twittered. "I am so honored to meet you. Anyone who knows the president is always welcome here."

"He was very complimentary about your home and domestic servants, and I understand that you took very good care of him and Nancy while they were here."

"Such a nice couple," she said, her voice high-pitched and girlish. "And even though they were Hollywood types, they seemed quite well bred."

A Hollywood president, married to Nancy? The *Reagans*? And Bruiser knew them? Sometimes I forgot that he was over a hundred years old. While he took care of the particulars, I reconnoitered the house. The downstairs was something like out of a movie set or the way really rich people lived, with antique wood furniture juxtaposed with more modern comforts, parquet floors in tri-colored woods, silk rugs, copper-coffered twelve-foot ceilings, and a maid and chef, which meant we wouldn't leave a mess or have to cook. There was a living room, dining room, kitchen, butler's pantry, wine closet, coffee bar, wet bar, billiards room, music room, TV room, servant's toilet, powder room for guests, a coat closet bigger than a small garage, and a mudroom with a full bath off the back entrance. I stuck my head out and saw a six-car garage to the left and a pool in the center of the enclosed garden. The wall around the backyard was over eight feet tall. No one would be getting in unless they could jump like I could or pole-vault in. The upstairs had eight bedrooms and five baths, and slept sixteen easily, more in a pinch—plenty of room for the rest of the men when the gear truck got here. The third story, up under the eaves, was where the servants slept and I backed out quickly when I realized I was in private quarters.

The place was amazing. I did not fit in here. Not at all. But I wasn't complaining.

I picked the smallest room and crawled into the bed. It was like lying down on air, and I punched the mattress. It swallowed my fist and then slowly returned to a flat plane. It was that memory foam stuff. I kicked off my boots, tossed my bra to the side and my weapons on the bed, curling up next to them. I had a feeling that I would get no sleep while I was here, so I was going to catnap when I got the chance. I was asleep in minutes.

I woke to the sound of gunfire, my hands grabbing for weapons.

CHAPTER SIXTEEN

And Then He Changed His Pants

I analyzed the sound patterns as I checked the Walthers, stuck one in my waistband against my spine, and shoved extra magazines in pockets. The gunfire was coming from downstairs, and I hadn't seen a shooting gallery. It was still daylight out, which meant no vamps, and I was betting there were no weres or witches living openly here; therefore it was a good guess that we were under attack by humans. De Allyon's people had heard we were here, and decided on a preemptive attack. "Dang small-town gossip factory," I whispered.

I opened the door and slid into the hallway, trying to get my sleep-clogged brain up to speed and remember the layout of the house. I shut the door behind me and quickly checked the other rooms. I didn't smell anyone, but it would be stupid to risk leaving an enemy behind me in case the external security had already been breached. Each room was empty and I closed the doors, leaving myself in shadow.

Beast moved up through me, padding softly, her head low and shoulder blades high, stalking. My vision sharpened as she slid into the forefront of my brain. I moved right, to the stairs, and down, my back against the wall, my bare feet silent, listening to the number and placement of shots, and wishing I had grabbed up my nine-mils. The weapons had better stopping power.

The gunfire was coming from the front and the back, which told me that they hadn't gotten inside yet. By the level of gunfire, I could tell that there were three bogeys at the front entrance, but only one defensive shooter inside. There were at least five bad guys in the backyard. So much for only pole-vaulters getting in over the back wall. A shotgun sounded from the back, a double-barreled boom-boom. We hadn't brought any shotguns. Had someone gotten inside?

A .380 held at my thigh in a two-hand grip, I stuck my head around the back entry opening, looked around, and stepped back, assimilating what I had seen. Eli and Wrassler were on either side of the back entrance. In the mudroom, the back window was busted out, and Esmee stood there, an old pump shotgun at her shoulder. Her scarlet hair was in disarray, and she had a fierce grin in place as she reloaded. Three pistols were on a tall stool by her hip. Oookaaay. An eighty-year-old Annie Oakley. I peeked back again. A small black low-riding SUV was parked in the yard; it hadn't been there before. Wrassler was taking aim at the wall of the garage, and when a head peeked out, he fired, a fast three-tap. He killed some brick, but the man jerked back.

"How many?" I called out between shots.

Eli swiveled his head over his shoulder as he ejected one magazine and slammed in another. "Five that I can count." His face was set in the emotionless lines of the soldier under fire, but his eyes were fierce. "Alex is in the garage. He went back out to get one of his electronic things. I don't think they know he's there."

I dialed Alex's phone, hoping it was on vibrate or that the sound of his ring tone was hidden under the gunfire. When he answered, I said, "Are you safe?"

"Are you freaking kidding me?" he whispered. "There are people with guns everywhere!"

"Are. You. Safe?"

"Yeah. For now."

"Where?"

"I locked myself in the limo."

I chuckled. "Good move. Stay there."

I ended the call and said, "Kid's good. He's locked in the limo."

Eli fired off three shots. Wrassler fired off three shots and ejected his magazine. In the mudroom, Esmee fired off two rounds and I nearly went deaf.

"I'll reload," Wrassler said, starting on the empty magazines.

"I really need to teach the Kid how to shoot," Eli grumbled. But some of the fierceness had left his eyes.

"I'll check on the front," I said. "It's gone quiet." Placing my bare feet carefully, I stepped through the house, from room to room, checking each one as I moved. When I reached the front of the house, I spotted Bruiser on one knee behind a sofa, which would provide zero protection from bullets, but did hide him from sight. Three empty magazines and a semiautomatic were at his knee. He was out of ammo or his nine-mil had jammed. In a two-hand grip was an old, long-barreled pistol, one I hadn't seen before. He was waiting for a frontal assault to come through the door. Idiot.

A shadow moved near the entrance. Then another. Two forms rushed through, moving with the speed of freshly fed blood-servants. I started to lift my weapon.

Bruiser *moved* and everything happened out of order. Faster than I could process. He straightened his back, raising above the sofa. Fired four shots, so close atop one another that they seemed to overlap, with the barest hint of a pause between shots two and three as he readjusted his aim. The two blood-servants fell, the one in front sliding sideways, hitting an easel holding an ugly painting, sending both spinning. Bruiser practically flew across the sofa and caught the painting. The other blood-servant fell with a hollow thump. Bruiser set the painting on the sofa. The easel landed with a crash on the floor. He checked the two he had dropped.

I whipped back behind the wall. *What the heck?* I had never seen anyone except a vamp move so fast. I remembered Katie saying to him, "*You will live. And still mostly human . . .*" What was Bruiser now? How close to being a blood-sucker was he?

I made a faint sound and stepped out. Bruiser was at the front entrance, scanning the yard. "We're clear here," he said, without turning around. He closed the front door with a snap, and the dead bolt settled into its slot.

"Good," I said, sounding almost normal. "I'll go help with the back, then."

Bruiser turned to me, his brown eyes taking me in. His roaming gaze paused at the sight of my bare feet, lifted, and stopped at my chest. *Oh yeah. No bra. White T-shirt.* A warm smile lit his face and he met my eyes. Beast's claws dug in hard as she stared back. Heat hit me. That deep, limb-numbing heat of unexpected, pure lust. Electric shocks sizzled through me, settling in the palms of my hands, soles of my feet. My breasts tightened. Heaviness weighted my lower belly with need.

I should be mad at Bruiser. *I am mad at him,* I thought. *He betrayed me.*

Mine, Beast thought. Which explained a lot.

Gunfire sounded from the rear of the house. A scream echoed in the backyard. I should have been moving that way. Instead, I was standing, gun gripped in both hands, as Bruiser crossed the room, slowly this time. He moved like a dancer, all lithe grace, the soles of his shoes making no sound beneath the concussive damage to my ears. Beast held me down and unmoving.

The gunfire at the back of the house fell silent. Our side had won, I guessed.

Bruiser holstered the long-barreled weapon in a shoulder holster and took my Walther out of my hand. His other slid around my nape, under my braid. He leaned into me, his body so heated it radiated through my clothes. Burning. His mouth landed on mine. Crushing, his teeth hitting, clacking against mine. I dropped my head back into his palm, and some feral sound came from my mouth, part moan, part purr, all need. His tongue slid between my lips. He smelled like caramel, like heated brown sugar, with a hint of something spicy. He cupped my backside, the gun hard and cold, his hand, holding it and me, felt like heated velvet.

I melded to him, his taller body fitting over mine as if we were made for it. He shoved me to the wall at my back. The cold gun vanished. His hot hand lifted me, his fingers so close—*so close*—to where I wanted them. He lifted me, and my legs went around him, my ankles locking at his spine. I pressed my center against his hard, long length. Wanting ...

His other hand slid down the side of my neck and across my collarbone, floated over my breast, slowing, tightening, fingers pulling at my nipple through my T. My hands were inside his shirt, sliding across his shoulders. Buttons flew.

A bark of pain sounded above renewed gunfire at the back. We jerked apart, our eyes holding, our breathing fast, oxygen starved. "This is nuts," I whispered.

"Bad timing. A bed. Later." He dropped me and handed me my Walther. Drew his long-barrel. In sync, we moved down the hall, Bruiser at point. I tried to remember how to breathe.

Wrassler should have been down, as a wound bled at his left side near his waist, soaking his dark blue pants black, but he was on one knee, firing single shots out the back, clearly low on ammo. Esmee was at the window, sighting down a target pistol. Eli was outside; he sprinted across the yard, zigzagging. Esmee took three steady shots, cover fire. A form behind the pool fell forward and then rolled back into the foliage. Eli tore for the garage. Someone rose from the garage roof, aiming down. I started to shout, but Bruiser raced through the short hallway and into the yard, into the sunlight, raising his weapon. *Moving.* Faster than I had ever seen a human move. Or almost human.

He leaped, his body going horizontal over the hood of the car. In midair, he fired. Up. Three shots. He landed on the other side, somehow on his feet. Wrassler cursed at the speed and the perfect landing. The man on the roof fell forward and slid down the roof tiles. Dead.

That was seven shots. Bruiser had to be almost out of ammo. "How many bad guys left?" I called out.

Esmee shouted from the mudroom, "One in the yard, three o'clock. I got him in my sights."

"One in the garage," Wrassler said.

"Esmee, hold fire," I shouted. I dove into the yard. Esmee did not hold fire. Instead she laid down cover fire, each shot behind me but so close I wondered if they were tearing through my clothes. I reached the side of the garage, stepping over the dead human on the ground. He was staring at the sky, his mouth open, eyes already drying. I smelled feces on the cool air.

Bruiser whirled at my movement, checking himself before he fired. "There's one in the garage with Eli," I said. "Blood-servant." Which meant faster than human, better eyesight than human, better reflexes than human. Eli was good, no doubt, but none of us knew how good yet. "Kid's supposed to be in the limo," I reminded him.

Bruiser nodded once. "I'm faster."

Yeah. He was. I checked the yard. Safety'd, tossed him my Walther, and drew the one at my spine, surprised it had survived the romp in the hallway. "Go," I said.

Bruiser leaped straight off the ground in a move so cat-like that Beast hacked with delight. Still in the air, he soared through the open garage door. I heard him land, a faint scuff of sound. Two shots sounded, echoing in the garage. Behind me, Esmee fired two shots. The last bogey in the yard fell into the bushes. I ran from cover and checked each of the downed. One was still alive, gut-shot, in agony. He'd probably live if he got to a hospital in time.

A barrage of shots sounded in the garage, then silence. Eli and Bruiser carried a woman from the garage and tossed her to the dirt. Dead. The Kid peeked around the garage door, his face white and eyes wide, an armful of electronic devices clutched to his chest.

It was only then that I realized I hadn't fired a single shot. I started laughing.

This wasn't something that we could cover up. Sirens sounded in the distance, closing fast. Neighbors, or maybe Esmee, had called 911. To avoid questions, I took my unfired gun upstairs and secured it. In minutes the house was surrounded by cops. Esmee trotted out to them, a big smile on her face. She had taken the time to smooth her hair and put on lipstick, and she looked the perfect hostess in her bright floral scarf and her pearls. Bruiser, still in his dress slacks with an unbuttoned shirt, the tails billowing out behind him, followed her, his cell phone to his ear. He looked like a fashion shoot from *GQ*—one titled "The Morning After." Around and in the house were dead humans, their blood soaking into the parquet flooring and the sculpted garden loam.

Only in the South.

An ambulance pulled up, the EMTs treating Wrassler's wound and the wounded bad guy before leaving with the injured man and two cops riding shotgun. More cops arrived—more than half the cops in the county and the town gathering, with plenty of plainclothed guys all trying to be the big dog. Alex and I were the only ones who hadn't fired a shot. To prove that assertion, neither of us had any GSR on us. The others of our group were herded into different parts of the house and questioned, the cops relentless and suspicious. Alex and I sat on the couch, Alex intent on his electronic searches, shaking from time to time, his body odor sour with hormones, fresh panic, and old fear.

At one point, however, the OIC—officer in charge of the shooting scene—made a call. Then, newly elected Adams County sheriff Sylvia Turpin, who was the many-times great-granddaughter of the county's first sheriff, drove up in her marked car. Turpin took her job very seriously, especially when she discovered that Leo Pellissier's primo was on-site. Seemed that Leo had contributed a hefty sum to her election campaign. After that discovery, Turpin made a series of phone calls, several of the plainclothes cops took calls, and things began to move along.

Within half an hour, the state crime lab had arrived, bringing a medical examiner, and we were free to go, though not free to leave town. I wondered who had called in the big guns. Remembering the cell phone at his ear, I was guessing Bruiser. As the MOC's primo and point man, he might be the most powerful human—part human—in the South, governors and senators included, and when he called in favors, things would naturally go his way. A New Orleans blood-servant pulled up in an SUV and consulted with Bruiser, the cops, and the petite, pretty, redheaded little sheriff. While the powers-that-be conferred, the rest of us retired to the dining room.

The unflappable chef had laid out a feast. Or I'd thought him unflappable until I heard him telling the cops he'd hidden under a small table in the butler's pantry during the shooting. And then he'd changed his pants. It was his vehicle out back. He had been grocery-shopping when we arrived, which was why I hadn't seen the SUV.

We gathered for snacks in the dining room, which had a carved mahogany table and chairs, and a wall-long hand-carved and painted china cabinet. The room would seat twenty easily, and the chandelier over our heads was the real thing—twenty-four-karat gilt and hundreds of lead crystals. The snack, thrown together in minutes, was brie, fresh fruit, sliced homemade rye bread, and ten pounds of rare roast beef with sandwich makings dished up in cut-crystal bowls. There was also red beans and rice and barbecued Andouille sausage. Finger-licking, to-die-for sausage. The fighters were starving, adrenaline breakdown needing fuel. I hadn't been involved in the fighting, but with my skinwalker metabolism, I was always hungry. Which likely had something to do with the little clinch in the hallway. But still . . .

I ate two sandwiches, mostly meat and brie, remembering Bruiser's hands on me, his mouth on me, while the guys discussed what we had to do.

"We can't stay here and wait until nightfall when our full backup arrives," Wrassler said.

"We can't storm the three-story building without them," Eli said. "It would be stupid."

"We're down to two healthy shooters," Bruiser said.

"Three," I said through a mouthful of food. "What am I? Chopped liver?"

"A woman," he said.

My eyes went cold and narrow. The table went silent, all the eyes on me. Bruiser stopped, a sandwich halfway to his mouth. He held it there, his mouth open, thinking. He turned his eyes to me, his head not moving. I didn't smile. He blinked once, took a bite, and chewed, still thinking, letting his eyes roam the room and out into the hallway where we had recently had that very unsatisfying clinch. When he swallowed, he said, "Four shooters, one injured. Forgive the automatic, ingrained stupidities of an old man."

Alex snickered into the silence. I finished chewing my bite and swallowed. "Don't let it happen again." Eli looked at Bruiser, at me, and to the hallway, his eyes considering. I reached for an apple and bit down, the crunch seeming to break the tension.

"So we have four shooters and they're down seven. And they won't be expecting us," Wrassler said.

"It's daylight. The fangheads will be asleep, right?" Alex said.

"Fiction. They can stay awake if they have to, and they can stand a little sunlight, especially the old ones." Wrassler emptied a Coke down his throat and popped the top on another. "From the intel—"

"What intel?" I asked.

"One of Leo's blood-servants is related to one of Hieronymus' servants. He asked some questions and provided us some answers. We've got maybe ten old ones in there, plus their blood-meals. No way we can take them."

"Most Mithrans travel with two blood-servants apiece," Bruiser said, "so if they hold true, then we would be facing ten masters and the remainder of their servants, thirteen humans."

Alex asked, "Do we have access to a helicopter?" Every head in the room turned to him. He spun the laptop around so we could see a schematic of the roof of the three-story building the vamps had taken over. There was a large, new air-conditioning unit and plenty of room for a helo to land, providing the structure could handle it, or for soldiers to drop down if not. And the AC vent was a specific weakness to the entire building.

Bruiser started to smile.

CHAPTER SEVENTEEN

I Disliked Her on Sight

The helo would be in position over the building in thirty minutes. We were parked down the street, geared up, watching the place from the back. Grégoire was not going to be happy when he saw the damage incurred on his new limo in the shoot-out. My official cell vibrated in my pocket. Ricky Bo LaFleur's picture appeared on the front. My heart did a little flutter. I opened the cell and said, "Hi." There must have been something odd about my tone, because all the men looked at me at once. I turned my back to them and heard Rick say, "Where—you?" There was a horrible roar in the background and he was breaking up.

"In Natchez. Where are you?"

"In a helicopter wi . . . razy former marines."

I put it together fast. "You and Derek are on the way *here*?"

"Yeah . . . mi. . . . and once this little problem . . . we can take off . . . play." The call clicked off. I wiped my mouth, hoping I was smearing off the goofy smile. I turned back around. "We have official government backup from the Psychometry Law Enforcement Division of Homeland Security."

Bruiser nodded. "I wasn't sure he'd be able to pull it off."

"*You* did this?"

"Yes." His eyes met mine. "As primo."

"Ah," I said, my heart plummeting. That was that. So much for the hot and heavy clinch in the hall. His duty to Leo came first, and keeping us on the right side of the law was a big part of that. Not that I could complain. Ricky Bo was coming and my big-cat was happy.

"Masks," Eli said.

I pulled the mask over my face. Eli had found them for sale at a gun shop in New Orleans and identified them as "Israeli M-15 military models with Nato filters." Whatever. I just wanted mine to keep me alive. I settled the mask in place and tested it by breathing deeply before Eli released the foul-smelling smokeless bomb in the confines of the limo. Stink filled the car. I didn't smell a thing, though breathing wasn't easy and the mask was hot and uncomfortable. But I smelled nothing gross and gave Eli a thumbs-up.

Eli had informed us that sleeping gas didn't exist, but the military had something that worked short-term on humans. He'd be using that on the building. I didn't ask what it was or where he got it, and he didn't volunteer. I vaguely recalled that the Russians had tried something on a theater full of people once and managed to kill most of them. I just hoped the U.S. military stuff worked better.

Thanks to Derek's suppliers and the truck that had followed us up here, we were all dressed in night camo with Kevlar vests, combat boots, utility belts, shooting gloves— the kind with the knuckles and fingertips bare—ear protectors that doubled as radio receivers, and enough gear to start a small war. Bruiser had guns holstered everywhere and carried the pump shotgun borrowed from Esmee. Wrassler had a totally illegal, fully automatic, compact machine gun and enough magazines to shoot for fifteen minutes at full auto. Enough ammo to melt the barrel of his gun, assuming the heat buildup from firing didn't jam it first, which was all too likely.

I had all my blades and stakes—including two new, longer, special-made ones—in sheaths and loops, and my Walthers holstered at my spine and under my left arm. One was loaded with silver for vamps and the other with standard ammo. My M4 Benelli was loaded for vamp with seven silver fléchette rounds, and I had another seven in special loops in a thigh pouch. But if I needed to reload, I would likely be dead before I could finish. The shotgun was slung at the ready and strapped in place under my right arm. The positioning was Wrassler's idea, and though I'd never fought with the M4 strapped there, it felt good. I wouldn't have to pull the shotgun from its spine sheath and ready it for firing. I just had to stabilize, point, and shoot. The webbing left me room to maneuver the weapon enough to aim and fire, and was relatively easy to pull free for full manual positioning.

"Com check," Derek said over the radio. Instantly, we could hear the helo in the radio system background. He called our names or monikers out one at a time, and when he said, "Legs," I replied, "Got 'em." Everyone laughed. It was hard to see his expression with the mask in the way, but I thought Bruiser's eyes were twinkling.

"Canisters?" Eli asked Bruiser and me.

I touched the three canisters at my belt; they were marked CS. It was the new pressurized colloidal silver stuff for use on vamps and I didn't know how they would work. No one did. When the canister was activated, it would spew an ionized silver mist into the air. Every time vamps took a breath—if they did before it dissipated—they'd get a lungful. It wouldn't mean instant death, but it might slow them down and poison them.

"On my go," Eli said. This was his gig. I had no training for paramilitary raids. My combat style was more along the lines of stake 'em and run. Eli pulled his mask off, grabbed a black mesh bag, and slid out of the car. He disappeared into an alley at a fast jog.

He had reconnoitered the alley earlier and found some old wood back stairs on the two-story building adjacent to the three-story one, housing our target. He was going to ascend the steps of the two-story building, make his way to the roof, toss a grapnel across to the adjacent walled roof, and then haul himself up to the roof next door. The last part was an eighteen-foot climb. Which I would like to see, but I wasn't part of the roof assault.

Six minutes later he said, "I'm in. Gas is a go." Which meant in six minutes he had climbed up the fire escape, then to the roof adjacent, found an access for the air conditioner, removed its air intake panel, and started the gas. Go, Rangers, go, army.

Based on estimated cubic feet, Eli had calculated the number of canisters needed to knock out the building, and how long it would take. Then he added two canisters. Waiting sucked. I looked at the time. Sunset was in fourteen minutes. In fourteen minutes, the vamps could take an attack into the streets. We were cutting it close.

I could hear the helo's rotors beating the air. The helo got closer, the noise louder. Leo's helicopter wasn't a sleek, modern, quiet-operating model, but an older helo, a refurbished Vietnam Era Bell Huey, with heavy armament and retrofitted with lots of modern bells and whistles. I was pretty sure that most of the bells were not entirely legal, and owning the whistles was likely a felony but well worth the risk. If we had to shoot the vamps with missiles, the helo had the capability, I thought dryly.

The helo was directly overhead, the tail rotor over the alley. Dark blobs dropped out—Derek Lee and his buddies. I wondered if Angel Tit was among them, and knew he must be, the Tequila Boys as well. There were too many men for just the Vodka Boys cadre. I wondered which one was Rick.

If I thought it was weird to have so many men I was interested in all in one place, my inner cat was just happy about it.

"Go. Go. Go," Eli said over the com, and Bruiser, Wrassler, and I leaped from the limo. Because of his injury, Wrassler's job was to cover the back entrance and make sure no one got away or came in to help the bad guys. Bruiser and I raced through the alley for the frontal assault, my breathing doing that whole Darth Vader wheeze inside the mask. I pulled on Beast's speed to keep up with him. We rounded the front together, and sent two women screaming away. I had a glimpse of a sleeping baby in a backpack.

Bruiser took out the front window with a ball-peen hammer. Glass shattered and fell, the sound muffled by the ear protectors. Bruiser raked the glass out with the hammer and leaped through. I followed, glass still falling. He disappeared behind the silver velvet draperies. My first job was to yank the draperies down and let in sunlight. The velvet came down fast, along with the metal track that supported it, flooding the space with light and revealing only an entrance to a hallway that opened both left and right.

Bruiser had disappeared to my right. I entered the hallway to the left, sliding my spine against the wall. I heard nothing except my heavy breathing, smelled nothing except the filtered air, and saw even less, thanks to the mask. On the upper floor, the guys were clearing rooms: I could hear it through the communication gear. On the roof, Eli was supposed to be doing his magic and reversing the powerful AC fan to air out the gas from the building so the guys could pull off the masks and pull on low-light-vision gear, but it would take time, and every second would just be pissing off the vamps. Fortunately, I didn't need low-light gear. I had Beast.

She rose in me like a wraith, and my vision sharpened, turning the world silvery bright. My heart pounded steadily in my ears. I moved down the hallway. There were no doors except at the ends, which was odd. I was hearing nothing. Except the radio chatter of the men. No one was on the third floor. No one at all. *Again—odd.*

I stepped through the doorway at the end of the hall into an open room. It looked like a reception room, and a woman was facedown at a desk. I raced over and checked her pulse. Steady, if a little slow. I secured her hands behind her back with two zip strips and moved around the desk to a door in the back. Carefully, I opened it. The room beyond was pitch-black except for tiny red and green lights, like on computers when they're asleep, or on battery backups. But I couldn't use my nose to smell vamp, which I hated. I was head-blind.

I pulled a flashbang and tossed it inside. Turned my head away and closed my eyes. It exploded, the flash white through my closed lids. I raced in and stopped, listening, hearing nothing. I had to get out of this headgear. As soon as I could breathe.

From nowhere, I took a blow to my chest that threw me across the room. I rolled to my feet and pulled two blades. I couldn't fire a gun—there might be sleeping humans in the room. I felt, more than saw, movement and struck out with the blades, cutting in a figure-eight pattern. I hit nothing. And I took another blow. This one to my head. It knocked my mask askew. I took an involuntary half breath and smelled sleep-bomb and vamp. The scents were vaguely like boiled eggs and vamp-spice tea, an unpleasant combo to my

Beast-enhanced nose, though the humans the vamp hunted probably liked her spicy scent. Holding my breath, I pulled the mask back in place. I yanked loose a CS canister, set it on the floor, and activated the nozzle. Hit the halogen light on my vest.

The room lit up like stadium lights and revealed a vamp right in front of me. She gripped my right arm and snapped down, around, and would have pulled me off my feet, except I knew that move and I followed her, dropping with her. I grabbed her ankle, threw it into the air. Dove under her legs. CS mist coated my mask, further depleting my view of the world. I wiped at it, smearing it worse. The halogen light bounced around the room, revealing and hiding, illuminating and throwing bizarre shadows dancing drunkenly on the walls. It was disorienting and Beast hurled more speed and her spatial awareness into my bloodstream.

The light hit the vamp in the face. She was vamped out, two-inch-long fangs and pupils like black saucers. Her face was bleeding. Her eyes were bleeding and watering. She took a breath and started coughing, the action so unexpected to her that she fell to her knees. She looked up at me, her face shocked. I wondered how many centuries since she'd had to cough. The CS was working in ways I hadn't expected. The vamp rolled to her back, breathing and coughing, clutching her throat. I pulled one of the special stakes and stabbed downward with both hands. The stake was way longer than my usual ones, at thirty inches. I rammed it into her belly. Blood sprayed up, but not the fountain I sometimes saw. I had missed her descending aorta. Caught on her belt buckle. I put my back into it.

The stake had a silver cap on the sharp end with a steel tip that I drove into the floor, pinning her down, poisoning her blood on the way through, in addition to the silver spraying into the air. She wasn't true-dead, and she might even survive, but she was in a lot of pain. She wouldn't be getting up anytime soon.

Over the com gear, I learned that one of the rooftop teams was entering the second story. They had already secured three humans, all of whom were starting to wake up. I also heard heavy, steady breathing and the sound of blades clashing.

Clicking off the halogen light, I moved on through the room and out another door, into a larger room, maybe half the total square footage of the bottom story. The open area was dim, lit by a single bulb hanging from the ceiling. Bruiser was already in the room. Part of the panting I heard over my com channel was him. He was fighting two very old, and very strong, vamps, one armed with a long sword and one bare-handed, claws extended.

I could barely follow the moves, the swoosh of afterimage giving it all a filmlike speed. Bruiser was fighting with a midsized blade in each hand and it was almost beautiful, poetry in motion. I had given him the blades two months ago, after I took them from the body of a vamp I'd killed. Bruiser had been mesmerized by them, calling them something Asian, in a language I didn't recognize. He had obviously been practicing, and even more obvious—he was no novice. With the vamp-blood in his system, he was a master work of art. He flew through the moves, the blades an extension of his will and his mind. The vamps were bleeding. And Bruiser had removed his mask. I yanked mine off and it fell to the end of the flex strap to dangle behind me out of the way. I took an exploratory breath and smelled the egg-stink, but felt fine.

On the other side of Bruiser, a door opened and three more vamps entered. They were far closer to Bruiser and his fight than I was. Bruiser was good, but not one-on-five good. I ran right at them, screaming in challenge, a big-cat scream of rage. I pulled and tossed a flashbang and a CS canister at them. Shouted, "Flash!" hoping Bruiser would understand. I leaped right at the closest vamp, sliding my hand around the stock of the M4 in midair. Tucked my feet out of the way, and fired, closing my eyes.

The flashbang and CS went off. I opened my eyes just in time to land. I kicked laterally into a vamp's knee joint. Heard the crunch over the ear protectors. He was falling down and away, coughing, his blood spouting from neck and chest, bubbling from the silver shotgun wounds. He was one of the vamps with acidic blood. It burned where it splattered on my exposed knuckles. I staked him in the belly, low down. Flipped him over and secured his hands with three zip strips, knowing they weren't made for a vamp's strength, but hoping the injuries and the silver he was breathing would weaken him enough to hold him for a while. He was coughing like he had a bad case of pneumonia or had just been pulled from the water, drowning. So were the other two vamps who had come in with him, both on the floor coughing and bleeding from the eyes, the silver mist in the air burning their skin. They looked like they both had really, *really* bad sunburns. Just to make sure they stayed down, I staked them both in the lower bellies and secured them with zip strips. I'd have to get some silvered strips. Yeah. Why hadn't I thought about that before now?

I clicked off the light and turned to see Bruiser finish off the two he'd been fighting. He stabbed, twisted, and slid the blade out of one. That vamp fell to his knees. Bruiser cut across a biceps of the last one, hitting bone, and caught the long sword the vamp dropped. Using the new blade, he took the vamp's head, whirled, and took the head of the other one.

"There can be only one," I murmured, and started laughing. Bruiser turned to me so fast I felt the air blow past my face. He swung the long sword back to attack. Beast slammed into me and I leaped away, across the room, landed, and pulled both Walthers. "Bruiser? It's Jane."

The room went still. Bruiser's face was emotionless, a mask. No recognition, no warmth. He hesitated for a space of three heartbeats. He advanced on me, stepping fastfast-fast.

"Don't make me shoot you," I said, backing away.

One of the vamps I had staked and secured kicked out at me, drawing Bruiser's attention. That was all I needed. I dove at him, swinging, knocking his head with the butt of the gun in my right hand. Not a nice way to treat a handgun, not to mention a head. They hit together with a satisfying thud and Bruiser dropped, catching himself with his open sword hand, holding the long sword with only a finger and thumb. When he looked up, he shook his head. "Jane?"

"Yeah. We'll talk about this later. Six vamps down. Weapons fire from upstairs." I pointed across the room. "We need to check that." *That* was the old bank vault and the specially built safe room to its side.

We moved slowly across the open space to the room. It

was built from cinder block reinforced with rebar and concrete. It had its own roof, flat and smelling of tar paper, about three feet from the warehouse ceiling. My eyes had acclimated to the dimness of the windowless place, but the inside of the room was blacker than pitch. I pulled the halogen light from my belt and shined it into the room.

The room was twelve feet square, with a six-foot-across circle in the middle made of salt. There was no pentagram, no runes, no magical elements to guide a witch in a working. But there was a body. A recently dead body. She was hanging from the rafters by a rope, her big toes barely touching the floor. She was naked. With a stake in her heart. Her fangs were small, marking her as, maybe, a hundred years old.

"Sacrifice," Bruiser said.

"Yeah. And her blood smells funny."

"One of the sick ones."

"I'd say so," I said, turning for the old bank vault. I shined my light inside. The metal shelves were bare. Whatever had been planned for this room either hadn't been finished or had been carted out already.

"Report," Eli said into my earpieces.

The fighters upstairs started reporting in. "One old vamp DB. Two humans contained. No injuries. Did not sight de Allyon." In the shorthand Derek used for ops, *DB* meant dead body, *contained* meant uninjured and restrained. *No injuries* referred to the men under Derek's command. *Not de Allyon* meant the vamp wasn't the one we were after.

"Danced with three humans, now contained. They were waking up and we had to hurt 'em some. No injuries. Did not sight de Allyon." It sounded like Tequila Blue Voodoo, proving that Derek had brought a mixed party of his men.

"One young fanghead DB, two humans contained. We're beat all to hell and back, but don't need anything except beer," Angel Tit said. "Did not sight de Allyon."

"One vamp, age indeterminate, DB, two injuries. Medic needed for John. Not life-threatening. I need a couple of stitches," an unfamiliar voice said. "Did not sight de Allyon." I thought it was El Diablo, who I had last seen feeding a vamp on the field of battle.

Eli said, "One old sucker DB. I'll be joining you for those

stitches and that beer." The men chuckled. "Cheek Sneak and I did not sight de Allyon."

"No vamps encountered," Rick said. "Three humans contained, no injuries, did not sight de Allyon.

Bruiser said, "Two old vamps DB." The mics went silent for that one. Bruiser had taken down two *very* old vampires. Single-handedly. "Did not sight de Allyon," he said. "But we did find one younger vamp, DB, on ice, true-dead." He looked at me and grinned, teasing. "Legs? That leaves you."

I frowned at him. Into my mic I said, "One human contained. Four old vamps contained." The radio traffic went silent. "No injuries. Did not sight de Allyon," I added, that important piece of info just hitting me.

"She buggered the rest of you and left us some vamps to chat with," Bruiser said. "Janie wins the pool."

There was a pool?

"This I gotta see," one of the guys said.

"Not until we go over this place with a fine-tooth comb. Lock it down," Eli said. "We want de Allyon."

Bruiser and I quartered off the lower floor and went through it again. There weren't many rooms, only one unisex toilet, and no closets or hiding places. It was fast work. "First floor clear," I said into the mic. We started up to the second floor. Five steps in, I heard something and looked back. "Correction. Two coming this way."

That was when we were hit with the second wave. Vamps came rushing out of the new, empty safe room and up the stairs with reptilian speed and grace, vamped out, screaming. *Hungry.* I could smell their hunger and their sickness. These were infected, and I had no idea where they had come from. The dang vault and cinder-block room had been empty.

I fired the shotgun, hitting the first one midcenter. Beside me, Bruiser stepped down two steps and took the head of the second one, the long sword in one hand, one of the lovely midsized swords in the other. Blood fountained up from her stump. I fired at the third vamp, knocking him back. Bruiser took the head of the two I had hit while I finished up the rounds in the M4. When all seven rounds were gone, I pulled the Walthers and started in with head shots, slowing them down, Bruiser to my side, finishing them off. Soldiers poured down the steps to back us up, and we took the fight down to the first floor, spreading out. And still the vamps came.

There was no grace, no finesse. It was just battle. Just blood and the stink of gunfire. I saw two of ours go down in the melee, and vamps fell on them to drink. Eli and Derek waded into them, stakes and blades flashing. I took a set of talons across one arm, a fist to the gut, and a round-house kick to the kidneys. It was three on one and I went down. Rule number one when fighting vamps. Stay on your feet.

I was still falling when the first vamp fell on me. Oofed out a breath it didn't need and went flying, a boot in the air in front of my face. A short sword followed, taking off another vamp's forearm with one swipe. Rick reached down and pulled me up, his fingers like steel bands on my unhurt arm. He swung me around and supported me with an arm around my waist until I was steady. Until I had drawn two vamp-killers. "Payback isn't *always* a bitch," he said.

I laughed. I'd saved his life a couple of times. Now he'd saved mine.

It went on and on. And when it was over, Bruiser and Rick were standing back to back, heaving breaths. Derek and I were against a wall, two downed soldiers at our feet, where we were protecting them. Three other of the men he had brought were still standing, but all were wounded. Two were dead. Derek hit 911 and called for medic.

Around us were fourteen vamps. *Only fourteen?* It seemed like hundreds. But none of them were de Allyon. Lucas de Allyon had not been in his base camp.

All the blood and fighting and death had been for nothing. Wasted. My eyes filled with tears that I blinked away. I wiped my face. Vamp blood was burning me. "*Crap.* Crap, crap, *crap*," I whispered.

Near me, a man moaned. I opened my cell and called Leo. Fortunately, he was already on his way. He'd be here quickly and would heal the injured humans. I closed the cell and looked up to see six humans emerge from a wall. Not a doorway, but a wall, a hidden opening to a hidden room. It hadn't been on the plans submitted to the planning commission. Vamps who broke the law. Imagine that. I almost started laughing until I got a whiff of the blood-servants. They all smelled of the vamp sickness.

Derek covered them and made them sit down with their hands on their heads. I thought about the sick and bleeding Asheville vamps. Here was a treatment that might save them until we figured out how Sabina had healed that guy ... the vamp ... the dumb pretty one whose name was totally gone from my exhausted brain. Callan! Yeah. Callan. I texted Leo. "Humans here have antibody to illness. Send to Asheville?"

Instantly he texted back "On the next plane."

Gotta love modern forms of communication. Then I texted to Adelaide "Got treatment. Will send ASAP." I closed my phone. And slid down a wall to sit on the floor.

Eli wandered over, his combat face still in place, looking hard and remote. He stood next to me, staring out over the battlefield, and when he spoke, his lips didn't move, a sotto voce not even vamps could have overheard. "The marine called Cheek Sneak. I caught him taking pics and texting. I took his phone. You want I should give it to Alex?"

"Yeah," I said, and closed my eyes. Had we finally found our other tattletale? "If you prove he's been talking to the enemy, tell me first. Not Derek."

Eli breathed a low laugh through his nose. "Copy that." He meandered away.

"You're hurt."

I opened my eyes and looked at Rick. "So are you," I said. He was burned and limping, and blood crusted his knuckles as if he'd hit a wall. Or maybe beat in a vamp's face. Either one sounded like him.

"My were-taint will heal it," he said, offhand. "But yours is bad." He knelt, lifted my arm, and I saw that blood coated my sleeve. He peeled back the cut cloth to reveal the injury, three oozing wounds, parallel, made by vamp talons. The lacerations were about two inches across and cut into the deltoid muscle deeply enough that when he pressed it open, a tiny pulse of blood started, rhythmic and steady. A tiny artery had been severed.

"I'll heal it when I shift," I murmured.

Rick sat beside me and opened a military med kit on his belt. Inside was a tourniquet, the kind a medic put on a severed limb to stop the bleeding, packages of sterile gauze and alcohol pads and cleanser. Stuff to sew up a wound, black thread and tiny curved needles. A syringe of clear fluid. It was marked MORPHINE.

"You are not sewing me up," I said.

Rick laughed. "No. I'm not. But I will pack it until we can get out of here."

"Okay. Sure."

I watched as he tore away my sleeve and cleaned and bandaged my wound. He tied the gauze snugly and wound cling wrap around my arm. It *hurt*, but I watched his hands, sure and steady as he worked. I smelled his scent, sweat and blood and cat. When he was done, he raised his eyes to me and smiled, flashing that small crooked bottom tooth. A shiver cut through me, burning and icy.

Rick lifted a hand and touched my burned face. Gently. So gently. I closed my eyes, inhaling him. Wanting him, and knowing that I couldn't have him without risking contracting the were-taint. "You smell so good," I whispered.

"I miss you," he whispered.

"I miss you too," I said. "This so sucks."

He chuckled. "Yeah. It does. What's worse, now I have a job that's likely to pit us against each other way too often." And then he was gone, taking his med kit and its little syringe to a soldier we had thought was dead but who was still with us. In agony.

I looked up to find Eli's gray eyes on me, a strange look on his face, an odd amalgam of something sharper than mere curiosity, more intense than suspicion. And maybe something like longing. It took me by surprise. He studied me and I studied him. And then he turned away.

A bit less than an hour after sunset, Leo arrived in a rented, extra-long stretch limo. With him was Sabina, the outclan priestess, healed of the disease that had taken her down, and three blood-servants chosen for battle experience, more so than beauty. Lounging on the beautiful upholstery was Grégoire, Leo's *secondo* heir, dressed in sky blue silk pajamas. Next to him on the long seat were the surprises. Rick introduced his unit—a werewolf stuck in wolf form, and Pea, a juvenile grindylow—and with them was his supervisor at PsyLED. Her name was Soul. She was gorgeous.

Soul could have been anywhere from forty to sixty, the kind of woman who was ageless and sexy and sultry, and made all the men in visual distance perk up and think about taking her to the nearest hotel. She had smooth olive skin and black, flashing eyes and platinum hair, the kind nature gives some formerly black-haired women. It hung down her back in long, supple waves. And she had curves in all the right places. I disliked her on sight.

I stepped back behind the wall and studied her. Soul was wearing some kind of long, floating, diaphanous dress made of layers of silk gauze that brushed her feet. Over it she wore a watered silk coat to her knees. She was wearing a pair of black dancing shoes with straps over the instep that I coveted. Around her neck was a thin gold chain with a solid gold apple depending from it. In Beast sight, she glowed with the heat of magical energies, not witch, not were, but something not human. She was also carrying a staff with a psy-meter mounted on the top. A supernat working for PsyLED. *Great. Just freaking ducky.*

Soul, the wolf, and Pea went straight to Rick. Leo came straight to me. Instantly I flashed on the forced feeding, the pain and the fury and the helplessness. My hands clenched, but I forced down my reaction, knowing that anything I felt he could read in my body language, or smell drifting from my pores. I took a slow breath and blew it out.

"Report," Leo said. It sounded like a military command and I was forced to remember that Leo had fought in wars for centuries, Grégoire at his side, as he was now. Or leading the way. Despite his slight build, delicate form, and silk pjs, or perhaps because of it all, Grégoire was a fierce warrior. I'd seen him jump in front of a bound demon armed with nothing but a sword and zeal. Leo was scary in totally different ways. The MOC was just freaky powerful.

"We beat 'em. I guess. But your enemy wasn't here. Sorry, Leo."

He lifted one black brow in that elegant and infuriating way he had, and said, "You are bleeding. Humans are dead. Mithrans are dead, and their blood smells of disease. I require details, *my Enforcer.*"

I sighed. And there it was. The instigating factor of all the crap I was in just now—my claim to be his Enforcer.

And then Leo leaned in, his nose near my collarbone. He sniffed once, delicately, and stood back, his face puzzled. He turned to his second and said, "Something is different."

Grégoire leaned in as well and sniffed. He said, "Your bonding with your Enforcer has undergone a metamorphosis."

Oh, crap. They could tell that by my *smell*?

Grégoire clasped his hands behind his back and walked in a half circle around me like I was a mare he might buy. I narrowed my eyes at him. If I hadn't been so weak from blood loss, I might've socked him. "Interesting," Grégoire said.

To a blood-servant standing at his back, Leo said, "Bring my injured *servant* a chair before she falls supine."

CHAPTER EIGHTEEN

One Punch with a Set of Brass Knucks

I refused the chair. I was feeling stubborn and ornery. I sat, bloody and exhausted, on the floor of the first level, my back to the wall, watching the cleanup. My involvement here was done. The battle between Leo and de Allyon had resulted in the death of humans, attacked by diseased vamps. Two of Derek's men had sustained life-threatening injuries, Vodka Martini and Vodka Lime Rickey. Even with a good supply of vamp-blood to heal them, they might not make it. Vampira Carta had been bypassed, we had a vamp war on our hands, and I had no idea where de Allyon was. I hated to think that things couldn't get much worse—because they always could. They always did.

A congressional committee had been looking at the supernatural problem as it related to law enforcement for ages, trying to come up with a way to apply human law to supernatural creatures. So far, they had not been successful, but scuttlebutt in the vamp hunting community said that PsyLED had been granted sweeping powers to deal with it. With us.

The human police agencies were now involved in this situation, and PsyLED, with Rick acting as OIC and PI, the officer in charge and principal investigator. It was his first big case, and he was coming up with a laundry list of legal charges against the enemy vamps still alive. Rick had called in the crime scene investigators from PsyLED HQ. He had also informed us that the witch circle in the middle of the cinder-block room had been a portal to a cell holding hungry vamps. Like, how was I supposed to know that? And how did he?

Soul followed Rick around like one of his pets, observing and evaluating, agreeing with everything Rick said. Rick was her prized pupil. My arm throbbed. My skin burned. Jealousy skulked through me on pointy little claws.

Close to midnight, Rick finally circled back to me. He knelt near me and said, "You look like hell. You need to shift."

"You say the sweetest things."

He chuckled, looking over his crime scene, and went suddenly silent. His wolf was sitting beside Soul, and the werewolf had dropped his head. His hackles rose. He stood and prowled across the room toward us slowly, lifting his paws one at a time, as if he'd just sighted prey. And the prey was me. I watched the huge white wolf, not moving, freezing like a rabbit in the grass. The wolf wasn't a real wolf, but a werewolf who had been zapped with angel power and was now stuck in wolf form. Pea rode his back, the green catlike grindylow's claws caught in the beautiful fur. The wolf sped up, almost trotting, his eyes on me, and Pea hissed in warning, tightening her grip.

"Brute, hold," Rick commanded. The wolf stopped, but his growl went up in volume. Soul studied us across the room, surprised. Pea chattered and yanked on the wolf's fur, agitated. Rick said, "What's gotten into him?"

"Me, I think." To the were, I said, "I took you down once. I can take you down again. And your pet Pea will slit your throat if you bite me. You better think about that before you try to get back at me."

"You took him down?" Rick asked.

"Yeah. When he was in human form. One punch with a set of brass knucks. I think I broke his jaw."

Brute, which was a good name for the werewolf, growled deep in his throat, more a vibration than a sound. His silver-blue eyes bored into me. Pea hissed and dug in with her claws; the scent of werewolf blood flooded out. I started laughing, which was probably not the smartest thing I could have done, but I was so tired I couldn't hold it in.

Rick stepped to the pair and put his hand on Brute's side. The vibration stopped. Brute lowered his head in threat, but it was a future threat, not one he'd fulfill right now. He snarled, his eyes not leaving mine. The wolf huffed in disgust and dropped to his stomach, putting his head on his paws. Pea mewled and petted the were, grooming his white fur. Rick shook his head. "I have the weirdest life," he muttered, and he walked off.

A moment later he was back, holding a key. He pointed it at his animal unit. "Stay with Soul, guys." He lowered his other hand to me for a hand up. "Come on. We're going for a ride." I let him pull me to my feet, feeling the new power in his body as he lifted me effortlessly. I followed him outside, my body aching and exhausted.

We ducked under the crime scene tape and went directly to Grégoire's limo, where Rick pushed me into the passenger seat and drove us out of the city, stopping at a Piggly Wiggly grocery store. Without a word he went inside, and I lay back in the seat and closed my eyes. I had gotten a nap, but my arm was throbbing, and my skin was burning where the vamp-blood had landed. I must have fallen asleep, because he was back in five seconds with three hams, a box of protein bars, and a ham sandwich. He expected me to shift and heal myself. Rick restarted the limo and took my hand as he pulled out of the lot.

Holding hands, silent, he drove down through Natchez Under the Hill, into the dark, the town's lights throwing dark shadows into the car. He parked next to the river, the limo engine silent. He stared out over the black water. It was moving fast, eddies and swirls and little fluffs of foam here and there.

"The docks and warehouses and old homes here were all built on the backs of slave labor. Just like New Orleans," he said. "Now, a century and a half after the fall of slavery, it's beautiful and awful all at once."

That was a very un-Rick-like comment. I looked out over the massive waterway, weeping willows and fall-painted trees on its verdant banks. Downstream, where a stream joined the river, there was a small rookery of white egrets, looking like a cloud caught in the branches of dead trees. Rick studied the water, and I turned to him, wondering how much the were-taint, and all he'd been through, had changed him. Was still changing him. I finally broke the silence. "You're healed," I said.

He shrugged. "I heal fast now."

I thought about that. "How was the last full moon?" I asked.

"I did okay." He shrugged again. "Solved a crime. Got a badge." After a moment, he said, "Lost my girl."

Beast rose in me, watching him, intent as if he was prey. *Mine,* she murmured. "I haven't gone anywhere," I said.

"I can't have sex. If I have sex with you, Pea will kill me. Then she'll kill you."

Unexpected tears blurred my vision. I tightened my grip on his hand. He returned the pressure, his gaze still on the river. "There's more to love than sex," I said.

He didn't look at me. "Do you love me, Jane?"

I swallowed past the sudden pain in my throat. "Yeah. Do you love me?"

"Yeah." He smiled then. "We're so damn romantic."

I laughed, fighting down tears. We were holding hands so tightly we'd have broken the bones of a normal human. "We'll find a way through this eventually," I said. "Both of our species are long-lived, barring fatal accidents like getting eaten." Rick's brows went up at that one, but he still didn't turn to me. "Just because we can't be together today doesn't mean we won't be able to be together tomorrow."

"Our jobs, you for the vamps, me with PsyLED, put us at odds." He had said that earlier and the repetition made me listen more closely. "I haven't told anyone what you are, but you're a skinwalker and I'm a cop." He stared hard into the night, and I got a bad feeling about what Rick might say next. "If you went renegade and, say, ate someone's liver—"

"*U'tlun'ta,*" I said. The Cherokee word was pronounced "hut luna," and was what one of my species became when we got old, went crazy, and started eating humans.

Rick let the ghost of a smile cross his mouth and said, "Yeah. That. We studied American tribal mythology as part of our training." He stared out over the Mississippi, her waters a muted susurration and a deep thrum, like the heartbeat of the world. "Don't make me have to kill you. Shoot you with silver."

I thought about that while the river ran past and my arm throbbed. "If I started killing humans, I'd want you to shoot me."

After a longer moment, he said, "Glad we got that straight. Like I said. Romantic. But we can't be together." It was half a question, and I shook my head in a silent no. We couldn't be together because sex would infect me with black were-leopard blood-taint. At the thought, tears gathered in my eyes.

Rick made a ruminating sound, halfway between a thoughtful *hmmm* and a grunt. "So, in the meantime we ... what? Date others?"

Mine, Beast thought.

I wondered if his dating others included the witch, Soul. My heart hurt when I said, "Seems only fair. See each other when we can."

Rick turned to me then, his cat rising in his eyes. "Play when we can?" He meant play in bed, which we'd done once and which had been pretty close to fantastic. Okay, had been totally fantastic.

My heart lightened and my lips curved up slightly. "Play. Yeah. Play."

"I can smell your blood," he said. "I can smell that you've lost a lot, too much, and you're still bleeding. You need to shift." He opened his door and pulled me across the seat and out. I felt faint-headed from standing so quickly, and leaned against the car as Rick grabbed the groceries, a blanket, and slid an arm around my waist to support me, which felt all kinds of weird. I wasn't used to being supported. In any way. But Rick was inhumanly strong now, my weight almost nothing on him. He led me down, toward the river, away from the lights of the city on the bluff and from the noise of Natchez Under the Hill, and into the shadows. The night was chill, with a faint wind. I could smell the water and the egrets and the hams. I had never fed Beast ham, especially not cooked ham, and I wondered how she would like the sugar-crusted honey-baked one and the bacon-wrapped one. My mouth started watering just thinking of the meat. Yeah. I needed to shift.

In a secluded spot Rick spread out the blanket, put the hams on the grass, and ripped them open. He lay down on the blanket. "Strip," he commanded.

I spluttered, thinking, *So much for any thoughts of romance.*

"I dare you." He lay back on the blanket with his hands behind his head.

"I've always thought taking dares was stupid."

"I've always thought you naked was wonderful."

Which put a totally different characteristic on his command. I felt in my pocket and found the lion's tooth I used when I needed to shift in an unexpected place or time. My arm was throbbing. I *had* lost a lot of blood. I sighed and started dropping blades. They made an impressive pile. Next to them I dropped the utility belt and the lightweight Kevlar vest, followed by the holsters and weapons. Then I pulled off combat boots and socks. The grass prickled my bare soles. When I unbuttoned the camo pants, Rick's eyes started a soft yellow-green glow. I could smell his cat, musky and hot-blooded.

I held his eyes as I slid the pants off, my body hidden by shadows and the long tails of the black shirt. The cold November night air hit my legs. Chill bumps rose on my skin. My body tightened all over.

I unbuttoned the shirt cuffs, exposing my wrists. Started on the buttons down the front of the shirt. Rick's eyes glowed greener. His cat scent filled the night, merging with the powerful water-fish-pollution stench of the enormous river. I slowed, a heaviness filling me. His eyes holding me.

Slowly, I pushed the shirt off my shoulders. Let it fall to the grass. It caught at my wound, the dried blood like glue. I felt fresh trickles across my skin. The cut was pounding, aching beneath the bandage. Ignored. My breath came fast. I unbuckled the black bra. Let it fall. The night caressed my stomach and across my breasts. Rick's eyes seemed to follow the wind. My nipples tightened and a turgid warmth settled low in my belly.

I hooked my fingers in my panties and slid them down. When I stood, Rick was watching me, his eyes a bright, sharp green-gold glow. The scent of our cats caught up on the slow breeze and played lazily in the small clearing.

Mine, Beast thought. And she slammed down through me. I knelt on the grass and bent over Rick, purring. I rubbed my cheek to his, his rough nighttime beard scratching. I scraped my jaw along his, scent-marking him. He was purring now too, the twin vibrations filling the air.

His hands clenched, as if to keep from grabbing me. "Shift," he said, his voice tight. "Or we're gonna be in trouble. You smell too good."

I laughed, my voice deeper than my own, and sat back on my heels. His eyes traveled over me as I arched back and wrapped my fingers around the tooth. Beast was so close to the surface that the transition started instantly. My spine whipped back, hard. Pelt sprouted. I entered the gray place of the change.

I came to, on the grass beside blanket. Ricky Bo was there, green cat eyes watching me. I panted, smelling his lust and Jane's on the air. Watched him. Liked the smell of the cat inside him. Different from smell of Beast-cat, but fertile and young and full of strength. I pulled paws under me and stretched, arching back, stretching out front legs and chest and spine. Yawned, showing killing teeth. I padded across blanket. Rick's body went still. Smelled his scent change. I huffed. *No need to fear.* I leaned over him, sniffing, sucking air in through mouth, over scent sacs in mouth. Liked his scent.

"Jane?" Rick asked, his voice tight. "Are you there?"

I licked his face, rough tongue on his pelt and skin. I rubbed my jaw over him, depositing scent. He did not move. He stayed still, not sure if he was prey or mate. I draped legs across him and lay on him, belly to belly. Licked again. Stared him in face, in eyes. *Mine. Always mine.*

Rick raised hand. Stroked along Beast side. Scratched under jaw and up near ears. I huffed and laid head on his chest. Heard his heartbeat grow steady. I closed eyes. Let Rick groom me.

Later, I opened eyes and rose, moving slowly. I turned to dead pig and settled to eat, belly to ground. Ate old watery pig meat. Rick relaxed beside me, scent signature changing again. He opened his pig meat and bread food and ate. He started laughing. I turned eyes to him.

"This is the weirdest damn picnic I ever had."

I chuffed with laughter. Licked pig juices from ground. Was not so good as boar killed with Beast claws, but was tasty.

I dressed while Rick watched. His eyes were human again, black as the night, Frenchy black and beautiful. Finally I said, "What did Beast do?" At his puzzled look, I said, "She held me down. Sometimes I don't have access to the world through her." Which just sounded all weird, since I hadn't told Rick about the second soul living inside me, or how she got there.

Rick grinned slowly. "She scent-marked me."

My brows went up.

"Then she draped herself across me and licked me. I figured she wanted to be petted, so I did. Then she ate her dinner and I ate my sandwich. And she shifted back. I think she was *claiming* me."

"Yeah," I said, uncomfortable with the subject of Beast's feelings for Rick. "She was." I buttoned the shirt and tucked it back into the pants. The blood was stiff and dried. I left the boots off. "So, what now?"

"Now we go back to town and finish the crime scene."

One of the phones vibrated on the grass. It was the official cell given to me by Leo. I picked it up, and Leo's picture was on the front. "Yellowrock," I said.

Bruiser growled, "Katie was attacked at sunset. Natchez may have started out as our foray, but once our forces were split, they used it to their advantage. We need to get back to New Orleans *now*."

"On the way," I said. Rick was already picking up the blanket and our stuff. I grabbed up my gear and we raced back to the limo. It was gonna be a long night, and for some reason, I was feeling all mellow and peaceful and easy. I smiled as we ran.

We left our luggage for later pickup in the house we had rented and damaged, and tore back toward New Orleans. I was in Grégoire's limo with Alex, Bruiser, Derek, and Eli. The limo had taken some hits during the fight with the blood-servants, and I wasn't looking forward to telling Grégoire that his ride was now damaged. Derek's other men, the injured and the healthy, were in the truck that had brought our gear and in the rented limo that Leo and Grégoire had arrived in. Leo had commandeered his own helo and he and Grégoire were already halfway back to New Orleans.

So much was left undone. We had never met or confronted the master of the city, the vamp whose name I couldn't pronounce, Big H. It was a serious breach of vamp protocol to enter an MOC's city without going the first night to say howdy. Of course, it was a worse breach to go in and shoot up and behead his guests, so maybe I was overthinking things. Or maybe I'd just made another fanghead enemy. Go, me.

In the limo, Alex was intent on something on his electronic gear, shoving in little finger-sized drives, saving, adding other files, oblivious of us. He had a plastic Coke bottle with a tall straw in the drink holder meant for crystal champagne flutes. Eli and Bruiser were discussing tactics and strategy for securing the humans and vamps, and on the phone to Leo and Grégoire and once to NOPD. Laying out plans.

Bruiser was in charge of this gig, not me; I was just muscle, a shooter, and I was stretched out on the rear seat, letting the events of the night flit through my brain like bats in candlelight, small things illuminated for a moment before darting away. I was aware of everything. The smell of dried blood and sweat on all of us, the stench of sick and dead vamp, tired humans, blood-servant, and the smell of cat caught in my clothes. The limo engine purred. The softer sounds of Alex's electronics whirred and clicked. The night, like black velvet, pressed against the windows. The men glanced back at me often, their puzzlement a faint tinge of scent on the air. The road bucked constantly beneath us, the expansion joints making the car rock.

I knew that Rick was in a car somewhere behind us. I could feel him. His concentration. His intensity. I guessed he was driving and talking and giving orders. Cop stuff. I knew that his inhuman unit and Soul were with him, but I was no longer jealous. I could feel his relationship with Soul and it was nothing like what he felt for me. She was his mentor, friend, and teacher. He honestly just liked her. I wasn't sure that knowing what Rick was feeling and doing was a good thing, and though it was nice on one level, I hoped it would fade soon. It was distracting.

And I could feel something else, like a disconnect in the fabric of the world. That was a little poetic, especially for me, but there it was. Something was wrong. We were under attack. We had caught one traitor, so . . . how had de Allyon known we were in Natchez? *Was* there another traitor in the close-knit group, maybe someone near the top of the vamp-chain? Not someone at the top of Leo's group, because a master vamp knew the heart and mind of everyone he drank from. That left the lower-level vamps and Derek and his men. Again. I scrubbed my face with my palms and pressed them against my eyes. We had lost the opportunity to use Angel Tit to feed our enemy info when we captured his assassin. Was there a way to use that?

I pulled my cell and sent a text to Alex. "Is Cheek Sneak our bad guy?"

He texted back "Still looking." Which was no help at all. With Eli taking his cell, he knew we were onto him. If he was the bad guy, he wasn't likely to make another mistake.

"How about the others?" I texted again. "Anyone likely?"

Alex looked up at me a moment later and nodded, a scant movement of his head, and sent me a text back. I read it, closed my cell, and put it away. So. Alex agreed with me. It was one of six people, with Cheek Sneak at the top of the list He was probably dirty. Not definitively. Which was no help at all, really. I remembered thinking recently that once a list of suspects rose above five, things got complicated. Like now. And the Kid had some new info for me, stuff he'd downloaded off the computers at de Allyon's before Rick took over. I remembered the green and red computer or battery-backup lights in the room where I'd fought the first vamp. The Kid had gotten in there and downloaded all the PCs. He was freaky smart. He was gonna be a huge help to me, even though he did need a shower again something bad. Stinky little fart.

The limo was breaking every traffic law there was. We passed no cops, lucky us, thanks to someone's interference, maybe Leo's. Maybe he had called in a few favors. Or Bruiser had. Operations involving vamps meant that the system worked differently—that whole "Some pigs are more equal than others" deal. I just rested through it all, letting the world pass me by for once. Not fighting for once.

When New Orleans' bright lights lit up the horizon, Bruiser's cell rang. "George Dumas," he said. He got a funny look on his face. His eyes slanted up and met mine. His accent went all British and snooty as it did when he was under stress or worried or really, really angry. Based on the way his eyes went dead, I was betting on anger this time. "Yes. I know who Lucas Vazquez de Allyon is. If you harm Katie, your blood, and the blood of your people, will run in the streets."

I sat up slowly.

"We are," Bruiser said. His eyes bored into mine. "Have you replaced your dead Enforcer? Yes. Jane Yellowrock is with us." A cold smile lifted his lips. "Good. We accept."

I had a bad feeling that the "we" part, of the "We accept," actually meant me.

That cold little smile stayed in place as Bruiser hit END and speed-dialed another number. I was more shocked than anyone when Sabina answered.

CHAPTER NINETEEN

Dumber Than Dirt

After Bruiser hung up the phone with Sabina, the tension in the limo was as sharp as lightning, all of us staring at Bruiser. I said, "Let me get this straight. I just got accused of the murder of Ramondo Pitri, and according to vamp law, I have to go to trial. Like now."

Bruiser nodded, his lips pressed tight. "Not tonight. But soon. Within two days."

"But that murder accusation could prove to be a political error on the part of de Allyon, who was angry, probably ticked off by the attack on his Natchez property. But for whatever reason, he blamed me and is using the death of Pitri to get back at me."

The men reacted to the "for whatever reason" part of the statement with various amounts of amusement. I ignored them and went on. "By accusing me of murder, de Allyon opened the door to forcing his blood-feud back under the Vampira Carta. Right so far?"

When Bruiser nodded, I said, "And so, based on that accusation, you got Sabina to call a parley, under the flag of truce, with de Allyon, ostensibly to iron out details about my trial. But at the parley, Sabina intends to force him back under the rule of the Vampira Carta, all by her lonesome. Oh. And I can't refuse the trial. Is that about right?"

Bruiser chuckled, the sound unamused and harsh. "Yes.

Not that anyone expects the trial to go against you. But during the parley, which should last two hours, Leo will be getting a feel for de Allyon's forces, while Leo's scions will rescue Katie."

I sat back in my seat at that one. "Ah," I said, finally understanding. Everything about the parley was a feint except that last part—finding Katie. The limo had been idling in front of my house for five minutes while Bruiser detailed the facts of our current situation, and my place in it all, to our small crew.

"If I go to trial and get convicted, the penalty is death."

"No," he said gently "The penalty for this particular charge is to be turned by the accuser, and to serve under him for all eternity."

I thought about that for a moment. About being de Allyon's plaything forever. About the risk of Leo using a parley to rescue his heir. About the fact that Sabina would not be informed of the subterfuge. It was audacious. It was sneaky and devious. I liked it. Well, I liked everything except the part about me having to go to a trial. *Crap*.

I looked out the tinted windows at my house. I'd called it my freebie house for ages, refusing to claim it. But lately I'd been calling it what it was. My house. My place. I was part of the world of vamps whether I liked it or not, and that meant being part of vamp politics. I *hate* politics.

Jane wants to be first with all her mates, Beast thought at me, smug. *And Jane needs good den.*

"And . . ." Bruiser took a slow breath and I tensed. "If you'll bond with Leo properly, and not do whatever you did to loosen the bond when he tried last time, he will be able to use you in the parley," he finished.

And theeeeere it was. I knew my face changed, because Eli said to him, "Man, you are dumber than dirt. To have lived as long as you have, you really have no clue about women."

I could smell Bruiser's sense of insult, tart and bristly on the air. I didn't look away from the house. "You need to get Leo and the other vampires to a safe haven for daybreak," I said, barely moving my lips, "someplace not on any record, and with lots of protection around. Protection armed with high-caliber weapons. Bazookas if you have them. I think

Grégoire has a lair in the Garden District. I also think there may be a lair beneath the Nunnery in the Warehouse District."

"I know my duty," Bruiser answered, confusion in his tone. "Leo and all his remaining personal possessions have been moved to a safe location."

"Well, goody for you," I said, and my tone was adult and understanding and gracious. Not. I opened the door and left the limo, stomped to my house, and let myself in. I slammed the door. "He really has no clue. He is dumber than dirt," I said to the empty house. I went to my room and closed the door. Turned the small lock, though I knew it was no impediment to Eli.

Once I shifted, my flesh wasn't dirty or bloody anymore, but my clothes were still grotty. I stripped in the dark, tossed my ruined clothes into one pile and the ones that were just bloody into another, showered, and dressed quickly in the dark, pulling on jeans, boots, and a long-sleeved knit T-shirt under my armored, vamp-fighting leather coat. I didn't expect to be fighting anyone, but the last few days had been hard on my wardrobe. I didn't have a lot of fashion choices left.

I could hear the guys moving around in the house, one upstairs showering, one in the kitchen. I left without seeing either, kicked Bitsa on, and took off. I had no desire to check out the security at Grégoire's place—the Arceneau Clan Home—but it was part of the job whether I liked it or not. I'd left the Pellissier Clan Home in the hands of Leo's true Enforcer and primo blood-servant, and that just got the place burned down. It wasn't going to happen again.

I got to the clan home in the Garden District near two a.m. and pulled through the six-foot-tall, black-painted, wrought-iron gate, the twisted bars in a fleur-de-lis and pike-head pattern at the top. As I braked at the back bumper of the black limo, one of Grégoire's identical twin blood-servants stepped to the porch holding what looked in the night like a small Uzi. I killed the engine, unhelmeted, and unwound my legs from the bike.

"Little Janie. I assumed you would be by here sometime tonight."

"Security check. Will Leo and Grégoire be close by day?

Close enough to be protected by you guys?" I asked as I walked up to the porch.

"Close enough," the B-twin agreed. "And the lair is hard-wired in to the security here at the clan home." The three-story house was larger and deeper than it looked from the street, forty-six feet across the front and nearly twice that deep, taking up most of the small lot. It entered into a foyer with dining room and parlor on opposite sides and a wide staircase to the right leading up to the second floor, the stairs carpeted with a blue, gray, and black Oriental rug.

Nothing décorwise had changed since my last visit except the clutter in the dining room. Stacked on the floor and on the hand-carved cherrywood dining table and chairs was a bunch of junk. By the sour stench of smoke, it was Leo's junk, which meant expensive art and collectibles. Over the scent, I smelled tea and coffee and something sweet, like freshly baked pie or cake. My mouth watered.

The twin, who had no mole at his hairline, thus identifying him as Brian, closed the door and murmured into his mic, "Janie inside. Resume patrols."

"How many do you have patrolling?" I asked.

"Two shooters in the attic at front and back, five on the grounds. Brandon is at the back entrance, and I have the front."

I let a small smile form on my lips. "You know what I like about you and your ugly brother?" He cocked his head in question. "You don't get your panties in a wad when I ask questions."

"Boxers, not panties," he said, showing his teeth in what could only be called a rakish grin.

"Whatever," I said, laughing. I pointed to the dining room. "I didn't think anything had survived the fire."

"The servants got everything out of the library, all the paintings off the walls, and most of Leo's more valuable collectibles out before the fire spread. Grégoire had them transported here until we can arrange for storage elsewhere. Until Leo can rebuild. Sabina wanted you to have this. The Master of the City agreed."

Brian was holding a leather-bound book and a pair of white cotton gloves. I looked the question at him and he said, "Gloves. To protect the book."

I slid them on and took the small, very heavy book. I didn't know much about old books, but I had a feeling that this one was *very* old. The leather felt slightly slimy even through my gloves, the paper inside was thick, like paper handmade out of old cloth, and there were pictures in the margins. The print was weird too, with lots of curlicues. Then I realized it was hand-scribed, not printed, each letter and each painting inked by hand. This was a *really* old book. Maybe from the Middle Ages. I saw a few words that might have been Spanish or maybe Latin. What did I know? I couldn't read a word. "What is it?" I asked Brian.

He reached around me and opened it. On the right-hand page was a stylized drawing of a vampire. There was no title on the cover or the spine, but I did find one on the third page. "La Historia De Los Mithrans en Las Americas," I said. I might not read Spanish, but I got this one. "Oh, crap," I whispered.

Brian chuckled. "Yeah. Those Mithrans love to see themselves in print and paintings," he said, sounding very upperclass New Orleans in that moment. "It's for interesting reading. Sabina, the priestess, thinks you will find page 134 of particular interest."

I turned to page 134 and found a drawing that slowly stole the breath from my lungs. It was a drawing of a Spanish conquistador, his plate armor shining, one boot resting on the fallen form of an Indian. The man beneath his boot was naked, his hair unbound and tangled on the ground. He was dead, his blood leaking into the dirt from a large throat wound. And his hands were furred and clawed. Silently I mouthed the word "Skinwalker."

There were other naked Indians on the ground at the feet of the Spaniard; two had yellow eyes like mine, one was a woman. She was alive, fear etched on her face in stark black ink lines. "Can you read this?" I asked, tapping the text on the page.

"I am possessed of a classical education," Brian said with a pretentious sniff, "but that book isn't Latin, Greek, French, Italian, or modern Castilian Spanish. It's some archaic form of Spanish. I can make out the name of this vampire, however."

He reached around me, his body heat enveloping me like

a warm blanket, and turned one page back. I had sparred
with the B-twins once and their body heat had made the
windows of the room sweat. I was cold now and wanted to
lean into him. But I didn't. I couldn't. Grégoire's blood-
servant pointed at the subtitle on the top of the page. " 'Lucas Vazquez de Allyon. El Rival de la Muerte.' Death's
Rival."

I took a slow breath, the air painful against my tight
throat tissues. Lucas had known skinwalkers. Had killed
skinwalkers. De Allyon was not just Leo's enemy. He was
mine as well.

"I have to get back to the door," he said. "You'll need to
talk to Leo about the text. He can read it." Brian walked
away.

I remembered seeing books in the Pellissier Clan Home
before it burned, secured in small, locked cases in his library
and in his music room. How could I ask Leo about the text
without having him see the yellow eyes of the prostrated
Indians and draw a conclusion I wanted him to avoid? He
had already seen me in a partial shift. He knew I was some
kind of supernatural cat, though not a were. I didn't smell
like a were. Unless I left the vamps, and the hefty paychecks
they offered, the time was coming when my secret would be
made public, whether I wanted that to happen or not. But I
wanted it to be a time of my choosing, not something that I
let happen with no direction, no control.

I studied the small painting beneath de Allyon's name. It
was a pen-and-ink miniature of a vampire in his fully human guise, his eyes and hair dark brown, his nose large and
Roman, jaw firm, forehead wide, with a beard and mustache
in the style that used to be called a Vandyke. He wasn't
pretty, not even handsome, but he looked powerful, force-
ful, domineering, a man who never took no for an answer.
The artist had managed to catch the brutal curl of his lips,
and his disdain for anything and anyone who wasn't him.

The heavy paper moving stiffly, I turned the page back
to the picture of the conquistador and his dead prey, staring
at the yellow-eyed woman, terrified at de Allyon's feet. I
realized that he wanted all of his enemies beneath his feet,
and probably all his women. Captive and fearful.

On the next page was another miniature, but now de Allyon was wearing cloth pants and an animal skin over his shoulders. It was a mountain lion pelt, the puma's head propped on one shoulder, showing killing teeth. The chill I was feeling spread and my fingertips tingled. Lying dead at his feet were more mountain lions. One had a human head. Another had human hands and feet. One was a black panther, the melanistic *Puma concolor*, a mythical beast as far as science was concerned. All were bound and bleeding from many wounds, but the largest wounds were at their throats where fangs had torn them out. De Allyon had killed my kind and drunk their blood.

Sabina had said, "Your enemy will know you by your smell." She knew.

The protectors of the Cherokee had been captured and slaughtered to feed the blood appetite of a Naturaleza vampire. I felt tears prick at the back of my eyes and I breathed deeply to control my reaction, but my hands grew icy and my breath came short and fast.

The vamp was sitting in a gilded chair, vamped out, fangs down, his eyes black and scarlet, and he was holding a golden bowl, filled with blood. Blood streamed from his mouth and down his naked chest. De Allyon looked odd. It took a moment to figure out why he looked so different from any other vamp I'd seen. He was . . . not fat, but not cadaverously skinny. Most vamps looked . . . starved. Yeah. That was the difference.

Things started to click into place in my mind as I stared at the bloody, violent creature on the page. With the blood flowing down his chin and chest, it was clear the artist had been trying to show us that de Allyon had been drinking blood. A lot of blood. When vamps drank a lot of blood, they were well fed and powerful. Only the Naturaleza drank as much as they wanted.

I had fought a Naturaleza once, but the fight had been too fast, too violent for me to pay attention to his body. That and the fact that he'd nearly killed me. I closed my eyes and thought back to the kaleidoscopic images from the day. Thomas had drained and killed several humans. When I killed him, he had been mostly naked, but I hadn't seen any ribs, stark through his flesh. No jutting collarbones. No chiseled jaw or sharp cheekbones. Yeah. Vamps got flesh on their bones when they drank a lot of blood. This vampire drank whatever and whoever he wanted. This vampire was why there were so few of my kind left in the world. He had killed them. Killed them and drunk down their blood.

Before, the fight against de Allyon had been a job. Now it was something far more. This *thing* that threatened me and my charges needed to be killed. And that was what skinwalkers did. We fought for our people.

Skinwalkers took vengeance on our enemies. I didn't think that when God said vengeance was his, he meant for skinwalkers to act in his behalf. But I was. I was going to be the hand of God that took down Death's Rival.

I turned another page and saw the last drawing, this one too tiny to see details. I looked around the room but didn't see what I was looking for. I had been in Arceneau's Clan Home and there was a library in the back, on the other side of the stairs. I hadn't been invited to roam, but I carried the book with me, back to where I had once smelled books and the mold that clings to them. I opened the door to find the library empty and looked around. Books lined the walls from floor to the twelve-foot-high ceiling; comfortable reading chairs with low tables and ottomans were scattered around. A gas fire crackled merrily in a small hearth. There was a large magnifying glass on a bronze-hinged arm clamped to an antique desk, and I crossed the hardwood floor to it, holding the book's page beneath. It was a drawing of a priest holding a sword in one hand, a cross in the other. He was running, his dark robe flying out behind him. The cross was blazing like a torch. In the distance a black horse raced, a man perched on its back. De Allyon outracing the Inquisition, maybe? It would explain why the man had disappeared so often. I wandered back through the house, the book in both gloved hands, one finger holding my place.

I was back in the dining room, surrounded by Leo's priceless things and the stench of smoke, when I realized the most important thing of all. Lucas Vazquez de Allyon would know what I was the moment he saw me. The moment he smelled me.

CHAPTER TWENTY

I'd Save the Last Bullet for Me

I sat on my bed surrounded by readouts, stacks of printed paper, and a pad, as well as my laptop, with half a dozen tabs open online and twice that many files open. I was studying several things at once: the Vampira Carta, the deep background histories of Leo's people and Derek's Vodka and Tequila Boys. I was also looking for a way out of the trouble I was in, the trouble Leo was in, and was searching for the traitor we still had to have in Leo's ranks. Though I couldn't totally rule out *anyone*, I had narrowed it all down to two vamps—both longtime troublemakers: Amitee Marchand and Fernand Marchand—and two Tequila Boys, both new men on Derek's team: Tequila Sunrise and Sneak Cheek. Both had been present at the raid on de Allyon's three-story building in Natchez, and both had significant financial troubles. Worse, I didn't know them well enough to make a judgment on their trustworthiness or lack thereof. Just in case, I sent texts to Bruiser, warning him to either keep all four away from the parley or keep eyes on them. I could deal with the problem people—alive and undead— later, when other situations were handled, and concentrate for now on the parley, and what I might do to fix things.

The day was mostly gone when I figured out what I could do. *Could* do. Maybe. *If* I could pull it off. I fell back on the bed and stared at the clean ceiling, thinking. Working it through. *Crap.* This was gonna be a booger. Leo and Bruiser were dead set (pun intended) on a parley with the murderer de Allyon and his scions, and I was going to be there, under-cover, so to speak.

I'd had little sleep in days. Little sleep, less rest. The par-ley was fast approaching. Beast, normally so active in my mind, had been silent, watching, as tense and expectant as I was. She knew we were about to face an enemy, and she chose now to put a paw on my mind and force me into a deep sleep.

It was nearly sunset, two days before the new moon, and I was dressed for hunting, not in pelt and claws, but wearing guns and blades and lots of silver. And, weirdly enough, wearing makeup.

"So. Whadda you think?" Christie asked. She was pop-ping gum, a black eyeliner pencil in one hand and a large dusting brush in the other. Her clothes were opaque, thank God, or the lights in my bathroom would have revealed far more than I wanted to see.

"She looks hot," Deon said from the corner chair, his voice awed. "And scary as a demon." He crossed himself.

I didn't react, except to turn, my reflection turning with me in the mirror. I was wearing thirteen wood stakes and thirteen silver-tipped stakes in pouches and loops. I wore armored leathers, butt-stomper combat boots, and I was carrying newly sharpened blades—three heavily silvered vamp-killers and four throwing knives—and my vial of holy water.

I carried the two red-gripped Walthers in Blackhawk vertical shoulder holsters, on top of a skintight vest and T-shirt, the M4 on my back in its old harness, a short-sword-length vamp-killer in one boot, and a nice little, dependable .38 revolver in the other. A nine-mil was strapped against my spine under the vest and another was at my waist in a belt holster, next to two CS canisters. Two flashbangs were on the other hip, so I didn't get the canister-style grenades mixed up with the colloidal silver ones. My gold nugget necklace now also carried my emergency shifting tooth, the tooth of the biggest *Puma concolor* I had ever seen. I had wired the tooth into a loop and now wore the nugget and tooth on the double gold chain underneath the double vamp-collars that protected my throat from vamp-teeth and talons. I was carrying a good twenty pounds of gear, enough to clank when I walked. But I had spent the time adjusting everything to make sure that I didn't.

Christie handed me a tube and I slashed on crimson lipstick, the same shade as the Walthers' grips. My hair was in a queue so tight my scalp hurt, and my tiny derringer was knotted into the bun, a last-ditch weapon. I figured if I got down to that one, I'd save the last bullet for me.

I studied myself in the mirror, my coppery skin a rich hue against the black of my clothes and my hair. My eyes were all wrong, and that might save my life. I was sporting heavy eyeliner in an ancient Egyptian style, eye shadow in a storm-cloud gray, and—most importantly—a brand-new pair of colored contact lenses. I now had eyes so dark they looked vamp-black. They made me blink, but they weren't completely uncomfortable. I looked like a pureblooded *Tsalagiyi*, not like a skinwalker. Not at all. As long as I stayed far enough away from de Allyon so that he couldn't smell me, I should be safe. *Yeah. Right.*

"Well?" The single word was laced with emotion and meaning—sarcasm, mockery. If Christie had added, "You idiot," to the question, her meaning would have been no clearer.

"I look like an Enforcer," I said.

"Yes, you do."

I turned to see Bruiser standing at my bedroom door and I almost did a double take. I had seen the primo in a tux, in a business suit, in casual dress, in night camo, and in jeans. I had also seen him soaking wet in my shower. But I had never seen him wearing Enforcer garb. Not ever. My breath drew in over my tongue, and Beast peeked out at the world through my eyes. I lowered my lashes, so he wouldn't see my black contact lenses, knowing he would think I was being coy or shy, rather than devious.

"Now, *that* is hot," Christie said, crossing the room to him. "To-tal-ly hot. Sugar, if you want to come work off some excess energy before the parley, I am your girl." She ran her hand from his collarbones, across his chest, and down his abs. He caught her wrists before she could head farther south. I could hear Deon gulp from across the room, and the pheromones of lust and excitement filled the air.

A slight smile lifted Bruiser's mouth, but his eyes never left me. "Thank you, Christie. But I am fine."

And indeedy he was. Bruiser was wearing armored leather and weapons from top to toe, formfitting, clearly handcrafted, matte black leather, four guns that I could see, two knives, and the two short swords I had given him at his waist, the scabbards set for a cross draw, or whatever they called it in sword fighting. His brown hair was slicked back, the goop he'd used making it look nearly as dark as mine.

Bruiser crossed the room to me and stood behind me for a moment. Fast as a magician, he slipped my silver and titanium throat protector around my neck. I hadn't seen it since that awful night in Leo's lair when Katie had removed it from my neck and I had discovered just how little protection it really was. Bruiser latched it, the metal icy on my throat, his fingers hot. "I'm sorry," he said. I nodded, the motion jerky.

He stood beside me, our reflections side by side in the mirror, his fingers still touching my throat. "We are perfect together," he said. And though I didn't know if he meant perfect as a fighting pair or as a couple, my Beast purred. Bruiser's smile widened. He took my hand and lifted it, curling my knuckles under. His lips pressed into them, hotter than human, and that heat seemed to zing through me like lightning on roofies. A memory of big-cat scent followed on the trail of the heat. *Rick . . .*

Christie said, "Son of a bitch. I never guessed."

Deon swatted her. "Language," he hissed.

I never got the chance to ask her what she had never guessed because Bruiser turned me in a dance step as elegant as anything from a Victorian ballroom and led the way to the front door. Eli waited there, geared up in black-and-gray camo combat clothes, night-vision gear on a strap around his neck, with crosses, silvered blades, and trank guns in among his regular battle gear.

He looked us over, expressionless, taking in our enmeshed fingers and our lookalike clothes. "Just so you know," he deadpanned, "no way am I dressing up in leather. Not now, not ever. Don't ask."

"Never crossed my mind," Bruiser murmured. "My lady, your carriage awaits." He opened the door, I picked up my go-bag, and Eli pulled his headgear in place, crouched, and took point. Alex followed.

In a standard security detail, we had four vehicles, Derek's men driving SUVs before us and after, his cadre of men geared up for battle, one I hoped to avoid. Wrassler drove the limo, Vodka Hi-Fi was in charge of the SUV in front. Angel Tit, redeemed and forgiven, drove the point vehicle, with Eli and Tequila Sneak Cheek in the back: Eli was keeping a eye on Sneak Cheek for any signs he was our mole. If he was, I wouldn't want to be him if Eli went all Ranger on his butt. Chi-Chi and Sunrise were in an SUV directly behind the limo. The SUVs were full of Leo's best fighters, all decked out in evening wear. Kabisa and Karimu—sworn to Grégoire and Clan Arceneau, and looking like Egyptian monuments—were in identical designer sheaths that sparkled with crystals sewn into the cloth and blades strapped to their thighs. Koun and Hildebert wore tuxedos, Koun's Celtic blue tattoos stark on his pale skin, his sword at his waist. Sabina, the priestess, rode with them. I was surprised to see Lorraine and Cieran, who had been part of an uprising against Leo only a few months past, but maybe they volunteered to make points with the boss. Ronald, the Texan, heir to and sworn to Bouvier's coleaders, was in jeans and boots, with six-shooters at his hips. Alejandro and Estavan, both of Spanish origin wore swords. Five others I didn't know. Until tonight, I had been included in the decisions for choosing the vamps who would be present in difficult parleys, but I had left the plans to Bruiser and the details to Eli and Derek. I had other things to concentrate on. Like staying alive.

Derek and the rest of his men were waiting for Alex to tell them where to search for Katie. They were decked out for armed search and rescue and soon they would be waiting near Leo's helo, and two armored Humvees ready to fly—or drive fast—as soon as we got coordinates for Katie.

Leo, Grégoire, Bruiser, Eli, and I rode in tense silence. Leo had something up his sleeve, something I had not been informed about. If I had been preparing security on this gig, that would have made me a tad antsy. Okay, it would have

made me mad. But I was not security. I was an Enforcer.
Except, not really. I had shifted enough and Beast had
loosened—maybe broken—Leo's binding on my soul, just
in time to actually need some good vamp power. Go, me.
My timing sucked. Bruiser had suggested I'd be safer if I
was bound more tightly to Leo. I figured I'd rather be in
danger, thank you very much.

"Where are we going?" I asked.

Leo said softly, "The Nunnery."

"Ah. Of course." The Nunnery was a converted warehouse in the Warehouse District of New Orleans, and was
owned by the Council of Mithrans. It was used by the clans
for soirees and events, and for self-help workshops on the
top ten ways to seduce a human for dinner, for all I knew. It
also had a steel-barred cage in the basement suitable for
holding werewolves through the full moon, or a rogue vamp
until it could be dealt with. I'd seen the cage once, when I
was trying to help Rick deal with his first full moon. That
seemed like ages ago now.

"Are you sufficiently prepared?" Leo asked.

I wanted to screech, "No!" like Beast, but I kept it in.
"I'm good," I lied. "I'm okay."

Bruiser had sent me instructions on the parley and my
part in the two-hour meeting. Vamps in parley used a form
of parliamentary procedure similar to Robert's Rules of
Order, and Bruiser had sent me the words I was supposed
to say when discussion turned to the accusation of murder
and the trial. I had memorized the phrases that would keep
de Allyon and his scions busy for as long as it took Leo's
people to locate and rescue Katie, but that rescue was no
way guaranteed, even with Reach and Alex both working
on invading every cell phone carried by the enemy and
tracking every GPS, call, and text made on the units in the
last two days. Yet, even if everything went off without a
hitch, nothing about tonight was guaranteed. I might be
forced into a trial. Katie might not be found, not in only two
short hours.

So I had come up with my own plan in the hours of my
study of the Vampira Carta, a plan that was sure to tick off
everyone but would give us adequate time to rescue Katie.
Like maybe all the hours until dawn. I didn't have to do it.

I could just stand in my place and keep my mouth shut and hope for the best. I could take the easy way out. But I wouldn't.

"Everyone, don't forget to turn off your cells or leave them in the limo. That decreases any chance the Kid will waste valuable time tracking the wrong signals."

Alex snorted, as if such a mistake was impossible. It probably was.

We pulled down the narrow roadway between perhaps a half dozen vehicles and up to the building. The Nunnery was an old-brick, Spanish-style warehouse with wrought-iron curlicues protecting the blown-glass windows, the lights inside wavering through like water. There were porches on each of its three floors, and the grounds were planted with semitropical flowers and shrubs. Heavy limbs of live oaks wound sinuously across the ground.

The car pulled to a stop and Eli murmured into his mic to Derek, who was not on the premises but was waiting to initiate the hunt for Katie. It felt seriously weird to have only limited access to the security channels, but I didn't want to be distracted by com chatter, so I had elected to wear only the general channel in my earbud. I shook out my arms and rotated my head on my neck. I was tense—not healthy around vamps.

Wrassler opened the limo door and Eli was out like a flash, listening to security babble, moving fast through the night. A moment later, Wrassler assisted Leo and Grégoire out. George followed, and I was last, feeling totally off my game. Bruiser leaned in close and placed his lips at my ear, murmured, "This time, don't play nice."

My mouth curled up in the first real smile all day. His command was the exact opposite of the one he gave the last time we had attended an event at the Nunnery. "Are you telling me to do something really stupid, or really violent?"

"You are anything but stupid, Jane Yellowrock. Anything but. And you look dangerous and gorgeous and violent and deadly tonight."

I knew it was absurd, and way too girlie for me, but I could I feel my nerves settle with his words. It was a description I could live with, even if the gorgeous part made no sense whatsoever.

Wrassler led the way, Leo behind him, and the rest of us followed like good little servants. Beast padded to the forefront of my mind and flooded me with her strength, speed, and night vision. The world went sharp and bright, full of greens and silvers and oddly tinted blues. The shadows lightened until I could see the men standing in them, Derek's boys—one of whom might be a traitor. As we ascended the short steps, other cars began to arrive, the rest of Leo's vamps and blood-servants showing up for the parley.

Inside, warm, dry air fought the sudden cool spell, dropping from overhead vents. The smell of vamp was muted but distinct, and it made me her hackles rise. Beast peeled back her lips and showed me her teeth, hissing softly, eager and powerful. For this night, the Nunnery was neutral territory, where Leo might meet and parley with the invading master vamp.

The front half of the building was one huge open area with three-foot-thick brick walls, slate floor, and thirty-inch-diameter brick pillars holding up the second floor, which was fifteen feet overhead. As always, gas-flame sconces lit the area, flickering in the artificial breeze. The entry floor was used for entertaining, with a dining area to the right big enough to seat a hundred at the long table, which was pushed against the wall.

The last time I was here for a party, the air had been redolent of meat and spices. Tonight it just smelled empty, vampy, slightly moldy, and the chill that wafted off the old brick would have been uncomfortable except for Beast's energy pulsing through me.

To the left of the entrance, where usually there was an area set up like a parlor with couches, chairs, tables, and a fireplace scaled to fit the warehouse, tonight there were two dozen chairs set up in two Vs, twelve facing twelve, with the apex chairs only six feet apart. The twenty-fifth and twenty-sixth chairs were between them, set back, on the opposite ends of a square. One was the place for Sabina, the priestess. The other one was for . . . I had no idea.

Before I could ask, I smelled the priestess arrive, her scent the aroma of old blood and dried rose petals and wind from a desert, stripped of moisture. It caught on the air currents and filled the lower floor. Her nunlike white robes swishing, her hands held clasped at her waist, hidden in her voluminous sleeves, she stepped through the doorway and Leo moved to her. He bowed from the waist in an old-world gesture, like something he might have done to royalty in his youth hundreds of years ago.

When he was at the lowest point of his bow, Sabina said, "Tonight, I am not your outclan priestess, Leonard Eugène Zacharie Pellissier, Blood Master of New Orleans. I am the emissary of the Outclan Council of Mithrans."

If Leo had been human, he would have started. As he was a vamp, he just did that still-as-death thing they do. I knew Leo had contacted the council, but I'd thought it would be a long time before they responded. Until last night, I hadn't known that Sabina had a phone line or cell at the cemetery where she slept by day. Now she talked to the council? By his slight pause, I knew Leo had been factoring this new info into his plans for the evening, plans that included trickery and deceit. Things one did not do when the Outclan Council was involved. Only a heartbeat too slowly, he rose and smiled at her. I had no clue if all this was a good thing or a bad thing.

I slid my eyes to Bruiser, but he was watching Leo like a hawk, and then his gaze moved to the entrance, and his eyes widened. I felt de Allyon as much as saw him, his power firing into the room like a torch, like a dozen lasers, like a flashbang going off. His energies prickled against my skin and made the hair on the back of my neck want to curl up and hide. And then I smelled him, that odd, beery scent that seemed all wrong for vamps, the scent on the man I'd killed in my hotel room, the death of the Enforcer that had started all this. *Crap*. I knew what it was. It was the scent of a blood-drunk master vamp. A Naturaleza who had been drinking his fill of humans for centuries was going up against Leo, who had been drained to the point of insanity recently. I remembered the note he'd left on the dead body in the Learjet: "You killed my Enforcer, Ramondo Pitri. You will die with your Master, in a massacre such as you have never seen. This, at a time of my choosing."

Except that it would be at a time of my choosing, not his. Some of the tension eased out of my body at the thought. *My choosing. Not his.*

Lucas Vazquez de Allyon was dressed in a tuxedo, the cummerbund and one of those little handkerchiefs in the color of old blood. His black beard was the same pointy Vandyke style he'd worn in the small pen-and-inks of him in the history book. He looked like a modern-day version of the devil. Satan in Armani. Death's Rival in a ten-thousand-dollar suit that caressed his body like living hands.

As he stepped closer, the power in the room ratcheted up, my skin feeling parched and prickly. Now I wished I had broken down and asked Leo to translate the text in the book for me. This guy wasn't just a master vamp. He was something more, something other. Arrogance and condescension oozed from every pore—assuming that vamps had pores. It occurred to me that drinking all that skinwalker blood so long ago might have done something to him. I looked at Leo, wondering what my blood had done to *him*, and if the old master would be able to tell. If so, then he would know that Katie had sipped a little too. So much to know; no time to discover anything useful. Without raising my head, I scanned the room and located the air vents, making certain that I stood well away from any that might take my scent to my enemy.

I remembered that Sabina had spoken inside my head, telling me that my enemy would know me by my scent. And he would if I got close enough, if he hadn't forgotten what skinwalkers smelled like. I surely would not be that lucky.

Leo and Sabina stood their ground, letting the conquistador cross the room to them, his footsteps oddly hushed in the suddenly silent room, his people fanning out behind him. They were all vamps, all vamped out, showing the three-inch fangs and long talons of the old, old, *old* vamp. As they all entered, the sense of power grew; I could feel it pressing against me, hot and electric. I knew that Leo's legal team had stipulated a maximum of twelve vamps, the rest blood-slaves and the new Enforcer. Somebody had come prepared to make a point or start a blood-feud in earnest. Maybe both.

De Allyon met Leo and Sabina in the center of the huge room, the beery stink of blood-drunk vamps, dried herbs, funeral flowers, dissipation, and the scent of sickness whooshing ahead of them. Our visitors had brought sick vamps with them, but none of the others seemed to notice. I found it odd that the vamps couldn't smell the only disease that could kill them. I touched my mouthpiece for the first time tonight and informed the crew, including Bruiser, that some of our guests were less than healthy.

"Acknowledged," Bruiser said into his mouthpiece. "Can you tell numbers? Which ones?"

"Not without getting a lot closer than I want," I said. Which brought up an image of a big dog sticking his snout into a vamp's crotch. Then of me doing the same thing. Bet that would liven up the proceedings. I curled my bottom lip in and bit down slightly to keep from grinning. The level of tension Bruiser had reduced with his compliment earlier decreased another notch, and my shoulders relaxed. I took a few steps back from the group clustered around Leo. Studying. Planning. Waiting.

De Allyon got in the first sally. "We are Lucas Vazquez de Allyon, Master of the Cities of Atlanta, Sedona, Boston, and Seattle. We present our heir, Hellene de Romanova, our *secondo* heir, Adam Jonas, and our Enforcer, Jude Talley." The royal "we" was a bit much, and de Allyon did it unconsciously, as if he considered himself the king of, well, of America. Which was a scary thought.

Point to de Allyon.

His heir and spare were an odd couple, Hellene looking like the bust off an ancient Greek coin, from the shape of her nose to the light brown braids woven around her head, while Adam's ethnicity was indeterminate. He looked Mediterranean European, as though he had been swarthy skinned when he was turned.

Leo inclined his head to indicate he had heard and spoke his title. "Leonard Eugène Zacharie Pellissier, master of the territory of Southeastern United States, south of the Mason-Dixon Line, east of the Texas border at the Sabine River to the Atlantic, and south to the Gulf, with the exception of Florida and Atlanta." He paused a bare moment, and added, "the largest single hunting territory in these United States." De Allyon didn't react and Leo went on. "My heir you have met and shackled. My acting *secondo* scion is Koun." He gestured to the Celt.

"*Acting secondo*?" de Allyon asked. The room went

quiet. Interrupting a vamp while he's speaking is a gross offense. Leo didn't react except to let a small smile touch his face.

"Grégoire is occupied elsewhere." Meaning that unlike their guest, he'd not put all his eggs in one basket. De Allyon blinked slowly, realizing that if he had miscalculated, if Leo attacked and won, he could lose his entire crew tonight.

Leo's smile widened and he went on. "And my dual Enforcers, George Dumas and Jane Yellowrock. Yellowrock who has been accused of murder, yet who first was attacked, unprovoked, in her hotel room."

Point to Leo. And a line that worked toward my plan. *Thank you, Leo.*

Before de Allyon could respond to the claim, Sabina said, "I am Sabina Delgado y Aguilar, outclan, and emissary of the Outclan Council." De Allyon's reaction was even less intense than Leo's, but his scent changed. In fact, the scents of all his people changed, growing tart as they calculated the meaning of a hurried response from the Europeans. No one had known the council was getting involved in this little war. Point to Sabina, and maybe to Leo. We would see.

"Lucas Vazquez de Allyon," Sabina said, "you have broken truce. Twelve of your scions may stay. Choose which Mithrans you keep at your side, and which will go. If you refuse, then *I* will choose."

De Allyon's Enforcer, a big man with oiled black skin, a bald head, and weapons up the wazoo, stepped slightly to the side, as if he was getting ready to rumble if his master needed muscle. Bruiser shadowed his moves. I didn't bother. I knew how powerful Sabina was, and if she said she was in charge, then she was totally in charge, and she had the metaphysical weapons to back up her claim.

"And how would you enforce such a demand?" de Allyon asked. It sounded like real curiosity, not a taunt, but his facial expression didn't shift from arrogant, and I got the feeling that de Allyon thought he could take the priestess. *Dumb-ass.*

"I am the bearer of the BloodCross." Sabina pulled her hands from the sleeves of her habitlike robe, revealing that she wore thick gloves. In one gloved hand was a black cloth, which she allowed to drop to the floor. "Behold the sliver of

the all-powerful BloodCross." The sliver of wood she had
hidden beneath the cloth began to glow. De Allyon threw
up a warding hand and took two steps back before he
caught himself. His people cringed even farther, leaving a
space around the old vamp. "I have wielded this weapon for
millennia," Sabina said, "and should you refuse my will,
while I act as the emissary of the Outclan Council of
Mithrans, I will thrust it into your flesh until you burn
brightly." The room suddenly smelled of fear pheromones,
the odd, musky, old herb scent of most vamps growing
stronger, bitter.

The old conquistador kept his head averted from the
sliver of wood and lifted one finger at his *secondo*. The man
quickly pointed at the vamps he was kicking out of the proceedings. I might be wrong, but I thought they looked relieved to be sent away. They didn't scurry like rats from a
sinking ship, but they didn't dawdle either. By the change in
scent, I could tell that most of the sick vamps had left the
building. I was guessing that the *secondo* wanted to keep
the healthy ones around for a fight that now had even odds.

When the numbers of vamps were equal, Sabina snapped
her fingers and de Allyon's *secondo* bent to the floor, rising
with the black cloth. I was pretty sure he hadn't planned to
bend and pick it up. The look of shock on his face was pure
comic relief, and when he backed away, he ended up in the
back of the crowd, his eyes on Sabina. Sabina tucked the glowing length of wood back into its covering and slid her arms
into her sleeves.

"There is no reason for the Outclan Council to interfere
in this parlay," de Allyon said. Which took a lot of nerve, I
thought.

"You drew the eyes of the legal apparatus of this nation
with the debacle in Natchez. You will be judged and governed no matter the outcome of this parley. Take your
seats." Sabina walked between the enemies and across the
room. Sat in her chair. *Point to the priestess*.

I held my breath, waiting, watching the thoughts flit
across de Allyon's face. Moments passed, and I let my hand
drop to my hip and the weapon there. But the old conquistador knew when to fight and when to talk. He moved after
Sabina and took the seat to her right. Leo took the seat to

her left. Their vamps filled in the places in the expanding rows behind them.

"We are now *gathered*," Sabina said. Cold energy sparked through the air as her power shot out, and I heard gasps from de Allyon's people. *Yeah. Go, Sabina.* "De Allyon has issued accusation of murder against the Enforcer of Pellissier. Therefore de Allyon has first salvo."

And that was my cue, which had come way too early. Bruiser's men had *better* be rescuing Katie. "Point of order," I said from the back of the room.

Leo turned shocked eyes to me. Surprise must be a difficult thing for an old vamp to experience. After a few centuries of life, there is nothing new. Right? Wrong.

"While acting as Pellissier's Enforcer, I was attacked, without cause, without proper challenge. I was forced to act in my own self-defense. That unwise action on de Allyon's part precipitated a blood-feud and this accusation of murder. Therefore, as per the history of the Sedorov versus Nikitn blood-feud of the fourteenth century, and the Sergius versus Giovanni murder trial of the tenth century, I challenge the new Enforcer of the Master of the City of Atlanta to personal mortal combat, as a way to determine my innocence or guilt."

The place went dead silent, not a vamp breathing, everyone thinking, putting together what I had just done. Sabina blinked once, an unusual motion on the face of the ancient priestess. Then she turned her head to me and smiled. It was not a happy moment for me. I was hoping she had figured out what I was trying to do and approved, but she was just as likely to be happy that I was about to be killed.

"Does anyone wish to speak to this point of order?" Sabina asked.

Bruiser, his voice careful and measured, said, "I wish to speak to the point of order. The challenge of mortal combat as a means to determine innocence or guilt is an outdated legal concept."

Sabina said, "Outdated, but well within her rights." The place went silent again, and I could feel the weight of Bruiser's eyes on me. He was ticked, and I had no idea if he would understand what I was doing or why.

Whether I lived or died, Leo would win, because my

challenge, if accepted, would force de Allyon back under the directives of the Vampira Carta. Of course, if de Allyon didn't accept, we were back where we started, with me going to trial, but I was betting on hubris and ego to make him accept, and also betting that he didn't know what was in the VC codicil about personal mortal combat.

The Enforcer, Jude Talley, raised his eyes to me and grinned, exposing huge, white fangs.

Crap. De Allyon's new Enforcer was a vamp, an old, powerful vamp. I had fought a master vamp once, and I would have lost had Leo not been snared in the insanity of grief, and run off. This guy was at least as old as Leo, and better trained. A warrior.

Beast pressed down on my mind. *Beast is not afraid,* she thought at me. *We will hunt him and eat his heart. His mass will make him slower than other vampires. I/we are fast, have silver-edged claws and Beast strength.*

Which made me feel better, but still...A vamp with three-inch fangs was no easy prey. Jude was more than six feet six, and his muscles had muscles. The ones on his chest started dancing beneath his thin-knit shirt. If he had been wearing pasties, they would be twirling. Beast hacked with amusement at the image, and suddenly I grinned. *Eat his heart, eh?* I thought.

My good humor seemed to surprise the big guy. He blinked and vamped out fast, his pupils going wide, sclera suffusing with blood. Jude didn't have much control for an old vamp. If he didn't overpower me and kill me in the first rush, I could use that against him. Maybe. If I was very, very lucky.

"This *woman* murdered our previous Enforcer," de Allyon said. His expression didn't change. It hadn't changed the entire time he'd been in the room. But his scent changed, and I could tell he was not a happy fanghead.

"Point of information," Bruiser said, his eyes on me. There was speculation in his gaze, and something else. Something like trust. I gave him a slight nod. He said to the gathered, "Personal defense is not murder. There were no witnesses, no challenge, and no resolution. All human police reports were sent to the Outclan Council and we await their ruling." Which was news to me.

"Human police are of no interest to us," de Allyon said.

"Maybe not in the past," a voice said from behind me.

I whipped my head to the back of the room. *Rick*. The arm of the law. Beside him were the white wolf and the neon green grindy. To his side was Soul, looking like an escapee from a realm of succubae, dressed in layers of misty, shiny gauze that moved in the room's air currents. I looked over at the chairs, and knew who the fourth chair in the proceedings had been set for. The Psychometry Law Enforcement Department of Homeland Security.

Why was PsyLED involving itself with a blood-feud? My heart started beating fast, too fast, and I took a breath to calm its racing. But the vamps were too focused on Rick to even notice me. Sabina's face stretched into an unfamiliar, satisfied smile. I thought back to her words, *"You drew the eyes of the legal apparatus of this nation with the debacle in Natchez."* Sabina had hatched plans of her own to end this war? Sabina had called PsyLED to the parley? If not her, who else? I looked around the room. No one else. *Dang. Go, priestess.*

Rick took his place in the vacant seat across from the priestess and said, "PsyLED is interested in these proceedings, and wishes to know how the Vampira Carta handles rogue, Naturaleza vampires." De Allyon's vamps bristled at the term "rogue" being applied to them. It was an insult. Rick knew better, which meant he had used the word deliberately. "We are also looking into numerous deaths and disappearances in the Atlanta area among the homeless, as well as the use of possible weapons of mass destruction in Sedona, Seattle, and Boston."

Weapons of mass destruction? I thought. *Oh yeah. Plague was considered a WMD. Now, that I did not consider.*

De Allyon's mouth curled down. "We are not humans, we are not cattle, to be brought beneath the hand of the human law and the human world."

Sabina said to the gathering, "The Outclan Council has approved the presence of this nonhuman and his nonhuman creatures, and observation by the human law enforcement agency, at this parley.

"The human police have determined that the evidence," she continued, "in the attack in the city of Asheville, is consistent with personal self-defense, not formal mortal combat, nor murder. The Outclan Council will rule shortly on the conclusion reached by the human law enforcement. For now, we must rule on this point of order."

To de Allyon she said, "How say you? Do you accept the challenge of Pellissier's Enforcer? If so, such combat will take place immediately, before the discussion on the agenda resumes."

De Allyon's lips drew down in the faintest of frowns. "We accept."

My breath eased out between my lips. Oddly, though I now had to fight an old, powerful vamp, I relaxed. By his fighting me, the entire blood-feud could be averted and de Allyon would be back under the Vampira Carta and the rule of the Outclan Council. Whether I lived or died, others would survive the bloodbaths recounted in the histories.

Sabina said, "Combat is approved by the council. As Pellissier made the challenge, de Allyon has choice of weapons. Pellissier will have choice of location. De Allyon will decide the number of rounds, not to exceed ten, and no fewer than three. Combat will begin at my count. De Allyon? Weapons."

"Bare hands," the Enforcer said. "No defensive gear, no weapons except skill and muscle and what the combatants find in the field of battle."

Ice flushed though me. That was *not* what I wanted to hear. Not when I was wearing such cool weapons and when Jude was such a hulk. Not when the field of battle was a bare floor and brick walls. If I shifted, would it be considered cheating? If I shifted, my secret would be out in a very real and dangerous and final way. Beast put a clawed paw on my brain and pressed down, the claws bringing both pain and relief. Unlike my opponent, I wasn't alone.

Beast sent me an image, and I wondered what would happen if I just pulled a gun and shot the Big Guy. Though there was no guarantee that a bullet would actually pierce the wads of muscle. It might take an RPG. My grin widened, and the bag of muscle's confidence slipped for a whole second. And then the perfect location for this little fight popped into my mind and I hoped Big Guy remembered that lapse when I killed him.

"Pellissier. Location?"

I was still smiling when I said, "Couturié Forest in the New Orleans City Park." De Allyon's Enforcer blinked at that one. So did Leo. Heads turned to me. Yeah, I'd kept something from them, a lot of somethings actually—like being a skinwalker—and if I was going to be outed as a supernat tonight, or killed saving Katie, then I was going to do it on my terms. Beast growled low in my mind, a warning, a challenge. Her strength flooded through me.

Sabina was the only one in the room to show no surprise, and she set her dark eyes on me in consideration. Her head tilted slightly, acknowledging much more than just my choice of location. Acknowledging what I was. "Number of rounds?" she asked de Allyon, while keeping her eyes on me.

"The full ten rounds. But if our people are in the park, how are we to know when a round is complete?" the old vamp asked.

Sabina considered me, the faintest of smiles on her pale, pale face. "Each round shall be one half hour long. If the combat is concluded with the death of one of the participants before the end of the specified number of bouts, or if a participant should surrender and concede the challenge prior to the termination, the bout will end."

Concession sounded like a pretty great thing on the surface, but I'd learned that if I conceded, the referee—Sabina—would offer me the coup de grâce and kill me. Conceding was a way to ask for mercy when one opponent was totally beaten and the other guy was just playing with him. Like the way Beast played with her food while it was still alive. It was a mercy stroke, not a way to stay among the living.

"Point of clarification and . . . maybe point of privilege," I said, trying to remember the Rules of Order for asking for something personal before the bout started. "Clarification—no weapons means we fight with the abilities and gifts nature gave us, right?" I didn't want to be beheaded after the fact for drawing on Beast or shifting.

"That is correct," Sabina said, her black eyes glinting. Except for Rick, Sabina knew more about what I was than any other supernat here. "And what is your point of privilege?" she asked.

"I would like to keep my personal jewelry with me." I

almost laughed at Leo's expression, and I thought Bruiser was going to choke. It was such a girlie request. Even better, the bag-a-muscle Enforcer smirked, as if I'd just proven how easy I was going to be to dispatch. Might as well go with the helpless and dumb female act—it seemed to be working. "My gold necklace, and this." I held up the lion's tooth. "It's like, uh, my lucky rabbit's foot."

Sabina smiled again, her face softening. It was such a rare thing that for a moment I just stared. "Does de Allyon refuse or reject the personal point of privilege?"

"The *woman* may do as she wishes," the vamp said, his tone both irritated and insulting.

"We will retire to the Peristyle, in the City Park, where stairs lead down to the edge of Bayou Metairie. There, the bout will begin upon my order." Sabina turned to Leo. "Bring the carriages around." Leo bowed again and Bruiser spoke into his mouthpiece. De Allyon's people backed toward the door. Pellissier's vamps followed Leo, leaving me alone in the center of the Nunnery.

Rick walked up to me, standing close. I knew it was him, without looking, and I could feel his concern. "Can you take him?" he whispered. "Bare hands and teeth?"

"Bare claws and fangs," I said. I turned and met his black eyes with my own black ones, and felt him start, shock shooting through him.

And then he grinned. "I like the new look. So, what?" He glanced after de Allyon. "He knows?"

"He killed my people. Drank their blood. It's in a history book Leo has."

"Beautiful woman, undercover, with guns and knives and things that explode. I'm in love."

I laughed, the sound filling the quiet warehouse. The remaining vamps turned to look, hearing my laughter. "Great lotta good it's doing me."

"Being in love or the weapons?" Rick asked.

"Yeah. Both."

Rick lifted a hand and stroked my jaw. I closed my eyes and leaned into his caress. "Are you going with us to City Park?" I asked.

"I'll be there. We'll follow in our vehicle. Don't get yourself killed, Jane."

"I'll do my best." I opened my eyes and met his. "I may have to break some rules."

"Like I said. My kinda girl. Just don't kill any humans and eat their livers, not even with fava beans and a good Chianti."

"Not planning on either."

Moments later, we were on the way.

I was silent on the drive, looking away from the others in the limo, staring into the night. The new moon was in two days' time, and the final challenge between the masters, de Allyon and Leo, would take place then, assuming I died tonight or failed in some other way.

I had planned as well as I could for this fight, but I had planned to fight a human, not a vamp with three-inch fangs. I needed something to create an edge for myself so I could survive the night. I needed something deadly. Some game-changer. *Something* to defeat a vamp warrior. But my mind was blank.

CHAPTER TWENTY-ONE

Beast Saw Gorilla on TV

The Peristyle was a fancy neoclassical arena—not a building exactly, because it had no walls, only a roof with large Greek-style columns. One of City Park's oldest structures, it was built in 1907 as a dancing pavilion, and I had seen the place from a distance when roaming as Beast, but I had never been inside it.

Now, as the limo pulled up, the four concrete lions that guarded the open-air structure felt like an omen—that I might survive this coming bout—even if they were African lions and not *Puma concolor*. Real ducks, geese, and swans were nesting on the banks, sleeping, most with heads under their wings, and as the vamps and I emerged from our vehicles, some of the water birds stirred, wings shifted uneasily. Wind rustled the leaves overhead. A security guard bent to the limo's window and verified who we were before scampering away into safety. Not that there was any safety here tonight. The Naturaleza were here and they'd guzzle down the plump guard like a cheap beer if they wanted to.

I wandered to the edge of the bayou and looked out over the water. Beast saw an alligator resting near shore, nostrils the only part of it that was above the surface. *Small gator. Big birds. Good hunting.*

Big Vamp Guy is your prey tonight, I thought at her.
I will be hungry after shift. I will eat big vampire?

No. But you can have all the Canada geese you can catch.
Beast hacked with delight. *Good hunt. Hunt and kill Big Prey. Eat flying birds.*

Sabina called out, "*Gather*." An icy wind came out of nowhere and blasted through my clothes to chill my skin. Leaves swirled down in a dense cloud, sounding like the uneasy souls of the recently dead. The call to *gather* was as old as the Mithrans themselves, and among the most powerful of their obligations and rituals, and everyone knew that ritual was almost as powerful as magic itself. At that, a thought occurred to me, and I smiled. *Yes.* I had found my edge—if I could call it that. Edges were for pain and cutting, edges were blades for battle. What I was planning was more like sleight of hand—the art of the stage. If I could pull it off.

The vampire priestess' magic was cold, like the grave, heavy and cloying. It smelled of old, spoiled blood and despair and ancient pain. I'd felt it before and the weight of it made de Allyon's power feel minor, like the sting of static electricity when measured against being struck by a lightning bolt. Nothing by comparison. I rubbed my upper arms. I walked from the bayou bank to the covered area, seeing Bruiser and Rick standing close together talking. Seeing the drivers, all human, standing at the cars and trucks. The Tequila Boys, looking vigilant.

I found Wrassler's eyes on me and I lifted a hand, palm up, questioning. He shook his head. Nothing yet. Katie was still a prisoner; Alex and the Vodka Boys were still searching. He tossed me my go-bag from the car, and I caught it one handed.

"The contestants will remove their weapons," Sabina said. It was a command, and I felt the urge, the *need*, to comply. I'd gone to a lot of trouble to look like this; it was a shame to ruin it. But I stepped to a table at the far side of the pavilion and unstrapped the harness for the M4, laying it on the surface. Started to pull guns, ejecting the magazines and the rounds in the chambers, and laying them beside the shotgun. The long knives followed, while I thought about the gun in my hair. I could get it out, but I'd rather no one know it was ever there, so timing was important. When Jude pulled out a knife with a jewel-encrusted handle, attracting the attention of the vamps, I lifted the braid and eased the tiny gun out, setting it with the .38 from my boot. The short-bladed throwing knives followed, then the stakes. My protective collars. My crosses in the tiny lead-lined pouch that was sewn into my pants. Rather than causing an incident, I ripped the pouch out. Leo's designer would be livid, and if I survived, I'd suffer for this one.

Across the way, the Big Guy was now weaponless—except for the muscles, teeth, talons, and his skills, which I expected were enough all on their own—and was wearing black jeans and a black T-shirt, boots, and a happy, fanged grin. I had the feeling that if he caught me first, he was going to play with me for a while before killing me. And that play wouldn't involve kiddie games and coloring books.

I unbuttoned the tight vest, placed it by the guns, and pulled the tee over my head, the boots off my feet. My skin pebbled in the icy air. I slid a pair of flip-flops onto my feet, leaving the go-bag on the table. When I was done, I was wearing only pants, undies, jogging bra, flip-flops, my necklace, and the contact lenses. The vamps were all looking at me now, taking in the bare skin, my coppery coloring bleached out by the night and the park lights, my scent whipped away by the wind. *My edge,* I thought. *Time to see if I can do this.*

I reached up and started to unbraid my hair, moving slowly, letting them look. I took measured steps, circling the Peristyle with slow precision. When I reached a stone lion, I let my hands flow across the mane, the stone cool and rough on my fingers. I bent my body across the lion and scraped with my gold nugget so I could find my way back to this spot, even if I lost myself in Beast.

I lifted my hands back to my hair, and it danced in the breeze like Medusa's snakes as I unbraided it, whirling and whipping in the wind. My black eyes stared the vamps down, calm and dispassionate. My half-bound hair whipped across the lion, and I could feel the power of the vamps' combined gazes, watching me. I had no magic of my own except to shift form, but if I survived, I wanted these vamps to remember me, maybe with something like fear. That was a magic all its own.

Sabina said, "Time?"

De Allyon's heir said, "Ten twenty-five."

Sabina looked back and forth between the contestants as I worked on my hair and watched the Big Guy Vamp I was going to have to kill. I didn't want to. I really had no desire to kill him. But I would have no choice. Literally, it was him or me. My hair whipped in the rising breeze, flowing like black snakes in a slow current. Big Guy was watching me, staring at the hair-handle I was providing him, confident to the point of stupidity, which I wanted to encourage. I grinned at him and shook out my hair, timing it perfectly. "Catch me, catch me, if you can," I sang out, "you big, bumbling buffoon."

"Begin," Sabina said.

Before the word was half-formed, Beast slammed her speed into me and I took off, racing like the anxious wind, into the night. Beast's sight took over, turning the world bright and silvery. I was into the shadows before anyone saw me move. I ripped off the bra, the pants and panties, running between trees, the concrete path bruising my soles through the flip-flops.

I couldn't hear the Big Guy behind me. Vamps are silent predators, even at full speed. I was betting everything on him wanting to play cat and mouse with me, hunt me slowly, thinking to wear me out physically and then drain me painfully, not attack and kill fast. I turned sharply left and raced along a rabbit path, moving hard crosswind now, hoping the cold breeze would carry my scent away from the pursuing vamp.

I reached up and wrapped one fist around the mountain lion tooth. *I'm gonna need a fast shift, Beast.*

Will hurt.

Yeah. It will. Do it anyway. As I ran, I let my mind drop into the gray place of the change, the place where skinwalker magics rested. The place of the snake that rests at the heart of all beings. I rounded into another narrow path and dove into the brush, dropped to my belly, and crawled deep into the scrub. *Now,* I thought.

Beast rushed up at me, fierce and furious, killing teeth bared. *I will be big,* she thought.

No! There's no stone to draw mass from! Pain took me,

ripping down my spine like dozens of minuscule blades, like scalpels flaying my flesh from my body.

Stone lions, she thought back, victory in her tone.

No! I shouted at her. *They're not stone! They're concrete! They may have organic matter in them!*

I will be big!

In the distance I heard the sound of exploding concrete and the screams of vampires as shards of broken lion shattered over them. Then the gray place of the change took me.

I lay in the trees and small plants, panting. Painpainpain was in bones and flesh. Even pelt hurt with pain of change. But I was big. Not as big as I wanted, but as big as the snake at the heart of the stone tooth would allow. Maybe big enough. Maybe. I stood and looked back at my body, seeing mass and muscle. *Yessss. Big.* Maybe big as female African lion. Maybe big as rhino or bison. Did not know for sure.

Was less hungry than usual. Stomach was empty, but did not cramp. From taking mass from not-stone lion? Jane had not expected that. I huffed in pleasure. Beast was smart to hide many things from Jane. Jane was like kit, to be protected. Shook head and felt Jane necklace, tight on big-Beast neck. Was *big!*

I pushed Jane clothes into the dark and nudged the contact lenses she had worn. They all smelled of Jane—skinwalker smell. I listened. In the distance, I heard vampire-prey stumbling closer, taking narrow path, path too small for his body. Stupid prey, but big. Had wanted to hunt big prey for a long time. I stretched through spine and chest and down legs. I liked being big. I trotted into path, looking for place to hide. To hunt. Ambush hunt. Easy hunt, except for killing big prey. Killing big prey was hard, dangerous work.

Ear tabs flicking, Beast kept track of stupid big prey, while looking up and up, into trees. Was big now. Needed bigger branch to ambush from. Saw one. Low enough to ground to leap into, high enough from ground to drop down from. Lifted snout into air, feeling wind in pelt, thinking about scent in wind. *Yesss. Good limb for ambush.* Good limb of tree, hanging over narrow path Jane had taken.

I leaped up into tree, claws scratching and digging into bark, and settled on limb to wait. Flexed claws into bark, pulling, shredding, grooming claw sheaths. Bark fell onto path. If sun was high, it would be stupid kit mistake to groom claws here, but moon was two-horned and dying, and man lights were far away. Bark would not be seen.

Stupid big prey crashed louder, closer, took a breath like dying gorilla. Beast saw gorilla on TV one time. Would be good big prey to hunt. Jane said no to hunting gorilla. I hacked. I was hunting big prey now. Big vampire prey. Thought about Jane. Fast change and mass gain had sent Jane to back of Beast mind, had put her deep asleep. *Beast is alpha. Beast is in control.*

Big prey came closer. Closer. Beast opened mouth and pulled in air with soft *screeee* of sound. Prey stopped, had heard. But Beast sucked in air again, over scent sacs in mouth. Fleshmen behavior, used mostly for scenting mating pheromones, was good for scenting prey too, scenting to find, scenting to determine sickness or not-sickness. Big prey was not sick. Was not vampire who had fed upon sick humans like sick vampires in hot, dry place of Sedona. "I hear you, little girl," prey called. "If you come out, I'll kill you fast."

Beast could hear lie in the words. Only vampires and humans lied. Pumas would tease, but did not lie. Beast did not understand lies. Humans were confusing. I hacked. Vampire prey stepped along path, placing feet carefully now, but was still loud. Stupid hunter, stupid prey.

"Come on, little girl."

Beast made puling sound like sick kit, soft and fearful. Then thought about sick fearful sound. That was lie. Was not sick kit. Was Beast. I hissed. Lies were confusing.

"Where is she, where is she?" prey whispered. Big prey appeared, walking slow along path. Was carrying knife.

Beast narrowed eyes. Vampire had . . . cheated. Jane would call him cheat. Beast thought he was worthy prey to hide knife and carry it. *Good hunt.* I gathered paws close underneath belly. Felt muscles tighten. Vision narrowed to watching prey. Watching. Prey moved closer, step, step, step, beneath limb. Two steps past. Five steps more.

Beast leaped, dropped, fell, onto prey. Landed. All the weight of big lion on prey's back.

Prey stumbled, fell to path, Beast riding his back, claws sinking deep. Bit down on back of neck. Hard crunch through spine and muscle. Shook prey, growling, hissing. Heard spine snap. Big vampire prey fell to earth. Fell onto own knife. Big vampire screamed. Loud vampire screams of dying prey. Hurt ears. Lowered ear tabs to cover ear holes. Beast shook jaws and head, breaking spine more, crunch-crunchcrunch. Screams stopped. Vampire lay still, making sounds of dying prey.

Vampire prey was breathing, almost like human, breathing fast in fear. Lungs worked, but arms and legs were dead. Dead but would heal if Beast did not take his head. Beast pulled killing teeth from vampire-prey-flesh. Licked jaw. Tasty vampire blood. Lay on top of prey. Waiting. Smelling blood. Smelling fear. Heard sound from path ahead. Footsteps.

Beast thought. Waited. Thought more. Footsteps grew closer. I stood to feet and stepped from fallen prey. Walked around to look into eyes of prey. Saw fear. Fear was good. But saw cunning also. Footsteps came closer. Saw joy in prey's eyes. Prey had cheated and had brought pack to hunt. *Hate pack hunters!* Beast hacked. Prey's eyes grew large, looking hard but unable to turn head to see path and footsteps of approaching pack hunter.

Beast stepped into shadows. Crouched and waited.

Human man raced down path and made breathing sounds when he saw big vampire on ground. Fear-sweat-stink was wetting clothes. Man was carrying two knives, long knives like Jane-claw. He turned around and around, staring into shadows, looking for Jane. Finally he bent over vampire and whispered, "Are you still with us, man? Blink once for yes, two for no. Crap, what'd she do? Break your neck. Sorry, big guy, but you'll live. She still alive? Stop blinking so fast. I can't read your lips. I'll get her, don't you worry." Human man stood and held knives before him. He wore jewelry like Jane: rings and silver and steel through ear.

Beast drew paws close under body, watching new prey.

Jane said to keep humans alive. Never kill humans. But I hate pack hunters, and Jane slept. When human pack hunter turned his back, I leaped. Landed on his back and screamed in human's ear. Human man tried to turn, tried to cut with steel claws. Beast sank killing teeth into his neck and tore flesh, shaking hard. Breaking spine high against skull. New prey fell, steel claws beneath him. Unable to breathe. Dying.

Beast stood over human hunter until life drained from him. Saw life spill from his eyes. And when human was dead, snuffled through his clothes, learning his scent. And smelled . . . magic! Tingly gray magic with blue spots of power, like magic of Molly-witch, Jane's friend.

Heart started to beat fast. Had smelled this magic before on amulet from hot, dry Sedona place, place where Beast had eaten goat and not told Jane. Witch amulet was important.

Snuffled and scented. Found amulet in clothes at human man's waist. Sank teeth into cloth and pulled, tearing cloth. Magic smelled good, smelled like meat! Tore into man shirt and man pants, ripping and tearing. Tasted blood and flesh and . . . stopped.

Was tearing dead human body. Was tearing human flesh. Spat flesh onto dirt. Tasted of magic and meat. Amulet magic was meat magic. Did not understand. Anger rose and Beast screamed. Turned to vampire on ground. He was breathing again. Was healing from broken spine. But when Beast's eyes met his, he squeaked like rabbit. Like rabbit with much fear. Beast smelled prey's death fear. Beast pawed big vampire prey over, pushing big prey with big lion mass. Prey rolled over, dead meat, slow heartbeat, but still alive. Must kill prey.

Lay across vampire, feeling heartbeat grow fast, fastfastfast. Hearing vampire breath. Bit down on throat, killing teeth piercing thin skin of vampire. Crushed windpipe of prey. Breath stopped. Held throat, watching prey eyes. Vampire eyes grew wide, vampire teeth folded back into vampire mouth with sharp snap like stone falling onto stone. Prey's heart raced now, too fast to follow beneath Beast paws. Beast bit down more, killing teeth cutting. Vampire blood flooded mouth. Tasty. Good blood. Strong blood.

Jane always said *do not eat*. Stopped cutting with teeth

and lapped blood. Jane did not say do not drink. Good vampire blood. Strength flooded into Beast. Blood slowed and Beast bit down again. Lapped blood again. Watching vampire eyes. When blood stopped and healing began, Beast bit down. Lapped fresh blood. Did this many more than five times, watching prey eyes. Time passed. Blood slowed. Beast licked jaws and muzzle. Watching prey eyes. Stood on prey chest, staring down, thinking, *Will kill now.* Bit down hard and tore flesh away from throat. Spat vampire meat to path. Bit down and spat again. Did not eat. Tore through muscles and flesh until only broken bones of neck were left. Then twisted prey head to side and bit down hard on neck bones. *Crunch.* Spat bones to side.

Vampire heart slowed. Heartbeat stumbled like feet of injured prey in forest. Stumbled again. Prey died.

Beast butted head away with chin. Screamed in victory. Beast was big. Beast had killed big prey. This was Beast's territory. Screamed and screamed and screamed.

Hunger gripped stomach in claws. Had killed but could not eat dead prey. I padded to bayou. Birds were awake on banks, startled by Beast's territory victory scream. Two Canada geese were on bank close to Beast. I crouched, leaped. Up and across and down bank to bayou edge. Caught one goose in jaws. One goose with claws. Killed both and landed on edge of water. Small alligator hiding in reeds blinked. I dropped geese and stared at gator. *I am Beast. I am big tonight. I will kill and eat gator.* But small gator sank below water. Gator was afraid.

Either that or it's never seen a two-hundred-pound mountain lion with feathers sticking out all over her face, Jane thought, her words sleepy.

I/Beast hacked with displeasure and turned back to geese. I settled and ate.

I came to in the night, lying on dirt and leaves, covered by plants that blocked out the sky. My head was on my piled clothes, angled to look down the path. In the dim light I made out a heap of dark flesh and dark clothes, the Enforcer I was supposed to kill. Had killed.

Beside him lay a human. Crap. Beast had killed a human too? I put it together quickly, realizing that the vamp had cheated and sent a human into the park on a different tangent, so that if I did get the drop on him, the other guy could take me out.

I pushed up slowly and dragged myself to the bodies. I had killed two beings tonight, one human. From the looks of the body, Beast had gone a little bonkers over the kill. She had savaged the human's side. Not good. She knew not to eat, but killing two opponents must have led her to the brink. She had tasted human flesh.

I closed my eyes and held them shut for a long moment, not sure what my religion permitted about this. Not sure how to pray. For that matter, I wasn't certain what my tribal forefathers would pray in a time like this either. I settled on the truth. "I didn't want to kill," I murmured to God. "Forgive me that I am violent and cold and a killer. Forgive me that I tasted my enemy when he attacked." For a moment, I could taste human blood on my tongue and my stomach roiled. I remembered the words of my cruel grandmother. *"We do not eat the bodies of our enemies. It is forbidden. It makes us sick."* What it did was make us even less human and drive us closer to the threshold of *U'tlun'ta.* Now I understood.

I had no tears. I felt oddly empty, as if God hadn't heard. As if God would never hear me again. I had killed and tasted human meat. My stomach rebelled, twisting in pain. Something else to deal with someday. Maybe. For now, I stripped the jewelry from his clothes, leaving his weapons beneath him. I didn't want my fingerprints on them anywhere. While I searched, my fingers tingled with magic and I pulled a pocket watch amulet from his pocket, just like the amulet carried by the blood-servant I had taken down in Sedona, the one Rosanne Romanello drank from. Now I had two magic things that I had no idea what to do with, three if I counted the blood-diamond in the safe-deposit box. I was amassing a hoard of magic things I couldn't use but was honor-bound to protect. Ducky.

I dressed in the night, surprised that my clothes still fit. Beast had stolen mass from the concrete lion and given it back, seemingly perfectly, despite the possible presence of organic matter—shells, maybe. I shuddered at the thought of organic matter buried somewhere in my body. I had no idea what it might do to me later. Maybe nothing. Maybe . . .

I would look the same to the gathered vamps, all except for my eyes, which were yellow now, the contact lenses lost in the shift. I pulled my hair back into a coil and slid into the flip-flops, shivering in the cold breeze.

I walked down the path to Big Guy's head and stared down at him, his eyes looking up into the sky. Dead. By my hand. "I'd honor you, if you were honorable," I said. Instead, I lifted the head by his ears and walked down the path to the Peristyle, my hair blowing in the icy wind, my feet aching from the cold. Hungry, needing to eat.

The wind was at my back, blowing my scent and the scent of blood before me.

I was determined to end this night as I had started it, with moxie and magic. Holding the head by one ear, I pulled my hair around and let the wind carry it before me across my left shoulder. A long gray and white flight feather was caught, tangled in my hair, and I pulled it free, holding the feather out to the side with the head.

The Peristyle came into view, the vamps lined up in the center, staring upwind, toward me. When I was close enough I raised my voice and called out, "Pellissier wins. De Allyon's Enforcer is dead at my hands and teeth."

De Allyon stepped forward, his entire body vibrating with emotion, his fists clenched. "That is not possible!" he shouted into the wind.

"Why? Because you gave him a knife?" I called back. "Because you sent a human behind him to make sure I died? Your Enforcer fell on his knife and lost his head. And your human is dead with him." I threw the human man's jewelry into the Peristyle, and it clanked as it landed.

"Did de Allyon deceive us?" Sabina asked. "Was there deception in a *gather*?"

"The human woman lies!" the enraged vamp screamed. "It was her own knife!"

"Not mine." I called on Beast's speed, racing past the table holding my weapons and through the pavilion, palming what I needed in the hand, hiding one behind my lower arm and the extension of the twelve-inch feather, holding another along the length of my leg—more sleight of hand, dependent on the sight of the severed head and the feather to keep their eyes from the weapons I'd grabbed. "And I am not *human*." Beast glared at de Allyon through my eyes and I knew they glowed golden. I/we growled.

De Allyon drew back. "You cannot *be*. I drank down all of your kind."

"Wrong. I'm alive." I tossed the severed head at him. Beast shoved her strength and speed into me. The world went silvery gray. Everything around me dilated and slowed. I turned the stake in my left hand, its base against my palm. De Allyon caught the head, looking down into the face. He looked back up at me, disbelief in his eyes, his neck exposed.

We ambush, Beast whispered to me. I had all the time in the world. I dropped the white feather that had been caught in my hair. As it fell, I stepped back, twisted my body forward, stabbed with the stake I had hidden. The sharpened steel tip parted de Allyon's ribs, pushed through his cartilage, deep into his flesh. The heart muscle resisted, rubbery and moving. I could feel it beat once, up through the wood in my grip. The steel tip pierced the heart and slammed through, the four inches of silver plating and the ash wood poisoning him. The wing feather was still falling as my fist hit against his chest.

The wood and silver in his chest should have immobilized him, should have stopped his heart. But his heart kept beating.

I released the stake. Continuing the arc of my momentum. Bringing up the vamp-killer.

I cut once, a single hard slash across his throat, severing tendons, muscles, and blood vessels. His head fell back, his blood pulsed out. Human warm. In a gush over me. The silvered blade caught in his spine with a dull thud that jarred up my arm and through my frame. It changed my trajectory, shoving us both around in a twisting spiral. His blood pumped again, showering me, burning like acid. De Allyon dropped, pulling me with him.

Faster than my eyes could follow, the vamps facing me vamped out and attacked.

Leo screamed and charged past me. Bruiser pulled weapons and started firing.

I rode de Allyon down, my blade trapped in the crevices of his spine. I landed on top of him, one leg to either side.

De Allyon was watching me, his eyes still open. The flesh around the blade began to reknit, the restorative powers of the Naturaleza healing him. I yanked up on the knife, jerking it back and forth until it released from the spine's bony processes, then pressed, cutting the healing tissues. Slicing deep. "You killed my people," I whispered as I cut. "You killed my people. I am the hand of God tonight, because you *killed my people.*"

The battle raged around me as I cut. I smelled Leo's blood. Smelled Bruiser's, and felt the heat from his body on either side of me. He had straddled de Allyon and me, his weapons firing with steady precision. I smelled Rick nearby, injured. I scented human blood on the awful wind, and heard gunshots from near the cars, the drivers fighting. Heard other cars roaring up. More humans coming.

Sabina's power was a barbed icy meat hook pulling on my blood-chilled skin. I rose and cut down, putting my weight into the knife blade.

I had killed a Naturaleza before, and I knew how hard it was to bring one true death. I sawed at his spine, the bones catching and grinding on the silvered blade. De Allyon's blood pumped again, burning, pooling beneath us.

I severed his head. The blade hit the flooring beneath and rang like a bell, scoring deeply into the floor. Lucas de Allyon's head rolled to the side and swiveled, as if looking at me. The remainder of his blood gushed out. I grabbed the hair of his head and pulled my legs beneath me. Pushed against his chest, steadying myself on his body. Bruiser stepped aside from me, spinning the twin short swords I had given him. Both blades were bloodied. I chuckled, and he slid his eyes to me, seeing my blood-drenched state and the head in my hands. A grim smile hardened his features. I held the head aloft and shouted, "De Allyon's blood-feud is over!"

Sabina shouted, far louder than I had, "Enough!" Her power shot through the room like frozen lightning. Everything stopped. All the vamps, all the humans near the cars.

"This is finished," she said more quietly. "De Allyon's territory and hunting grounds are forfeit to Pellissier." De Allyon's heir and spare started forward, vamped out and bloody, but seemed to lose the ability to walk. Both settled slowly to the floor in ungainly heaps, the priestess' cool gaze following them down. All de Allyon's other vamps went still, immobilized by her power. They looked at the priestess with something akin to awe.

Sabina said, "Any practicing Naturaleza who is tainted with *Sanguine pestis* will be held captive until such time as a cure is found. Any Naturaleza not tainted with *Sanguine pestis* will put aside the evil and practice Fame Vexatum or suffer the penalty of the council and my wrath. All of de Allyon's scions and loyal subjects who still adhere to the ways of the BloodCross will be accepted into Pellissier's clans under his authority. So do I rule, and so shall I be obeyed."

The icy wind dropped and disappeared. I searched out Leo in the crowd. He was standing with Koun, his back against a pillar at the edge of the Peristyle. At his feet were three dead vamps, staked and bloody. He watched as I walked to him, holding the head of my enemy out in front of me, his blood dribbling from the severed stump. The words that came from my mouth were stilted and formal, and sounded nothing like me at all, yet they were perhaps more like me than any words I had ever uttered. "Lucas de Allyon killed my people. He killed the *Tsalagiyi*—the Cherokee." *The people my kind had sworn to protect.* "He enslaved us, killed us, and drank us down. He destroyed us. Despite the fact that you betrayed me and forced a binding, I am in your debt for the favor of his death at my hands."

Leo took the head by the hair, accepting the gift. "In recompense of your debt and in honor of your service, you may choose a gift from among mine. Choose wisely," he said.

I shrugged my acceptance. The Peristyle was a bloody battleground. Five vamps were lying dead, three of them Leo's—Kabisa and Karimu, sworn to Grégoire and Clan Arceneau, had died fighting back to back. Koun was kneeling over the body of Hildebert, a German vamp whose name meant "bright battle," and who had died fighting, still wielding a blade as his head hit the floor. Hildebert and Koun were the warriors of Clan Pellissier, and Koun bent his head low over Hildebert's chest, bloody tears dripping, to run across his friend's body.

In the far shadows, Rick walked out of the wood, along the path I had taken during my battle with the Enforcer and his human accomplice. I remembered the human Beast had savaged; her claws and killing teeth had marked his flesh. I had some explaining to do soon. I didn't think it would be a pretty discussion.

I looked down at my hands, the blood drying and cold. It seemed I'd always had blood on my hands, from the time my grandmother had given me my first blade. De Allyon's hair and blood were caught under my nails. The hair was coarse and black as the night sky. I took a breath at the sight of them, the action of my chest erratic, the muscles jerking and stabbing. Tears flooded my eyes. I curled my fingers under, the blood tacky on my skin. A sob rose in my chest, gathering a scream with it, tangling into some huge snarled pain, like roots twisting tight and choking. They were stuck, wedged in place, blocked by some organic dam that kept the agony of my soul from finding release. Tears gathered and settled inside, floating close to the surface, but obstructed, unable to find freedom. I clenched my hands, the blood sticky.

Ahead of me, Eli pointed a rifle at Sneak Cheek, the Tequila Boy we had suspected of being leak number two. During a debriefing, I'd have to ask what Eli had seen. Later. Much later. I nodded to two Vodka Boys and three Tequila Boys, talking quietly about getting good and drunk before dawn.

I passed El Diablo, standing by himself, and he gave me a small nod, touching his combat helmet, like some old-time Western cowboy. I lifted a finger at him, and though I didn't manage a smile, I did manage to keep my sobs in.

When I passed the last marine, I took a breath, painful and coarse sounding, dropped my hands, and walked to Bayou Metairie, sliding out of my flip-flops as I went. I waded into the water, feeling Beast looking out through my eyes. She spotted the gator in the distance, nostrils above the surface, but it wouldn't bother me, not with vamp blood on my skin. I looked up in the black sky and found the North Star, orienting myself to face east. There was no ritual for my kind of Christian who had faced battle and killed. Maybe the Roman Catholics had one. Absolution.

Something. The Cherokee would have one, and Aggie One Feather would guide me through it some morning soon. But I needed something now, when the night and the blood of my enemies coated me, their deaths pressing on me.

In two steps, the water rose up my thighs. Without looking, I knew that Rick was standing on the bank, watching me, Leo and Bruiser and Eli behind him. Rick's wolf and his Soul stood beside him. Something like pain cut through me, a steel blade of misery and grief, sharp and burning cold. But nothing in life was set in stone and nothing in life is promised us. Not happiness, not joy, not love. Everything was variable and mutable and inconstant. Perhaps Rick and I still could be together. Someday. But I couldn't count on that. I couldn't count on anything except God, death, and myself, and sometimes not even myself.

I looked up into the eastern sky. "I call on the Almighty, the Elohim, who are eternal. Hear me. See me." I knelt, dropping slowly below the muddy surface, the cold water closing over my head, washing away the blood of my enemies. I stood just as slowly, letting the water run through my clothes and hair and over the drying blood on my skin.

The water trickled off me, into silence. Nothing moved now that Sabina's magics had died away, the trees of the park motionless. Even the vamps had stopped moving, standing, all of them, friends and enemies alike, watching me.

I turned to my right, facing north, and whispered, knowing that the vamps and weres would hear, and not caring. "I call upon my *Tsalagiyi* ancestors, and upon the grandmother and father of my kind. Hear me." I knelt and dropped below the surface of the water. When I rose, my skin felt cleaner, my soul less soiled. Cold prickles lifted my flesh and water ran from me, cleansing.

I blinked against it. When the water draining down my face cleared, I caught a glimpse of humans in night camo standing in the crowd of enemies over de Allyon's clan, guns at the ready. The Tequila Boys. One stood beside de Allyon's heir, now the clan leader. Another stood beside his *secundo* scion. Guarding. If we had enemies among our own, that was finished now. They were free of obligation and coercion. Leo was safe now.

I turned west. "I call upon my guardian angel, Hayyel.

Hear me." I heard the wings of a night bird on the far bank, but resisted the urge to look behind me. My human and vamp watchers were not alone. Not anymore. I knelt, letting the water close over me, cleansing me. Purifying me. When I gained my feet, the water pulled through my hair and it lay on the surface like a veil.

I faced south. "I call upon the Great One, God who creates." A predawn breeze blew along the length of the bayou, growing harder, stronger, smelling of wet and leafless trees and water birds and the soil of the earth. I dropped once again below the surface, and as the water closed over me, it took the last of the blood with it, leaving me clean. Leaving me at peace. I stayed that way, kneeling in the mud, under the water, waiting, feeling the unaccustomed cleanliness of my unconventional baptism.

I stood, the water cascading from me, and turned right, facing east again. I felt the current swirl around me, and I knew the alligator was swimming close for a look, tasting the flavor of water and the strange blood in it. But I was still unafraid of the creature.

"I call upon the Trinity, the sacred number of three." Beast growled low in my mind, the sound a rumble as I dropped below the water. I rose and said softly, looking at the night sky, "I call upon the Redeemer, the blood sacrifice, for peace and for forgiveness. I seek wisdom and strength, purity of heart and mind and soul." In the distance an owl called, loud and long, the hooting echoing. Nearby another answered, three plaintive notes.

I had survived the vamp blood-feud, alive and unhurt. I had turned that feud on my enemy and taken his head. Though the vamps now had better confirmation that I wasn't human, they weren't much closer to knowing what I was than they had been. I smiled up at the nearly new moon.

Rick stepped into the water, approaching me slowly, and I looked away from the night sky to watch him come. His face was hard, his eyes dark. Suddenly I remembered his words, lightly spoken on the bank of the Mississippi. I remembered the human with his side torn open by killing teeth. And I remembered his words. *"Don't make me have to kill you. Shoot you with silver."*

I opened my mouth to speak, to tell him that I hadn't

eaten the human. Rick's hand came up. The night exploded. Pain hit me in the chest, left side, up high. The world went dark. I fell back. Black water closed over my head, filled my mouth, my nose. But I wasn't breathing. I had no desire to. I could see under the water, Beast's vision taking over, but the world was telescoping down into darkness. Rick, the cop, had done his duty, thinking I had gone *U'tlun'ta,* had become the liver eater, the evil of my kind.

Beast shoved at me, hard, her pelt abrading my skin, her claws tearing at my fingertips.

My heart isn't beating.

Heart shot.

Shift! she screamed.

No time to shift.

I'm dead.

CHAPTER TWENTY-TWO

I Was Alpha. I Was Big-Cat. Wanted to Eat Gator

I woke to the taste of blood in my mouth, hot, spicy blood. My heart thumped once, sounding wrong, sounding mushy. My vision cleared to see Leo over me, his black eyes fierce, his wrist slashed and bleeding. Into my mouth.

"Vous devez boire, mon amour. Boire, et vivre."

I had no idea what that meant, but I swallowed. Heat slammed through me. My heart beat again, sounding strange, broken. But its movement sent that heat into my veins, into my arteries. I took a breath and could hear the wheeze of blood in my lungs. I drank. My heart beat again. And again. And picked up speed. I dropped inside my own mind, into the dark, into the cavernlike place where I took my spirit journeys. It was ... different.

And I drank.

The small dark cloud in my soul, the place where Leo had bound me, took strength from the blood. It rose from its place in my mind, as if alive. As if scenting.

My heart beat. I breathed. The black form of the binding seemed to breathe too. It solidified, smelling of old papyrus, black pepper, and metal. In the deeps of my mind, I reached out and touched the black form. It was frozen iron, so cold my fingers burned. It was solid. *This is not good,* I thought. It opened its eyes and stared at me. This thing was Leo.

I leaped back, away. Landing on the far side of the cavern of my mind.

From the binding, a black chain slithered across the floor of my soul, reaching for me. The links sounded like scales. *We are not prey!* Beast thought at me. She smashed into me, through my mind, through my heart and lungs, and into my cells. Her pelt ground against me as if she rolled around inside my skin. Her claws pierced through my fingertips. "No!" In the real world, I pushed Leo's wrist away. I caught sight of my hand. Golden-furred fingers, plump, with knobby knuckles and extruded claws at the tips.

I rolled away, landing on the floor of Grégoire's limo. I fell into the gray place of the change. "No, no, no, no, no—"

The iron chain snapped hard, the sound echoing.

Far into the change, Beast did . . . something. The chain warmed. Silvered. And I was lost.

I pawed away from Leo and Bruiser and Rick. Clawed at them, at the leather of the car. I leaped. Twisted in midair, kicking free of Jane clothes. Landed. Looked back and met Rick's eyes. His were golden green. Big-cat eyes. I snarled at him. At the woman beside him, her eyes wide. Nothuman woman named Soul. Rick's Soul.

I growled at Bruiser, his mouth open in shock. Hissed at Leo, who was staring, his fangs down. Good strong predator. Would take him as mate one day. To show my interest, I swiped at him, drawing blood. Then thrust from them, spiraling in midair, claws out. Landed in brush. Raced into night.

Hunger tore at me. Side ached, place where Rick gun bit me. Place that nearly killed me/us. Raced along bayou, scattering geese. Caught one. Crushed neck with snap of jaws. Dropped it. Caught another. Crushed neck. Leaped out over water, thick tail spiraling, front claws reaching. Caught neck of flying goose and broke it with single sling of big-cat claws. Landed in muddy water. Paddled in circle and swam to shore, carrying goose in killing teeth. *Have three geese. I hunger! Will eat.*

I dropped goose and shook pelt, slinging water. Settled to muddy bank and tore into dead bird. Good greasy bird, crunching bones, swallowing feathers and ugly webbed feet.

Ate entire bird and bit into goose two. Ate it all. And goose three. Lay on muddy bank, panting. Belly full. Chest aching.

I yawned and licked bloody jaws and thought about Jane. She was not awake, but slept in mind. Thought about binding of Leo. It slept too, black form curled in corner of Jane spirit. The form looked like monkey. Monkey-cat. Ugly thing. Had metal chain that trailed across floor to Jane, asleep on floor of den place in mind. But chain to Jane was broken. Chain was lying on the floor of mind-den, not touching Jane. Chain also trailed across floor to Beast.

I snarled. Saw cuff on back leg. Sniffed at cuff. Ugly silver metal. Ugly smell of Leo and shackling. I growled. I had tried to stop binding during shift to Big-Cat. Used angel Hayyel power, but was not angel. Was big-cat. But did not work like I expected. Needed to think about cuff. Needed to think about binding. Long thoughts. Jane thoughts. Could not understand metal-cuff-binding in spirit den. Not now.

Heard vampires in distance. Pulled away from mind-den, away from dark place in thoughts. Looked-listened-scented at world outside mind-den. Vampires and werewolf were hunting Beast. I stood and stretched body, pulling at muscles and sinews. Stretched hard along spine and chest. Chest should not still hurt. Needed more shifting.

Would think about chain. Later.

I was alpha. I was big-cat. Wanted to eat gator. Wanted to hunt.

Looked out into darkness of night. Was near tree where Beast had ambush-hunted and killed human and big vampire. Could smell dead human and dead big prey on cool wind. Dead and dead again. Did not understand twice-dead things. Did not understand things that were alive and dead. Like Bitsa. Like vampires.

Could smell vampires on wind, hear vampires. Vampires were hunting Beast. Wanted to go far away from hunters. Wanted to think. I huffed and padded into dark.

At road, I climbed tree and lay on limb hanging over road. Jumped from limb over road to top of small truck and set claws to metal. Holding on. Truck was like bison, big and fast and stupid. But truck had no blood and bones. Truck was alive and not alive, like vampires were alive and not alive. Did not understand truck or vampires. But truck was moving toward city lights, toward place of Jane-den. Stupid truck turned away soon, and Beast jumped down to ground. Prowled on before finding other truck heading toward Jane-den. Changed trucks three more times. Less than five. Was good number.

In French Quarter, truck stopped at place of sleeping and eating. Hotel, Jane called it. Jumped from back of truck to street and padded into shadows. I moved through French Quarter place smelling of many more than five humans and man-food and man-spices and gasoline and many more than five vampires. Went to Katie's place. Place where enemy of Jane had hunted Katie and taken Katie.

Could smell Katie and Derek and other humans inside. Derek had hunted Katie and brought her back to her den. Derek was good hunter. Wondered if Derek and Katie were mated now. Katie needed strong mate. But smelled blood. Much blood. Katie was wounded and drinking from more-than-five humans. Heard sound of pain from Katie-den.

I chuffed. Did not like smell of human blood. Did not like taste of human flesh. Remembered taste from fight. Jane was right. Should never eat humans. Did not understand vampires—good hunters who ate humans. I turned and trotted into night.

I woke in a stinking alley behind a restaurant, lying on the pavement. Next to a wino so drunk he smelled like a brewery. I crawled to my feet and met his eyes.

"You're naked, you know."

"I noticed."

"I got a blanket I'll sell you."

"It isn't like I have any money on me."

His eyes gleamed and he showed me broken, brown teeth as he looked me over.

I chuckled softly. "How about this? You loan me your blanket, and I'll come back with fifty dollars and a brand-new blanket."

He thought about that for a good half minute while I shivered. "And a pillow. And a waterproof tent. A tiny one I can drape over things when it rains."

I was standing buck naked in an alley at dawn, bargaining with a wino for his flea-infested blanket. Which was stupid on so many levels. "Whatever it takes to get me the blanket." The wino scratched himself and I didn't look at where or at the sight of his black fingernails.

"Done."

"How about I give you a hundred and let you live?" a soft voice said.

I froze. Rick. Who had just shot me. I turned my body at an angle, making a narrower target. But his hands were empty. His white wolf sat at his side, panting.

Rick saw my reaction and he opened his mouth, breathing in. He went dead-still for a moment, not breathing now, not doing anything, reading me like a cat might. His voice went dead, no tonal shifts or flex. "You think I *shot you*? You think *I* shot you?" he exploded. "I've been hunting you all night. Thinking that he had killed you, that you shifted too late and only Beast was left." Rick ripped his coat off and threw it at me. I caught it, something heavy banging into my kneecap. "There is a nine-mil in the right pocket. Take it and shoot me, you crazy bitch."

I held the coat in front of me, one hand gripping the pocket that held the gun. I could feel it, warm from his body heat, and it did feel like a nine-mil. I held the coat in front of me like a shield, but of course if he had another gun and really wanted me dead, now was the time to fire. He didn't.

"You told me you had orders to shoot me if I killed a human. I killed a human. Your hand came up. I was shot. Soooo."

Rick's face twisted with some emotion I couldn't name. "You really think I shot you." He lowered his lids and dropped his head to keep me from seeing what might be on his face. "You killed him in self-defense, not a blood-magic spell or a killing frenzy." When I didn't say anything, he added, "I'm a cop. I'm trained to notice little things like that."

"Who shot me?"

"You call him Diablo."

I let my mind wander back over the last moments of my life, putting two and two together, and hopefully reaching four. I remembered the humans guarding the remains of de Allyon's clan. The Tequila Boys. I remembered Diablo, pounding a downed vamp in the pasture after the battle, the night that Leo's clan home burned to the ground. Had he been putting on a show? Had he agreed to snitch later, in return for something? Drugs? Women? A place in a vamp's household and the increased life span that offered? Money? Money always talks, and most of the time it talks too much.

"Oh," I said. Sounding totally lame. "Crap."

Even I—with my limited social skills—knew I had hurt Rick. I could smell the anger and misery rushing through his veins. See it in his body language, in his expression, in his eyes that were fading from golden green back to black.

"You really thought I'd shoot you," he said, the sound raw.

"What about my money?" the wino asked.

Rick tossed him a handful of bills without looking, turned on his heel, and walked back down the alley. I slid into the coat, warm from his body.

"Star-crossed lovers, is what you two are," the wino said. "Or maybe he's right and you really are a crazy bitch."

"Yeah," I said, blowing out a breath. "Right now I'm going with door number two."

The wolf huffed with what sounded like disgust and showed me his teeth before turning in a sharp circle and lifting a leg on a Dumpster. He huffed again to make sure I knew he would rather be peeing on me. He dropped his leg and padded back down the alley. If a wolf could show disdain, he just had.

"Well, crap," I muttered.

The rest of my day just got worse. Bruiser needed me to find and corral the humans de Allyon's death had left running around without a master. De Allyon had used a lot of compulsion on his servants, and when that control disappeared suddenly, there were a lot of displaced, panicked humans running around, most with some version of PTSD from being in his service.

Someone had to deal with the CDC about the vamp plague. They had joined in with Leo's private lab, working on finding a true cure. Again, me, since PsyLED was a police agency, not a government health agency. Meanwhile, Rick wrapped up his case and left New Orleans without a word—Rick, his unit of nonhumans, and his Soul. I watched him drive off in a new SUV—the kind that looks like a sta-

tion wagon. It had rental plates, and somehow it looked ...
domestic. I didn't let tears pool in my eyes until the rental
pulled around the corner. Then I blinked them away and
went back to work. What else could I do? I worked around
the clock with Wrassler and Bruiser and then, all at once, it
was all done. Finished. My job was done.

It was midnight, on the night of the new moon. And I
was alone.

I got a job offer two weeks later. It was from the elusive
Hieronymus, the Master of the City of Natchez. Seemed he
had a problem with the remnants of de Allyon's ungovern-
able Naturaleza running amok in his city and the nearby
hunting territory. He was estimating there were at least
twenty vamps hunting humans, and he wanted them removed. The council of Mithrans had offered thirty thousand
a head—literally—to take them down. I was thinking about
it. A change of scenery sounded like a good idea, and if I
took the Younger boys, it would be a good way to test out
this partnership idea. Frankly, I was surprised that he'd want
one of the people who had shot up his town and left it in
disarray to come back, but maybe he felt I needed to clean
up my own mess.

I hadn't heard from Bruiser. Hadn't heard from Rick, despite the numerous apologies I'd left on his voice mail. Either
I'd hurt him so badly with my accusation and lack of trust
that he'd just walked away—maybe forever—or he was already in the field again and hadn't checked voice mail. I could
hope it was something simple, though the more time passed,
the less likely it was a voice mail problem. I had told him I
loved him and then accused him of shooting me. Go, me.

My life was sublimely uncomplicated right now. Which
could be a good thing. But was probably not.

I went that night to hunt, deep in bayou country. In the
middle of the shift, as the place of the change took me over,
and gray light sparkled with the energies of my magics, I
discovered Beast's secret. I found the chain that ran from
Beast, across the floor of my soul house to the sleeping
form of Leo in the corner of my mind.

As we stood in the silence of the magics of the change,
both fully skinwalker and fully cat, I said, *He bound you.*

Not me. He bound you. How . . . ? Oh, crap. It must have been because his blood was in your mouth, in my mouth when we shifted. Even caught in the magic, I felt my breath hitch. *I had vampire blood in my mouth at the time of the shift into cat.*

Beast was bound to Leo Pellissier. I stared at the silvered chain and cuff that encircled her foreleg.

Best huffed, amused. *Leo will be good mate.*

The pain of the shift slid into me. "Well, crap."

Love Jane Yellowrock? Then meet Thorn St. Croix. Read on for the opening chapter of *Bloodring*, the first novel in Faith Hunter's Rogue Mage series. Available from Roc.

No one thought the apocalypse would be like this. The world didn't end. And the appearance of seraphs heralded three plagues and a devastating war between the forces of good and evil. Over a hundred years later, the earth has plunged into an ice age, and seraphs and demons fight a never-ending battle while religious strife rages among the surviving humans.

Thorn St. Croix is no ordinary neomage. All the others of her kind, mages who can twist leftover creation energy to their will, were gathered together into enclaves long ago; and there they live in luxurious confinement, isolated from other humans and exploited for their magic. When her powers nearly drive her insane, she escapes—and now she lives as a fugitive, disguised as a human, channeling her gifts of stone-magery into jewelry making. But when Thaddeus Bartholomew, a dangerously attractive policeman, shows up on her doorstep and accuses her of kidnapping her ex-husband, she retrieves her weapons and risks revealing her identity to find him. And for Thorn, the punishment for revelation is death....

I stared into the hills as my mount clomped below me, his massive hooves digging into snow and ice. Above us a fighter jet streaked across the sky, leaving a trail that glowed bright against the fiery sunset. A faint sense of alarm raced across my skin, and I gathered up the reins, tightening my knees against Homer's sides, pressing my walking stick against the huge horse.

A sonic boom exploded across the peaks, shaking through snow-laden trees. Ice and snow pitched down in heavy sheets and lumps. A dog yelped. The Friesian set his hooves, dropped his head, and kicked. "Stones and blood," I hissed as I rammed into the saddle horn. The boom echoed like rifle shot. Homer's back arched. If he bucked, I was a goner.

I concentrated on the bloodstone handle of my walking stick and pulled the horse to me, reins firm as I whispered soothing, seemingly nonsense words no one would interpret as a chant. The bloodstone pulsed as it projected a sense of calm into him, a use of stored power that didn't affect my own drained resources. The sonic boom came back from the nearby mountains, a ricochet of man-made thunder.

The mule in front of us hee-hawed and kicked out, white rimming his eyes, lips wide, and teeth showing as the boom reverberated through the farther peaks. Down the length of the mule train, other animals reacted as the fear spread, some bucking in a frenzy, throwing packs into drifts, squealing as lead ropes tangled, trumpeting fear.

Homer relaxed his back, sidestepped, and danced like a young colt before planting his hooves again. He blew out a rib-racking sigh and shook himself, ears twitching as he settled. Deftly, I repositioned the supplies and packs he'd dislodged, rubbing a bruised thigh that had taken a wallop from a twenty-pound pack of stone.

Hoop Marks and his assistant guides swung down from their own mounts and steadied the more fractious stock. All along the short train, the startled horses and mules settled as riders worked to control them. Homer looked on, ears twitching.

Behind me, a big Clydesdale relaxed, shuddering with a ripple of muscle and thick winter coat, his rider following the wave of motion with practiced ease. Audric was a salvage miner, and he knew his horses. I nodded to my old friend, and he tipped his hat to me before repositioning his stock on Clyde's back.

A final echo rumbled from the mountains. Almost as one, we turned to the peaks above us, listening fearfully for the telltale roar of an avalanche.

Sonic booms were rare in the Appalachians these days, and I wondered what had caused the military overflight. I slid the walking stick into its leather loop. It was useful for balance while taking a stroll in snow, but its real purpose was as a weapon. Its concealed blade was deadly, as was its talisman hilt, hiding in plain sight. However, the bloodstone handle-hilt was now almost drained of power, and when we stopped for the night, I'd have to find a safe, secluded place to draw power for it and for the amulets I carried, or my neomage attributes would begin to display themselves.

I'm a neomage, a witchy-woman. Though contrary rumors persist, claiming mages still roam the world free, I'm the only one of my kind not a prisoner, the only one in the entire world of humans who is unregulated, unlicensed. The only one uncontrolled.

All the others of my race are restricted to Enclaves, protected in enforced captivity. Enclaves are gilded cages, prisons of privilege and power, but cages nonetheless. Neomages are allowed out only with seraph permission, and then we have to wear a sigil of office and bracelets with satellite GPS locator chips in them. We're followed by the humans, watched, and sent back fast when our services are no longer needed or when our visas expire. As if we're contagious. Or dangerous.

Enclave was both prison and haven for mages, keeping us safe from the politically powerful, conservative, religious orthodox humans who hated us, and giving us a place to live as our natures and gifts demanded. It was a great place for a mage-child to grow up, but when my gift blossomed at age fourteen, my mind opened in a unique way. The thoughts of all twelve hundred mages captive in the New Orleans Enclave opened to me at once. I nearly went mad. If I went back, I'd go quietly—or loudly screaming—insane.

In the woods around us, shadows lengthened and darkened. Mule handlers looked around, jittery. I sent out a quick mind-skim. There were no supernats present, no demons, no mages, no seraphs, no *others*. Well, except for me. But I couldn't exactly tell them that. I chuckled under my breath as Homer snorted and slapped me with his tail. That would be dandy. Survive for a decade in the human world only to be exposed by something so simple as a sonic boom and a case of trail exhaustion. I'd be tortured, slowly, over a period of days, tarred and feathered, chopped into pieces, and dumped in the snow to rot.

If the seraphs located me first, I'd be sent back to Enclave and I'd still die. I'm allergic to others of my kind— really allergic—fatally so. The Enclave death would be a little slower, a little less bloody than the human version. Humans kill with steel, a public beheading, but only after I was disemboweled, eviscerated, and flayed alive. And all that after I *entertained* the guards for a few days. As ways to go, the execution of an unlicensed witchy-woman rates up there with the top ten gruesome methods of capital punishment. With my energies nearly gone, a conjure to calm the horses could give me away.

"Light's goin,'" Hoop called out. "We'll stop here for the night. Everyone takes care of his own mount before anything else. Then circle and gather deadwood. Last, we cook. Anyone who don't work, don't eat."

Behind me, a man grumbled beneath his breath about the unfairness of paying good money for a spot on the mule train and then having to work. I grinned at him and he shrugged when he realized he'd been heard. "Can't blame a man for griping. Besides, I haven't ridden a horse since I was a kid. I have blisters on my blisters."

I eased my right leg over Homer's back and slid the long distance to the ground. My knees protested, aching after the day in the saddle. "I have a few blisters this trip myself. Good boy," I said to the big horse, and dropped the reins, running a hand along his side. He stomped his satisfaction and I felt his deep sense of comfort at the end of the day's travel.

We could have stopped sooner, but Hoop had hoped to make the campsite where the trail rejoined the old Blue Ridge Parkway. Now we were forced to camp in a ring of trees instead of the easily fortified site ahead. If the denizens of Darkness came out to hunt, we'd be sitting ducks.

Unstrapping the heavy pack containing my most valuable finds from the Salvage and Mineral Swap Meet in Boone, I dropped it to the earth and covered it with the saddle. My luggage and pack went to the side. I removed all the tools I needed to groom the horse and clean his feet, and added the bag of oats and grain. A pale dusk closed in around us before I got the horse brushed down and draped in a blanket, a pile of food and a half bale of hay at his feet.

The professional guides were faster and had taken care of their own mounts and the pack animals and dug a firepit in the time it took the paying customers to get our mounts groomed. The equines were edgy, picking up anxiety from their humans, making the job slower for us amateurs. Hoop's dogs trotted back and forth among us, tails tight to their bodies, ruffs raised, sniffing for danger. As we worked, both clients and handlers glanced fearfully into the night. Demons and their spawn often hid in the dark, watching humans like predators watched tasty herd animals. So far as my weakened senses could detect, there was nothing out there. But there was a lot I couldn't say and still keep my head.

"Gather wood!" I didn't notice who called the command, but we all moved into the forest, me using my walking stick for balance. There was no talking. The sense of trepidation was palpable, though the night was friendly, the moon rising, no snow or ice in the forecast. Above, early stars twinkled, cold and bright at this altitude. I moved away from the others, deep into the tall trees: oak, hickory, fir, cedar. At a distance, I found a huge boulder rounded up from the snow.

Checking to see that I was alone, I lay flat on the boulder, my cheek against frozen granite, the walking stick between my torso and the rock. And I called up power. Not a raging roar of mage-might, but a slow, steady trickle. Without words, without a chant that might give me away, I channeled energy into the bloodstone handle between my breasts, into the amulets hidden beneath my clothes, and pulled a measure into my own flesh, needing the succor. It took long minutes, and I sighed with relief as my body soaked up strength.

Satisfied, as refreshed as if I had taken a nap, I stood, stretched, bent, and picked up deadwood, traipsing through the trees and boulders for firewood—wood that was a lot more abundant this far away from the trail. My night vision is better than most humans', and though I'm small for an adult and was the only female on the train, I gathered an armload in record time. Working far off the beaten path has its rewards.

I smelled it when the wind changed. Old blood. A lot of old blood. I dropped the firewood, drew the blade from the walking-stick sheath, and opened my mage-sight to survey the surrounding territory. The world of snow and ice glimmered with a sour-lemon glow, as if it were ailing, sickly.

Mage-sight is more than human sight in that it sees energy as well as matter. The retinas of human eyes pick up little energy, seeing light only after it's absorbed or reflected. But mages see the world of matter with an overlay of energy, picked up by the extra lenses that surround our retinas. We see power and life, the leftover workings of creation. When we use the sight, the energies are sometimes real, sometimes representational, experience teaching us to identify and translate the visions, sort of like picking out images from a three-dimensional pattern.

I'm a stone mage, a worker of rocks and gems, and the energy of creation; hence, only stone looks powerful and healthy to me when I'm using mage-sight. Rain, ice, sleet or snow, each of which is water that has passed through air, always looks unhealthy, as does moonlight, sunlight, the movement of the wind, or currents of surface water—anything except stone. This high in the mountains, snow lay thick and crusted everywhere, weak, pale, a part of nature that leached power from me—except for a dull gray area to the east, beyond the stone where I had recharged my energies.

Moving with the speed of my race, sword in one hand, walking-stick sheath, a weapon in itself, in the other, I rushed toward the site.

I tripped over a boot. It was sticking from the snow, bootlaces crusted with blood and ice. Human blood had been spilled here, a lot of it, and the snow was saturated. The earth reeked of fear and pain and horror, and to my mage-sight, it glowed with the blackened energy of death. I caught a whiff of Darkness.

Adrenaline coursed through my veins, and I stepped into the cat stance, blade and walking stick held low as I circled the site. Bones poked up from the ice, and I identified a femur, the fragile bones of a hand, tendons still holding fingers together. A jawbone thrust toward the sky. Placing my feet carefully, I eased in. Teeth marks, long and deep, scored an arm bone. Predator teeth, unlike any beast known to nature. Supernat teeth. The teeth of Darkness.

Devil-spawn travel in packs, drink blood and eat human flesh. While it's still alive. A really bad way to go. And spawn would know what I was in an instant if they were downwind of me. As a mage, I'd be worth more to a spawn than a fresh meal. I'd be prime breeding material for their masters.

I'd rather be eaten.

A skull stared at me from an outcropping of rock. A tree close by had been raked with talons, or with desperate human fingers trying to get away, trying to climb. As my sight adjusted to the falling light, a rock shelf protruding from the earth took on a glow displaying pick marks. A strip mine. Now that I knew what to look for, I saw a pick, the blackened metal pitted by ichor, a lantern, bags of supplies hanging from trees, other gear stacked near the rock with their ore. One tent pole still stood. On it was what I assumed to be a hat, until my eyes adjusted and it resolved into a second skull. Old death. Weeks, perhaps months, old.

A stench of sulfur reached me. Dropping the sight, I skimmed until I found the source: a tiny hole in the earth near the rock they had been working. I understood what had happened. The miners had been working a claim on the surface—because no one in his right mind went underground, not anymore—and they had accidentally broken through to a cavern or an old, abandoned underground mine. Darkness had scented them. Supper . . .

I moved to the hole in the earth. It was leaking only a hint of sulfur and brimstone, and the soil around was smooth, trackless. Spawn hadn't used this entrance in a long time. I glanced up at the sky. Still bright enough that the nocturnal devil-spawn were sleeping. If I could cover the entrance, they wouldn't smell us. Probably. Maybe.

Sheathing the blade, I went to the cases the miners had piled against the rocks, and pulled a likely one off the top. It hit the ground with a whump but was light enough for me to drag it over the snow, leaving a trail through the carnage. The bag fit over the entrance, and the reek of Darkness was instantly choked off. My life had been too peaceful. I'd gotten lazy. I should have smelled it the moment I entered the woods. Now it was gone.

Satisfied I had done all I could, I tramped to my pile of deadwood and back to camp, glad of the nearness of so many humans, horses, and dogs that trotted about. I dumped the wood beside the fire pit at the center of the small clearing. Hoop Marks and his second in command, Hoop Jr., tossed in broken limbs and lit the fire with a small can of kerosene and a pack of matches. Flames roared and danced, sending shadows capering into the surrounding forest. The presence of fire sent a welcome feeling of safety through the group, though only earthly predators would fear the flame. No supernat of Darkness would care about a little fire if it was hungry. Fire made them feel right at home.

I caught Hoop's eye and gestured to the edge of the woods. The taciturn man followed when I walked away, and listened with growing concern to my tale of the miners. I thought he might curse when I told him of the teeth marks on the bones, but he stopped himself in time. Cursing aloud near a hellhole was a sure way of inviting Darkness to you. In other locales it might attract seraphic punishment or

draw the ire of the church. Thoughtless language could result in death-by-dinner, seraphic vengeance, or priestly
branding. Instead, he ground out, "I'll radio it in. You don't
tell nobody, you hear? I got something that'll keep us safe."
And without asking me why I had wandered so far from
camp, alone, he walked away.

Smoke and supper cooking wafted through camp as I
rolled out my sleeping bag and pumped up the air mattress.
Even with the smell of old death still in my nostrils, my
mouth watered. I wanted nothing more than to curl up, eat
and sleep, but I needed to move through the horses and
mules first. Trying to be inconspicuous, touching each one
as surreptitiously as possible, I let the walking stick's
amulet-handle brush each animal with calm.

It was a risk, if anyone recognized a mage-conjure, but
there was no way I was letting the stock bolt and stampede
away if startled in the night. I had no desire to walk miles
through several feet of hard-packed snow to reach the nearest train tracks, then wait days in the cold, without a bath or
adequate supplies, for a train that might get stranded in a
blizzard and not come until snowmelt in spring. No way.
Living in perpetual winter was bad enough, and though the
ubiquitous *they* said it was only a *mini*–ice age, it was still
pretty dang cold.

So I walked along the picket line and murmured soothing words, touching the stock one by one. I loved horses. I
hated that they were the only dependable method of trans-
port through the mountains ten months out of the year, but
I loved the beasts themselves. They didn't care that I was an
unlicensed neomage hiding among the humans. With them
I could be myself, if only for a moment or two. I lay my
cheek against the shoulder of a particularly worried mare.
She exhaled as serenity seeped into her and turned liquid
brown eyes to me in appreciation, blowing warm horse
breath in my face. "You're welcome," I whispered.

Just before I got to the end of the string, Hoop sang out,
"Charmed circle. Charmed circle for the night."

I looked up in surprise, my movements as frozen as the
night air. Hoop Jr. was walking bent over, a fifty-pound bag of
salt in his arms, his steps moving clockwise. Though human, he
was making a conjure circle. Instinctively, I cast out with a

mind-skim, though I knew I was the only mage here. But now I scented a charmed *something*. From a leather case, Hoop Sr. pulled out a branch that glowed softly to my mage-sight. Hoop's "something to keep us safe." The tag on the tip of the branch proclaimed it a legally purchased charm, unlike my unlicensed amulets. It would be empowered by the salt in the ring, offering us protection. I hurried down the line of horses and mules, trusting that my movements were hidden by the night, and made it to the circle before it was closed.

Stepping through the opening in the salt, I nodded again as I passed Audric. The big black man shouldered his packs and carried them toward the fire pit. He didn't talk much, but he and Thorn's Gems had done a lot of business since he discovered and claimed a previously untouched city site for salvage. Because he had a tendresse for one of my business partners, he brought his findings to us first and stayed with us while in town. The arrangement worked out well, and when his claim petered out, we all hoped he'd put down roots and stay, maybe buy in as the fourth partner.

"All's coming in, get in," Hoop Sr. sang out. "All's staying out'll be shot if trouble hits and you try to cross the salt ring." There was a cold finality to his tone. "Devil-spawn been spotted round here. I take no chances with my life or yours 'less you choose to act stupid and get yourself shot."

"Devil-spawn? Here?" The speaker was the man who had griped about the workload.

"Yeah. Drained a woman and three kids at a cabin up near Linville." He didn't mention the carnage within shooting distance of us. Smart man.

I spared a quick glance for my horse, who was already snoozing. A faint pop sizzled along my nerve endings as the circle closed and the energy of the spell from the mage-branch snapped in place. I wasn't an earth mage, but I appreciated the conjure's simple elegance. A strong shield-protection-invisibility incantation had been stored in the cells of the branch. The stock were in danger from passing predators, but the rest of us were effectively invisible to anyone, human or supernat.

Night enveloped us in its black mantle as we gathered for a supper of venison stew. Someone passed around a flask of moonshine. No one said anything against it. Most took a swallow or two against the cold. I drank water and ate only stewed vegetables. Meat disagrees with me. Liquor on a mule train at night just seems stupid.

Tired to the bone, I rolled into my heated, down-filled sleeping bag and looked up at the cold, clear sky. The moon was nearly full, its rays shining on seven inches of fresh snow. It was a good night for a moon mage, a water mage, even a weather mage, but not a night to induce a feeling of vitality or well-being in a bone-tired stone mage. The entire world glowed with moon power, brilliant and beautiful, but draining to my own strength. I rolled in my bedding and stopped, caught by a tint of color in the velvet black sky. A thick ring of bloody red circled the pure white orb, far out in the night. *A bloodring.* I almost swore under my breath but choked it back, a painful sound, close to a sob.

The last time there was a bloodring on the moon, my twin sister died. Rose had been a licensed mage, living in Atlanta, supposedly safe, yet she had vanished, leaving a wide, freezing pool of blood and signs of a struggle, within minutes after Lolo, the priestess of Enclave, phoned us both with warnings. The prophecy hadn't helped then and it wouldn't help now. Portents never helped. They offered only a single moment to catch a breath before I was trounced by whatever they foretold.

If Lolo had called with a warning tonight, it was on my answering machine. Even for me, the distance to Enclave was too great to hear the mind-voice of the priestess.

I shivered, looking up from my sleeping bag. A feasting site, now a bloodring. It was a hazy, frothing circle, swirling like the breath of the Dragon in the Revelation, holy words taught to every mage from the womb up. "And there appeared another wonder in heaven; and behold a great red dragon. . . . And his tail drew the third part of the stars of heaven, and did cast them to the earth: and the dragon stood before the woman. . . . And there was war in heaven: Michael and his seraphim fought against the dragon; and the dragon fought, and his seraphim." The tale of the Last War.

Shivering, I gripped the amulets tied around my waist and my walking stick, the blade loosed in the sheath, the prime amulet of its hilt tight in my palm. Much later, exhausted, I slept.

Lucas checked his watch as he slipped out of the office and moved into the alley, ice crunching beneath his boots, breath a half-seen fog in the night. He was still on schedule, though pushing the boundaries. Cold froze his ears and nose, numbed his fingers and feet, congealed his blood, seeped into his bones, even through the layers of clothes, down-filled vest, and hood. He slipped, barely catching himself before hitting the icy ground. He cursed beneath his breath as he steadied himself on the alley wall. *Seraph stones, it's cold.*

But he was almost done. The last of the amethyst would soon be in Thorn's hands, just as the Mistress Amethyst had demanded. In another hour he would be free of his burden. He'd be out of danger. He felt for the ring on his finger, turning it so the sharp edge was against his flesh. He hitched the heavy backpack higher, its nylon straps cutting into his palm and across his shoulder.

The dark above was absolute, moon and stars hidden by the tall buildings at his sides. Ahead, there was only the distant security light at the intersection of the alley, where it joined the larger delivery lane and emptied into the street. Into safety.

A rustle startled him. A flash of movement. A dog burst from the burned-out hulk of an old Volkswagen and bolted back the way he had come. A second followed. Two small pups huddled in the warm nest they deserted, yellow coats barely visible. Lucas blew out a gust of irritation and worthless fear and hoped the larger mutts made it back to the makeshift den before the weather took them all down. It was so cold, the puppies wouldn't survive long. Even the smells of dog, urine, old beer, and garbage were frozen.

He moved into the deeper dark, toward the distant light, but slowed. The alley narrowed, the walls at his sides invisible in the night; his billowing breath vanished. He glanced up, his eyes drawn to the relative brightness of the sky. A chill that had nothing to do with the temperature chased down his spine. The rooftops were bare, the gutters and eaves festooned with icicles, moon and clouds beyond. One of the puppies mewled behind him.

Lucas stepped through the dark, his pace increasing as panic coiled itself around him. He was nearly running by the time he reached the pool of light marking the alleys' junction. Slowing, he passed two scooters and a tangle of bicycles leaning against a wall, all secured with steel chains, tires frozen in the ice. He stepped into the light and the safety it offered.

Above, there was a crackle, a sharp snap of metal. His head lifted, but his eyes were drawn ahead to a stack of boxes and firewood. To the man standing there. *Sweet Mother of God ... not a man. A shadow.* "No!" Lucas tried to whirl, skidding on icy pavement before he could complete the move. Two others ran toward him, human movements, human slow.

"Get him!"

The first man collided with him, followed instantly by the other, their bodies twin blows. His boots gave on the slippery surface. He went to one knee, breath a pained grunt.

A fist pounded across the back of his neck. A leg reared back. Screaming, he covered his head with an arm. A rain of blows and kicks landed. The backpack was jerked away, opening and spilling.

As he fell, he tightened a fist around the ring, its sharp edge slicing into his flesh. He groaned out the words she had given him to use, but only in extremis. The sound of the syllables was lost beneath the rain of blows. "Zadkiel, hear me. Holy Amethyst—" A boot took him in the jaw, knocking back his head. He saw the wings unfurl on the roof above him. Darkness closed in. Teeth sank deep in his throat. Cold took him. The final words of the chant went unspoken.

ABOUT THE AUTHOR

Faith Hunter was born in Louisiana and raised all over the South. She writes full-time and works full-time in a hospital lab (for the benefits), tries to keep house, and is a workaholic with a passion for travel, jewelry making, orchids, skulls, Class III white-water kayaking, and writing.

Many of the orchid pics on her Facebook fan page show skulls juxtaposed with orchid blooms; the bones are from roadkill prepared by taxidermists or a pal named Mud. In her collection are a fox skull, a cat skull, a dog skull, a goat skull (that is, unfortunately, falling apart), a cow skull, and the jawbone of an ass. She would love to have the thigh bone and skull of an African lion (one that died of old age, of course) and a mountain lion skull (ditto on the old-age death).

She and her husband own fourteen kayaks at last count, and love to RV, traveling with their dogs to white-water rivers all over the Southeast.

3 1901 05366 0157

R0123